The bronze giant, who with his five aides became world famous, whose name was as well known in the far regions of China and the jungles of Africa as in the skyscrapers of New York.

There were stories of Doc Savage's almost incredible strength; of his amazing scientific discoveries of strange weapons and dangerous exploits.

Doc dedicated his life to aiding those faced by dangers with which they could not cope.

His name brought fear to those who sought to prey upon the unsuspecting. His name was praised by thousands he had saved.

DOC SAVAGE'S AMAZING CREW

"Ham," Brigadier General Theodore Marley Brooks, was never without his ominous, black sword cane.

"Monk," Lieutenant Colonel Andrew Blodgett Mayfair, just over five feet tall, yet over 260 pounds. His brutish exterior concealed the mind of a great scientist.

"Renny," Colonel John Renwick, his favorite sport was pounding his massive fists through heavy, paneled doors.

"Long Tom," Major Thomas J. Roberts, was the physical weakling of the crowd, but a genius at electricity.

"Johnny," William Harper Littlejohn, the scientist and the greatest living expert on geology and archaeology.

**WITH THEIR LEADER, THEY WOULD
GO ANYWHERE, FIGHT ANYONE,
DARE EVERYTHING—SEEKING
EXCITEMENT AND PERILOUS
ADVENTURE!**

Two Complete Adventures in One Volume

THE CZAR OF FEAR
and
FORTRESS OF SOLITUDE

Kenneth Robeson

BANTAM BOOKS
TORONTO · NEW YORK · LONDON · SYDNEY

THE CZAR OF FEAR #22
FORTRESS OF SOLITUDE #23

*A Bantam Book / published by arrangement with
The Condé Nast Publications, Inc.*

PRINTING HISTORY

The Czar of Fear *was originally published in* Doc Savage Magazine,
*November 1933. Copyright 1933 by Street & Smith Publications, Inc.
Copyright renewed © 1961 by Street & Smith Publications, Inc.*
Fortress of Solitude *was originally published in* Doc Savage Magazine,
*October 1938. Copyright 1938 by Street & Smith Publications, Inc.
Copyright renewed © 1966 by The Condé Nast Publications, Inc.*

Bantam edition / September 1982

ISBN 0-553-22619-3

Published simultaneously in the United States and Canada

*Bantam Books are published by Bantam Books, Inc. Its trademark,
consisting of the words "Bantam Books" and the portrayal of a rooster,
is Registered in U.S. Patent and Trademark Office and in other
countries. Marca Registrada. Bantam Books, Inc., 666 Fifth Avenue,
New York, New York 10103.*

PRINTED IN THE UNITED STATES OF AMERICA

O   0 9 8 7 6 5 4 3 2 1

CONTENTS

THE CZAR OF FEAR

CONTENTS

Chapter I
GREEN BELL

The midget radio squawked away noisily beside a cardboard sign which read: "Our Special To-day—Roast Beef Plate Lunch, Twenty-five Cents."

The man on the lunch-room stool sat sidewise, so he could watch the door. His eyes were staring; pale fright rode his face. He wolfed his sandwich as if it had no taste, and gulped at his fourth mug of scalding coffee. He was tall, light-haired, twentyish.

One of the two women beside him was also tall and light-haired, and in her twenties. She was some degrees more than pretty—hers was a striking beauty. A mud-freckled raincoat and a waterlogged felt hat seemed to enhance her charm.

Her eyes were dark-blue pools of fear.

The other woman was a pleasant-faced grandmother type. Around sixty was probably her age. She had a stout, efficient look. Her cheeks were ruddy as apples, and pleasant little wrinkles crow-tracked from her eyes.

Her jaw had a grim set, as if she expected trouble, and was steeled to meet it. She was not eating, and she was watching the door more intently than the man.

The young man and the girl were obviously brother and sister. The elderly woman was no relative, but they called her Aunt Nora.

"You had better eat, Aunt Nora," said the girl. Her voice was liquid, quiet, with a faint quaver that went with the terror in her eyes. "It is more than an hour's drive to New York. And we may be very busy for several hours, trying to find Doc Savage."

"Eat!" Aunt Nora snorted. "How can I, Alice? The way you and Jim are acting takes a body's appetite away. Bless your Aunt

1

Nora, honey! You children are acting like two rabbits about to be caught!"

The girl forced a faint smile, reached over impulsively, and gripped the older woman's arm.

"You're a brick, Aunt Nora," she said gratefully. "You are just as scared as we are. But you have control enough not to show it."

"Humph!" Sniffing, Aunt Nora grabbed her sandwich. Squaring both elbows on the white counter, she began to eat.

Rain purred on the lunch-room roof. It crawled like pale jelly down the windows. It fogged the street of the little New Jersey town. The gutters flowed water the color of lead.

The little radio made steady noise. It was picking up canned music from Prosper City, a manufacturing town in the Allegheny Mountains. Aunt Nora had tuned it to the Prosper City station when they first entered the lunch room.

"Good little set," she said, nodding at the instrument. "Prosper City is quite a ways off, and the set brings in——"

She stood up suddenly, splayed both hands tightly to her cheeks, and screamed.

The young man whipped off his stool and spun to face the radio. His face was distorted; his eyes bulged.

His sister also leaped erect, crying out shrilly. Her coffee cup, knocked to the concrete floor, broke with a hollow crackle.

Even the noise of the breaking cup was not enough to drown the strange sound which had come abruptly from the radio.

It was a tolling, like the slow note of a big, listless bell. Mixed with the reverberations was an unearthly dirge of moaning and wailing. The din might have been the frenzied crying of some harpy horde of the ether, shepherded by the moribund clangor of the hideous bell.

The lunch-room proprietor got off his stool behind the cash register. He was startled, but more by the terrified actions of his three customers than by the hideous uproar from the radio. However, the bewildered stare he directed at the set showed he had never heard this sound before.

The fanfare in the radio ended as unexpectedly as it had arisen. The lunch-room owner smiled, evidently from relief at the thought that he would not have to pay a repair bill. The three customers stood in a sort of white-faced, frozen immobility.

Rain strings washed moistly on the roof and swept the street like the semi-transparent straws of a great broom.

Aunt Nora was first to break the rigid silence.

"Prosper City is around three hundred miles from here," she said hoarsely. "It's not likely the Green Bell was tolling for us —that time!"

"I suppose—not," blond Alice shuddered violently. "But that sound was the Green Bell, and it always means death!"

Jim made his voice harsh to hide a quaver. "Let's get out of here!"

They paid a puzzled, curious proprietor for their lunch, and also for the broken cup. He watched them leave, then shrugged, winked at his cook, and tapped his forehead. He had decided his three late customers had been slightly touched with insanity.

A somewhat ancient touring car stood at the curb, forlorn in the rain. The side curtains were up, but the windows were cracked, some entirely gone, and the car interior was almost as damp as the drizzling dusk.

"Got plenty of gas, son?" Aunt Nora asked with gruff kindness.

Jim roved his fear-ridden eyes alertly. "Sure. You remember we had her filled at the last town. The gauge isn't working, but the tank should be nearly full."

Starter gears gritted worn teeth. Sobbing, the motor pulled the old car away in the streaming gloom, in the direction of New York.

A few seconds after the elderly machine had gone, a blot stirred under the trees which lined the village street. In the dripping murk, it seemed to possess neither substance nor form.

Down the street, a lighted window made pale luminance across the walk. The moving black blotch entered this glow. It suddenly became a thing of grisly reality.

There was, however, little of a human being about its appearance.

It was tall, tubular, and black. It might have been a flexible cylinder of black rubber standing on end, had an observer chanced to glimpse it in the fitful light.

On the front of the thing, standing out lividly, was the likeness of a bell. The design was done in a vile green.

Close against the sepia form hung a tin pail of ten gallons capacity. It was full to the brim with gasoline. Gripped in the same indistinguishable black tentacles which held the pail was a long rubber siphon hose of the type used to draw fuel from automobile tanks.

The dusk and the rain sucked the eerie figure into a wet black maw.

A moment later, a moist slosh denoted the bucket being emptied. Smell of gasoline seeped along the street, arising from the gutters where the stuff was flowing away.

Silence now enwrapped the small town, broken only by the sound of the rain and the occasional moan of a car down the main street, which was traversed by one of the main highways leading to New York.

The ancient touring car was laboring along at perhaps forty miles an hour. Jim drove, hunched far over the wheel, wan face close to a small arc the swiping windshield wiper kept clear of water.

The two women huddled in the rear, raincoats drawn tight against the spray which sheeted through the broken side curtains.

"I guess—that belling—couldn't have been meant for us," the girl, Alice, said jerkily.

"I wouldn't be too sure of that!" Jim called back sharply.

Aunt Nora leaned forward, jaw out, arms akimbo.

"Jim Cash, you know something you haven't been telling us women!" she said, almost screaming to get her voice above the roar of car and rain. "I can see it in your actions! You know more about the Green Bell than you let on—what the thing is, or something! You can't fool me! You do know!"

Jim Cash replied nothing.

Aunt Nora snapped: "Answer me, boy!"

"You're a good guesser, Aunt Nora," Jim managed a gray smile.

"What is it?" Aunt Nora bounced forward anxiously. "What do you know?"

"I'm not going to tell you."

"Why?"

"For the good and simple reason that it would mark you for death! Alice, too! The Green Bell would kill you so you couldn't tell what you know!"

"Rubbish!" Aunt Nora tried to sound as if she meant it. "They would have no way of telling——"

"Yes, they would, aunty. It looks like they know everything."

Aunt Nora whitened. The tendons stood out on her plump hands.

"Listen, sonny—is the Green Bell aware that you know what you do?"

Jim Cash squirmed, almost losing control of the car.

"I don't know!" he cried shrilly, wildly. "Maybe he does! I'm not sure! The suspense—expecting death any instant, and in the same breath wondering if I'm not safe enough—has been getting me! It's driving me crazy!"

Aunt Nora settled back on the wet cushions. "You're silly not to tell us, Jimmy. But that's just like a man, trying to keep women out of trouble. It don't show good gumption, but I respect you for it. Anyway we'll soon be talking to Doc Savage and you can get it off your chest."

Jim Cash muttered doubtfully: "You seem to have a lot of faith in this Doc Savage."

"I have!" Aunt Nora sounded vehement.

"But you admit you don't even know him."

Aunt Nora snorted like a race horse. "I don't have to know him! I've heard of him! That's enough."

"I've heard a little talk of him, too." Jim Cash admitted. "That's the only reason I let you and Alice talk me into going to him."

"A little talk!" Aunt Nora sniffed. "If you would have kept your ears open you would have heard more than a little talk about him! Doc Savage specializes in things like this. He makes a life work out of going around getting other people out of trouble and punishing lads who need it."

Jim Cash began skeptically: "I don't think any man can——"

"Doc Savage can! Take the word of an old woman who knows enough to discount half of what she hears. Doc Savage is a man who was trained from the cradle for the one purpose in life of righting wrongs. They say he's a physical marvel, probably the strongest man who ever lived. And moreover he's studied until he knows just about everything worth knowing from electricity and astronomy to how to bake a decent batch of biscuits."

"Maybe you've been putting too much stock in wild talk Aunt Nora?"

"Didn't I tell you I only believe half of what I ever hear?" Aunt Nora demanded.

Jim Cash smiled. The elderly lady's optimism seemed to cheer him.

"I hope Doc Savage is up to expectations," he said grimly. "Not only for our sake but for those other poor devils back at Prosper City."

"You said a mouthful!" Aunt Nora agreed. "If Doc Savage isn't able to help us and Prosper City I hate to think what'll happen!"

The touring car rooted on through the rain and gloom for nearly a mile. Then the engine gave a few pneumatic coughs, died, coughed a few more times and silenced completely.

"You're out of gas!" Aunt Nora snapped.

Jim Cash shook his head. "But I just got gas. It must be water on the distributor——"

"Out of gas!" repeated Aunt Nora firmly. "I know how these old wrecks act!"

Easing into the drizzle Jim Cash got a measuring stick from under the seat, walked to the rear and thrust it into the tank. His gasp was startled.

"Empty! I don't understand how that could happen!"

"Maybe that filling station was a gyp!" called blond pretty Alice Cash. "They might not have put in any gas."

"I guess that was it honey," Aunt Nora agreed. She opened a road map, peered at it by the glare of a flashlight. "There's a little jumping-off place down the road about two miles. You'd better walk to it Jim."

Jim Cash hesitated. "I don't like to leave you two."

Aunt Nora opened a capacious leather hand bag. She produced two big, businesslike blue revolvers. She gave one of them to Alice Cash, and the blond young woman handled it in a way that showed she could use it.

"Anybody who monkeys with us won't find it healthy!" Aunt Nora said dryly. "You go on, Jim. We'll be all right."

Relieved at sight of the weapons, Jim Cash slopped off through the rain. He walked on the left side of the pavement, where he could see the lights of oncoming cars and evade them.

A few machines passed him, going in both directions. He did not attempt to flag them, knowing it would be useless. Motorists who pick up strange pedestrians late at night are few and far between.

He descended a small hill. At the bottom, he crossed two bridges—one over a stream, the other spanning the line of an electric railroad.

He had barely crossed the second bridge when several flashlights gushed brilliant white upon him. In the back glow of the flashes, he could discern the figures holding them.

Each was a tall cylinder of black. And upon every figure was the green likeness of a bell.

There was something hideous in the way the raven figures stood there, saying nothing, not moving. The rain, streaking down their forms, gave them a shiny look.

Jim Cash stood as if blocked in ice. He had been pale before, now he became positively white.

"Green Bells!" he said thickly. "That radio—the tolling was meant for us as a——"

His own words seemed to snap the chill spell which held him. He exploded in action. His right hand dived into his raincoat pocket like a frightened animal. He wrenched wildly at a pistol which he carried there.

Another eerie black form glided out of the murk behind Cash. It whipped convulsively upon him. Taken by surprise, he was carried down.

The flashlights now went out, as if directed by some occult signal. The cavernous gloom which followed was filled with swishings and slappings, as the ebony-cloaked, green-belled figures charged.

Cash's gun was dislodged, and went *clank-clanking* across the pavement.

His raincoat tore. He tried to scream. The yell was throttled, and ended in a sound which might have been two rough rocks rubbing together.

The fight noises trailed off. Several moments of ominous quiet followed. Then the entire group moved back to the bridge spanning the railroad.

They turned off and came to a high fence. There was another short, terrific fight while Cash was being put over the fence. Then they descended to the railway tracks.

Once a light came on briefly. This disclosed the darksome figures in a compact wad, with Cash helpless among them.

The railroad was electrified. The current, instead of being carried by an overhead line, was conducted by a third rail which ran close alongside the track. Use of such third rails was common in the vicinity of New York, where the presence of numerous switches and sidings made overhead wiring too intricate. The charged rail was protected by a shedlike wooden shield.

A light came on. A wad of black cloth between Cash's jaws kept him from crying out.

He was thrown headlong at the electrified rail. With a frenzied contortion of his muscles, he managed to avoid landing upon it.

The somber figures pounced upon him, and again hurled him at the rail. Again he saved himself. He was fighting madly for his life. The shed protector over the rail helped him.

But one touch upon the strip of metal beneath, which bore a high voltage, would mean instant death.

The third time, Cash got an arm across the wooden shed and preserved his life. He tore the gag from his jaws with a desperate grasp and emitted a piercing bleat for help!

The Green Bells swarmed upon him, silent, murderous. This time, they pitched him at the rail feet first. One of his legs fell across the highpowered conductor.

There was a tiny hissing play of electric flame. Cash's body seemed to bounce up and down. It convulsed, tying itself in a tight knot around the rail of death.

It stayed there, rigid and still. A wispy plume of brownish smoke curling upward might have been the spirit departing from his body.

The Green Bells eased away in the rain-moist night like dread, voiceless ghouls from another existence.

Chapter II
VISITORS

The Triplex was New York's newest, gaudiest, and most expensive hotel. It catered to its guests with every comfort and convenience.

Guests arriving by taxi, for instance, did not find it necessary to alight at the sidewalks and enter before the stares of *hoi polloi*. There was an inclosed private drive for the cabs.

This drive was a semicircular tunnel done in bright metals and dark stone, after the modernistic fashion. In it, a taxi was disgorging a passenger.

The newcomer was a tall snake of a man. The serpentine aspect was lent by the fact that his body was so flexible as to seem boneless. His hair was carefully curled, and had an enameled shine. His eyes were ratty; his mouth was a crack; his clothes were flashy enough to be in bad taste.

He paid the taxi with a bill peeled from a fat roll. Entering the lobby, trailed by a bell boy bearing two bags, he leaned elbows on the desk.

"I'm Mr. Cooley," he said shortly. "I wired you for a reservation from Prosper City."

The man was conducted to his room. The bell boy was hardly out of hearing when he picked up the telephone.

"Gimme Judborn Tugg's room," he requested. Then, when he had the connection: "That you, Tugg? . . . This is Slick. What room you got? . . . O. K. I'll be right up."

The man rode an elevator up six floors, made his sinuous way down a corridor, and knocked at a door. The panel opened, and he said familiarly: "Howzza boy, Tugg!"

Judborn Tugg looked somewhat as if he had found a wolf in front of his door—a wolf with which he must, of necessity, associate.

"Come in," he said haughtily.

Tugg was a small, prosperous-appearing mountain. His dark pin-stripe suit, if a bit loud, was well tailored over his ample middle. His chins, big mouth and pale eyes rode on a cone of fat. A gold watch chain bridged his midriff, and formed a support for several lodge emblems.

"Slick" Cooley entered, closed the door, and said: "We don't have to worry any more about Jim Cash."

Judborn Tugg recoiled as if slapped. His head rotated on its foundation of fat as he glanced about nervously.

Slick quickly folded his arms, both hands inside his coat, where he carried automatic pistols. "What's the matter? Somebody here?"

"Oh, my, no! It would be too bad if there was! You should be more careful!" Tugg whipped out a silk handkerchief, and blotted at his forehead. "It is just that I cannot get used to the cold way you fellows have of handling things."

"What you mean is the Green Bell's way of handling things." Slick leered.

"Yes, yes; of course." Judborn Tugg ground his handkerchief in uneasy hands. "The Green Bell will be glad to know young Cash is satisfactorily disposed of."

Slick took his hands away from his armpits, and straightened his coat. "I didn't get any time alone with Cash, so I couldn't question him before he was tossed on that third rail."

"Your orders were not to question him," Judborn Tugg said smugly.

Slick sneered slightly. "You don't need to pretend to be so damned holy with me, Tugg. We understand each other. We'd both like to know who the Green Bell is. Jim Cash knew. By questioning him, I might have gotten the lowdown. But I didn't dare. There was too many guys around."

"Ahem!" Judborn Tugg cleared his throat and glanced about nervously.

"One of these days, we're gonna find out who the Green Bell is!" Slick said grimly. "When that happens, we'll rub him out, see! And, presto, we've got the gravy."

Judborn Tugg shuddered violently.

"Oh, goodness, Slick!" he wailed. "Suppose the Green Bell —suppose some one should overhear us! Let us not talk about it!"

"O. K.," Slick leered. "What're me and you to do now?"

Judborn Tugg put his handkerchief away, and fiddled with the ornaments on his watch chain. "Have you ever heard of a gentleman by the name of Doc Savage?"

"Kinda seems like I have." Slick smoothed his coat lapels. "New York is not my stompin' ground, and this Savage bird hangs out here. I don't know much about him. Kind of a trouble buster, ain't he?"

"Exactly! I understand he is a very fierce and competent fighting man, who has a group of five aids."

"A muscle man with a gang, eh?"

"In your vernacular, I believe that is how you express it. The Green Bell had me investigate Doc Savage. I did not learn a great deal about him, except that he is a man who fights other people's battles."

"Yeah? And what about this guy?"

"The Green Bell has ordered me to hire Doc Savage. I am to obtain the services of the man and his five aids for our organization."

Slick swore wildly. He stamped around the room, fists hard, mean face twisted with rage.

"I won't stand for it!" he gritted. "I was to have charge of the rough stuff in this business! I was to be third in command—takin' orders only from the Green Bell and you! Now the Green Bell is fixin' to ring this Doc Savage in!"

Judborn Tugg patted the air with both hands.

"My dear Slick, you misunderstand," he soothed. "You are to retain your position. Doc Savage is to work under you! The Green Bell made that very clear."

"He did, eh?" Slick scowled, but seemed mollified. "Well, that's different. But that Doc Savage has gotta savvy that his orders come from me!"

"Of course. That will be made clear."

Slick lighted an expensive cigarette. "Supposin' Doc Savage considers himself a big shot, and don't want to take my orders."

"Any man will take commands, if the pay is sufficient," Judborn Tugg said, with the certainty of a man who has money and knows its power.

But Slick was still uncertain. "What if Doc Savage ain't the kind of a guy who hires out for our kind of work?"

"There, again, my statement about payment applies. Every man has his price. The Green Bell needs more men, needs them badly. He does not want ordinary gunmen. Therefore, I am to approach Doc Savage."

"O. K. Where'll we find 'im?"

Judborn Tugg shrugged. "I do not know. We shall see if the telephone information girl can tell us."

He put in a call. The swiftness with which he was given Doc Savage's address seemed to daze him. He blinked his pale eyes and hung up.

"Doc Savage must be rather well known!" he muttered. "The phone operator had his whereabouts on the tip of her tongue. Come, Slick. We shall go see this man."

The two quitted the hotel room.

The skyscraper before which Slick Cooley and Judborn Tugg eventually alighted was one of the most resplendent in the city. It towered nearly a hundred stories.

"What a joint!" Slick muttered in awe. "Doc Savage ain't no cheap skate if he hangs out here!"

"These surroundings show Savage is good at his business,"

Judborn Tugg replied stiffly. "That is the kind of a man we want. You, Slick, will wait in the lobby."

"Why?" Slick demanded suspiciously. "How do I know but that you'll pay this Savage more money than I'm gettin'?"

"Nothing of the sort, Slick. You will stay here in case Alice Cash and Aunt Nora should put in an appearance. They were coming here to hire this Savage to do their fighting. They cannot pay Savage as much as we can, but it would be better if they did not see him."

"Yeah," Slick agreed with bad grace. "I'll stick below, then."

An express elevator which ran noiselessly and with great speed, lifted Judborn Tugg to the eighty-sixth floor. He strutted pompously down a richly decorated corridor.

Sighting a mirror, Tugg halted and carefully surveyed his appearance. He wanted to overawe this Doc Savage. That was the way to handle these common thugs who hired themselves out for money.

Tugg lighted a dollar cigar. He had another just like it which he intended to offer Savage. The fine weeds would be the final touch. Doc Savage would be bowled over by the grandeur of Judborn Tugg.

Tugg did not know it, but he was headed for one of the big shocks of his career.

He knocked on a door, puffed out his chest, and cocked his cigar in the air.

The door opened.

Judborn Tugg's chest collapsed, his cigar fell to the floor, and his eyes bulged out.

A mighty giant of bronze stood in the door. The effect of this metallic figure was amazing. Marvelously symmetrical proportions absorbed the true size of the man. Viewed from a distance, and away from anything to which his stature might have been compared, he would not have seemed as big.

The remarkably high forehead, the muscular and strong mouth, the lean and corded cheeks, denoted a rare power of character. His bronze hair was darker than his bronze skin, and it lay straight and smooth as a skullcap of metal.

The thing which really took the wind out of Judborn Tugg, though, was the bronze man's eyes. They were like pools of fine flake gold, alive with tiny glistenings. They possessed a strange, hypnotic quality. They made Judborn Tugg want to pull his coat over his head, so that the innermost secrets of his brain would not be searched out.

"Are—are—you Doc Savage?" stuttered Judborn Tugg.

The bronze giant nodded. The simple gesture caused great cables of muscle to writhe about his neck.

Tugg felt an impulse to shiver at the sight. This bronze man must possess incredible strength.

In a quiet, powerful voice. Doc Savage invited Tugg inside. Then he gave him a cigar, explaining quietly: "I hope you'll excuse me, since I never smoke."

That cigar was the final shock to Judborn Tugg. It was a long, fine custom weed in an individual vacuum container. Tugg happened to know that cigars such as this could not be obtained for less than ten dollars each.

Judborn Tugg was a pricked balloon. Instead of overawing Doc Savage, he was himself practically stunned.

Several moments were required before Judborn Tugg recovered sufficient aplomb to get down to business.

"I have heard you are an—er—a trouble buster," he said, in a small voice, very unlike his usual overbearing tone.

"You might call it that," Doc Savage agreed politely. "More properly, my five companions and myself have a purpose in life. That purpose is to go here and there, from one end of the world to the other, looking for excitement and adventure, striving to help those in need of help, and punishing those who deserve it."

Judborn Tugg did not know that it was a very rare occasion when Doc Savage gave out even this much information about himself.

Tugg did not like the speech at all. He mulled it over, and reached a conclusion—the wrong one. He decided this was Doc Savage's way of hinting that he and his men hired out their services. The man, of course, could not come right out and say he was a professional thug.

"My case is right in your line," Tugg said, managing a faint smirk. "There are people who need help, and some others who need punishing."

Doc Savage nodded politely. "Suppose you tell me the situation."

"It's this way," said Tugg, lighting the costly cigar. "I am one of the leading business men in Prosper City. I own Tugg & Co., the largest cotton-milling concern in the town."

Tugg folded his hands and looked pious. "Some months ago, because of terrible business conditions, we were forced to cut the wages of our employees. Much against our wishes, of course."

"I thought business was picking up," Doc remarked.

Tugg acquired the expression of a man who had been served a bad egg unexpectedly.

"Business is terrible!" he said emphatically. "It's worse now, too, because all of my employees went out on a strike! And the workmen in the other factories and mines went on strikes. It's awful! Conditions are frightful!"

Doc Savage asked gently: "Did the other concerns cut wages before or after you did?"

Judborn Tugg swallowed a few times. He was startled. With that one question, Doc Savage had grabbed the kernel of the whole situation in Prosper City.

The truth was that Tugg & Co. had cut wages first, and the other concerns had been forced to do the same in order to meet the low prices at which their competitor was offering goods for sale. Tugg & Co. had turned itself into a sweatshop, paying their employees starvation wages.

When this had happened, there had been no necessity for it. Business had indeed been picking up. The whole thing was part of a plot conceived by that mysterious, unknown being, the Green Bell.

Other concerns in Prosper City had been forced to cut wages, although not as much as Tugg & Co. But the cuts had been enough to give agitators hired by Tugg & Co. an argument with which to cause numerous strikes. The hired agitators had even been directed to urge the strike at Tugg & Co. who paid them.

For months now, the agitators, under the direction of Slick Cooley, had kept all business at a standstill. Any factory which tried to open up was bombed, burned, or its machinery ruined. Every workman who sought to take a job was threatened or beaten, or if that failed, the Green Bell had a final and most horrible form of death, which was in itself an object lesson to other stubborn ones.

The whole thing was part of the scheme of the unknown master mind, the Green Bell. No one knew what was behind it. Judborn Tugg, if he knew, was not telling anybody.

Tugg carefully avoided Doc Savage's weird eyes, and decided to handle the bronze man warily.

"We were all forced to cut wages about the same time," he lied uneasily: "But the salary whacks were not at the bottom of the trouble. It is all the fault of the agitators."

When Tugg paused, Doc Savage said nothing. He had settled in a comfortable chair. Several of these were in the outer office. There was also an expensive inlaid table and a massive safe. A costly rug was underfoot.

Adjoining, was a library containing one of the most complete collections of scientific tomes in existence, and another room which held an experimental laboratory so advanced in its equipment that scientists had come from foreign countries, just to examine it. The presence of these rooms was masked by a closed door, however.

"Conditions in Prosper City are pitiful," continued Judborn Tugg, secretly wondering if he might not be entirely mistaken about this bronze man. "People are starving. There have been bombings, beatings, killings. It is all the fault of these agitators."

Doc Savage maintained a disquieting silence.

"Aunt Nora Boston is the leader of the agitators," Tugg said, telling an enormous lie without blinking.

Doc might have been a figure done in the bronze which he resembled, for all the signs of interest he showed. But that did not mean he was missing anything. Doc rarely showed emotion.

Tugg sucked in a full breath and went on: "Aunt Nora Boston is aided by Jim Cash, his sister Alice, and a young man named Ole Slater, who is hanging around Prosper City, pretending to be a play writer gathering local color for a manufacturing-town drama. Those four are the ring leaders. They're the head of a gang they call the Prosper City Benevolent Society. That organization is back of all the trouble. They're just low-down trouble-makers. I'll bet they're paid by some foreign country."

This was so much more falsehood.

Judborn Tugg had not intended for his talk to follow these lines. But he was afraid to broach the truth. It was those eyes of the bronze man's. Tugg would have been glad to get up and walk out, but he feared the wrath of the Green Bell.

"I want to hire you to—er—punish Aunt Nora Boston and her gang," he said bluntly. "I'll pay you plenty!"

"My services are not for sale," Doc Savage said quietly. "They never are."

Judborn Tugg's head seemed to sink in his fat cone of a neck. What manner of man was this?

Doc went on: "Usually, individuals who are assisted by my five men and myself are generous enough to contribute a gift to worthy causes which I name."

Tugg stifled a smile. So this was the dodge the bronze man used to make it seem he was not a hired thug. Tugg thought he saw the light. This Doc Savage could be hired, all right!

"Just how big a gift would you want?" he asked cannily.

"In your case, and provided conditions are just as you have outlined," Doc replied promptly, "the gift would be a million dollars."

Judborn Tugg narrowly escaped heart failure.

Down in the skyscraper lobby, Slick Cooley was also experiencing a shock; but from a different cause.

Slick had caught sight of Alice Cash and Aunt Nora Boston.

The two women were mud-spattered, bedraggled, and sodden from the rain. They left wet tracks across the polished lobby tiling. Their faces were pale, frightened, and they seemed overawed by the magnificence of the giant building.

They trudged for the elevators, Aund Nora in the lead, strong jaw thrust out.

Slick gave his brain a mental whipping. He had best do something! Should the two women get upstairs, they might complicate things. Aunt Nora would do that, at least. She was an old war horse when she got mad. A brilliant idea hit Slick. He dashed forward. Before the two women saw him, he grabbed them savagely and jerked.

Aunt Nora's big purse sailed to the floor.

Slick pounced upon the bag. He had his roll of bills concealed in one hand. Furtively, he got the purse open. He slipped the money inside. In doing this, he saw the two revolvers.

He now seized the women. A violent tussle ensued.

"Robbers!" Slick bellowed. "These two dames held me up!"

Aunt Nora gave him a poke in the eye which made him bawl in real agony. Pretty Alice Cash administered a few blows of her own.

A policeman dived in from the street. In a moment, he had stopped the fight.

Slick jabbed a hand at the two women. "These women held me up to-night! I recognize 'em! Search 'em officer! I'll bet they've got the rods they used, and my coin!"

The officer opened Aunt Nora's bag, found the guns and the money. He counted the latter.

"How much did you lose?" he asked.

Slick gave him the exact amount of the roll.

"This is it!" the patrolman said grimly. He collared the two women.

Alice Cash shrieked angrily: "We did not rob him!"

"Evidence says you did!" rumbled the officer. "Even if you didn't, you're carryin' guns, and that's against the law in New York."

"You scut!" Aunt Nora flared at the smirking Slick. "You framed us! You low-lifed, slippery-haired sneak! I'll wring your snaky neck!"

She jumped for Slick, who back-pedaled hastily.

"None of that!" shouted the officer. "It's into the jug for you!" He propelled his prisoners for the door.

Chapter III
THE COMEBACK

As the women were leaving, the gorilla ambled upon the scene.

This personage had, to give him his due, some man-like qualities. His finger nails were manicured, even if the job had been done with a pocketknife. His little eyes glistened with keen intelligence in their pits of gristle. His face attained that rare quality of being so homely that it was pleasant to look upon.

His clothing was expensive, although it did look like it had been slept in. He would weigh every ounce of two hundred and sixty pounds, and his hairy arms were some inches longer than his bandy legs.

He ambled up and stopped in front of Slick.

"I saw you slip the money in that purse," he said in a voice so mild that it might have been a child's.

Then he hit Slick. Hit him on the nose!

Slick's curly hair was varnished straight back on his head. The blow was so hard that it made the hair stand out suddenly in front, as if blown by a wind from behind.

Describing a parabola, Slick lit on his shoulders and skidded a score of feet. His nose had been spread over most of his weasel face.

Aunt Nora began to bounce up and down in ribald delight, and to shout: "Glory be! Just what I wanted to hand him!"

Entrancing Alice Cash bestowed a grateful smile on the fellow who looked like a furry gorilla.

The cop shouted: "You say this squirt planted that roll of bills?"

"He sure did," said the hairy man.

Growling, the officer rushed for Slick.

Slick shoved up dizzily from the floor. He sprinted for the door. Glancing around, he saw the policeman was sure to overhaul him. He spaded his hands inside his coat, and brought out two revolvers. Each was fitted with a compact silencer.

The guns began to *chung* out deadly reports. The bullets missed the fast-traveling patrolman. But he veered for shelter, tugging at his own weapon.

Slick hurtled through the door. A taxi chanced to be cruising past. With a wild spring, the fleeing gunman got into it. He jammed the hot silencer of a revolver against the shivering driver's neck.

The cab jumped down the street as if dynamite had exploded behind it.

The officer raced out, but did not shoot because of the traffic. He sped back into the skyscraper and put in a call to headquarters, advising them to spread a radio alarm for the taxi.

"The guy as good as got away!" he advised the huge, furry man and the two women, when he rejoined them. "Now—you two ladies! We've still got to settle about them guns you were carryin'!"

"The ladies tell me they were on their way to see Doc Savage," the hairy fellow advised in his babylike voice.

The cop blinked. Then he grinned from ear to ear.

"That makes it different," he chuckled. Then he walked away, acting as if he had never seen the two women.

Alice Cash looked prettily incredulous at the magic which mention of Doc Savage's name had accomplished.

Aunt Nora gulped several times, then smiled. "Bless you, you homely monkey! How'd you get us out of that? I know they're very strict about people packin' guns here in New York."

The human gorilla laughed. "The fact that you were goin' to Doc Savage made it all right."

"Doc Savage must have a big reputation in this town," Aunt Nora said wonderingly. "You ain't him, are you?"

"Who, me? Hell—I mean, oh my—no! I'm just one of Doc Savage's five helpers."

"What's your name?"

"Lieutenant Colonel Andrew Blodgett Mayfair."

Aunt Nora snorted. "I'll bet you're not called that much!"

"Not enough for me to know who's bein' wanted when I hear it!" the hairy fellow grinned. "Call me Monk."

"Monk" might have added that he was a chemist whose name was mentioned with reverence in scientific circles of both America and Europe. But he was not addicted to blowing his own horn.

The speedy elevator lifted them to the eighty-sixth floor. When they were near the door of Doc Savage's office, the murmur of a voice within was distinguishable.

Aunt Nora gave a start of angry surprise. "I'd know that voice anywhere!" she gasped. "It's Judborn Tugg!"

Monk's little eyes showed interest. "Who's he?"

"A fat, conceited jaybird! He's no friend of ours! Slick Cooley —the fellow you pasted downstairs—follows Judborn Tugg around like a Man Friday. They're tarred with the same brush —both crooked!"

Monk considered this, then waved the women back. He opened the office door, and stood in the aperture. His big, hirsute hands moved nervously, as if he were embarrassed.

"Oh, excuse me! I didn't know you had company." He started to back out.

No one, other than Doc, had noticed that the apparently aimless movements of Monk's hands had spelled out a message in the deaf-and-dumb sign language.

"Come out here without alarming your visitor," Monk had signaled.

Doc arose, saying to Judborn Tugg: "If you will excuse me—I wish to speak with this man!" He strode rapidly to the door.

For all of his great weight and swiftness of stride, he made no appreciable sound. There was an uncanny silence about his movements, a natural lightness which indicated enormously developed leg muscles.

Fat Judborn Tugg, instead of suspecting anything, was rather glad to have Doc step outside for a moment. Tugg had not yet recovered from the shock of having Doc suggest that his services would call for a million-dollar donation. He welcomed the chance to regain his balance.

Doc closed the corridor door. Shortly later, he was in the presence of the two women.

Aunt Nora let her mouth hang open in unashamed astonishment at sight of the giant bronze man. Then she cocked her arms akimbo and smiled, wrinkles corrugating every inch of her motherly face.

"Glory be!" she chuckled. "You're the answer to this old girl's prayers!"

Alice Cash did not exactly let her jaw drop, but her lips parted slightly, and her blue eyes became round with amazement. Her next act was to glance down disgustedly at her muddy, disheveled raiment.

Doc Savage usually affected pretty young women like that—set them wondering about their appearance. Feminine eyes were inclined to be quick to note that Doc was unusually handsome, a fact which escaped men after they saw his amazing muscular development.

Monk performed the introduction.

"What has Judborn Tugg been tellin' you?" Aunt Nora questioned anxiously.

"A great deal," Doc replied quietly. "He is one of the most profuse liars. I have ever encountered."

This would have pained Judborn Tugg exceedingly, had he overheard it. It was his belief that he could tell a falsehood as smoothly as the truth. He would have been shocked to know that Doc Savage, by close attention to his voice tones, had spotted almost every lie.

Aunt Nora clenched her work-toughened hands, and gave Doc a look of genuine appeal.

"I need your help!" she said earnestly. "But I haven't got a cent with which to pay you!"

Doc's strange golden eyes studied Aunt Nora and attractive Alice Cash. His bronze features remained as expressionless as metal.

Without speaking, he turned. He entered his office.

"I do not think I am interested in your proposition," he told Judborn Tugg.

Tugg picked the costly cigar from his pursy mouth, as if it had suddenly turned bitter.

"I can pay you plenty," he pointed out. "I might even pay you that million, provided you can do the work that I want done."

"No!"

Judborn Tugg purpled. To him, it was inconceivable that any man would dismiss a million so abruptly. He would probably have keeled over had he known that Doc intended to help Aunt Nora Boston, who had admitted she could not pay him a copper cent.

"If you change your mind, you'll find me at the Hotel Triplex!" Tugg said in a loud, angry tone.

"There will be no change of mind," Doc said, reaching out and grasping Tugg by the coat collar.

Before Tugg knew what had happened, he was hoisted off the floor. His coat tore in two or three places, but held.

Helpless as a worm on a stick, Tugg was carried into the corridor and deposited urgently in an elevator.

"If you want to retain your health, you had better not let me see you again!" Doc advised him in the tone of a physician prescribing for a patient with dangerous symptoms.

The elevator carried Tugg from view.

Monk, an innocent expression on his homely face, ambled up and asked: "Didn't I hear that bird say he was staying at the Hotel Triplex?"

Doc nodded; then invited Aunt Nora and Alice Cash into his office.

Grinning, Monk ambled to a public telephone in the corridor. He got the number of the Hotel Triplex from the phone book, then called the hostelry. He asked the hotel operator for the night manager.

"You have a guest named Judborn Tugg," Monk informed the hotel man. "Doc Savage just threw this fellow out of his office."

"In that case, we'll throw him out of the Hotel Triplex, too," Monk was advised.

Hanging up, Monk fished an envelope out of his pocket and addressed it to the Unemployment Relief Fund.

From another pocket, he produced Slick Cooley's fat roll of bills. Monk had managed to harvest this in the excitement downstairs. He sealed the money in the envelope, applied stamps then put it in a mail box. The envelope was so bulky that he had to insert it in the lid marked for packages.

Whistling cheerfully, Monk tramped for Doc's office.

When Judborn Tugg reached the Hotel Triplex, he found his bags waiting for him on the sidewalk. The night manager in person was watching over the valises.

"I am sorry," the manager said coldly. "We do not want you here."

Judborn Tugg, after nearly choking, yelled and cursed and waved his arms. He threatened to sue the Triplex for a million dollars.

"Get away from here, or I'll have you arrested for disturbing the peace!" snapped the manager. Then he walked inside.

A moment later, a dark limousine rolled up to the curb. The rear was heavily curtained.

The driver leaned from behind the wheel and advised: "Get in!"

It was Slick Cooley, partially disguised by a raincoat and a low-pulled hat.

Judborn Tugg placed his bags in the front, then got in the back. At this point, his hair almost stood on end.

The rear seat held a figure incased from head to foot in a black sack of a garment. On the front of the raven gown was painted a big green bell.

The unholy apparition in black held two silenced revolvers in dark-gloved hands.

"Do not mind the guns," said a hollow, inhuman voice from the murksome form. "I am the Green Bell, and the weapons are merely to remind you not to snatch at my hood in an effort to learn my identity."

The limousine now rolled out into traffic.

"I was walkin' down the street when *he* called to me from the back of this car," Slick advised. "There wasn't any driver——"

"I simply parked the car ahead of you, before donning my hood," interposed the sepulchral tones of the Green Bell. "Incidentally, this machine is stolen. But I do not think the owner will miss it for some hours. Tugg—what happened to you?"

Judborn Tugg started. He had been cudgeling his brain in an effort to identify the Green Bell's voice. But there was nothing the least familiar about the disguised tones.

Rapidly, Judborn Tugg explained the unhappy outcome of his visit to Doc Savage.

"You have served me very inefficiently!" Anger had come into the booming voice of the Green Bell. "This Doc Savage is not at all the type of man you thought him to be!"

Tugg, still smarting from his reception at the hotel, said angrily: "This is my first mistake!"

The Green Bell gazed levelly at him. The eye holes in the jet hood were backed by goggles which had deep-green lenses. The effect was that of a big, green-orbed cat.

"I do not care for your angry tone!" said the dark being. "You are fully aware, Tugg, that I can get along without those who do not coöperate fully with me. You are no exception! You are of service to me only as an agent, a figurehead through which I can work. You pretend to be Prosper City's leading citizen, and I choose to let you. Your milling concern, Tugg & Co., was ready to fail when I came upon the scene, thanks to your bad management. You have retained control of the company only because I have furnished you money with which to pay the interest on your loans. You are but a cog in my great plan."

Judborn Tugg collapsed like an automobile tire which had picked up a nail.

"I did not mean to offend you," he mumbled. "I was excited because of the treatment Doc Savage gave me."

"I am going to take care of Doc Savage!" the Green Bell said ominously.

Tugg shivered. "The man is dangerous—especially if he has the brains to match his unbelievable physical strength!"

"We do not want Savage against us," replied the Green Bell. "I have already put a plan in operation which will keep Savage so busy that he will have no time to stick a finger in our pie."

"I'd like to see him dead!" said Judborn Tugg savagely.

"You may get your wish!" tolled the Green Bell. "My little scheme will undoubtedly result in Doc Savage dying in the electric chair!"

Ordering Slick down a dark street, the Green Bell eased out of the car, and was swallowed by the drizzling darkness. A bit farther on, Judborn Tugg and Slick Cooley abandoned the stolen limousine.

Walking away from the car, they could see in the distance what appeared to be a tower of gray freckles in the wet gloom. This was the skyscraper which housed Doc Savage's aerie.

Chapter IV
THE MURDER WITNESSES

In his eighty-sixth-floor headquarters, Doc was listening to Aunt Nora Boston and Alice Cash tell their story. The homely Monk lingered in the background, furtively admiring Alice Cash's loveliness.

"My brother!" Alice said, whitefaced. "He has vanished! We ran out of gas in New Jersey, and Jim walked ahead to find a filling station. That was the last we saw of him!"

"We thought we heard Jim scream," Aunt Nora amended grimly. "But we couldn't find him."

Alice put her fingers over her pale lips and said between them: "And just before that, we heard the Green Bell from the radio!"

Aunt Nora grimaced. "The sound of the Green Bell over the radio nearly always means some innocent person is to die!"

Alice shuddered, wailed: "Poor Jimmy! I have a feeling something terrible happened to him!"

Doc Savage could do remarkable things with his powerful voice. He now made it calm and soothing, a tone calculated to quiet the excited women.

"Your story is a bit disconnected," he told them. "Suppose you start at the first."

Aunt Nora clenched her hands and stared steadily at them as she talked.

"The trouble in Prosper City started many months ago, when Tugg & Co. cut wages. That caused the first of a series of strikes——"

"Judborn Tugg told me about that," Doc interposed. "All business in Prosper City is at a standstill. A gang of men, pretending to be agitators, bomb or burn every factory and mine which attempts to start operations, and terrorize all men who want to go back to work. Tugg said you were the chief of the agitators."

"The liar!" Aunt Nora flared, "All I have done is organize my Benevolent Society to help some of the poor souls who are out of work."

"Aunt Nora has kept lots of people from starving!" Alice Cash put in. "She has spent all of her money, and all she can borrow, in feeding those unfortunates."

"You shut up!" Aunt Nora directed gruffly.

"I will not!" Alice snapped, "I think Mr. Savage should know the truth! You're an angel!"

Aunt Nora blushed and stared at her big, muddy shoes. "I ain't no angel—not with them feet."

"What about these agitators back of the trouble?" Doc asked.

"They're hired thugs, of course!" Aunt Nora declared. "But just who they are, nobody knows. When they appear they're always in robes that look like black sacks, with green bells painted on the front."

"Their leader is not known?"

"No!" Aunt Nora made a fierce mouth. "Alice and her brother and Ole Slater have been helping me try to find out who the Green Bell is."

"Who is Ole Slater?" Doc Savage wanted to know.

"A nice young lad who thinks he can write plays. He's stricken with the charm of Alice, here. He's gathering material for a play, and he stays at my rooming house. I forgot to tell you that I run a boarding house."

Doc asked: "And you think Judborn Tugg and Slick Cooley are in the Green Bell's gang?"

"I ain't got no proof!" asserted Aunt Nora. "But they could be! One of them might be the Green Bell, himself."

Monk entered the conference, asking gently: "Hasn't the police chief of Prosper City done anything about all this?"

"That old numbskull!" Aunt Nora sniffed. "His name is Clem Clements, and he thinks Judborn Tugg is the greatest man alive and the soul of honor. I don't think Chief Clements is crooked. He's just plain downright dumb!"

"How come Tugg exerts such a sway?" Monk wanted to know.

"Judborn Tugg tries to make himself out as the leading business man of Prosper City!" snorted Aunt Nora. "He's fooled a lot of nitwits, including Chief Clements. Tugg has been spreading the story that I am behind the Green Bell. He has made Chief

Clements and plenty of others believe it. I've thought several times they were going to throw me in jail!"

"They haven't quite dared do that!" Alice Cash explained. "The poor people Aunt Nora has been helping would tear down the jail if she was in it. I don't think they've dared harm Aunt Nora for the same reason."

Aunt Nora laughed grimly. "I've told everybody that if anything happens to me, it'll be Judborn Tugg's doing! If the Green Bells should murder me, or drive me insane, my friends would lynch Tugg. That's why I haven't been harmed."

"What's this about insanity?" Doc interrupted.

Alice Cash shivered. "It's something that happens to workmen who are persistent about going back to their jobs. No one knows how it is done. The men simply—go crazy. It's happened to more than a dozen of them."

For a few moments Doc and Monk mulled over what they had been hearing. It was an amazing story, the more so because the motive behind the affair was unclear.

"Why hasn't martial law been declared?" Monk demanded.

"Chief Clements claims he has the situation in hand!" Alice Cash replied. "The distressing situation in Prosper City has come about gradually. To an outsider, it merely looks like strike trouble."

Aunt Nora had maintained a short, tense silence. Now she exploded.

"Jim Cash as much as admitted he had found out who the Green Bell is!" she announced. "And that very thing makes me think he has been killed!"

Alice Cash gave a soft, grief-stricken moan, and buried her face in her hands.

Monk got up as if to comfort her.

There was a loud interruption from the corridor outside. Blows chugged. Men grunted and gasped.

Doc glided over and whipped the door open.

Two men stood in the hall, hands lifted, facing a third man who held a flat automatic.

The hands which one of the men held up were so huge it seemed a wonder they did not overbalance him. Each was composed of considerably more than a quart of bone and gristle. He had a somber, puritanical face.

This man of enormous fists was Colonel John Renwick, known more often as "Renny." Among other things, he was a world-renowned engineer, a millionaire, and loved to knock panels out of doors with his big fists.

The other fellow with upraised arms was slender, with a somewhat unhealthy complexion. He had pale hair and eyes. Alongside his big-fisted, rusty-skinned companion, he seemed a weakling.

He was "Long Tom." The electrical profession knew him as Major Thomas J. Roberts, a wizard with the juice.

Renny and Long Tom were two more of Doc Savage's five aids.

The man with the gun was a chap Doc had never seen before. He was tall, athletic, and not unhandsome.

The fellow backed to an elevator, sprang inside, and the cage sank.

Renny and Long Tom looked sheepishly at Doc.

"We came upon that bird listenin' outside the door!" Renny said, in a roaring voice, suggestive of an angry lion in a cave. "We tried to grab him, but he flashed his hardware on us!"

Doc was gliding down the corridor as these words came. He reached the endmost elevator. His sinew-wrapped hand tapped a secret button. Sliding doors whistled back.

This lift was a private one, which Doc maintained for his own use. It was fitted with special machinery, which operated at terrific speed. The ordinary express elevators were fast, but compared to this one, they were slow.

The floor dropped some inches below Doc's feet, so swiftly did the descent start. For fully sixty stories, he hardly touched the floor. Then came the slow, tremendous shock of the stop. Doc's five aids, all strong men, were usually forced to their knees when this happened.

So powerful were the bronze man's thews that he withstood the shock without apparent effort.

He flashed out into the lobby of the towering building. The cage bearing the young man with the gun had not yet arrived.

But it came within a few moments. The young man got out, backing so as to menace the elevator operator with his weapon.

Doc grasped the fellow's arms. Bronze fingers all but sank from view as they tightened.

An agonized wail was forced through the man's teeth. He dropped his gun. The excruciating pressure on his arm muscles caused his fingers to distend like talons.

He tried to kick backward. But pain had rendered him as limp as a big rag. His head drooped; his eyes glazed. He was on the verge of fainting from the torture.

Doc tucked the slack figure under an arm, entered the speed elevator, and rode back to the eighty-sixth floor.

Aunt Nora, Alice Cash, and the others were waiting in the corridor.

Doc's prisoner was hardly able to stand. His knees buckled. Doc grasped him by an arm, not too tightly, and held him erect.

Aunt Nora stared at the captive, popeyed.

Amazement also engulfed Alice Cash's attractive features as she gazed at the young man.

"Know him?" Doc asked quietly.

"He is Ole Slater!" Alice exclaimed. "My—er—the boy who likes me!"

Half carried into the office, and deposited in a deep chair, Ole Slater found his tongue.

"I got worried and followed you to New York," he told Alice and Aunt Nora.

"You should not have been sneaking around that door," Aunt Nora informed him severely.

"Don't I know it!" Ole Slater touched his arms gingerly, then eyed Doc Savage's metallic hands as if wondering how they could have inflicted such torment. "I stopped outside the door a minute to listen. I was just being cautious. Then these men jumped me. I guess I lost my head—I thought they were Green Bells!"

Aunt Nora smiled at Doc. "This young man is our friend. I'm sure he didn't mean any harm."

"Of course he didn't!" Alice Cash added her defense.

"I'm terribly sorry about this," Ole Slater said meekly. "I was, well—worried about Aunt Nora and Jim and Alice."

Grief returned to Alice Cash's refined features. "Jim has vanished, Ole."

Ole Slater now received the story of what had happened on the New Jersey road, beginning with the awesome belling sound which had come unexpectedly from the radio.

Aunt Nora Boston added a few more details about conditions in Prosper City. Although Doc questioned her closely, he learned little that had not been brought out already.

Alice Cash, it developed, was private secretary to Collison McAlter, a man who owned the Little Grand Cotton Mills. The

Little Grand was the main competitor of Tugg & Co., in Prosper City, but was now closed down, like all the rest of the industries.

The master mind, the Green Bell, for some reason as yet unclear, was keeping all Prosper City business at a standstill by use of a reign of terror. That was what it amounted to.

They had been talking the situation over for about half an hour when two men dashed excitedly into the office.

One gesticulated with a slender black cane, and barked: "Doc! You're in a frightful jam!"

The cane which the man waved looked innocent, but it was in reality a sword cane with a blade of fine Damascus steel. The gentleman who carried it was slender, with sharp features and a high forehead. His clothing was of the latest style and finest cloth.

He was Brigadier General Theodore Marley Brooks—"Ham" to Doc's group, of which he was a member. He was by way of being the most astute lawyer Harvard ever turned out. He was also such a snappy dresser that tailors sometimes followed him down the street, just to observe clothes being worn as they should be worn.

"You've been accused of a murder, Doc!" exclaimed the second of the newcomers.

This man was tall, and so thin he seemed nothing more than a structure of skin-coated bones. He wore glasses, the left lens of which was much thicker than the right. The left lens was a powerful magnifying glass. The bony man had lost the use of his left eye in the War, and since he needed a magnifier in his profession of archæology and geology, he carried it in the left side of his spectacles, for convenience.

He was "Johnny"—William Harper Littlejohn, one-time head of the natural science research department of a famous university, and possessor of an almost universal reputation for proficiency in his line.

The addition of these two completed Doc Savage's group of five unusual aids. Each was a man with few equals at his trade. They were men who loved excitement and adventure. They found that aplenty with Doc Savage. The strange bronze man seemed to walk always on paths of peril.

Undoubtedly the most amazing fact about this remarkable company of trouble busters was the ability of Doc, himself, to excel any one of his helpers at his own profession. Doc's fund of knowledge about electricity was greater than that of Long Tom, the wizard of the juice; the same supremacy applied to the others in their fields of chemistry, geology, law, and engineering.

"What's this about me being a murderer?" Doc asked sharply.

"The New Jersey police have a warrant for you!" declared Ham, still flourishing his sword cane. "They have four witnesses who say they saw you throw a man against the third rail of an interurban line and electrocute him!"

"And they're bringing the witnesses over here to identify you!" Johnny added. Excitedly, he jerked off his spectacles which had the magnifier on the left side. "They'll be here any time, now!"

Ham nodded vehemently. "They will! A police officer in New Jersey, knowing I usually take care of the law angles in our troubles, called me and tipped me off about the thing."

"Who am I supposed to have murdered?" Doc queried dryly.

Ham tapped his sword cane thoughtfully. "A fellow I never heard of. His name was Jim Cash!"

Alice Cash sank soundlessly into a chair and buried her face in her arms. Her shoulders began to convulse.

Monk, who had prowled over to the window, and stood looking down, called abruptly: "Look at this!"

Doc flashed to his side.

Far below, a car was sweeping in to the curb. Men got out. In the darkness and rain, it was impossible to identify them. They numbered nine.

Faint light spilled from the front of the skyscraper, revealing, painted on top of the car for easy identification from airplanes, the lettered symbols of New Jersey State Police.

"The New Jersey officers with their witnesses!" Monk muttered.

Chapter V
PERIL'S PATH

Doc backed from the window. Without apparent haste, but none the less with deceptive speed, he crossed to the massive table and touched several inlaid segments. These depressed under his fingers, but immediately sprang back into place, so as to conceal the fact that the table top was one great cluster of push buttons.

"Monk, you and Ham stay here and stall these fellows!" Doc directed.

Monk surveyed the sartorially perfect Ham and made an awful grimace. "O. K. I'll try to put up with this shyster!"

At that, Ham glared and hefted his sword cane suggestively. His expression said that nothing would give him more pleasure than to stick the blade into Monk's anthropoid frame.

"Some of these days, I'm gonna take that hairy hide of yours home for a rug!" he promised.

This exchange, accompanied by fierce looks, was nothing unusual. Ham and Monk were always riding each other. Their good-natured quarrel dated back to the Great War—to an incident which had given Ham his nickname. To have some fun, Ham had taught Monk some highly insulting French words, telling him they were the proper adjectives with which to curry the favor of a French general. Monk had used them—and landed in the guardhouse.

Shortly after his release from the military calaboose, the dapper Brigadier General Theodore Marley Brooks had been hailed upon a charge of stealing hams. Somebody had planted the evidence. The nickname of Ham had stuck from that day.

What irked Ham especially, was the fact that he had never been able to prove it was Monk who had framed him.

Monk only leered nastily at Ham, and asked Doc: "Where are you goin'?"

31

"If you do not know, you can tell the truth when those fellows ask you where we are," Doc informed him dryly.

Every one but Monk and Ham now left the office. They entered the high-speed elevator. A breath-taking drop followed. Doc sent the cage to the basement level.

The New Jersey officers and their four witnesses had undoubtedly been passed somewhere en route.

Doc led his party along a white passage. They entered a private garage which the bronze man maintained in the basement. This held several cars, all excellent machines, but none in the least flashy.

Doc stepped to a large limousine. He produced two objects from a door pocket. One of these resembled a greatly overgrown wrist watch. The other was a flat box with numerous dials and switches, and a harness by which it could be carried under a coat, out of view.

The two objects were joined by a flexible conduit.

Doc flicked switches. On the glass dial of the oversize wrist-watch contrivance appeared a picture of the office upstairs.

Aunt Nora looked at this picture, noting the presence of the big, furry Monk and the dapper Ham. Her eyes threatened to jump out of her head when she saw the two go to the door and admit a string of men.

"Land sakes!" she gasped. "A television machine! I didn't know they made 'em that small!"

"The only ones of that size are in Doc's possession," Long Tom advised her, with the natural pride of an electrical expert discussing a remarkable accomplishment in his profession. "Doc made them. The transmitter is concealed in the wall of the room upstairs."

"But I didn't see it turned on!"

"Doc did that when he pressed the inlaid table top."

There was a radio set in the limousine. Doc spun the dials. The words which came from the loud-speaker showed the set was tuned to a transmitter relaying sounds picked up by secret microphones in the office room above.

Between the televisor and the radio, Doc and the others were able to follow what went on above almost as perfectly as if they had been present.

Four of the men who had just arrived wore uniforms of New Jersey State Troopers. A New York detective was also with them.

If an arrest was to be made, he would have to make it, jailing the prisoners until they were extradited to New Jersey.

Any water-front dive might have been combed to get the other four. They were attired in suits, neckties, and hats which looked brand-new. This was productive of a suspicion that they had been dressed up for the occasion.

"Where is Doc Savage?" demanded one of the troopers.

Monk's homely face was very innocent. "Search me, officer."

"This is a regretful mission for us," said another of the policemen. "Knowing Doc Savage to be a man of fine character—"

"He ain't so damn fine!" sneered one of the four somewhat sinister witnesses. "We saw 'im murder a man!"

Ham beetled his brows and bent a hard stare on the quartet. This was Ham's element. As a lawyer, he had handled many lying witnesses.

"You saw the murder?" he challenged.

"Yeah!" they chorused sullenly.

"And you are sure it was Doc Savage?" Ham's tone of voice called them frauds as plainly as words could have.

"Yeah! We've seen the bronze guy's picture in the newspapers! It was 'im!"

Ham leveled his sword cane dramatically at the four. "The Green Bell showed you Doc Savage's picture, and gave you money to swear that he murdered Jim Cash! Isn't that right?"

This blunt accusation failed to have the desired effect. The spokesman of the quartet winked elaborately at one of the troopers.

"This guy must be nuts!" he said. "We don't know anything about any Green Bell. We saw Doc Savage push that poor feller onto that third rail. Like honest citizens should do, we told the police!"

"That's right!" snarled another of the four. "We don't have to stand here and listen to this little snort of a mouthpiece razz us, either!"

"Shut up!" growled one of the officers. Then, to Ham: "Can you tell us where we can find Doc Savage?"

"I do not know where he is," Ham said. This was the truth to a letter.

Ham now stepped into the library. He came back, bearing a large group picture. He held the print up before the four men who claimed they had seen the murder.

"Let's see you pick out Doc," he invited.

Doc Savage was not in the picture at all. Ham hoped to trick the men into a false identification.

It failed to work.

"What d'you think we are!" jeered one of the men. "Savage ain't there!"

Ham wondered if he looked as worried as he felt. These charlatans, he was now sure, had been shown a picture from which they could identify Doc.

This meant that Doc was certain to face a murder charge.

The police of both New York and New Jersey held the bronze man in great esteem. But that would not keep Doc out of jail—not with four witnesses saying he had committed a murder.

There was no such thing as bail on a murder charge.

"Can you tell us whether or not Doc Savage will give himself up?" asked one of the officers.

"Naw—he won't!" Monk rumbled. "Not to get himself throwed in jail on a fake charge!"

The officers became somewhat grim at this. "Then we'll have to spread a general alarm for him."

"Don't pay any attention to what this hairy dope says!" Ham interpolated, glaring at Monk. "He hasn't got good sense, so he don't know what Doc will do. I am sure Doc will take every measure to help the police."

The troopers showed plainly that they were distressed about the whole thing.

"This is—a case of murder, you know," the New York detective said reluctantly. "I am afraid we shall have to issue an immediate pick-up order for Doc."

The officers and the quartet of mountebank witnesses now took their departure.

"You had better watch those four closely!" Ham warned the police.

"Don't worry," replied the trooper. "We're going to pop 'em in the can an' keep 'em there!"

Doc Savage gave the officers an interval in which to get out of the building. Then he went to a telephone in the garage and called the office upstairs.

"The thing looks pretty bad!" he advised Ham. "If I surrender myself now, I'll have to go to jail. I couldn't get bail on a charge that serious."

"That's right," Ham groaned.

"The thing to do is to get out of town. So we're leaving for Prosper City at once."

"Great!" Ham brightened. "We'll go and clean up on this Green Bell right in his own belfry!"

"*You* are not going!" Doc advised.

Ham squawked in disappointment. "But listen, Doc——"

"Some one must stay in New York and fight this murder charge," Doc pointed out. "You're elected."

Ham was groaning loudly when Doc hung up. The thought that he might miss out on some excitement was a big blow to Ham. He was the logical one to remain behind, however, because of his profession.

It was Doc's custom to assign his men tasks for which their particular profession fitted them. This was an emergency calling for a lawyer, which happened to be Ham's specialty. It was his hard luck if he was forced to remain behind and miss anything.

Monk soon entered the basement garage. His homely grin was so wide that it threatened to jam his little ears together on the back of his head. He was well aware of Ham's disappointment—and tickled in proportion.

"We shall leave for Prosper City in half an hour," Doc stated. "Can you make it?"

The query was directed at Aunt Nora, Alice Cash, and Ole Slater. As for his own men, Doc knew they would have no trouble getting away in that interval.

"Our bags are in our old car in a parking lot near here," Aunt Nora told him. "When we get our grips, we'll be ready to hike."

"It will not take me long to get my Gladstone from the railway station check room, where I left it!" Ole Slater offered.

As guards to accompany Aunt Nora and Alice Cash, Doc dispatched Renny and Monk—much to Monk's pleasure. A pretty girl always took Monk's eye.

Ole Slater declared he would need no protection. "I doubt if they know I am in New York, anyway."

It was noticeable that Ole favored Monk with a faint scowl when the homely fellow offered the attractive young lady a gallant arm.

Each of Doc's men assembled equipment which they might need. This was their usual procedure.

Monk, for instance, had a marvelously compact little chemical laboratory which he took. Long Tom had an assortment of parts from which he could assemble an almost unbelievable number of electrical devices. Big-fisted Renny had a few engineering instruments.

Johnny, the archæologist and geologist, carried most of his equipment in his head in the form of knowledge. So he burdened himself with machine guns, ammunition, and grenades, as well as a set of bullet-proof vests.

The machine guns which Johnny packed were remarkable weapons. They resembled slightly oversized automatics, with big curled magazines. Doc had perfected them. They fired shots so swiftly that they sounded like gigantic bull fiddles when they went into operation.

These weapons were carried more for the terror they caused foes, than for lethal use. Doc and his aids never took human life if they could help it.

However, Doc's enemies had a way of perishing in traps which they themselves had set for the bronze man.

The group gathered in the skyscraper basement and entered the large limousine. A special lift carried the car to street level. Few persons, other than the building attendants, knew of the presence of the garage.

Ham, tapping his sword cane disconsolately against a polished toe, saw them off from the curb. He figured he was in for a dull time.

As a usual thing, when there was danger, Doc rode either in an open car or outside, clinging to the running board. He did this as a matter of safety. The manner in which his strange golden eyes could detect a lurking enemy was uncanny.

Doc broke his rule this time, and ensconced himself on the rear seat. To ride outside, where he could be seen, would mean difficulties with the police.

With Renny at the wheel, the car rolled toward the Hudson River.

Except for an occasional lonely drop, the rain had ceased. The streets glistened wetly. Out on the wide Hudson, two tugboats were hooting deep bass whistles, each stubbornly contesting for the right of way.

Warehouses loomed—flat, monster hulks.

Renny drove directly toward one of these. The headlights brought out a name on the front of the structure.

THE HIDALGO TRADING CO.

If one had taken the trouble to investigate, he would have learned the Hidalgo Trading Co. owned nothing but this one warehouse. Also, Doc Savage was the whole concern.

At Doc's quiet warning, no one got out of the limousine. By now, they had all noted that the windows were bullet-proof glass, more than an inch thick, and the body of the machine itself was armor-plate steel.

Renny depressed a switch on the instrument board. This produced no visible phenomena. But big doors in the front of the warehouse opened silently.

Actually, Renny had turned on a lantern which projected ultra-violet rays invisible to the human eye. These had operated a special photo-electric cell concealed in the front of the great barn of a building. This cell had set the door mechanism in action.

As the car glided forward, the lights illuminated the warehouse interior. Aunt Nora, Alice Cash, and Ole Slater emitted three gasps of surprise which blended as one.

The place held several planes. These ranged from a vast, tri-motored craft which was streamlined to an ultra degree, to various small gyros and auto-gyros. Every ship was an amphibian —capable of descending on land or water.

The automobile heaved gently over the threshold, and rolled several yards into the vast warehouse hangar. Every one alighted and began unloading the duffel.

"Hey!" Monk ripped. "Lookit what's comin'!"

Seven ominous figures materialized soundlessly from the darkness outside. There was barely room for them to come abreast through the large door. They resembled a charge of crows.

Each was mantled from crown to toe in a black sack of a garment. The bells, painted on the fronts of the gowns, had a green hue which seemed particularly vile.

Three figures held automatics; the others gripped sub-machine guns. Extra ammunition drums for the rapid-firers were suspended around their necks by thin strings which could be broken with a jerk.

The seven sinister figures ran a few feet within the warehouse. "Give it to 'em!" snarled one.

Automatics and machine guns opened up in a hideous roar!

Empty cartridges chased each other from the breeches of the automatics, and poured in brassy streams from the ejectors of the rapid-firers. Powder noise cascaded through the capacious warehouse in a deafening salvo.

Alice Cash shrieked, and showed Aunt Nora into the shelter of the sedan. Quick thinking, that! Ole Slater followed them with a leap.

Doc Savage and his four friends merely stood there empty-handed, and watched the exhibition of murderous fury.

Something mysterious was happening to the bullets. A few feet from Doc and his men, the slugs seemed to stop in mid-air and splatter like raindrops. Some halted and hung in space, strangely distorted.

None of the bullets were reaching Doc's group.

The truth dawned on the gang of Green Bells. They ceased shooting as abruptly as they had started. They goggled at the bullets which seemed suspended in the air.

Their leader tried to yell a command. Amazement had gripped him so strongly that he made several unintelligible choking noises before he could get words out.

"Beat it!" he gulped. "This joint is hoodooed, or somethin'!"

As one man, the seven veered around and pitched for the outer darkness. What had just occurred was startling. But what happened now was far worse—at least to the Green Bells.

They seemed to smash headlong into an invisible wall. Bruised, noses spouting crimson, they bounced back. Two piled down on the floor, stunned.

The survivors now realized what had happened. Walls of glass —thick, transparent, and bullet-proof—had arisen in front and behind.

The one in front must have been up when they entered; the rear panel had arisen after their feet had operated a hidden trip in the floor.

Howling in terror, they flung themselves against the transparent barricade. They shot at it. The bullets only splattered, or stuck. They could see tiny cracks radiating like cobwebs from points where the bullets made contact. This fact had escaped their notice before.

They skittered their hands along the cold, vertical expanse, seeking an escape.

Doc Savage glanced at his companions, and said quietly: "Hold your breath—at least a minute, if you can."

Drawing several small glass globes from his clothing, Doc advanced. The bulbs were thin-walled, and held a liquid.

Before the almost invisible barrier, Doc sprang high into the air and flung a fistful of the glass balls over the top. The tiny squashing noises as they broke was lost in the frightened wailing of the trapped Green Bells.

Doc waited. He was holding his breath; his friends were doing likewise. The two women and Ole Slater had followed suit, without knowing what it was all about.

The Green Bells began to act like men who had gone to sleep on their feet. They collapsed in quick succession. Some fell heavily; others reclined with more care, as if tired. The two who had dazed themselves by butting the glass wall, ceased their nervous twitchings.

Perhaps a minute elapsed.

Then Doc gave a signal, and his companions began to breathe.

Chapter VI
FEAR'S DOMAIN

"Land sakes!" Aunt Nora sputtered. "What happened? I don't mean the glass walls! What put 'em to sleep like that?"

The homely Monk took it on himself to explain, probably for the benefit of pretty Alice Cash.

"There was an anæsthetic gas in the glass balls. It spreads quickly, and produces instant unconsciousness if breathed. After mixing with the air for something less than a minute, the stuff becomes ineffective."

Working rapidly, Doc Savage operated small levers at one side of the warehouse. The glass walls sank noiselessly.

"Put the Green Bells in the big plane," he directed. "The police will be drawn by those shots, and we want to get out of here before they arrive."

This order was carried out with swift efficiency.

Aunt Nora bounced about, highly excited by the lightning speed of recent events.

"This disguised hangar—these planes—that office of yours!" She waved her arms. "These things have cost a lot of money! You must be rich as sin!"

The bronze man only gave her one of his rare smiles.

The somewhat fantastic truth about Doc's wealth was destined to remain a mystery to Aunt Nora, just as it was an enigma to the rest of the world.

Doc possessed a fabulous hoard of gold. The trove lay in a lost valley in the remote mountain fastness of a Central American republic. Descendants of the ancient Mayan race lived in this valley and mined the treasure.

When Doc was in need of funds, he had merely to broadcast, at a certain hour, a few words in the Mayan language. This was picked up by a sensitive radio receiver in the lost valley. A few days later, a burro train laden with gold would appear in the capital of the Central American republic.

The cargo was always deposited to Doc's credit in a bank. It was a slim trip when one of these burro trains did not bring out a treasure of four or five million dollars.

The warehouse floor sloped downward. The outer end, a concrete apron, was under water. The big plane was quickly rolled down and set afloat. Electric motors pulled great doors back on oiled tracks.

Doc took the controls. The motors started. They were equipped with efficient silencers, and made only shrill hissings.

A few minutes later, the giant plane was streaking over the surface of the Hudson; it cocked its nose up in a steep climb.

Looking backward, using binoculars, Doc's men could see red lights crawling about in the vicinity of the warehouse. These were police cars putting in a tardy arrival.

Prosper City lay to the westward, but Doc flew north. He soon turned the controls over to Renny. All of the bronze man's aids were expert airmen.

Moving to the seven sleeping prisoners, Doc stripped off the green-belled black gowns.

Aunt Nora eyed the faces which were disclosed, and snapped: "I've seen those rats loafing around Prosper City!"

Alice Cash nodded, then relapsed into a white-faced silence. She was grieving over her brother's murder, and saying very little.

Ole Slater scowled, causing his features to lose some of their handsomeness. "I've seen them around town, too!"

Doc now used a hypodermic needle and administered a stimulant to one of the captives. This soon revived the fellow.

The man quailed from the bronze giant and began to whimper in terror. "It was all a mistake—"

Doc grasped the craven's face between muscular palms and began to stare steadily into the wavering eyes.

The onlookers soon understood what he was doing. Using hypnotism! But the victim was too frightened to realize what was occurring, or to combat the effects of the weird golden eyes.

The fellow finally became still, staring at Doc like a bird at a big serpent.

"Who is the Green Bell?" Doc demanded in a compelling tone.

"I dunno," the man mumbled tonelessly. "None of us knows."

Under normal conditions, Doc would not have believed a word the man told him. But now he knew he was hearing the truth.

"Who told you to spring that trap at the warehouse?" he persisted.

"The Green Bell telephoned us," was the droned answer. "He just said for us to follow you and kill you and your men when we got a chance. We were not to harm the two women and Ole Slater."

"Glory be!" exploded Aunt Nora. "Why didn't he want Alice and Ole and me done away with?"

Doc relayed this query to his source of information.

"It was on account of the effect their death would have on their friends in Prosper City," mumbled the Green Bell hireling. "They'd lynch Judborn Tugg. Tugg is important in the big scheme, whatever it is!"

Doc queried: "Do Judborn Tugg and Slick Cooley belong to the Green Bell's gang?"

"I dunno—I guess so. I don't know much. I'm a new man."

Doc tried one more question. "Did the Green Bell send you to New York, in the first place, to murder me?"

"I don't think so. He just sent us so we'd be handy in case something went wrong. His first idea was to get you on his pay roll. He thought you were a common muscle man."

"Did you and this gang here murder Jim Cash?"

"No. Some more of the Green Bell's men done that."

This summed up the information Doc was able to secure from

the man. He awakened the other six, and put questions to them, but learned little more. Nothing, in fact, that was valuable.

Renny veered the giant plane inland, toward the mountainous, thinly populated up-State portion of New York.

The huge speed-cowled motors were almost wide open. The ship was making a speed considerably in excess of two hundred and fifty miles an hour. It was one of the fastest craft for its size to be found.

Doc went to the radio transmitter and sent a brief message.

Later in the night, when they landed in a clearing in the northern wilderness, three ghostly ambulances were waiting. These had been summoned by Doc's radio message.

White-clad men, their faces lost in the shadows beneath their cap brims, loaded the seven prisoners into the ambulances. Few words were exchanged.

The ambulances departed. Doc took his plane off. The whole incident had been grim and spectral.

Aunt Nora was bewildered. "What'll happen to those seven men?"

"They will be taken care of," Doc said, and did not clarify the thing further.

Doc did not advertise what happened to wrongdoers whom he captured. The bronze man maintained a strange institution in this mountain wilderness. There, the seven men would undergo brain operations which would cause them to completely forget their pasts.

Next, they would be taught upright citizenship and a trade. They would be turned loose—honest men, unaware of their past criminal careers.

No crook, once treated in this manner, had ever returned to evil ways.

Doc's institution would have caused a world-wide sensation, had its existence become public.

A hissing meteor, the plane hurtled through the night, bearing the remarkable bronze man, his four unusual aids, and the three unfortunates whom he intended to help.

Prosper City—crisscrossed strings of street lamps far below—appeared some time before dawn.

"The airport is north of town!" Alice Cash advised.

The drome was unlighted. It was situated in the middle of an area of ripening grain which looked yellow in the moonlight —there was a moon shining on Prosper City. The flying field was turfed with grass, which was very dark as seen from the air.

Three rusty hangars were hunched at the edge of the tarmac. A junked plane stood behind one shed. Faded pennants of fabric clung to its naked skeleton.

As far as could be seen, there was no one about.

Doc cranked the landing wheels down out of the wells, into which they had disappeared for greater streamlining. He planted the big ship on the ground as lightly as if it had been a glider. They coasted to a stop perhaps two hundred feet from one of the hangars.

The sliding door of this hangar scooted back and let out a flood of men. They wore police uniforms.

An incredibly tall, rawboned man led the policemen. He had an enormous mustache, and a small red face. The combination was remindful of a cherry with a large brown caterpillar on it.

"The police chief—Clem Clements!" Aunt Nora snapped. "I'll bet some one has told him we're criminals, and Clem has believed 'em! Clem is sure pin-headed!"

Chief Clements was flourishing an official-looking document.

Doc Savage needed no close inspection to tell him what this paper was—a warrant for his arrest, perhaps, or a wire from New York, requesting the bronze man's apprehension.

A deduction that Doc would head for Prosper City would call for no great thinking on the mysterious Green Bell's part. But the master mind had moved quickly to give more trouble to Doc and his friends.

Doc did a bit of fast thinking, and decided the simplest thing he could do was to avoid Chief Clements for the present.

Turning in the pilot's seat, Doc glanced backward. There had been no rain in Prosper City recently. The prop stream was pulling dust from the grass roots, and squirting it back in a funnel. There was much more dust around the hangars.

Doc locked one wheel brake, and slapped the throttles open. This pivoted the plane. A dusty hurricane slapped the faces of Chief Clements and his men.

They were blinded. They yelled angrily, and fired warning shots in the air.

Doc dropped out of the ship. He seemed to flatten and vanish in the scrubby grass. He left the vicinity like a startled ghost.

Chief Clements dashed up to the plane, rubbing his eyes and blowing dust out of his big mustache.

"You done that on purpose!" he declared irately. He had a metallic, whanging voice.

Renny put his sober face out of the window. The twanging voice of Chief Clements reminded him of a taut barbed wire being plucked.

"We didn't think of the dust!" he said meekly. This was not a prevarication—Doc had thought of the dust.

"We're lookin' for a murderer named Doc Savage!" snapped Chief Clements.

Renny heaved a relieved sigh. The policemen had been blinded by the dust so effectively that Doc's departure had escaped their notice.

"Who put you up to this, Clem Clements?" Aunt Nora shouted wrathfully.

Chief Clements glared at Aunt Nora as if the motherly old lady had horns.

"None of your business!" he retorted, somewhat childishly.

Aunt Nora jumped out of the plane. "Was it Judborn Tugg?"

Chief Clements pulled the ends of his mustache down in a scowl, giving the impression that the caterpillar on the cherry had bowed its back.

"Now don't you start running down Judborn Tugg!" he twanged. "He's an upright man, and the best citizen this town's got! What if he did wire me from New York that you was mixed up with a murderer named Doc Savage, and might show up here? He was doin' the decent thing!"

"Tugg never did a decent thing in his whole evil life!" Aunt Nora said scathingly.

Chief Clements thrust his little red head forward. "I think you're behind this trouble, Aunt Nora Boston! I've just been waitin' to get some proof, so I could throw you in jail!"

Aunt Nora cocked her arms akimbo. "That sounds like some of Judborn Tugg's advice!"

"If I find Doc Savage in that plane, you're gonna be locked up on a charge of helpin' a murderer escape!" Chief Clements yelled.

"If you find Doc Savage in the ship, I'll go to jail willingly!" Aunt Nora snapped.

Chief Clements and his men now searched the giant trimotor.

Their faces registered a great deal of disappointment when they found no bronze man.

"We'll hang around the airport!" the Prosper City police chief whanged. "Savage may show up in another plane. I've got a guard around your house, too, Aunt Nora! And you're gonna be shadowed, every move you make. If Doc Savage tries to get in touch with you, we'll nab 'im!"

Aunt Nora sniffed loudly. But her wrinkled face showed concern.

"I suppose it's all right to call a car to take us into town?" she snapped.

"I'll send you in my car!" offered Chief Clements, figuring this would make it simpler for his men to keep track of Aunt Nora and her companions.

"I wouldn't ride in it!" Aunt Nora informed him. "I'll telephone for a hack!"

The cab which Aunt Nora summoned arrived something over half an hour later.

The driver was a shabby individual, who slouched low behind the wheel. He had a purple nose, bulging cheeks, and he seemed half asleep. He did not offer to open the door for his fares.

The luggage was piled in front with the chauffeur. The two women and Ole Slater got in the rear. Johnny and Long Tom turned down the drop seats. Monk and Renny, the giants of the group, rode clinging to the running board.

The taxi had not rolled far when it passed a pitiful little camp beside the road. There was a ragged tent and a litter of house furnishings which had been virtually ruined by the weather. It was a scene of utter poverty, even when seen in the mellow glow of the moonlight.

"There's a sample," Aunt Nora muttered. "A year ago, that family was happy and buying their own home. The husband was one who wouldn't go out on strike. Driver—stop the car! I want these people to hear something!"

The machine halted; the motor silenced. A sound which came steadily from the ragged tent could now be heard. It was a low, frightful gibbering. It kept up without end.

"That's the poor husband," Aunt Nora said brokenly. "He is insane! The Green Bell made him that way in some horrible fashion! As I told you, there's more than a dozen others like him. They're all men who wanted to stay at work, and keep the mills and mines operating. The Green Bell is tryin' to break every factory in this town."

Every one was silent as the car got under way again. To Doc's four men, this incident had been an appalling sample of what they were up against. It brought home to them the sinister power of this mysterious master, the Green Bell.

They soon saw other evidence of the terrible conditions in Prosper City. In more than one alley, there were furtive, slinking figures. These individuals were looking for scraps of food.

"The poor souls are starving!" Aunt Nora explained.

"It's ghastly!" Ole Slater groaned. "If I should put conditions such as these in the play I am writing, people in other cities would say it couldn't happen! And no one knows what's behind it all!"

Johnny, the gaunt geologist, took off his spectacles with the magnifying left lens. "Isn't there a community chest, or some kind of a charity fund?"

"All of those were exhausted long ago," Alice Cash told him quietly. "Nine out of every ten men in Prosper City are out of work. That seems inconceivable. But it is true!"

The car rolled on. It turned several corners, behaving somewhat uncertainly, as if the driver did not know where he was going.

"You're not going toward my house!" Aunt Nora rapped.

The driver shrugged. "Which way is it?"

"You don't know?" Aunt Nora asked incredulously.

"No!" said the driver with the purple nose and fat cheeks.

"Humph! It looks like you have never been in Prosper City before!"

"I haven't!"

Aunt Nora suddenly stood up and thrust her face close to that of the driver. She stared.

"Glory be!" she ejaculated. "You're Doc Savage!"

Chapter VII
CLEMENTS SETS A TRAP

The discovery that the chauffeur was Doc Savage surprised Monk and Renny so greatly that they almost fell off the running board. Ole Slater jumped as if he had been slapped. Alice Cash made silent whistling lips of wonder.

Long Tom and Johnny both chuckled. This was not the first time the bronze man had donned a remarkable disguise. He was a master of make-up, just as he was a master of innumerable other things.

"I was hanging around, and heard you phone for the cab," Doc enlightened Aunt Nora. "It was a simple matter to stop the machine and bribe the driver to let me take his place."

"Where's the driver?" Aunt Nora wanted to know.

"He is going to sneak past the guards, and be waiting in your house to take the car away. That will get me into your house without the knowledge of the watching policemen."

Aunt Nora settled back with a sigh which almost attained happiness. "If you ask this old girl, I'm betting Prosper City is soon going to see the end of its streak of hard luck."

The rooming house operated by Aunt Nora Boston was a large, rambling white structure of two stories and a set of garret bedrooms. Much neatly trimmed shrubbery surrounded it. Doc and his men thought the old-fashioned place rather attractive.

Doc's ruse for gaining admission to the house was carried to a successful completion. The real driver drove the taxi away, leaving Doc behind.

Chief Clements's cops, stationed just outside Aunt Nora's grounds, did not smell a mouse.

Aunt Nora's house stood on the outskirts of Prosper City, at the foot of a range of high, wooded hills, which the local citizens called mountains.

47

Coal mines were located in the mountains, Doc soon learned. Long galleries from these mines underlaid much of Prosper City itself.

Alice Cash grasped an opportunity to impart the information that Aunt Nora had secured a small fortune from the sale of this coal. The kindly old lady had expended all of her funds in providing for the needy, however.

The sun flushed up redly. With dawn, a fresh shift of policemen went on duty. There were four of the officers observing the house.

Doc was careful to keep out of sight.

The bronze man took his first steps aimed at improving conditions in Prosper City. From a pocket, he produced a sheaf of bank notes.

Aunt Nora rubbed her eyes when she saw the size of the bills. Some were hundreds, but most were of thousand-dollar denomination.

Doc passed the small fortune to Aunt Nora, along with instructions.

Aunt Nora paid a visit to the Prosper City merchants who had been most generous in contributing to charity. Each received a tremendous order for food and clothing, with cash on the line.

The delight with which the merchants greeted this business was moving. One old groceryman, who had been carrying his whole neighborhood on credit because he could not bear to see former customers in want, sat down and cried.

Before noon, arrangements were completed for the delivery of more than a score of truck loads of food and clothing to Aunt Nora's capacious yard. "By night," was the time insisted upon.

There were a few skinflint merchants who had given credit to none of the impoverished, and who had not contributed to charity. These fellows did not get a penny of Doc's business.

A circus was stranded in town. Aunt Nora leased the big top and the menagerie tent, and ordered them erected in her yard to shelter the supplies.

Working under Doc's directions, Ole Slater rented several open cars. These rolled through the streets. Slater, Alice Cash and Doc's four men stood in the back seats with megaphones, broadcasting the fact that there would be a food distribution and a meeting at Aunt Nora's place that night.

"Tell them," Doc directed, "that at this gathering a plan will be presented which will put every man in Prosper City back to work within the next two weeks."

To say this information created a sensation in Prosper City was putting it mildly. Few believed the thing could be done. But every man, his family, and his dog would attend the meeting to see what it was all about.

The mysterious master mind, the Green Bell, was not dormant. Hardfaced men—the agitators who had been prominent in the trouble from the first—mounted soap boxes at street corners, and began to label Aunt Nora as a sinister woman, and Doc Savage a murderer and worse.

The elderly lady, they said, was in league with "The Interests." Just who The Interests were, they neglected to mention explicitly, but included mill and mine owners in a general way. Aunt Nora was going to try to persuade men to go back to work at starvation wages, they declared. Why go to work and starve anyway, while the pockets of the rich were lined?

This argument would have been good, had it had any foundation in truth. These fellows did not give a hoot about the welfare of the workmen, although they claimed they did.

They were on the pay roll of the Green Bell. Their purpose was to keep the factories and mines closed. Why? Only the Green Bell knew.

The hired agitators held themselves up as protectors of the workers. They voiced threats against all who attended Aunt Nora's meeting.

"We ain't gonna go to work until we get decent wages!" one orator proclaimed. "You're fools if you listen to the soft-soaping words of that lying old lady——"

At this point, one of Aunt Nora's admirers knocked the spieler off his soap box. A dozen policemen were required to break up the fight which followed.

This was not the only incident of its kind. The day was marked by a dribble of bruised and battered agitators into the hospitals.

Chief of Police Clements appeared at Aunt Nora's house. His big mustache was a-bristle with rage.

"I forbid this meeting to-night!" he yelled. "You're just fixing to start more trouble! Even now, there's fightin' all over town!"

"Judborn Tugg must be back home!" Aunt Nora jeered.

Chief Clements became purple. It was a fact that Judborn Tugg and Slick Cooley had alighted from the noon train.

"What's that got to do with it!" he gritted.

"Didn't Tugg tell you to stop my meeting?" Aunt Nora countered.

This was the truth, and Chief Clements was not ashamed to admit it. Chief Clements was an honest soul, if a dumb one, and pompous Judborn Tugg was an idol in his eyes.

"Mr. Tugg is the best citizen this town has!" he declared with the firmness of an ignorant man with one firmly fixed idea. "It is true that he thinks your powwow will only cause trouble. I think so, too! And I'm going to break it up!"

"You're going to get your head broke if you try it!" retorted Aunt Nora.

This was hardly the argument to use on a bullheaded man such as Chief Clements. It only made his determination firmer.

Pretty Alice Cash came forward with the argument which really swayed the boss of the Prosper City police.

"We are going to distribute food to the starving to-night," she said gently. "Surely, you are not going to be cold-blooded enough to stop that?"

Chief Clements squirmed uncomfortably. He might be thick-headed and a worshiper of Judborn Tugg, but he was also a kindly man. If any hungry person was to be fed, he would be the last one to stand in the way.

The upshot was that he agreed to let the meeting be held.

"But I'm gonna have plenty of cops here," he warned.

Doc Savage had eavesdropped from the concealment of another room. He complimented attractive Alice Cash when she joined him.

"You were clever enough to avoid what might have been a nasty bit of trouble!" he told her.

Alice gave Doc a ravishing smile of thanks. She was, it could be seen plainly, experiencing a great attraction for the giant bronze man. Signs already indicated that, once grief over her brother's death was dulled by the passing of a little time, she was going to fall for Doc in a big way.

Ole Slater could see this. He failed to conceal a worried look. He was obviously enraptured with the entrancing Alice.

He might have been relieved to know that Doc Savage made it a policy to steer far wide of feminine entanglements. His perilous, active career made that necessary. Should he encumber himself with a wife, she would not only be always in danger of becoming a widow, but enemies would strike at Doc through her. He could let no woman lead a life like that.

Late in the afternoon, Ham telephoned from New York. He reported that he was investigating the past lives of the four men who had sworn falsely that they had seen Doc murder Jim Cash.

"I may be able to get something on them that will make them tell the truth," he said hopefully. "But, frankly, I'm not doing so hot."

Since Doc was forced to keep under cover, his four aids in Prosper City handled preparations for the night's conclave.

Big-fisted Renny, who had superintended construction of skyscrapers and bridges as an engineer, directed raising of the circus tents. Long Tom, the electrical wizard, installed a public address system, so that every word spoken from a rostrum at one end of the big top could be heard. He also erected powerful flood lights.

Gorillalike Monk, who had learned to command men as a lieutenant colonel in the army, organized a score of Aunt Nora's friends into a corps to handle the distribution of food and clothing.

Two banks remained open in Prosper City. The gaunt Johnny visited one of them, after ascertaining Judborn Tugg was a director in the other. The one Johnny entered was the smaller one.

When Johnny departed, he left a stunned set of bank officials behind. They held a check deposited in Doc Savage's name. The amount of the check crowded the space providing for writing in the figures. The bankers telephoned New York before they would believe the draft was good.

A rumor of this enormous deposit got out. The Prosper City *News* telephoned New York newspapers, asking who this Doc Savage was. They were informed that he was a bronze man of mystery, who possessed an unknown source of fabulous wealth, and who devoted his life to fighting other people's battles. They also learned that Doc now stood accused of murdering Jim Cash.

The *News* carried both stories on its front page that evening. The paper also printed an editorial, beginning:

Who is Doc Savage—Midas or murderer? Is he a being whose might and wealth is to save Prosper City? Or is he a charlatan and a killer with a sinister purpose?

Indications were that almost every one in Prosper City was going to attend Aunt Nora Boston's meeting in hopes of learning the answer.

Long before sundown, men, women, and children began trickling into Aunt Nora's great yard. The first comers were ragged, pitiful figures with pinched faces. Hunger had drawn them.

Some of the Green Bell's hired agitators appeared and started voicing threats. Monk's corps of trained helpers lit into these fellows with clubs. A pitched battle ensued.

An agitator drew a pistol and tried to kill Monk. The first shot missed.

Renny lunged in and flung a fist that was as big and hard as half a concrete block.

The gun wielder dropped, his jaw broken like so much gravel.

Chief Clements appeared magically, leading a squad of at least thirty officers. The latter had long billies, tear-gas bombs, and gas masks.

"I knew there was gonna be trouble here!" Chief Clements howled. "Every blasted one of you are under arrest!"

Monk waved at the agitators. "You mean those clucks are pulled, don't you?"

"I don't mean them! They're within their rights in makin' speeches! This is a free country! I mean *you!*"

Ole Slater was in none too good a temper, probably because he had been worrying all day over the unmistakable signs charming Alice Cash gave of falling for Doc Savage. Rage got the better of Slater.

He drew back and pasted the handiest cop.

Two policemen sprang upon Slater and belabored him with their clubs.

"Everybody's under arrest!" Chief Clements repeated shrilly. "Then we're gonna search the house! We got a tip that Doc Savage is in there!"

Monk rammed his homely face forward. "You what?"

"Judborn Tugg said one of his friends saw a bronze man hidin' in the house!" growled the police leader.

Doc Savage was stationed near an open window in the house, where he could listen. His strange golden eyes betrayed no emotion at Chief Clements's words.

The report that Doc was concealed in Aunt Nora's home was a puzzling angle, however. Indirectly, it had emanated from the mysterious Green Bell, of course. But how had he known Doc was there? Or had he only made a wild guess?

Doc glided to a rear window. Darkness had now fallen, but the grounds were brilliantly lighted by Long Tom's flood lamps.

Police were stationed in a cordon around the house. They stood close together. It was doubtful if a mosquito could escape past them without being discovered.

Doc was in a trap!

Back to the open front window, Doc moved. The wall of one circus tent was not many yards distant. He faced this. The remarkable muscles in his throat knotted into strange positions.

He spoke loudly, using ventriloquism. His words seemed to come from the tent wall. They were strange words—a not unmusical stream of gutterals.

It was the language of the ancient Mayans. Doc's men had learned it on their adventurous visit to the lost Central American valley which held Doc's golden trove. It was one of the least-known tongues on earth. Certainly Chief Clements did not understand it.

"Face the tent wall!" was Doc's first advice.

Monk and the other four instantly began staring at the tent. This enhanced the impression that the voice was emanating from that source. Doc knew very well that half the success of ventriloquism lies in getting the hearer's attention on something he *thinks* the voice is coming from.

Doc now added further commands, speaking rapidly. He got them all out before the policemen came to life.

Chief Clements dashed to the tent, lifted the wall, then looked baffled when he found no one. He spun on Monk and the others.

"Put your hands up!" he twanged. "You're carryin' them funny-lookin' little guns! We don't allow gun totin' in Prosper City!"

The "funny-lookin'" guns which he referred to were the tiny machine guns which would fire with such terrific speed.

Monk ignored the order.

"I gotta talk this over with my friends," he said in his small voice.

"You ain't gonna do nothin' of the kind!"

Monk and the others now drew their weapons. "Oh, yes, we are! If you don't let us talk, there's gonna be plenty of trouble!"

Chief Clements hedged angrily, eyeing the weapons. Finally he gave in.

"All right, But you gotta stay in plain sight!"

Monk and the rest did not follow this order to the letter. They retired within the tent. Monk entered the house and came back with hands empty, but with a suspicious package bulging his coat.

The conference lasted perhaps another minute. Then every one came out of the tent. They threw down their weapons.

"That satisfy you?" Monk demanded.

"We're gonna search you!" whanged Chief Clements.

The officers advanced. Counting Doc's four aids and the score of recruits for the food distribution, there came near being one prisoner for every policeman.

The search got under way. Monk coughed loudly. Instantly, every captive brought his right hand in contact with the face or hands of the lawman who was frisking him.

The policemen toppled over like mown bluegrass. They lay where they fell, snoring loudly.

Highly elated, Monk and the rest removed tiny metal thimbles from their fingers. These were fashioned to blend closely with finger tips. Only an intent inspection would disclose them, and the unsuspecting officers had failed to note the things.

Each thimble held a tiny hypodermic needle, which, upon contact with the skin, injected a drug producing a sleep of several hours' duration.

Doc, when he had spoken Mayan, had directed this operation to overpower the police. These thimbles were devices of his own invention.

Chief Clements and his men were carried to their parked cars and dumped on the cushions. Onlookers, vastly puzzled, agreed to drive them away.

"We're shut of that guy until midnight, anyway!" Monk grinned.

The crowd gathered with increasing speed. Among those coming now were substantial citizens—owners of mills and mines which were being thrown into bankruptcy by the enforced idleness.

It was a strange situation. The owners were anxious to operate their plants; the workmen wanted jobs badly. But the odious organization of the Green Bell was holding both at a standstill. To open a factory meant it would be bombed or burned. For a workman to take a job meant he was in danger of beatings or —worst of all—the weird, horrible insanity.

That there was some cold, relentless purpose behind it all, many realized. But they could not fathom the reason.

Why was the Green Bell trying to bankrupt every industry in Prosper City? Was he a fiend with a mad hate for the town? No one knew.

The crowd seemed reluctant to enter the tents. More than one man there had felt the vengeance of the Green Bell. They gathered in knots outside and talked. A few became frightened and left.

The agitators on the Green Bell's pay roll had not spoken entirely without effect.

In order to quiet fears, Long Tom tuned in a portable radio set and stood the loud-speaker near the microphone of the public-address system.

Dance music was now audible all over the grounds, and for some distance along the suburban roads in either direction. The tune came from the local Prosper City station.

Unexpectedly, an unearthly wail burst in upon the lilting of fiddles and the muted moaning of saxophones. The sound rose and fell, changing its tone. It was like the death cries of a monster, pouring from the loud-speakers.

A deep-throated, reverberating boom lifted over the bedlam of wailing. The throbbing sound seemed to fill all the night, magnified a thousand times by the address-system speakers. More of the weird notes came. A death-walk procession!

It might have been the tolling of some cataclysmic dirge.

The sound ended, and the jazzy dance tune poured from the loud-speakers as if nothing happened.

On the grounds men milled, grim of eye and pale of face. Women clung to their husbands, or mothered their children. The hideous tolling had stricken stark terror.

"The Green Bell!" a man mumbled.

"It means death or insanity to somebody! It nearly always does!"

Doc Savage, a motionless statue of bronze, surveyed the scene from the house. He had seen savage tribesmen in far countries, living in apprehension of something they did not understand. He had seen passengers on a great ocean liner aghast at approaching disaster.

He had never seen quite the depth of fear which was here before his eyes, induced by the gonging sound with which the Green Bell had associated himself.

The unknown brain back of this strange trouble—the being who was reducing a city to poverty for some secret reason of his own —had progressed far toward accomplishing his aims. Prosper City was a realm of fear, and he was its czar.

Chapter VIII
VOICE FROM THE EARTH

Some two hundred yards from Aunt Nora Boston's house, a man perched in a tree, laughing heartily. He was getting great glee out of the terror which the Green Bell's sound had wrought.

Slick Cooley held his side with one hand, and a limb with the other. He finally stifled his unholy mirth.

"That'll hold 'em!" he chuckled.

He pocketed a pair of binoculars and clambered out of the tree. Carefully avoiding the road, he strode northward. On his right, the low mountains frowned in the pale moonlight. He paralleled them.

When he had covered some distance, he veered over to the road, where walking was easier. A dog ran out and barked at him. Slick threw clods at the dog.

He went on. The dog had come from the last house; ahead was a large area of marsh land. A wealthy farmer had once tried to drain this swampy section to cultivate it, but had been forced to give the task up as a bad job. Great weeds and brush had overgrown the waste land.

A car came up behind Slick, and stopped when it was alongside him. The machine was Judborn Tugg's flashy roadster. Tugg in person sat back of the wheel. He inquired: "Lift?"

Slick got in.

"The bellin' noise scared that crowd plenty!" he boasted.

"I cannot understand what happened to Chief Clements!" Tugg snapped. "I visited the man at the hospital! He seems only to be asleep. But they can't wake him up!"

"If I was you, I'd lay off Chief Clements!" Slick leered.

"Why?"

"Some day he's gonna wake up to the fact that you ain't the goody-goody he thinks you are. When them knotheaded guys turn on a man, they can be just as strong agin' him as they were for him!"

"Nonsense!" Tugg retorted grandly. "Chief Clements is too dumb to ever suspect anything. And he is very valuable to me."

Slick squinted curiously at Judborn Tugg.

Noting the glance, Tugg added hastily: "Valuable to the Green Bell, I mean!"

The roadster pulled into a narrow lane through the brush. They soon parked the machine and went on afoot.

Slick walked in silence. He was wondering if Judborn Tugg could be the Green Bell. True, there were occasions when a hooded man appeared before them both and said he was the Green Bell. This happened in the car in New York.

But such appearances might be made by members of the gang. Slick himself had once been ordered to don a black gown and play the part of the Green Bell. Tugg might be the master mind, Slick reasoned.

Suddenly, he recalled the remark he had made in New York about slaying the Green Bell, once he learned the fellow's identity, and substituting himself as the unknown leader.

Slick was serious about that. But he wished now that he had been more reticent with his words. He shivered several times. If Tugg was the Green Bell, Slick had a feeling he was as good as a dead man.

A ramshackle old barn appeared in the moonlight. They rapped on the door, giving a peculiar, drumming signal.

"Come in!" said a weirdly hollow, booming voice.

They entered.

The ancient barn was concrete-floored. A black, ominous figure sat cross-legged in the shadows at the rear. The smoky robe sheathed it from head to foot. Although the form was seated, it also leaned back slightly against the rear wall. Through cracks in this wall, strings of moonlight were visible.

Most of the luminance within the structure came from two candles a few feet in front of the seated apparition. These candles were green, and their flame was sputtering and green. They cast a bilious light on the green-bell design of the seated one's robe, and on the green goggles which masked the eyes. The effect was eerie.

No other word was spoken.

Slick Cooley and Judborn Tugg both drew black hoods from within their clothing and donned them.

In the distance, a crashing of brush denoted men approaching. They filed in—eight in the first group, then by twos and threes and fours. Every man was draped in a sepian masquerade.

No word was spoken. They stood in a half circle, keeping their distance from the strange seated figure. The latter did not move in the slightest, or speak. Nor did the arrivals voice anything. They had come, these followers of the Green Bell, in answer to the summons tolled over the radio. The sound had warned them to gather here for orders.

"Are all present?" asked a voice from the seated form. It was hollowly booming, that tone! It seemed incredible that it could come from a human throat.

Slick counted the assembled men.

"All but about half a dozen," he said. "I guess they didn't hear the call."

"Speak louder!" commanded the sepulchral voice.

Slick fairly yelled a repetition of his statement.

"Very well!" came the croaked reply. "Judborn Tugg—are you there?"

Tugg came forward and shouted: "Yes!"

Slick backed away. It was always like this—the Green Bell pretending he was partially deaf.

The gloomy figure might not be the Green Bell, either, Slick reflected. It could conceivably be some member of the gang who had been ordered to serve in the Green Bell's place.

"I am far from satisfied with certain work done to-day!" tolled the seated form. "Chief Clements, for instance, was to have been persuaded to seize Doc Savage."

"Could I help that?" Tugg protested. "I did my part. But Chief Clements is so stupid that he let Savage run a whizzer on him!"

"I am not sure that Clements being stupid is entirely to blame," came the dull voice. "I sent seven men to get Savage in New York, and they vanished completely. They were not dumb fellows. Savage is a very dangerous foe!"

Tugg wiped at his fat forehead. His features were, of course mantled in the black hood, and the wiping gesture upon the cloth was somewhat ludicrous. Savage dangerous! Did he not know it?

"I been doing my best!" he yelled.

"And that was not good! Slick Cooley—I'll talk to you now."

"Sure!" Slick shouted.

He scuttled forward, a spooky vision in the green-belled hood. He did not mind the mention of his name. He knew every one here, anyway. Many of those present, however, were unacquainted with one another.

The seated figure had not moved perceptibly at any time.

"You did good work in noting Savage's reflection in a mirror in Aunt Nora Boston's house, when you were watching with binoculars!" said the fantastic voice.

Slick was slightly shocked. It was the first time he had heard the Green Bell bestow praise. It made him uneasy.

"I was just doin' my best!" he bellowed.

A short silence ensued. Uncanny quiet lay in the old wreck of a barn. No one moved. The creamy strips of moonlight in the cracks had a spectral quality.

"I need a trustworthy man for the work ahead!" tolled the Green Bell. "So I am selecting you. For this work, if you complete it successfully, you will receive a bonus, over and above your regular pay, of fifty thousand dollars."

Slick's startled gasp puffed out his hood like a small balloon.

"Concealed in the weeds beside the door of this barn you will find my device which produces insanity!" continued the Green Bell. "You will place this where Doc Savage will come close to it, preferably near the head of his bed."

"But I dunno how to work the contraption," Slick muttered.

"What?"

Slick had forgotten to yell. He did so now. "How d'you work it?"

"That is very simple. There is only one switch upon the box. You throw it. Be careful that the switch is not operated accidentally while you are carrying the container. And once you do work it, get away quickly. It takes only a few seconds for the thing to disrupt the functions of a human brain!"

"O. K.!" Slick bellowed.

"With the box, you will find a package of money—ten thousand dollars," continued the voice. "You will take the sum to Chief Clements's office after you plant the box. Wait for Chief Clements to appear; then post the ten thousand dollars as a reward for Doc Savage—dead or alive. This precaution is in case you fail."

"O. K. to that, too!" Slick barked. "I won't slip up!"

"That will be all, then. You other men remain in close touch with Slick or Judborn Tugg, so that you can receive orders quickly."

The men bobbed their hoods in understanding, then departed. They went swiftly, as if eager to quit the ghostly presence.

Slick Cooley remained behind, making a pretense at examining the box which he found in the weeds beside the door. The box was not large. It was shiny and black, with a tiny single-pole switch on the top.

There was also a bundle of money, which Slick pocketed.

He carried the box to the near-by brush and waited, eyes fixed on the barn door. He was watching for the Green Bell to appear. Slick intended to follow the master mind and learn who he was.

Minutes dragged by. No one put in an appearance. Almost half an hour passed.

Impatient, Slick crept to the door and peered in. The eerie black form had not moved. The sputtering green candles had burned quite low.

Slick debated, then decided to stake all on a desperate chance. He fished the two silenced guns from his armpits and shoved through the door.

"Put 'em up!" he gritted.

The seated figure did not stir.

Slick ripped another command. No response! He became excited. Both his guns coughed bullets!

The slugs hit the black form and the wall with smacking reports which were much louder than the *chung!* of the silenced weapons.

The apparition in black still remained motionless.

Frankly terrified, Slick pitched forward and brought a gun crashing down on the hooded head.

The whole figure collapsed, amid a loud cracking! It was nothing but a framework of sticks!

Cursing feverishly, Slick bent to examine the thing. A hole in the concrete floor came to view. This had been partially concealed by the black gown.

Slick lighted a match and held it over the hole. He saw the moldy red walls of tile.

Comprehension dawned on Slick. The farmer who had once

tried to cultivate this marsh land had put in an intricate system of tile drains. The hole in the floor admitted to one of these underground pipes. Or so Slick had decided.

Doubtless there were many other exits. The Green Bell might have been speaking from anywhere in the vicinity.

This, then, accounted for the necessity of yelling. It took a loud tone to carry through the tile labyrinth.

Using his flashlight, Slick carefully rebuilt the framework which supported the black gown. It was just as well, he realized, that his treachery should not be discovered.

Some time later, Slick appeared in the vicinity of Aunt Nora Boston's home.

Distribution of food and clothing to the needy was well under way, from the looks of the situation. There was a multitude in the two big tents and on the grounds.

Those who had received an allotment of necessities were not departing. They wanted to attend the meeting which was to follow. Especially did they want to see and hear this remarkable bronze man, Doc Savage.

The food in their hands was concrete evidence that the mystery man meant business. Doc had known the distribution would have this effect, hence he had ordered it to be made before the speeches. He needed every ounce of cooperation and confidence from these people.

The battle against the insidious forces of the Green Bell was just starting.

Presence of the crowd made it simple for Slick to snap his hat brim over his eyes and mingle among them. He worked to Aunt Nora's house. All attention was directed on the tent. It proved easy for Slick to enter the house, unobserved.

He made his furtive way to the room where, during the day, he had been lucky enough to observe Doc Savage's reflection in a mirror. He reasoned this was Doc's quarters.

Certain articles of the bronze man's attire hanging in a closet told Slick he was correct.

Numerous intricate mechanical and electrical devices stood about the room. Of these, Slick identified only a portable radio outfit. The other stuff was too complex for his rather limited understanding.

Slick disturbed nothing. He was too canny for that. Nor did he show a light. The moon furnished sufficient illumination.

Behind the head of the bed stood a large, dilapidated cabinet. To all appearances, this was not used. The front had no doors, but was masked by a gaudy print curtain.

"Just the place!" Slick whispered to himself. "I'll plant my toy there, then go to Chief Clements's office and wait for him to turn up!"

He placed the black box behind the curtain, and threw the deadly switch; then all but ran from the room.

Much to his relief, Slick was able to leave the house without being observed.

Just before he faded away into the night, he glanced at the circus tent. The canvas sides had been tied up because of the warmth.

Doc Savage was taking the speaking rostrum.

"That guy will be a gibberin' nut before mornin'!" Slick leered. Then he crept out of the neighborhood. Somehow, even a distant look at that bronze man made him feel like having a good shiver.

Chapter IX
PLANS

There was a great deal of talk in the big top, but it snapped into the silence of a graveyard when Doc appeared. In two spots, babies cried. The night breeze puffed the tent top and sucked it down with a hollow booming.

The quiet was a tribute to Doc's appearance. The giant bronze man, in the glare of a spotlight, was an arresting figure.

Alice Cash, also occupying a chair on the rostrum, seemed unable to take her eyes off his figure.

"This is not going to be a longwinded discussion," Doc announced, speaking in a modulated tone which the public-address system could handle with most efficiency. "You people who have received food and clothing here, tonight, do not need to embarrass yourselves with the idea that you are taking charity. Your names have been filed, and the stuff charged against you."

"Fat chance you have of collecting!" some one called grimly. "We haven't any jobs!"

"There'll be plenty of jobs!" Doc retorted.

"How soon?"

"I set the time limit at two weeks; but we should be able to beat that. Probably most of you will be drawing pay by to-morrow."

In the rear, a man jumped up and shrieked: "That's just wild talk! You're only a crazy murderer from New York!"

This fellow was one of the Green Bell's agitators who had managed to slip inside. He fled wildly when a dozen angry men charged him.

After the excitement subsided, Doc resumed speaking.

"Will the following individuals please come forward," he requested.

He now read a list of names which Aunt Nora had furnished him. It included practically every factory and mine owner in Prosper City.

The designated men seemed reluctant to assume the limelight —until the lead was taken by a sparse, gray-haired man who had a determined face.

"That is Collison McAlter, my employer," Alice Cash whispered to Doc. "That is—he was my employer when there was a job."

Other men followed Collison McAlter's example. They were quietly dressed, substantial-looking fellows, all of middle age.

The desperate situation in Prosper City was mirrored on their faces. Some were pale, nervous, openly worried. Others carefully masked their concern.

Doc Savage counted them. About two thirds of the list he had called were present. But he had not expected unanimous attendance. That even this many had attended Aunt Nora's meeting was remarkable.

"Will each of you sell me your factory or mine holdings?" Doc asked bluntly. "Provided I give you the right to buy them back at the same price any time within a year."

Jaws sagged among the worried industrialists. The proposition was a bit sudden for them. They were incredulous.

The idea that they should be recipients of an offer so strange was too much for their mental digestions.

"Understand me," Doc told them; "I am not taking any man's

plant off his hands at a handsome profit. The purchase price must be what is fair in the judgment of an impartial board."

Collison McAlter ran fingers through his graying hair. "I should like to know what your purpose is in making this offer."

"Your plants are simply being taken off your hands," Doc told him. "We intend to start every one working. If they are damaged, or we fail, you don't stand to lose anything."

"You mean that you're going to buy them, get them operating profitably, then let us have them back at what we sold for? Why, that's not good business! You won't make any profit!"

Aunt Nora Boston sprang up and said loudly: "You men get this through your heads: Doc Savage don't go around trying to make money! He goes around helping people! You fellows never met anybody like him before! He's probably the most remarkable man in the world!"

"This is too good to be true!" Collison McAlter smiled widely. "There must be a string tied to it."

"The only string is an agreement that the wages and working hours in effect, when you take the plants off my hands, must be maintained," Doc replied.

"The kind of a deal you are proposing will take millions!" Collison McAlter muttered doubtfully.

Doc now summoned the banker with whom Johnny had deposited the check for such an enormous sum.

"I want you to advise these gentlemen the size of my account with you," Doc requested of him.

The banker, more than glad to please the largest depositor his institution had ever seen, complied with the request.

The owners of Prosper City's inoperative factories and mines were becoming a bit dizzy. They looked like men who were having a pleasant walk in their sleep.

But they were hard-headed, conservative individuals. They began discussing the matter among themselves. Some wanted time to think it over. A week! Thirty days! Two months!

Doc's powerful voice stilled the babble of words.

"This requires swift action!" he announced. "You men know very well that a mysterious master mind known only as the Green Bell is behind this trouble! We must begin fighting him without delay!"

Doc knew human nature. If they got to talking about the thing, they might hem and haw for months.

For the second time that night, it was Collison McAlter who took decisive action. This might have been due largely to the persuasive nod given him by his pretty secretary, Alice Cash.

"I'll take you up, Mr. Savage!" he declared. "I'd be foolish not to. I don't stand to lose anything. I shall give you a bargain price on my concern, the Little Grand Cotton Mills."

Doc Savage stepped down and shook hands heartily. Getting the Little Grand concern was half his battle. It was second in size only to Tugg & Co. among Prosper City's industries.

Most of the other owners now came forward with oral agreements to surrender their properties. A few men, still suspicious, were reticent. But Doc had no fear that they would fail to come around, once public opinion was aroused.

This entire discussion had been picked up by the sensitive microphones of the public-address system. The vast throng within the tents and upon the grounds had heard each word.

Doc now addressed the crowd. "You have just heard an agreement entered into which will put most of the industrial plants in Prosper City in my possession. It will be two or three days before these sales are completed and money changes hands. Opening of the plants will have to wait that long. How many of you are ex-service men?"

All over the tents and the grounds a surprising number of hands shot into the air.

"Fine!" Doc called. "How many of you fellows are willing to go to work right now?"

Practically every hand stayed up.

"That's still better!" Doc told them. "You've got jobs. You'll draw pay for to-day. The salary is ten dollars a day."

Mention of the rate of remuneration called forth several pleased howls. The sum was well over the prevailing scale for labor in that section of the State.

"You fellows are going to earn that money," Doc told them. "You are going to form an armed guard to protect the plants as we open them. Some of you may be killed. But the family of any man who dies in the line of duty will receive a trust-fund income of two hundred dollars a month for the balance of life."

Perpetual monthly payments was the kind of insurance that appealed to the men. It was something their widows could not be swindled out of.

A visible change had swept over the crowd as developments chased each other. Earlier, the attitude had been the dull hopelessness of beings who felt themselves helpless victims of some Gargantuan monster which they could not understand. That was now changed entirely.

The concern of each man was naturally for himself. Where was the next meal for himself and his family coming from? What had caused the factories and mines to close down was something too vast, too vague and abstract, for them to grasp, unused as they were to thinking in large terms. Nobody, for that matter, understood the reason for this trouble.

They were like cattle caught in a hailstorm. They could feel the hail pelting them, but what had caused the clouds to form and the hail to fall, they did not comprehend clearly. What they wanted was a shed or something for protection.

Jobs which Doc was offering were figurative sheds. The men were overjoyed.

Doc had more bounty to distribute.

Four armored trucks lumbered into Aunt Nora's great yard. These were the type of vehicles used to convey factory pay rolls. Each had a grilled pay window.

Lines were formed, the ex-service men superintending operations. Each person to pass a barred window received a moderate sum of money. In return, they signed vouchers saying the amount was advance salary on jobs they were to get.

Through Johnny and the banker, Doc had summoned the money trucks, some of which had come from neighboring cities.

Distribution of this money was the climaxing sensation. Charity to the tune of a few dollars was one thing; philanthropy on such a stupendous scale as this was something else again. Such a thing had never before been heard of here.

Reporters from the Prosper City *Star* ran around like chickens with their heads off. Down at the newspaper plant, an extra press was dusted off. It was decided to double the size of the paper, and fill it all with news about Doc Savage. Stories about Congress, European troubles, and the murder of a big gangster were consigned to the wastebasket.

The insidious master mind, the Green Bell, whoever he was and wherever he was, had something to think about. The pall of fear which he had built up so painstakingly was being, in a single night, almost completely wiped away by the remarkable power of this man of bronze.

Doc knew very well, though, that the battle was just starting. The Green Bell's organization was still intact. The sinister czar's followers were now certain to concentrate on their bronze Nemesis.

This was as Doc wanted it. The innocent workmen of Prosper City would not suffer.

The night was far along when Doc went up to his room to get a few hours of sleep.

Doc's eyes roved the room as he stood in the door. Nothing suspicious met his eye—there was no detail to show that the little black box of insanity was concealed near the head of his bed!

Doc strode over, seated himself on the edge of the bed, and started to kick off his shoes.

He became rigid; his mighty body seemed to solidify into the metal it resembled. He brought both corded hands to his ears.

Then he leaped erect and whipped out of the room.

He stopped in the hall and waited there, tense. He shook his head a time or two. His expression was strange, curious, puzzled.

Through the open door, his eyes roved the room. They rested finally upon the curtained cabinet, near the head of the bed. This was the only logical hiding place.

Doc entered the room. He flashed to the cabinet, stripped back the curtain, and discovered the dark box. He clicked the switch off. His whole movement had taken but the flash part of a moment.

Curiously, Doc began examining the box. He loosened small screws and lifted the lid off.

Long Tom, the electrical wizard, came in.

"What in blazes is that, Doc?"

"The devil's own machine! Take a look at it!"

Long Tom scrutinized the device closely.

"Huh!" he ejaculated. "This is a mechanism utilizing quartz crystals and high-frequency electric currents for making ultrashort sound waves."

"Exactly," Doc agreed. "Sound waves which have strange effects upon many substances. There is not the slightest doubt but that this is the explanation of the strange cases of insanity in Prosper City. The sonic waves affect certain centers of the brain, rendering them inoperative, I believe."

Long Tom nodded. "But how'd you find the thing?"

"The waves are inaudible to a normal ear. Fortunately, I was able to detect certain sounds of peculiar nature. It is doubtful that these were the sonic waves themselves, but more probably they were heterodyne beats caused by some refracting phenomena."

It was perfectly clear to Long Tom how this could happen, although a scientific discussion lasting for days could have been waged over the subject.

No doubt the main explanation of Doc's escape was his remarkable hearing. From the cradle, Doc had each day taken certain sound exercises calculated to develop his auditory senses. For this purpose, he used a device which made sound waves inaudible to an ordinary ear. Through long practice, Doc was able to hear these notes.

Ole Slater, Aunt Nora, and the others soon arrived, anxious to see the hideous black box and hear how it worked.

Doc borrowed the magnifier in the left lens of the gaunt Johnny's spectacles, and went over the interior of the brain-paralyzing device.

Strange little lights came into his golden eyes as he examined it.

Into the room there came abruptly a low, fantastic sound. It was like the song of some exotic bird of the jungle, or the mellow trilling of a breeze filtering through a forest. It had no tune, though it was entirely melodious.

Those present stared. They looked frightened. Ole Slater backed nervously for the door, thinking the deadly sonic device was in operation. The weird sound was in all the room, seeming to emanate uncannily from no particular spot.

Doc's four friends showed no fear, however. They had heard this uncanny note before. They knew it was the sound which was a part of Doc—a small, unconscious thing which he did in moments of utter concentration. In the present case, they were sure it presaged an important discovery.

"What'd you find, Doc?" rumbled the big-fisted Renny.

"Finger prints," Doc told him. "The fellow who made this thing might as well have signed his name."

Collison McAlter came upstairs, along with some of the other Prosper City factory owners. He listened in amazement to Alice Cash, as she told him about the sonic device.

Doc Savage placed the black box on a table near the bedroom window. He walked to a rather bulky metal box which stood to one side of the chamber. This was decorated with various knobs and switches, together with circular glass lenses.

Doc opened it. Inside, mechanism was operating slowly. Two large magazines held a narrow movie film.

Collison McAlter's eyes popped. "A movie camera! And it's been operating in here all the time?"

"Doc had several of those," volunteered the homely Monk. "They operate silently, and they're handy to leave standing around to photograph prowlers. I'm betting the fellow who planted that black box got his picture taken!"

Collison McAlter wiped his forehead. "But it was too dark to take pictures in here!"

"This movie camera operates on ultra-violet light," Monk explained. "The rays are invisible to the human eye, but they affect photograph film of the type we use. In other words, that camera can take pictures in pitch darkness. And it carries enough film to run all day."

Monk further announced that the film, immediately after passing the lens, ran through a tank which automatically developed it.

Doc now put the film through a tiny projector. The images were thrown on the white plaster of the wall. The pictures were not attractive to the eye, since highlights and shadows contrasted starkly.

As portrayed by the film, the room seemed unreal, horrible. The creeping figure of Slick Cooley appeared. Every detail of his features was plainly discernible.

He was facing the camera at the moment he whispered to himself; then he planted the box and fled.

"So he is the culprit!" barked Collison McAlter.

Doc stopped the projector. He indicated the black sonic box on the table. "Make sure no one carries that off. The finger prints in it are important."

He glided for the door.

Collison McAlter gulped: "But where are you going?"

"To get Slick Cooley," Doc said dryly.

"But how do you know where to find——" Collison McAlter fell silent, for Doc was gone.

Doc's four aids exchanged knowing glances. They had a good idea how Doc knew where to locate Slick Cooley.

Slick had been facing the camera when he whispered: "I'll plant my toy there, then go to Chief Clements's office and wait for him to turn up!"

Doc Savage was a proficient lip reader.

The group now left Doc's room. Renny took up a position outside the door, armed with one of the tiny, high-speed machine guns. The room was on the second floor, and the grounds were flood-lighted.

Even if the Green Bell did know of the finger prints, it did not seem possible that he could get to the black box to destroy them.

Renny had not been on guard before the door for long, however, when certain portentous events transpired.

A tree, lifting between Doc's window and one of the flood lamps, cast a shadow over the portion of the house that was between the window and the roof.

Directly above Doc's room was the window of one of the garret chambers. This lifted silently.

A small package appeared, tied to the end of a string. This was lowered. A swinging movement caused the package to sweep in through the window of Doc's quarters. It was dropped within.

The string was permitted to hang between the two windows. It was small and dark and not likely to be noticed by any one.

In the garret cubicle, the murksome figure which had lowered the package now made for the door. This being wore a long black gown, on the front of which was a bell design in bilious green.

The little room under the roof chanced to be the one which had formerly been occupied by unfortunate Jim Cash.

The black-hooded personage quitted the garret.

A few minutes later, the group of factory owners took leave of Aunt Nora's house, discussing Doc Savage and his men, and the things they had seen that night. Collison McAlter was with them. He seemed greatly pleased with the events of the night. His step was jaunty.

Chapter X
THE MURDER SNARE

The Prosper City police station was a dingy, red-brick building, constructed in the shape of a "T." The stem of the "T" contained the barred cells for prisoners. The crosspiece held offices, including the one used by Chief Clements.

Chief Clements did not keep a very sightly office. Circulars concerning wanted criminals stuck to the walls like stamps. There were metal filing cabinets, all large and rusty.

On top of the scarred flat-top desk stood a box of five-cent cigars. About two thirds of them had been smoked.

Slick Cooley occupied the swivel chair back of the desk. His weasel face was screwed into a grimace over the cigar. Slick considered five-centers below his station in life.

Back of Slick, a window was open. He did not worry. This was the second floor. A night breeze rushed softly in through the window and pulled strings of gray smoke off his cigar end.

Suddenly, the breeze seemed to bring in a great bronze cloud. This cloud tied around Slick and became as real and hard as banding steel cables.

Air tore loudly out of Slick's lungs as he was squeezed. He made no other sound. He was planted, helpless, upon the desk, and relieved of his two silenced guns.

Slick tried to struggle, but he might as well have been a mouse in the clutches of a big cat.

The brick wall of the police station had offered no great obstacle to Doc Savage. It was not the smooth type of wall, but one which had fairly deep grooves between the bricks. Doc, with his tremendous strength and agility, had come up it much as another man would climb stairs.

Doc maintained a purposeful silence, not speaking even after he had disarmed Slick.

Cabled bronze fingers seemed to flow over Slick's person. They administered a wrench here—pressure there. Slick found himself mysteriously relieved of the power of speech by some weird paralysis of nerve centers.

"You're going to die," Doc told him—but neglected to mention the mortal date.

Slick naturally presumed Doc meant immediately. Doc had no intention of slaying Slick. He had merely stated a natural truth, and let Slick draw his own conclusions.

For some seconds Doc worked on Slick's frame with incredibly strong hands. His manipulations produced excruciating agony. So great was the torture that Slick began to think he was actually dying.

"Who is the Green Bell?" Doc demanded.

The bronze fingers kneaded Slick's nerve centers again, and he found the use of his tongue had magically returned.

He tried to bluff. "Honest, mister, I don't know anything about any Green Bell!"

"A lie!" Doc told him quietly. "You are one of the Green Bell's hirelings. You might be the Green Bell himself—except that you don't show any signs of having that many brains."

"You're crazy!" Slick snarled.

"Not as crazy as you hoped I would be when you planted that sonic device in my room."

"I didn't——"

"A movie camera was hidden in the room! It registered your actions!"

Slick did not doubt this. Remembering the intricate electrical apparatus standing in the bedroom, he wished he had investigated more closely.

"They won't hang a man for that," he mumbled.

"No!" Doc agreed. "They'll never hang you!"

Thinking this was a threat, Slick shivered. He changed his tactics.

"Now listen, Savage; maybe we can get together!"

"Who is the Green Bell?"

"I don't know! Honest, I don't!"

"But you are one of his men?"

Slick knew there was no use denying this. "Yeah!"

"You were one of the gang who murdered Jim Cash," Doc said.

That was merely a guess on Doc's part, stated as a fact. But

Slick goggled at the bronze man's features, saw no expression there, and came to the mistaken conclusion that Doc had learned of the deed in some mysterious fashion.

"What if I did? You can't prove it!" Slick squirmed desperately. "You can't prove anything on me!"

"Judborn Tugg is one of the gang," Doc said calmly.

"Sure." Then it suddenly dawned on Slick that he was being tricked. He cried desperately: "You can't prove a thing I've been telling you!"

The door opened, and a twanging voice said: "He don't need to prove it."

Chief Clements of the Prosper City police stood on the threshold. His cherry of a face was somewhat pale, and his bristling caterpillar of a mustache drooped slightly, making it seem smaller. Otherwise, he appeared none the worse for the hours of sleep induced by Doc's drug.

No surprise showed on Doc's metallic face. A few moments ago he had heard some one approach the door. This had escaped Slick's notice.

"You should have stayed outside a while longer," Doc advised Chief Clements. "You might have learned other facts."

Chief Clements's face wore the expression of a man who had suddenly discovered that his house had burned down. Jerkily he mopped at his small features.

"I've been played for a sap," he mumbled.

"All of us are taken for a ride occasionally," Doc assured him without malice.

This did not seem to relieve Chief Clements. He knotted his bony hands, captured a part of his dark mustache with his lower lip, and nibbled it, goat fashion.

"I talked to some people on my way here, and read an extra edition of the *News* put out," he twanged. "I found out what you done at that meeting tonight—passing out food and clothing and money to them starving people. A lot of them poor devils you helped were my friends."

Chief Clements was an honest, stubborn man, who had learned he was wrong. He was trying to apologize.

Doc helped him out. "Forget it! You were doing what you thought was right. No man can do more than that."

Chief Clements smiled gratefully. His knobby shoulders lost their droop.

"From now on I'm working with you," he said grimly. "What I

just heard proves you didn't murder Jim Cash. I'm not going to arrest you. And I'd like to see anybody from out of town pinch you. Furthermore, I'm going to arrest Judborn Tugg. Slick's talk proved Tugg is mixed up with the Green Bell."

"I'm afraid such slender evidence would not convict Tugg in court."

Chief Clements stared dismally at Doc. "You mean that we had better not throw Tugg into the can?"

"Tugg may be the Green Bell. Suppose we watch him closely. If he is not the Green Bell, he might still lead us to the master mind. With your very valuable help, we'll be sure to solve this."

The last statement was partly flattery. Undeniably, though, having Chief Clements on Doc's side would greatly facilitate matters.

"I'll slap this guy in the hoosegow, then we'll talk things over," Chief Clements said, and snapped handcuffs on Slick's wrists.

The lithe, snakelike Slick was led off in the direction of the cells in the rear.

Doc had been smiling in friendly fashion for Chief Clement's benefit. Left alone, his strong features now settled into repose. A warm light in his golden eyes indicated that he was well satisfied with the way things were going.

Chief Clements returned, stepping spryly.

"I wish you would tell me what you know about conditions here in Prosper City, Mr. Savage. I must confess I have been blinded by that flashy bluffer, Judborn Tugg."

"My facts are meager," Doc told him.

Then, without squandering words, he imparted his facts. He told of the capture of the Green Bell's seven thugs in New York City. But he made no mention of what had finally happened to them. No one, other than those connected with the place, knew of the strange institution in upstate New York.

"So Jim Cash was rubbed out because he got wise to who the Green Bell was!" muttered Chief Clements. "Cash was a good kid. I knew him. His sister is swell, too. That young Ole Slater has been rushing her lately."

"Know anything about Slater?"

"He's all right. I investigated him mighty close."

"How come?"

"That was when Tugg had me thinkin' Aunt Nora Boston was at the bottom of this trouble. I combed their records. I didn't find nothin' on Slater. He's written a couple of plays that have been produced on Broadway."

The discussion veered to plans for the future. Chief Clements suggested that the ex-service men guard for the mines and factories should be commissioned as members of the Prosper City police force.

This was an excellent idea, Doc agreed.

"I can supply most of them with guns!" Clements declared.

"I should like to have all the prisoners," Doc requested.

"I don't get you! What do you want with the Green Bell's bunch, if we catch 'em? Why not let 'em go to the pen?"

"My treatment is more effective than penitentiary terms or the electric chair," Doc said.

Chief Clements looked at the bronze man's face and squirmed uneasily. He had received the impression that Doc meant to slay the prisoners.

"No one will be put to death," Doc promised him.

"It's irregular," Clements said, "but if you want them, you can have them!"

Back in the jail, a shot banged. The sound was hollow—like a single grain of popcorn letting loose in a popper.

Doc whipped for the door. His movements seemed easy, but were executed with a swiftness which caused Clements to stare in amazement. This phenomenon of a man moving with such unearthly speed all but made Clements forget the shot. He heaved out of his chair and followed Doc.

A long, bare, cold corridor ended at a sheet-steel door. Chief Clements unlocked the panel.

A concrete alley, barred cells on either side, stretched beyond. Faces were jammed against the bars; excited questions babbled.

An iron stairway sloped down to the first-floor cells.

"I put Slick below!" Chief Clements shouted, and hammered his heels on the stairs.

Halfway down the passage, a steel grid of a door hung open. Two turnkeys huddled before it, peering into the cell. Both were rigid, bent forward grotesquely.

Doc and Chief Clements raced the corridor's length.

Light blazed in the passage, but not in the cells. The bars cast striped shadows on the cement floor. The shadow stripes seemed to crawl like black snakes over two figures in the dungeon.

One man was a jail flunky. He held an automatic. An empty cartridge glittered on the floor, and the place reeked of cordite.

The second man was a twisted pile. His position was so contorted that it seemed his body had been pulled apart, then dropped in a heap.

There was an ugly froth on his lips. His eyes were rolled in their sockets until they resembled white marbles. A bullet had knocked the top of his head out of shape. It was Slick Cooley.

The man with the automatic backed stiffly away from the body. "Something went wrong with him!" he cried shrilly. "He was havin' a fit. He grabbed my gun and got shot when we were fightin' for it. He was stark, ravin' crazy, if you ask me!"

Wheeling, Doc Savage sped back the length of the passage. He reached a metal door. A tiny, glittering tool appeared in his hand. He used this briefly on the door lock, and the panel opened as if he held a weird power over it.

Chief Clements ran to the door. His jaw was sagging. The door had been locked, and he would have sworn that it was burglar proof. He stepped out into the night, bobbing his small red head like a blinded chicken. It was a long minute before his eyes accustomed themselves to the gloom, and he could see Doc Savage.

The lots around the police station were vacant. On them some one had sown grass—and grown a profuse crop of weeds. Doc was wading through these, using a flashlight.

Rows of tiny windows, heavily barred, admitted to the cells. Doc Savage lingered under one from which came the low voices of the turnkeys gathered about Slick's body.

The ground bore faint marks where feet had recently trod. The earth was too sunbaked to retain definite footprints, but weeds, crushed by a recent tread, were slowly straightening.

Doc joined Clements.

"The Green Bell got Slick with one of his sonic devices which produce insanity!" he imparted.

Clements wailed: "We've lost our only witness who could prove you didn't kill Jim Cash."

Doc seemed not to hear the statement. He started away, hesitated, turned back.

"I'm going to Judborn Tugg's home! Want to drive me? You know the town."

"You bet!" Clements ran for his car.

Prosper City's most pretentious residential district was located on a knoll known to the local wags as Plutocrat Knob. As befitted a man who was not backward in holding himself up as a leading citizen, Judborn Tugg occupied the most flashy dwelling in the section.

The mansion was white, after the Spanish style—a thing of tiled roofs, overhanging balconies, and wrought-iron railings. Shrubbery was plentiful.

Several blocks from the place, Chief Clements got up speed, kicked out the clutch, and cut off the ignition. He coasted to a silent stop two blocks from the white castle.

Doc lifted out.

"Thanks," he said. "You might as well go back to the station."

Chief Clements jerked at his bristling black mustache. "But listen——"

He clamped his teeth on the rest. The bronze man had faded away silently into the night!

Chief Clements stood up, intending to call loudly, then thought better of it. The sound might alarm Judborn Tugg. He sat there, blanketed in disgust. He had hoped to be in on whatever investigation Doc contemplated.

The bronze man fascinated Clements; he wanted to see more of him.

Clements fiddled with the ignition, then made an angry finger-snapping gesture. This was provoked by recollection of how he had fallen for Judborn Tugg's trickery.

Clements suddenly decided to do some investigating on his own. If he could learn the identity of the Green Bell, his stupidity would be less reprehensible.

The thought occurred to him that he might interfere with some plan of the bronze man. Well, he would be careful not to do that.

Leaving his car, he eased through the shrubbery. He managed to make little noise.

The shadow of a manicured hedge led him close to a side door of the white palace. He crouched there, not ten feet from the door, wondering what he should do next.

The problem solved itself.

The door opened, and Judborn Tugg came out. Apparently he was getting a breath of the night air before turning in.

Tugg lit one of his dollar cigars and threw the match away. It landed beside Clements. Not extinguished by the fall, it flared up. The light disclosed the Prosper City chief of police.

Tugg dashed forward, drawing a pistol. Then he perceived the interloper's identity.

"My good friend, Chief Clements!" he exclaimed pompously. "What on earth are you doing here?"

Chief Clements heaved up on his knees. Within the last hour, he had acquired a great hate for this flashy man.

Clements was not only a slow thinker; he had a temper.

"Don't you call me a friend!" he snarled.

Tugg jumped as if kicked. His head seemed to dive down into his fat neck. He had been warned that Clements would be a deadly enemy if he ever learned the truth. And the police leader was now acting as if he had glimpsed light.

Armoring himself with dignity, Tugg began: "My dear man, what——"

"You damn murderer!" gritted Clements. "Don't you try to soft-soap me!"

Tugg appeared to swell in girth and shrink in stature. A paleness bleached his pursy jowls.

Chief Clements had only spoken rashly in his rage, but Judborn Tugg thought the officer was stating a charge, which he could prove. Fear crawled in Tugg's veins like red ants. He was desperate. He decided to try a trick.

"Call your other officers!" he snapped. "I surrender!"

"There's nobody else with me," rapped Chief Clements, falling neatly into the trap.

This was what Tugg had wanted to know. Jutting his gun at arm's length, he worked the trigger. The reports banged thunder. The bullets sledged Clements backward, tunneling through his heart and lungs.

Tugg continued shooting until his gun was empty. Then, from the corner of an eye, he glimpsed what to him was a terrible sight. A giant man of bronze! The figure came volleying across the lawn toward him.

Tugg snapped his empty gun twice at Doc, then veered around into the house.

"Help!" he called.

Several men, aids of the Green Bell, were in the house. Some had attended the sinister meeting in the dilapidated barn. Others were merely agitators, who did not work in the Green Bell's black robes, and, as a consequence, were paid less money. They were loafing in Tugg's company.

Flourishing weapons, these men rushed to Tugg's aid. When Doc Savage loomed in the door, their guns loosened a volley.

Lead gnashed splinters out of the door, or screamed on to slap into distance houses. None of the slugs touched Doc. He had seen the danger in time to twist away.

The Green Bell's gunmen, weapons ready, sidled nervously through the door, or dropped from near-by windows. Their bronze quarry was not visible. But there was much shadow-matted shrubbery near by, which could hold him.

Inside the house, Tugg ran to a phone. He called the Prosper City police headquarters.

"Doc Savage has just murdered Chief Clements out at my place!" he screamed. "I got half a dozen witnesses to it!"

The words were loud enough to reach Doc Savage, where he lurked in the shrubs. He glided rapidly away from the vicinity.

Five minutes would see half of Prosper City's police department on the spot.

The officers did not know Doc and Chief Clements had made their peace. They would be ripe to believe Judborn Tugg's lie. A terrific man hunt was certain, with Doc Savage as the quarry.

Hardly a flicker appeared in Doc's eyes when they caught the reflection of a street lamp. Their gold was dull. The charge of murdering Chief Clements was going to be a hard thing to combat.

At a rapid run he made for the outskirts of the town, where Aunt Nora Boston's house stood.

Chapter XI
DESTROYED CLEWS

Roosters were crowing four o'clock from distant farmhouses when Doc Savage neared Aunt Nora's rambling dwelling.

To one side of the house, Monk was drilling a determined squad of ex-service men.

On the other side of the house a score of individuals stood in a knot, staring upward. Their curious attention was centered on the window of Doc's room.

The window was wiped clean of glass. Part of the frame had been ripped out and hung dangling. Around the aperture, weather-boarding was splintered and torn until it looked furry.

Monk yelled, lumbering over to meet Doc. Monk's gorillalike face was hard and wrathful.

"There was an explosion in your room, Doc! The blast put the kibosh on a lot of your equipment."

"What about the Green Bell's sonic device?"

"Blown to smithereens!"

Doc received this news as expressionlessly as if it had been a comment on the weather. He had developed perfect control. He could take the greatest misfortune without emotion.

Why the black sonic box had been destroyed was perfectly clear. It had held the finger prints of the Green Bell, or some one who knew the evil czar's identity.

"The bomb was planted from inside the house," Monk grunted. "It was lowered on a string from an attic window and swung into the room. We found the string!"

Doc walked to the house, entered, and went upstairs.

The door was not only off its hinges, but lay in fragments along the hallway.

"Renny was on guard outside the door," Monk explained. "He got knocked head over heels!"

"Was he hurt?"

"That guy!" Monk snorted. "Nothin' can hurt him!"

Doc examined the room. Practically all his scientific devices had been ruined. This damage alone amounted to many thousands. Some of the mechanism was of such a complex nature that only Doc Savage's skilled hand and unique brain could recreate it.

Scummy brown stains smeared the floor, walls, bed—almost everything in the chamber. These seemed to be devouring whatever they covered. An acrid odor reeked in the place.

"Don't touch anything!" Doc warned.

"Yeah—I know!" Monk agreed. "The brown stuff is acid. It would eat the flesh right off a man. There must have been several bottles of it tied in with the bomb."

"It was intended to eat the finger prints off the sonic device in case the explosion failed to do the job," Doc decided.

Doc sought pieces of the sonic apparatus. The only segment of any size was the split end of a coil mounting.

This trophy Doc carried into the bathroom and washed thoroughly to remove the acid. He also scoured the voracious liquid off his own shoes soles. It was dissolving the leather.

Some moments later, Doc's hands abruptly became idle upon the towel he was using. He glided to a window and leaned out, listening.

In the distance, toward the center of town, he could hear spattering shots. The fusillade died in a banging series which might have been periods.

Monk lumbered over.

"That sounds bad!" he muttered. "It may mean Renny and the rest are in trouble!"

"Where did they go?"

"I forgot to tell you. Ham telephoned from New York that he had sent the body of poor Jim Cash by train. Renny and everybody else accompanied Alice Cash down to the station to get it. Everybody but me, that is. I didn't care about seeing the girl's grief."

"Let's get downtown!" Doc rapped.

They loaded into a touring car in front of the house. This was one of several fast machines which Doc had rented and was keeping on hand for general use.

Doc crouched out of sight on the rear floorboards. Monk drove. Tire treads shrieked as the phaëton careened onto the road. The exhaust moaned; the rush of air popped the top fabric against the bows. Doc braced himself in position, watching street lights bat past like white eyes.

"Angle over a bit to the right," he advised.

Keenness of hearing had enabled him to place the source of the shots.

A cop tweedled frantically on his whistle as the car went past like a meteor. Dwellings ceased; business blocks veered ahead.

Prosper City had erected a new Union Station when times were good. It was a lumpish gray building, with long train sheds radiating like fingers in the rear. The place resembled a mausoleum.

In the gloom in front of the station, Doc found a hearse, two cars, and an excited crowd. Blue uniforms of policemen freckled the assemblage.

Monk drew in close and stopped the car. Doc got out. He worked forward, almost brushing the elbow of a policeman, who was too occupied with craning his neck to notice.

Although dawn was threatening redly in the east, it was gloomy in the vicinity of the station. This, and the fact that all attention was focused on the hearse, aided Doc in avoiding discovery.

Big-fisted Renny and handsome Ole Slater stood near the rear of the hearse, talking to officers.

In one of the parked cars huddled Alice Cash, sobbing on Aunt Nora's ample shoulder.

Long Tom and Johnny were keeping the crowd from getting too near the two women.

Doc found a fat man, and a did a good job of masking himself in the gentleman's shadow. He threw his voice in the direction of the hearse. Not wishing to betray his presence, he spoke in Mayan.

"What happened here, Renny?" he inquired in the lost language.

A tightening of Renny's big fist betrayed his surprise. He pondered briefly on how to give the explanation without it seeming suspicious. Then he got it.

"I want you fellows to get this straight," he told the officers loudly. "We came down here to receive the remains of young Jim Cash. They had been shipped down from New York, one of the railway officials accompanying them. We had no more than——"

"You told us all that, before!" snapped a policeman.

"Shut up!" Renny thundered. "We had no more than taken the

coffin off the train when a gang attacked us. They all wore black hoods with the green, bell-like design on the front. They started shooting, and we had to hunt cover in a hurry!"

Renny made his voice even louder to emphasize the words which he particularly wanted to reach Doc. "The Green Bell's gang just examined the body. It didn't look to me like they took a thing."

This ended Renny's explanation.

Doc drifted a bronze hand into his clothing and brought out a bundle of small objects which might have been red sticks with strings sticking from the ends.

He touched a lighted match to one of the strings, and dropped them. So great was the crowd's interest in Renny and his story, no one noticed Doc's act.

Careful not to attract attention, Doc drifted nearer the hearse. A moment later, a series of loud explosions came from the spot which he had just quitted.

Doc always carried a few ordinary firecrackers with long fuses. These had proved convenient on many occasions.

A yelling hubbub arose over the fireworks. This hypnotized all eyes. No one observed a bronze figure which slipped into the hearse.

With a flashlight that spiked a white thread of a beam, Doc made an examination. His search was brief.

On Jim Cash's body, on the arm above the right elbow, were words.

From their metallic color, these letters might have been printed with the lead snout of a bullet. But Doc knew that they had been put there by a chemical—to remain unnoticed until the application of a second chemical brought them out.

They read:

IN MY FACTORY LOCKER

This, then, was what the Green Bell horde had sought.

Doc dropped out of the hearse. At that point, he lost the good luck which had attended his brazen efforts. A policeman saw him.

The officer gasped. Then he flashed his service pistol, and recklessly tried to put a bullet in Doc's bronze head.

The slug went a yard too high. Doc dropped to all fours. Keeping down, he torpedoed through the forest of legs.

A wake of yelling, overturned men marked his progress. Several individuals sought to seize him. They either missed their clutches entirely, or were shaken off. Some launched kicks, only to bruise their toes on a frame which was almost as solid as metal.

In the phaëton parked near by, Monk drew one of the tiny machine guns and began to rip bullets into the air.

Renny, Long Tom, and Johnny sent up deafening yells, and thrashed aimlessly about. These two disturbances were aimed at aiding Doc's escape.

Doc dived out of the crowd, raced for the station, and almost made it before a policeman saw him. It was necessary for the officers to fight clear of the crowd before they could use their guns. And long before they could do that, Doc was inside the depot.

The station was cleared of waiting travelers, porters, and loafers, thanks to the excitement outside. Doc crossed the colored tile floor and ran out under the train shed.

A line of Pullmans and day coaches stood under one of the shelters—evidently a train which was to depart at a later hour.

Doc crawled into one of the coaches. He ran between aisles of green plush seats incased in white protecting cloths. Through coach after coach he passed, shutting the intervening doors so the officers could not sight him by looking the length of the train.

At the far end he dropped off.

Although dawn was imminent, enough gloom remained to simplify the rest of the escape. Doc hurdled sidings, whipped under freight cars, and cleared a low concrete wall.

As if to climax recent ghoulish events, he found he had entered the stockyard of a monument concern. Grave markers of white marble, and more elaborately carved headstones, stood all about.

A long alley beyond the monument yard precipitated him into a side street.

Until Collison McAlter's Little Grand Cotton Mill had been forced to close, Jim Cash had been an employee of the concern.

The strange words on Cash's arm undoubtedly referred to his locker at the Little Grand plant.

For the Little Grand Mills, Doc set his course. They were many blocks away on the south side of Prosper City. Doc ran, haunting alleys and side streets.

He made no effort to get a taxi, after noticing that policemen were staioned at prominent corners, stopping passing cars and examining the interiors.

Doc had been without sleep or rest for many hours, yet his stride lacked nothing in elasticity. Through a lifetime of intensive exercises—two hours of it each day—Doc had developed a strength and stamina which was almost superhuman, as compared to that of other men.

The Little Grand Mills were situated like a gaudy blossom on a sweeping stem of railroad sidings.

The buildings were gray, red-roofed, neat. Grass on the ground was cropped so close it might have been a coating of green paint.

A high fence, of wire as thick as a lead pencil, surrounded the plant. A barrier of barbed strands circled the top. There was a wide entrance, steel gated, flanked by a watchman's turret. This later structure had a small, barred window.

A man peered out of the watchman's box—a pale man who looked scared.

"Who are you?" he quavered. "What do you want?"

"Let me in!" Doc commanded. "It will be all right with Collison McAlter!"

The watchman hesitated.

"Mr. McAlter is here now," he muttered finally. "I'll go with you and find out if he wants you around."

The watchman stepped out of the box, closing the door behind him. He wore a white linen suit badly in need of laundering. He kept his hand in his coat pocket, and the bulge in his pocket was longer than his hand should have been.

He unlocked the gate.

Doc's gold-flake eyes seemed to give the man the briefest of glances.

Then he suddenly flashed a corded arm.

Like a hard cleaver, it descended between the man's arm and his side. The pocket tore open. The fellow's hand and a stubby pistol were forced out.

Doc's sinew-wrapped fist seemed to gulp the gun from the fingers which held it. The watchman tried to flee, but a shove—it made him think of the nudge of a locomotive—sent him reeling against the wall of his cubicle.

Doc opened the door, hurled the man inside, and followed after him.

Propped in a corner, where he had been invisible from the barred window, sat a man. He wore greasy coveralls. A time clock, suspended from his neck by a strap, proved him to be the genuine watchman. He was unconscious from a head blow, and would remain so for some time.

Doc's prisoner gritted: "This fellow is my buddy—the assistant watchman! Somebody beaned him——"

"Did you have on your Green Bell hood when you struck the watchman down?" Doc asked dryly.

The man began to sputter. "I don't know what——"

Doc sent a hand to the man's shoulder, plucked away a long black thread.

"This is not the kind of thread which would come from your suit," he murmured. "It's silk."

"It's from my necktie!" the other barked desperately.

"Your necktie is a particularly unlovely shade of yellow," Doc reminded.

The man pitched backward, desperate to escape.

Doc started a swift gesture, aimed at recapturing him. His gaze, always alert and nearly all-seeing, went beyond the false watchman to the factory buildings. What he saw caused him to duck swiftly.

The factory walls were largely of glass, after the modern fashion. The windows were great tilting panels. Three of these had opened silently since Doc's last inspection. Ominous black rods were protruding.

The rods lipped flame. They were machine guns, and they trip-hammered mad strings of reports.

Bullets slashed completely through the thin walls of the watchman's turret. They chopped the planks off. A drawer under the little inspection window was hit. It jumped out of its groove and spilled its contents on the floor.

Gloves, a lunch pail—stuff belonging to the watchman—and a Green Bell hood! Evidently this last had been hidden there when Doc was sighted.

The fake watchman was slain by the first storm of lead. The slugs doubled him up, spun him around and around, knocking him out of shape.

Doc grasped the feet of the genuine watchman, who was slumbering from the blow over the head, and jerked. The limp form skidded flat on the floor.

The floor was of painted concrete. Around it ran a foundation wall, also of concrete. It would turn bullets.

The machine guns continued a deadly chatter. The men using them were coldblooded, intent on ridding themselves of the bronze man. In their blood lust, they had coldly sacrificed their fellow crook.

From the walls chunks of wood fell. Shingles were scooped off the roof; gray dust spurted from the concrete foundation walls. The wall cracked at one point, then another. But it held, furnishing protection.

The barrage ended. Silence reeked for a moment. Then men could be heard leaving the factory.

Doc lifted his head. Two men were running forward to see what kind of work their fire had done; both were armed. Both wore the gloomy hoods of the Green Bell.

Doc reached for the pistol which he had taken from the fake watchman. He rarely carried a gun himself. He held the opinion that a man who carried a firearm would come to put too much dependence on it, and accordingly, would be the more helpless if disarmed.

An ear could barely divide the twin roar which his shots made. The charging pair seemed to go lopsided, reel, then topple down, two loose bundles of arms and legs.

It was not because of any lack of skill in their use that Doc did not carry firearms. He had winged both men in the legs.

Machine guns promptly opened up again from the factory. Doc threw himself close to the floor. It would be suicide to shoot back.

The gunfire kept up for what seemed an age. The concrete foundation wall was getting thinner and thinner. A bullet lunged through.

But once more the shooting stopped.

Chancing a look, Doc saw that the two men had been moved to safety under cover of the fire. He could hear one of them wailing faintly in agony.

Two or three mysterious volleys of shots soon sounded somewhere in the rear of the factory.

Doc exposed himself briefly. He was not fired on. Quitting the turret he ran for the factory. He reached it and veered around a corner.

It was as he had guessed: the men in the Green Bell hoods were retreating. They had used their rapid-firer to batter the lock off a small gate in the rear fence.

They fled, carrying the two wounded. Tall weeds and small brush received them. They were lost completely to view.

Motors came to hooting life in the brush. A car lunged out of a thicket like a frightened black hawk. Another followed. The two streaked down a side road, pursued by a tumbling snake of dust.

Doc entered the factory. He knew the general layout of such textile plants as this. It did not take him long to find the room which held the workmen's lockers.

The lockers were tall, green metal boxes. Each bore a small frame which held a name card. One of the lockers was upset.

Doc turned it over so that he could see the name plate:

JIM CASH

Whatever had been concealed under the locker was now gone.

A sharp, brittle voice somewhere behind Doc rasped. "You will put your hands up!"

Chapter XII
THE BODY IN THE VINES

The lockers stood in a row, like drab metal teeth. The one which was upset left an opening.

Doc dived through.

The factory floors were rubber composition. This explained how the man had approached unnoticed. Too, the newcomer was not very close—at the end of the locker room, a good fifty feet away.

There was no shot. Light in the cavernous place was too dim to permit accurate marksmanship. It was even a bit too dark to identify faces. But Doc had recognized the new arrival's voice. It was Collison McAlter, owner of the plant.

Doc lighted one of the firecrackers and threw it. It was concealed from McAlter by the lockers. Striking the wall near him, the cracker exploded with a terrific report!

Collison McAlter cried out, fired his revolver—both at the same instant. Firecracker and gunshot were about of an equal loudness.

Doc Savage, big and bronze and grim, stood very silent. It was quite dark in the corner where the firecracker had loosened. Collison McAlter probably could not tell what he had shot at, or whether he had hit any one.

Doc was puzzled. Was Collison McAlter one of the Green Bell's men? Was he the Green Bell himself?

To determine the truth, Doc decided on a small ruse. He glided silently along the phalanx of lockers until he stood as close to McAlter as he could get, without being discovered. Using the voice which he employed in ordinary speech, but making it small, choking, and thin, Doc said: "McAlter—you wanted—to kill —me."

Collison McAlter's gun slipped from his fingers and planked on the floor.

He cried shrilly: "Doc Savage—good heavens! I thought you were one of the Green Bell's gang!"

Doc waited. If Collison McAlter was the Green Bell, this might be a sly trick to draw him into line for a bullet from another gun.

But McAlter came stumbling to the spot where he thought he had shot Doc. The bronze man drew his flashlight, gave the lens a twist to spread the beam widely, and splashed luminance.

Collison McAlter's hands were bare of weapons. He was trembling, pale. He looked worried.

Doc Savage showed himself. "It's all right; you didn't hit me."

McAlter spluttered. He swabbed a cold dew off his forehead, leaning flaccidly against the locker.

"What a horrible mistake I made!" he gulped.

"Did you just get here?" Doc demanded.

"I've been here at least two hours."

McAlter paused, apparently waiting for Doc to make a remark. The result was a dead silence.

"You see, I must confess I'm not a very brave man when it comes to physical danger," McAlter mumbled. "After I left the meeting at Aunt Nora Boston's to-night I went home, but couldn't sleep. So I came out here to the factory to look things over. I saw the Green Bell's men arrive and overpower the watchman."

He paused, shuddered violently, and drooped even more limply against the lockers.

"Frankly, I was afraid to show myself!" he groaned.

"I would hardly call that lack of nerve," Doc told him. "There were too many of them for one man to handle."

"Yes, that's what I thought," McAlter agreed. "Anyway, I don't know why they were here. They started shooting, but I couldn't see their target. I guess it was you! Even then I was afraid to open fire on them. I'll never forgive myself for that!"

McAlter peered anxiously in the gloom, trying to ascertain from the expression on Doc's bronze features whether or not his story had been accepted as true.

What he saw gave him little satisfaction one way or the other.

"What in the world could they have been after?" he asked.

"Jim Cash evidently had documentary proof of the Green Bell's identity," Doc replied. "He concealed the evidence under his locker here in the plant. He wrote the name of the hiding place in invisible ink on his arm. Just why he should follow that procedure is a mystery. How the Green Bell learned of the message is also unexplained."

Both these enigmas were answered indirectly when Doc appeared at Aunt Nora Boston's house.

Collison McAlter used his limousine as a conveyance to Aunt Nora's. Doc crouched on the rug in the ample tonneau. The police did not dare to stop a man of Collison McAlter's prominence and search his car.

Ham was calling by long distance from New York, when Doc arrived at Aunt Nora's.

"How's it coming, Doc?" he asked.

"It could be a great deal better," Doc assured him.

"I thought I'd report something queer!" Ham said rapidly. "It may be important. Our mail carrier here was kidnaped yesterday by men in black gowns. He managed to escape during the night. The object of the kidnaping seemed to be to get mail he was bringing us. He said there was only one letter. It was from Prosper City."

"That explains what just happened here, Ham! Jim Cash hid his evidence against the Green Bell, and marked the hiding place on his arm! He must have written me a letter from Prosper City, suggesting that, in case he was killed, I should look on his arm for the information."

"Confound it!" Ham gritted. "We're sure having our setbacks in this mess."

"Some of the Green Bell's men may still be in New York," Doc warned. "You'd better watch out for them!"

"Don't worry, I've been doing that," Ham said wryly. "I think I'm going to be able to scare those four lying witnesses into telling the truth, too."

"When you get that done, you can come down here and clear me of the charge of murdering Prosper City's chief of police!"

Ham snorted. "O. K. How is that hairy missing link, Monk, coming along?"

"He has his eye on Alice Cash," Doc said, knowing this was exactly what Monk would wish him to tell Ham.

The conversation terminated with a loud groan from the distant lawyer. If there was anything that pained Ham, it was to see his sparring enemy, Monk, making a hit with an attractive young lady.

Monk himself soon arrived. Renny, Ole Slater, Aunt Nora and the others accompanied him. Alice Cash was quiet, and her eyes were continuously downcast.

They had consigned her brother's body to a local funeral home.

Monk looked at Doc and shook his head slowly.

"The cops sure are combing this man's town for you!" he declared. Then, in a low tone which did not reach Alice Cash, he added: "They even followed us into the funeral home and searched the coffin, thinking we might be pulling some kind of hocus-pocus! And they frisked our cars two times on the way here."

"That's not half of it!" Renny put in grimly. "They're liable to show up here any minute!"

Renny stepped out. He came back with the latest extra edition of the Prosper City *News*. Through his spectacles with the magnifying lens, he stared owlishly at the headlines.

"They've got a decent crowd on that newspaper!" he grinned. "They carry a story saying Chief Clements was shot, but they don't mention Doc's name in connection with the affair! They simply say that there is not enough evidence to name the slayer."

Absently, Renny knocked his big fists together. This made a sound as if bricks were colliding.

"What about the gun with which Tugg shot Clements?" he pondered.

"Tugg will be too wise to keep it," Doc told him.

Ole Slater came dashing in from outdoors.

"Mr. Savage!" he ejaculated. "The police!"

Doc went to the door. Down the road somewhere, loud voices were making angry demands, and getting just as angry refusals. The gang of ex-service guards had evidently stopped the police.

Monk offered: "I told them to do that."

Doc nodded. "Fine! That gives us a few moments to work which should be enough."

Monk looked uneasy. "It's going to be plenty dangerous getting away from here!"

"I'm going to stay right on the grounds!"

"Holy cow!" exploded Renny, using an expression which came to his tongue whenever he was greatly surprised. "How're you going to manage that?"

Without answering, Doc stepped outdoors and circled the house. He did not know how he was going to remain without being ferreted out by the Prosper City lawmen.

He was looking for a hiding place which would not be suspected. Before he was halfway around the house, he discovered it.

A large galvanized iron tank stood at the rear of Aunt Nora's rambling old house. Eave spouts emptied into it. Aunt Nora Boston was a thrifty soul who did her own washing. She believed there was nothing like soft rain water for this.

The tank was two thirds full.

"Give us a shoulder!" Doc directed, and bent his efforts to moving the tank some distance away from the house. "Don't spill the water!"

A skeptical laugh escaped Ole Slater. "You can never avoid them by submerging yourself in the tank. The police are sure to prod around in the water with sticks."

"Dry up, sonny," Monk advised him. "Doc's scheme ain't anything as simple as that."

Ole Slater flushed angrily. He was not in a mood to take any cracks from Monk—piqued as he was because Monk had been giving charming Alice Cash marked attention.

Doc called Monk. They ran inside the house. Although Doc's equipment had been destroyed by the explosion in his room, Monk's chemical supplies were still intact. With a great clanking of test tubes and a fizzing of liquids, Monk went to work.

Doc entered Renny's quarters. Among other things the big-fisted engineer had brought from New York were compact diving "lungs." These consisted of little more than oxygen tanks with hoses running to a mouthpiece. The outfit included a clip like a clothespin for holding the nostrils shut.

Monk appeared. He was carrying two bottles—one small, one large. They held liquids of a widely different nature. He gave Doc the smaller bottle. They hurried outdoors.

The bronze man now picked up a large rock and immersed himself carefully in the tank. He sat on the bottom, the rock on his lap to hold himself down.

Monk dumped the chemical in the large bottle onto the water. Striking a match, he applied it. The stuff blazed up brilliantly, making a brownish smoke.

Homely Monk gave Ole Slater his best leer.

"This chemical burns without hardly any heat!" he chuckled. "The police will think we're burning trash in the tank. They won't know there's water in it. Now, do you believe they'll prod with sticks?"

Ole Slater looked sheepish. "No, of course not! But suppose Mr. Savage should want to get out of there? How could he do it without being burned?"

"Didn't you see the small bottle I gave him?"

"What's that got to do with it?"

"It's filled with an extinguishing fluid that floats. All Doc has to do is uncork the bottle—and the fire goes out."

Ole Slater rubbed his strong jaws. "Isn't there any limit to the number of tricks you fellows have up your sleeve?"

"Listen!" Monk grinned. "Nobody has ever put Doc in a jam he couldn't get out of!"

Word was now dispatched to the ex-service men, advising them it was perfectly all right for the police to approach. When the officers arrived, Long Tom and Johnny were making a great show of dumping trash into the flaming tank. They ceased this before the cops came close enough to observe that the "trash" was only tin cans, which would not add to the heat of the chemical fire.

"We're gonna search this joint!" a police sergeant declared loudly. "We're gonna search it good!"

"Go ahead!" Monk told him. "Just one thing, though! Don't start intimidating Alice Cash and Aunt Nora!"

"I'm gonna make damn sure they ain't seen Doc Savage!"

Monk gave a signal. His three pals crowded up threateningly. They were a grim-faced fighting crew.

"You can ask all the questions you want to!" Monk grunted. "But whether anybody answers them or not is something else!"

"Where's Doc Savage?"

"That's one we're not going to answer!"

The lawman glowered blackly. "You won't answer because you're afraid of givin' your pal away!"

"I ain't afraid of nothin' or nobody!" Monk hammered his chest like a bull ape. "I just don't feel like answering your damned question!"

At this point more policemen arrived. Three carloads! They bristled with sub-machine guns and double-barreled riot guns. A cordon was stretched around Aunt Nora's grounds.

The officers pushed their search. Beginning at the circus tents, they tore into every bale and box. They even climbed to the top of the tents to see that there were no trick pockets.

They ignored the flaming barrel, except to toss an empty cigarette pack in the flames.

They reached the house. At front and rear doors guards were posted. The scrutiny started in the basement. Walls and floor were brick. The bricks were examined, literally one at a time, to make sure no trapdoor gave into a secret room.

Other officers scattered over the remainder of the house.

Approximately two dozen newcomers arrived. These were the men who owned the mills and the mines of Prosper City. They had evidently held a conference, and had come in a body to discuss measures which would give Doc control of their property.

When they found the bronze man was being sought by the police, they exploded indignantly. No one would entertain the idea that Doc Savage had shot Chief Clements.

They landed on the officers with a verbal barrage. For a few moments the house was a bedlam of angry shouting. The police perspired and their necks became red. They could not tell these men to shut up and clear out. They were Prosper City's powerful citizens.

"The suggestion that Savage murdered anybody is preposterous!" insisted a mine owner. "We've been investigating! Savage is known all over the world for his remarkable deeds!"

Pompous Judborn Tugg had come upon the scene from somewhere. He entered the argument.

"My dear fellow business men and comrades," he said bombastically. "This man Savage is twice a murderer—probably worse."

"We do not believe that!" some one advised.

"I saw Savage murder Chief Clements!" Tugg shouted. "Half a dozen others witnessed the horrible crime, too! Furthermore, Savage is trying to buy your properties for a fraction of what they are worth! Can't you see that? He's not only a killer—he's a gigantic swindler!"

Renny's great voice roared: "When the time comes, Tugg, we'll either prove that you're the Green Bell, or that you're on his pay roll."

Both fists up and clenched, Tugg started forward as if to strike Renny. However, he stopped well out of reach of the enormous blocks of gristle which Renny called hands.

"Your lying words won't hurt me!" he said, with the air of an injured man.

After this, Tugg subsided. He could see plainly that every one but the police was against him.

"Go ahead with the search," commanded the sergeant in charge of police. "We're going to scour this place from top——"

He never finished. Feet rapped the porch. A uniformed officer dived inside.

"One of our men!" he yelled. "Hanging in the vines under a window! A knife is sticking out of him!"

There was an excited rush around the house. Vines which the excited officer had mentioned were wistaria. The creepers draped over a lightly constructed trellis.

Under one second-story window there was a vertical streak where the leaves were wet with dull, thick red. The blue-clad body of a policeman was the mountain from which this streak of crimson spilled.

The cadaver hung from the window by a rope around the neck. The officer had been stabbed several times, judging from the places where he had leaked blood. The knife had been left protruding from his chest after the last blow.

One of Aunt Nora Boston's carving knives! It had a black stag-horn handle. From below, the hilt looked not unlike the head of a black serpent peeping from the vest pocket of the dead man's coat!

Homely Monk stared at the window—and began to feel as if he was standing in a pool of ice water. It was *his* room from which the body was dangling!

"Holy cow!" Renny breathed in Monk's ear. "Why on earth was he murdered? And right under our noses, too!"

Monk tied his furry hands into knots, then untied them. He was visioning the inside of the Prosper City Jail.

The chances were good that every one present would be arrested. It was only in detective-story books that a houseful of people were kept on the scene after a murder, in order that the detective hero might trap the villain. These hard-headed cops would throw every one in jail.

Made silent and grim by the presence of murder, the officers ran into the house and upstairs.

The rope which suspended the slain man was one Monk had used to tie around a case of chemicals which he had brought from New York. It was not long enough to lower the body to the ground.

They hauled the corpse in through the window.

There was nothing to indicate why the bluecoat had been slain; no bruises to indicate a struggle.

"There couldn't have been a fight, anyway," Monk pointed out. "We would have heard it from downstairs. The fellow has been dead only a few minutes."

"Whose room is this?" demanded the police sergeant.

"Mine," Monk admitted. His small voice was even more tiny than usual.

The officer yanked a pair of handcuffs from his pocket, and bore down on Monk.

"Listen, big hairy, you're under arrest for murder!" he snapped.

Monk beetled his brows angrily. "You're forgetting something."

"What!"

"I haven't been out of your sight a minute since you arrived. The slain man was one of the men who came with you, so I couldn't have killed him."

Marked disappointment was registered by the policeman. He wanted to put Monk under custody. But Monk was obviously not the guilty person.

"Bring everybody up here in the hall!" the cop shouted. "We'll get to the bottom of this!"

The group of men, who represented Prosper City's mines and factories, protested vociferously to being herded about by the police. This, however, had no effect.

"This is mighty serious!" the bluecoats growled. "We got to investigate everybody!"

"That is exactly right, officer!" Judborn Tugg agreed loudly. "I will gladly submit myself to any examination. Personally, I think any one reluctant to do that, under the circumstances, has something to conceal."

Numerous dark glares rewarded Tugg for his speech. He replied with a smug smile. He knew the words had lifted him in the estimation of the officers.

Between ten and fifteen minutes of catechizing now ensued. The servants of the law did a rather thorough job. The information they obtained, however, only added to their perplexity. Almost any one, it seemed, could be the killer. Indeed, Doc's four aids were almost the only men who had been continuously at the side of some officer during the time the slaying must have occurred.

Collison McAlter, Aunt Nora, Ole Slater, Alice Cash—all others, in fact—found difficulty in proving exactly where they had been.

The little flock of Prosper City business men became frankly worried. Their efforts to prove by one another that they were accounted for at all times, were almost frantic.

"All of you stick here in the hall!" commanded the sergeant. "We're gonna finish our search of the house. Doc Savage may be around, and may have murdered the cop!"

Tall, bony Johnny had been using his spectacle magnifier on the hilt of the knife which had slain the bluecoat.

"It has been wiped clean of finger prints," he announced regretfully.

The police search progressed up from the basement. Plaster was scrutinized; walls were rapped; books and magazines were examined.

"You've got strange ideas of hidin' places!" Monk snorted.

"Don't get sassy!" he was ordered. "We're lookin' for the gun that shot Chief Clements!"

Monk gave a pronounced start. "Say, officer, did somebody suggest the gun might be here?"

"We don't broadcast the source of our tips!" snapped the sergeant. But a movement of his eyes toward Judborn Tugg was significant—the gun hint had come from Tugg.

A hoodoo seemed to have settled in Monk's room for it was there that the next unpleasant development occurred.

Monk had brought along a spare suit. It hung in the closet. From its pocket was produced the gun which had slain Chief Clements!

Proof that this was the particular gun would have to await examination of ballistics experts, though. Identification numbers had been filed off. Judging by the shiny condition of the file grooves, it was a safe bet this had been done since the fatal shooting.

Monk entertained no doubt about its being the murder gun. Some one had planted it in his room. He proclaimed this fact loudly.

"It explains the murder of the policeman!" he declared. "The cop happened to find the Green Bell or one of his men hiding the gun in this room! That's why he was killed!"

"The gun bein' here shows Doc Savage has been here," the sergeant insisted. "He could have done the killin'!"

Monk subsided. What was the use of arguing?

A fresh stream of objections now came from the Prosper City business men. If Doc Savage was guilty, they asserted, why arrest everybody? Some of them made the ominous prediction that, if this kept up, Prosper City would soon find herself with an entire new set of policemen.

The officers relented—partially. It was agreed that every one should remain at Aunt Nora's place under careful guard, Doc's four men—thinking of their bronze chief concealed in the water tank—were not pleased at this turn of events.

Flames still leaped from the top of the tank. It was the nature of Monk's chemical to burn slowly—it would blaze for another hour. Then what?

Doc stood an excellent chance of being discovered, and none at all of escaping from the grounds.

"We ought to warn Doc how things are stacking up," Monk whispered to pretty Alice Cash.

Alice now showed that she carried around something besides good looks on her shoulders. She secured permission from the policemen, and retired to the privacy of her room. On a sheet of stiff white paper she wrote a brief summary of what had occurred. She sealed this in a large-mouthed bottle which had once contained stick candy.

The roll of paper pressed against the walls of the bottle, due to its own stiffness. Hence the words it bore could be read through the glass.

Alice found a heavy paper weight, and tied this to the bottle to serve as a sinker.

The current fashion in gowns tended toward full sleeves. She was wearing the latest. She concealed the bottle in a sleeve, then managed to make her way outdoors without attracting suspicion.

She maneuvered toward the flame-crowned tank and tossed her message inside, without seeming she was doing anything unusual.

Descending through the water, the bottle and its weight landed on Doc's right knee. He grasped it. The fire above lighted the water more brilliantly than sunlight would have. Too, although the burning chemical was not supposed to make much heat, the water was getting unpleasantly warm.

Peering through the wall of the bottle, Doc read the message.

He reached a swift decision. Indeed, he seemed hardly to consider the matter at all, so rapidly did his brain analyze the situation and ferret out the best procedure.

The cork left the neck of the bottle which held the extinguishing compound. It was a milky fluid. In wreathing streamers, which resembled the smoke from a small fire, it climbed upward. The chemical flames were promptly snuffed out.

Removing the rock anchor from his lap, Doc got up and clambered from the tank.

Yells of surprise greeted his appearance. Alice Cash pressed her hands to her cheeks and looked startled.

The police sergeant dashed forward, gun in one hand, handcuffs in the other, shouting: "You're arrested! If you bat an eye, you'll get plugged!"

Chapter XIII
PIPED COMMANDS

Within surprisingly few seconds, Doc was centered in a bristling ring of gun mules.

Judborn Tugg bounced up and screamed: "Kill him, officer! Don't let him escape! He's the devil who murdered your chief!"

Long Tom chanced to be near Tugg at that instant. The

electrical wizard—slender, pallid, unhealthy-looking—did not seem half a match for the portly Tugg. But he sprang upon Tugg. His fists delivered a smacking volley.

Before Long Tom was hauled off, Judborn Tugg had lost three front teeth. His nose was awry. Both his eyes had received a pasting which would soon turn them a beautiful black.

Long Tom swung his fists recklessly at officers who grabbed him. Two dropped. The electrical wizard had the appearance of a weakling, but his looks were highly deceptive.

Ordinarily, Long Tom kept a level head; but on rare occasions, he flew into a great rage. He was having one of his tantrums now. The accusations against Doc had heated him to the exploding point.

A lawman got behind and whipped the back of Long Tom's head repeatedly with a blackjack. The electrical expert tumbled over, unconscious.

Doc Savage was now conducted into the basement of Aunt Nora's house, and ordered to undress.

Every piece of his clothing was taken. This indignity was suggested by bruised, trembling Judborn Tugg.

"You don't want to take any chances," Tugg told the police. "There's no telling what kind of weapon this bronze fiend might have hidden in his clothing."

An old pair of overalls and a blue shirt were handed Doc. His feet were left bare. The officers conducted him to a large police touring car.

The top was up, but there were no curtains. Doc sat in the rear, an officer on each side. Three more cops occupied the front seat.

When they headed for town and jail, two cars rolled ahead. Three came behind. In one of the latter Long Tom languished. They were going to jail the electrical wizard for his performance on Tugg.

Every one else was, it seemed, to be permitted liberty. Now that the police had Doc, they seemed to think everything was settled.

The official cars were driven slowly. Their motors were rather silent for such big machines.

As they entered a part of town where residences were more plentiful, a metallic squeaking of radios in houses could be distinguished. Evidently the Prosper City broadcasting station put on a program at this hour which was very popular with the housewives. A majority of sets were tuned in.

The autos progressed several blocks. Suddenly, all about them, a wailing and screaming came from the radio speakers.

The uproar had an eerie, banshee quality. Intermingled with the bedlam, rising above it, came a procession of dull gonging notes. These persisted for only a few moments, then the whole clamor died.

"The Green Bell!" a cop gulped.

The police looked at Doc as if suspecting the bronze man might have made the noise.

Doc showed by no sign that he had heard. His hands reposed on his knees. They rested close together, snugged by handcuffs. His ankles were also manacled.

Three railroads entered Prosper City. To avoid dangerous crossings, the tracks lay on high grades. Overhead bridges spanned the streets.

The police cavalcade crawled toward one of the bridges. Two passed under. Doc's machine came up within a score of feet of the structure. It traveled at a leisurely pace.

Flinging both fists above his head, Doc sprang upward. Driven by tremendously developed leg muscles, his body burst through the top fabric as if it were paper.

He twisted out on top. The bows were stanch enough to support his weight.

The shackles on wrists and ankles seemed to hamper him hardly at all. By the time the car reached the bridge, he was standing erect.

Springing upward, he grasped the bridge beams. A flip outward and upward hooked his toes over the rail. An acrobatic swaying —and he was atop the bridge.

Had Doc sought to make an escape in any direction other than upward, the police would have been in a position to riddle him. As it was, the tops of the cars spoiled their aim. Before they could lean outside, Doc was gone—sheltered by the high steel side pieces of the bridge.

In concealment, Doc tested the handcuffs against his bronze sinews. It was no mean feat of muscle he was attempting. The handcuff links were not undersize, nor were they of a special metal, so brittle it would snap easily—two dodges sometimes employed by professional strong men.

His sinews seemed to bunch, and crawl like animals under his bronze skin. *Snap!* went the links joining his ankles. Then another straining tug, and those on his wrists went the same way.

Down the tracks he ran, doubled as low as possible between the rails. Policemen were shooting, yelling, and scrambling madly up the grade!

It would have been an excellent time for a train to come along. But never was a horizon more barren of a snorting locomotive. Doc scooted ahead until a bullet squeaked dangerously close, telling him officers had gained the track.

He pitched right, and literally slithered down the grade on his stomach. The railway section men had sown a plentiful amount of clover on the slope—it was a sweet variety of clover which grew rank and offered excellent concealment.

Doc gained a fence, left pennants of his overalls on the barb wire getting through, and dived behind some one's chicken house, just as bullets began to smack the boards.

He crossed the yard, surrounded by a young tornado of frightened chickens. Racing past a small dwelling, he glided down the street.

He was safe. He made directly for Aunt Nora Boston's place.

The brief, hideous clangor of the Green Bell over the radio was the reason for Doc's escape. He had no proof as to the meaning of the unearthly radio noise, but he had concluded it could have only one purpose.

Rumor said the noise always presaged death or violence by the Green Bell's men. Therefore, Doc reasoned, the gong was a summons to bring the evil, hooded tribe to some point where they received orders.

Doc was certain that Judborn Tugg was one of the clan—if not its chief. He intended to watch Tugg's reactions to the radio call.

Doc reached a tall tree some distance from Aunt Nora's home. This was a lofty elm. It chanced to be the same perch from which the ill-fated Slick had watched. Small scuffs on the bark, a clinging thread or two which had been wrenched from Slick's suit, told Doc this part of the story as he climbed upward.

He stationed himself at the end of a large limb.

Some sort of disturbance was going on near one of the circus tents. Judborn Tugg was waving a fat arm and shouting. Monk and Johnny were dancing about him with threatening gestures.

Tugg's actions showed he was insulting Doc's two aids in studied fashion.

In a moment, Monk and Johnny seized the pompous man and threw him bodily out of the grounds.

Doc Savage, witnessing this bit of drama, felt a new respect for Tugg's sagacity. The fat man had managed to get himself kicked out so that his departure, so soon after the radio clangor, would not be suspicious.

Doc silently lowered himself from his perch and followed Tugg.

The fat man entered his limousine. However, he drove only a short distance, and that very slowly. Parking near a wide flat field which was overgrown with brush, he made for the ramshackle barn.

The sunlight was brilliant. At no time did Tugg take more than half a dozen steps without glancing alertly around. Yet Doc was hardly fourscore feet behind when his quarry ducked into the old barn.

Doc sidled near the structure, only to be forced back as he heard the approach of other men.

The Green Bell's pack was assembling!

They came by twos and by threes. Once, half a dozen in a group. The last arrival closed the door.

Each man to come to the spot had been incased in a long black garment with a green bell painted on the breast. No one remained outside on guard. That exotic masquerade would have been sure to attract attention of any chance passer-by. No doubt more than one watching eye was pasted to the cracks, however.

In assembling the vast knowledge which his remarkable brain held, Doc had made it a practice to learn from masters in each line; then, by intensive study, to improve on the best they were able to give. He had gone to animal hunters of the jungle to learn woodcraft, for these were the masters of stealth.

As noiselessly as a cloud-cast shadow, he drew near the ramshackle building.

A hollow, earthy voice mumbled within the structure. The words, as they reached Doc's ears, were almost too distorted for understanding.

The thing Slick Cooley had learned only by use of his eyes. Doc's keen ears discerned instantly! The voice was pouring from an underground pipe!

"Is every one here?" it was asking.

"Yes, sir!" Judborn Tugg shouted in answer.

"You are here for orders!" came the sepulchral tones of the

Green Bell. "Each of you, of course, made sure he was not followed?"

To this, there was general clamor, evidently meant for assent.

"Good!" boomed the voice from the ground. "We finally got Savage in jail. His men remain. It is to hear their fate that you were summoned."

Doc Savage listened with only half attention, for he was worming a slow way through the weeds, pressing an ear to the ground at frequent intervals. Due to the marshy nature of the earth, he did not believe the tiling could be deeply buried. Otherwise it would fill with water.

The Green Bell—wherever he was—must of necessity shout loudly to make his voice carry with volume. Doc thought he should be able to locate the tile by ear.

"Judborn Tugg!" donged the Green Bell.

"I am here!" Tugg shouted.

If he did not know the figure to which he spoke was a dummy of sticks and cloth, he must be very puzzled at being asked to identify himself.

"You will recall that, nearly a week ago, you were commanded to make certain preparations near Aunt Nora Boston's home!"

"Yes," howled Tugg.

"Just what did you do? I want to be sure!"

"I hid a big bottle of poison in a brush patch on the mountain slope, close to Aunt Nora's place! You can't miss the brush! Four large trees grow out of it. They're in a straight line—as if they'd been planted."

"Exactly where is the bottle?"

"Buried halfway between the middle two trees."

"What kind of poison?"

"Cyanide! The most deadly stuff I could find!"

Outside, Doc Savage dug silently with his fingers. His sensitive hearing had guided him well, for the hole he sank landed squarely on top of the tile. He spaded rapidly with his hands, lengthening his excavation along the tile.

The big clay pipes were not long.

The Green Bell's voice boomed: "Tugg, you will get that poison and go——"

In the midst of the gonging words, Doc struck a sharp blow with his fist. The pipe was not of very strong construction. It collapsed, eggshell fashion.

The Green Bell interrupted himself, roared: "What was that noise?"

"It sounded as if—it came from under you some place," Tugg yelled.

"Never mind," the master mind said hastily, apprehensive lest his hirelings learn the figure in the barn was only a stuffed dummy of wood and fabric.

Doc hastily cupped palms over the hole. This was to prevent escape of too much voice sound. Picking up several pinches of fine dust, he let it trickle slowly into the opening.

Entering the tile, the dust streams were sucked away from the barn. This showed a draft, and gave him the direction.

It was possible that the string of tiles turned before they reached their destination.

"Tugg, you will get the cyanide which you secreted near Aunt Nora's!" continued the Green Bell. "There is, I presume, a large quantity of it in the bottle."

"A lot!" Tugg shouted.

"Good! You will get it! To-night you will take a group of men and dig up the water main which supplies Aunt Nora's home. I happen to know that, due to the house being in an outlying district, the water line is very small—two-inch pipe. You will insert the poison. I am sure you can handle the mechanical details."

"I guess so!" Tugg replied uneasily.

Doc Savage glided away from the barn, following a trail used by the masked men. His gaze switched here and there—always on the ground.

Soon he found what he expected—a cigarette stub. He picked it up, then continued his hunt. He added two remnants of Judborn Tugg's dollar cigars to his assortment.

The prize find was a discarded paper matchbook—one match remaining. Doc had feared it was going to be necessary to start a fire Boy Scout fashion, twirling one stick upon another.

He moved back toward the dilapidated building. The cigarettes, cigars, and matches had been discarded by the Green Bell's men as they donned black hoods upon nearing the rendezvous.

Back at the tile, Doc crumpled the tobacco into a loose fistful. He put a match to the papers off the cigarettes, then added the tobacco. The draft made it burn.

A wisp or two of smoke escaped the baked clay pipe. This was not enough to lift above the weeds and be seen by the watchers in the barn.

Doc listened. Judborn Tugg was talking, giving a recital of what had happened at Aunt Nora Boston's.

Doc felt there was no need of Judborn telling the Green Bell what had happened at Aunt Nora's. The Green Bell had been upon the scene, and had murdered the policeman, Doc believed.

Collison McAlter—the group of Prosper City factory and mine owners—the others who had been on hand—one of these must be the Green Bell.

Doc circled widely, sensitive nostrils expanding and contracting as he sniffed the air. Tobacco smoke possessed a marked odor. He hoped to locate it where it escaped from the end of the tile. Daily from childhood, Doc had taken an exercise calculated to develop his olfactory organs. His sense of smell was phenomenal.

He ringed the place, without finding what he sought. The second time, he went entirely around. The last circle was wider. Doc quickened his pace; he had expected better luck.

Over toward the barn, he heard noises. Brush cracking. The Green Bell's gang leaving the trysting place! The séance had ended.

Doc let them go. Judborn Tugg was the important member. He would not be hard to locate. Doc concentrated on trying to find the mouth of the tile.

Judborn was one of the first to leave the barn. He walked swiftly from the vicinity. It was a hot day; his black hood was uncomfortable. He removed it as soon as he got out of sight.

Although his name was spoken freely at these sinister meetings, Tugg was always careful to keep his face hooded. This was merely an incidental precaution. If anything came up in court he could swear he had never attended the conclaves, but that the culprit must have been some one else masquerading under his name.

Entering his expensive car, Tugg drove back to town, taking his time. He smoked one of his costly cigars. There was nothing ahead of him for the remainder of the day.

As for getting the poison from the cache near Aunt Nora's home, that would wait until darkness.

Tugg eventually wheeled his machine up before his great white house. A few months ago, there had been a flunky to open the door; but there was none now. Tugg had dismissed all his servants, pleading financial stringency.

The real reason was that he did not want servants around where they might pick up dangerous information. Tugg was unmarried, and took his meals at Prosper City's leading restaurant.

He entered his sumptuously furnished library. The minute he stepped through the door, he jumped a foot in the air.

A somber black crow of a figure was perched in a deep armchair. The green of the bell insignia and the green of glass goggles were almost the same hue.

The apparition held a leveled gun.

The firearm alone was enough to tell Judborn Tugg that he was now facing the Green Bell in person. The czar sinister always held a gun when he showed himself, to make sure none of his followers took a notion to yank off his hood.

"W-what do you want?" Tugg spluttered. "I—I—I was just talking to you."

"And a fine mess you made of it, too!" The Green Bell's tone was deep, angry.

Tugg dropped his cigar, and it lay unnoticed, charring the rug. "What do you mean?"

"Savage followed you to the swamp! He listened to everything that was said!"

Tugg shook his head violently. "Impossible! The police have Savage!"

"He escaped!" The Green Bell's gun never wavered from a line with Judborn Tugg's heart. "The police—helpless fools—let Savage get away. And he followed you to the meeting in the barn."

"*Me!*" Tugg choked. "Surely not!"

"We will not argue about that!" the Green Bell clanged. "Savage was there! I heard him! I am certain! You will take the orders which I came to give you! Then I will go!"

"What is it?"

"You will ignore all orders pertaining to the hidden bottle of cyanide!"

Tugg blinked. Then his quick brain grasped the possibilities.

"Say, boss, if Savage overheard us talking about that poison, he's sure to go to destroy it. We can lay an ambush——"

"The ambush is already set!" intoned the Green Bell.

"But I didn't know you had gotten hold of any of the men——"

"This is a trap which does not use men. And it is the more effective for that!"

The Green Bell now took his departure, fading into the shrubbery.

Judborn Tugg, watching from a window, swore in disgust and wished he had not landscaped his place so profusely. He would have liked to follow and learned the identity of this fiend who was behind Prosper City's difficulties.

Chapter XIV
THE SUSPICION PLANT

Had Doc Savage been able to witness what had just occurred at Judborn Tugg's home, he would no longer have retained a suspicion that Tugg was the Green Bell.

However, Doc was not considering Tugg very seriously for the part of villain. His reason for this was simple. Tugg was too obviously connected with the Green Bell organization. The man actually behind the thing was too clever to let suspicion point at him in that fashion.

Doc had now made five circles around the barn ruin. He had detected no faintest odor of tobacco smoke. He was frankly puzzled. It was hardly possible that the Green Bell had been this distant from the rendezvous.

Disgusted, Doc returned to the ramshackle old farm building. By now, his bird had flown. He concluded to follow the tiling and learn where it actually did go.

The baked clay pipes were not buried deeply. By jabbing a sharp stick, he traced them. They ran perhaps two hundred feet, turning sharply at two points. Then they suddenly ended.

He dug. The discovery he made was unexpected. The tiles simply elbowed straight downward. After a depth of three feet, the shaft was steel pipe.

Doc compressed a small ball of clay, dropped it. The lump fell, he judged accurately, at least two hundred and fifty feet.

With great care, Doc now wiped out all traces of his presence, filling in the holes he had excavated, and scattering leaves and trash about.

He left the vicinity. His steps were careful; his progress noiseless. This, although there was no apparent danger. His was an instinctive caution.

Many days had passed since the last rain at Prosper City. Yet the ground underfoot was soft, wet. In some spots it was muck which oozed over his shoes.

It was not ground through which one could readily drive a tunnel. A few feet beneath the surface, the earth must be literally a thick soup. Yet the tile line had ended in a vertical shaft which sank straight downward more than tenscore feet.

Doc had a theory to explain this. He hoped it might play an important part in the eventual capture of the Green Bell.

Something over an hour later, the bronze man turned up in the vicinity of Aunt Nora Boston's home. Evading a covey of searching policemen had delayed him somewhat.

Numerous blue uniforms were scattered in Aunt Nora's yard. Others could be glimpsed occasionally, moving within the house.

Doc set a course for the mountain slope which began almost at the edge of Aunt Nora's abode. He had no trouble locating a patch of brush from which grew four perfectly aligned trees. This, from what he had overheard, was the hiding place of the deadly poison.

What he did not know, though, was that the Green Bell had set a death trap at the spot.

Old leaves made a gray-brown carpet under the brush and smaller trees. These would show tracks, for the undersides were dark and moldy, while the upper surfaces had been washed and bleached by the weather.

As Doc progressed, the brush thickened; trees of moderate size became more plentiful.

Doc crouched, then sailed upward in a great leap. His sinewy fingers trapped a limb. He swung easily to another branch, flipped atop it, glided its swaying length, and seemed to float outward in space to the next tree.

It was a remarkable exhibition of agility. Few jungle anthropoids could have done better.

The four extremely tall trees, he discovered, jutted from the midst of a thorn thicket. Moreover, a path grooved between the second pair. From the condition of the carpeting leaves, it was evident this trail received only occasional use.

Directly between the spindling trees, there was a small opening in the thorny trail walls. Almost a pit! This seemed a logical hiding place for the poison.

Doc balanced out on a branch of a smaller tree, some yards from the four giant sentinels. Lowering, he dangled from sinewy hands. Back and forth, he began to flip, after the fashion of a trapeze artist getting his swing going. The bough gyrated.

Releasing his clutch at the proper instant, the big bronze man arched upward through space. He made a perfect landing on the lowermost limb of a tall tree.

It was then that he encountered his big discovery.

A machine gun was lashed to the tree. Its ugly snout angled downward. Doc sidled along the limb, examined it. He sighted down the barrel. It was aimed at the tiny recess in the thorns, which probably held the poison.

A flexible wire, attached to the trigger, ran down through tiny, greased pulleys. A death trap! Any one who grasped the poison bottle would be instantly riddled.

Doc thought swiftly. He detached the trigger trip of the gun. Then, with a long, descending leap, he landed on the path.

Searching under the leaves, he quickly found the poison. He untied a small wire from the neck of the bottle. This was the trip for the rapid-firer.

A glance showed him the poison was genuine. The stuff was not in crystal form, but was an odorless, volatile liquid. Cyanic acid! One of the most deadly of poisons!

Doc carried the bottle some distance away, got rid of its contents in a hole which he dug in the ground, then refilled it with water from a stream trickling down the mountainside. This stream, due probably to the presence of mines above, had a foul color, not greatly different from that of the cyanic.

Replacing the now harmless bottle took only a moment.

Moving with the ease of a squirrel, Doc clambered into the tree which held the machine gun. He altered the position of the weapon slightly.

Doc took great pains with the work. Several times, he sighted along the fluted barrel. Then he replaced the wire on the trigger.

He quitted the vicinity as noiselessly as he had arrived.

In the distance, a freight train was whistling and puffing as it pulled out of Prosper City. It got under way slowly, and its snorting and bleating became fainter and fainter.

The freight was still audible when Doc appeared in the brush which fringed Aunt Nora Boston's spacious yard. He waited, watching.

A car approached from the direction of town. It rolled into the yard, bearing Long Tom.

The slender, pale, temperamental electrical wizard must have put up bail and received a quick release on the charge of battering Judson Tugg.

Perhaps five minutes, Doc waited, in order that the jubilation caused by Long Tom's return might subside. Then the bronze man's strange, mellow, trilling note saturated the vicinity.

Musical, yet entirely without tune, it ran up and down the scale. A bystander, looking at Doc's lips, could not have told it was from thence that the fantastic sound came. Yet the weird resonance possessed remarkable carrying qualities.

It penetrated across the lawn and soaked through the innermost reaches of the vast old house. Policemen glanced about wonderingly, with no idea where the cadence was coming from.

Doc's four men gave no indication that the eerie note meant anything to them. But a few minutes later, the quartet sauntered casually into the house. They used binoculars from upstairs windows.

It was gaunt Johnny, spectacles containing the magnifier cocked up on his forehead, who discovered Doc.

A strange bit of pantomime followed. Johnny's binoculars were powerful. Hence, Doc was able to converse with him by using deaf-and-dumb sign language.

Doc explained fully what he wanted. Then he eased away from the region.

Patrols of cops had taken to prowling the vicinity. He wished no contact with them which could be avoided.

The sun had marched two hours nearer meridian when Johnny, driving down the road in one of the rented cars, passed a certain culvert. Without stopping, he flung a paper-wrapped bundle from the machine. This hopped end over end, coming to a rest directly before the culvert.

Johnny drove on as if nothing had happened.

An arm—it looked like a beam wrapped with steel hawsers and painted with bronze—reached out of the profuse weed growth and snared the packet.

Both bundle and arm disappeared.

This seemed the end of the incident. The tops of the weeds shook a little; but that might have been caused by the breeze.

About eight minutes later, and about eight blocks distant, a householder's dog dashed madly through his back yard, barking. The householder looked out.

He saw, or he thought he saw—for he was not quite sure—a mighty bronze figure vanishing along the alley. The householder went back and sat down to his dinner, grinning widely. The police were after that bronze man! What of it? The viands on the table before him were some distributed by Doc Savage the night before.

The next incident of this sort occurred well on the other side of town, when a merchant, coming home to his lunch, was astounded to have a giant bronze man step from a grape arbor ahead of him, and calmly cross the street.

The merchant ran after the apparition. It was not in his thoughts to give an alarm. He wanted to thank this bronze man for a morning's business, which had practically saved his store from bankruptcy.

This merchant had been carrying scores of impoverished families on credit, and these, practically without exception, had been grateful enough to make a substantial repayment with the money which they had received from Doc.

The merchant, however, was forced to withhold his thanks. He failed to find the bronze figure which he had glimpsed. The form had vanished magically in a garden.

These two spots where the metallic giant was sighted were on a direct line between Aunt Nora Boston's home and Judborn Tugg's palatial white mansion.

Judborn Tugg had just partaken of an excellent dinner at Prosper City's leading restaurant. He returned to his home, driving his luxurious limousine.

Pausing before the front door, he made an elaborate ritual of clipping the end from one of his dollar cigars, and applying a match.

He opened the door, entered, stopped—his jaw seeming to disappear in his fat neck as he gaped.

He made an absent gesture at putting the cigar in his mouth, but missed that cavity fully four inches.

"I thought you—goodness gracious!" he stuttered uncertainly. "What is the trouble now?"

A figure in a raven-black robe occupied one of the living-room chairs. A green bell was painted on the front of the hood. The eyes were practically invisible. There were eye holes in the hood, but the wearer's face seemed to be bandaged heavily in white.

"Nothing is wrong!" snapped the somber figure in a hollow, gonging voice.

Tugg blinked, lifted his chin out of his fat neck, and found his lips with his cigar.

"You look much different than you did this morning!" he mumbled. "I guess it is because you are not wearing your green goggles. You have your eyes bandaged! I hope you have not met with an accident?"

"Don't worry about my health!" tolled Doc Savage, imitating the Green Bell's macabre tones.

At the same time, Doc wished he had known about those green goggles. He had resorted to the white bandages to disguise the distinctive gold color of his eyes, knowing they would give him away instantly.

This Green Bell gown had been in the bundle which Johnny had flung from his car. Johnny himself had tailored it.

"What do you want with me?" Tugg demanded anxiously.

"About the bottle of poison!" Doc returned, angling for anything which would give him a lead.

Tugg's head dived into his neck and came up as he nodded. "Yes, yes! When you were here this morning, you told me not to go for the poison, but that Doc Savage would probably appear on the scene and be caught in a death trap!"

This was illuminating. It told Doc nearly all he needed to know. The Green Bell had learned Doc was eavesdropping in the vicinity of the old barn. The czar of fear himself had later visited Tugg and countermanded the barn orders.

"That plan is changed!" Doc said in his assumed tolling voice. "The new scheme is for you to go get the poison, just as you were ordered at first."

"You mean I'm to go ahead——"

"Exactly! You are to poison the water main leading to Aunt Nora's place!"

"Oh, my goodness!" Tugg gasped. "Didn't Savage fall into the trap?"

"Entirely unforeseen developments came up! Savage, I regret to say, did not tumble."

"But maybe he'll be watching the hiding place of the poison?"

"He will not harm you!"

Tugg shivered, said: "I'm kinda worried——"

"You, Tugg, are to get that poison!" Doc ordered in his assumed tolling.

"You are to go in person. Above all things, you are not to send any one else! Understand!"

Tugg squirmed. "Very well."

Doc Savage, in his masquerade as the Green Bell, had accomplished his purpose. He did not want to stretch his luck. Consequently, he now took his departure.

His going was quite effective. Judborn Tugg, determined this time to follow the master mind, flung wildly to a window the instant the somber figure exited. Quick as he was, the sepia form had been swifter. The visitor had vanished, as if gifted with supernatural powers, or an agility which would put him across fifty feet of lawn while a fat man was crossing a room.

Exasperated, Tugg turned on an electric fan and seated himself in its windy breath. The taste of his excellent dinner had been ruined, and his digestion hampered.

Sometimes, he wondered if any good at all would ever come from his association with the Green Bell. He had, in fact, pondered this on numerous occasions.

He wished Slick Cooley was still alive. Slick had been intent on learning who the Green Bell was, then killing him.

That would have been highly satisfactory to Tugg. Slick had expected to take over the Green Bell's organization. Judborn Tugg smiled wolfishly, and mused how easily a bullet from his own hand would have finished Slick.

This brought an unpleasant thought—Slick's death!

Tugg snapped up very straight in his chair. Then he scrambled forward and shut off the fan. He was cold enough now without any artificial refrigeration. His spine, in fact, felt like ice cubes joined with a string.

The newspapers had said Slick Cooley had gone insane in his jail cell, and had been shot while trying to escape. Insane! That was the Green Bell's trademark!

Slick Cooley had been killed because, in the hands of the law, he was a danger to the organization. That was clear!

Judborn Tugg's head crawled in and out of his neck. Doc Savage suspected *him* of being one of the gang. Did that not make him—Judborn Tugg—a menace to the organization?

This was a frosty thought, for it suggested the possibility that the Green Bell might find occasion to dispense with Judborn Tugg.

Throughout the evening, Tugg wrestled these thoughts around in a mire of unease. He would go through with the poisoning—it was often fatal to ignore the Green Bell's commands—but he would be very careful.

Just before dark, furtive, slinking figures began dropping in on Tugg. These were disciples of the Green Bell—the fellows who were to help with the poisoning of the water main.

Tugg directed each of them to meet him at a spot some distance from Aunt Nora's house, then bundled them out. He considered it a strain on his dignity to associate with such riffraff.

An hour and a half after the street lamps of Prosper City had been turned on, Tugg neared the four sentinellike trees on the mountain slope. He was rushing the job. He wanted to get it over.

He carefully scouted the vicinity of the trees and the thorn patch. No lurking figure was flushed out by this strategy.

"Maybe I am wrong in thinking myself in danger," Tugg argued with himself. "Of course I am! The Green Bell will not murder a man of my importance to the organization. I would be hard to replace."

His mental balloon received a big prick when, a few moments later, he bent over and picked up the bottle of poison.

There was a deafening clatter behind him! It was as if a gigantic iron turkey had started gobbling. Bullets swooped over Tugg's head, chopped branches, and clouted the earth.

Tugg flattened, instinctively spinning. He saw the fire-lipping snout of the machine gun.

He had no way of knowing Doc Savage had aimed the weapon high enough that it could not possibly hit a man on the path. He had no way of knowing Doc Savage had been here at all! His only thought was—he had been doublecrossed!

The Green Bell had tried to murder him!

Judborn Tugg's actions for the next few moments were those of a frantic man. He scuttled down the trail, collecting numerous thorns in his haste.

Sweat bubbled from his forehead like grease from a cooking bacon rind. He fell to cursing the Green Bell.

"Tried to kill me like a dog!" he snarled.

It did not occur to Tugg that he might have been tricked. Up until a few minutes ago, he had held an evil admiration for the

Green Bell. That had evaporated. Rage had taken its place. Rage, and a lust to turn the tables.

Revenge! The thought flamed Tugg's brain. But how to get it? Tugg knotted his fat hands.

He reached a momentous decision. The attempt on his life meant that he needed protection from the Green Bell. Where better to get this than from the Green Bell's Nemesis, Doc Savage?

Judborn Tugg decided to go to Doc Savage, tell the bronze man everything, and ask sanctuary. If there was any safety at hand, the bronze man was it.

This was the exact train of thought which Doc Savage had foreseen when he had reaimed the machine gun and set the trickery trap for Tugg. Doc was psychologist enough to guess that Tugg, in protecting himself, would turn upon his master.

Doc Savage, in fact, was at that moment gliding along not fifty yards from the frightened and enraged Tugg.

The portly, terrified factory owner bee-lined for Aunt Nora Boston's home, so Doc let him go.

Monk, a towering, furry form in the night, challenged Tugg. Seeing who it was, Monk smiled grimly, reached out, and trapped Tugg's fat neck.

Tugg wriggled, squealing: "Now, don't hurt me! I came to see Savage!"

"Yah!" Monk growled. "I hope you don't expect to find him here, after your lying charge that he murdered Chief Clements!"

Desperately, Tugg pulled at the hirsute hands clasping his neck. But at the same time, his active little brain raced. Since he had himself murdered Chief Clements, he would have to make some sort of a deal. Any kind of a deal!

If it came to the worst, Tugg was willing to go to trial on a murder charge. With his influence in Prosper City, he believed he could get off. Tugg was a supreme egoist. He did not realize his influence was practically nil.

Better yet, he might strike a bargain with Doc Savage, whereby, for his services in trapping the Green Bell, he would be permitted to go free.

Tugg was also always the optimist. If he had known Doc Savage's true character, the iron determination of the bronze man, he would have entertained scant hopes of a deal.

"I think I made a mistake about that killing!" Tugg wailed.

Monk loosened his clutch. "You what?"

"I might have made an error!" Tugg said evasively. "If I can see Doc Savage and talk to him in private, I can tell whether my identification of him as the killer was correct!"

To all appearances, there was not room for a spoonful of brains in Monk's knot of a head. But he possessed a keen intellect. He perceived instantly what Tugg was driving at.

"You wanta make a deal?" he demanded.

Tugg did not commit himself. "If I could see Doc Savage——"

Monk shook him and said: "You'd what?"

Tugg remained stubbornly silent.

The mousy tufts which Monk wore for eyebrows crawled together as he thought deeply. The upshot of his reflection was that he conducted Judborn Tugg to the house.

They sought out the sergeant who was in charge of the detachment of Prosper City police.

"Prosper City's leading citizen thinks he made a mistake in calling Doc a murderer," Monk declared, elbowing Tugg roughly. "Ain't that right, fatty?"

The indignity galled Tugg's pompous soul. But he was desperate.

"I've got to see Savage!" he gulped.

"There ain't no need of that unless you can swear he wasn't the killer!" Monk said cannily.

Tugg writhed, perspired, and pulled nervously at his gold watch chain until he broke it. He had reason to know his own peril was desperate. In his extremity, he was willing to make almost any concession to get in touch with Doc Savage.

"I—I think I made a mistake!" he groaned.

"You think?" Monk scowled.

"I—I'm sure I did!" Tugg gulped. "Savage wasn't the killer!"

Monk whistled loudly. Renny and the others raced up, together with policemen.

Tugg was conducted into the house. Monk—his small voice for once a great roar—announced vociferously that Judborn Tugg was willing to swear Doc Savage was not Police Chief Clement's slayer.

Monk was exerting pressure, not giving Tugg a chance to back up. The proclamation broke up a meeting which the Prosper City business men were holding in the house.

This conclave was for the purpose of discussing the transfer of their holdings to Doc Savage. Although Doc had, of necsssity, been absent all day because of the police, his four aids were rushing his plans for the salvation of the manufacturing community.

Collison McAlter was a prominent figure in this conference.

Monk left Tugg inside, went out on the porch, lifted his voice. "Doc!" he bellowed. "Tugg is willin' to clear you! But he wants to talk! What'll we do?"

As if it were answering his howl, a shot banged loudly within the house.

Chapter XV
THE GREEN TRAP

Monk veered around. The screen on the front door had a patent lock which defied his fingers. So he walked bodily through, bearded hands pawing fine wire.

Inside the house, the only thing lacking to make the situation a perfect one for murder in the dark, was the lack of darkness. The lights were on brilliantly.

Collison McAlter and Ole Slater rushed up to Monk, crying questions. Other Prosper City industrialists boiled about.

"The shot was upstairs!" somebody yelled.

Big-fisted Renny came lumbering from somewhere. He grunted at Monk, and the two giants shouldered each other up the stairs. In the hallway, burned powder made a tang.

Since the evening was warm, most of the room doors were open to secure cross ventilation. The cordite reek was coming through one of these. Renny and Monk split, each popping their heads into a row of doors.

They fully expected to find a corpse. They were equally as certain that it would be Judborn Tugg.

"The Green Bell croaked Tugg before he could talk!" Monk wailed.

Their expectations were not realized.

In the first place, there was no body in any of the upstairs rooms. Now was there a lurking gunman.

In the wall of Aunt Nora's room they discovered a gouge in the plaster. This held a bullet. The slug was not distorted, and obviously had not hit the wall with much more force than could have been developed by a small boy's slingshot.

The explanation of the puny blow was scattered over a dressing table—the mangled remains of an ordinary electric toaster.

Monk snorted loudly. "Lookit!"

"The bullet was laid in the toaster, and the heat exploded it," Renny agreed.

"Sure! A plant! Somebody did it to draw attention!"

Monk and Renny had come up the stairs in haste, but they went back down with a great deal more speed. Indoors, a swift search was started.

Racing outside, Monk bellowed for every guard to keep his eyes on the house.

Both hunts drew blanks. Not only were there no murdered bodies around, but nobody had the slightest idea what the excitement was about.

However, the mystery lost its profundity before long.

Judborn Tugg, somewhat pale, his pudgy form drawn up in a stiff dignity, walked toward the door.

Monk collared him. "Where you goin', fat boy?"

"I wish to take my departure!" Tugg replied in a voice which he could not quite make pompous.

Peering at the fat man, Monk observed that a remarkable change had taken place. Tugg was still frightened, but he was no longer anxious to talk to Doc Savage. His greatest concern was now to get out of the vicinity.

Monk looked fierce, but groaned inwardly. He realized what had happened. The shot had been a trick by the Green Bell to secure an opportunity to speak with Tugg in private.

"So you've changed your mind!" Monk gritted.

Judborn Tugg's answer was an angry squirm for his freedom. Monk let him go. He had a hunch that, if he did not, Tugg would immediately reverse his previous declaration that Doc was not guilty of Chief Clements's murder.

Tugg left the vicinity in great haste. He made directly for his palatial white home on the other side of town.

Monk's conjecture that Tugg had received a communication from the Green Bell was correct. What Monk had no way of knowing, however, was that Tugg possessed no idea of who had delivered the words. They had been whispered through the crack of a partially open door, when every one was interested in the banging noise upstairs.

The verbal interchange had been short. In a single angry sentence, Tugg had told of the machine gun. With equal terseness had come the reply that the whole thing must be a clever ploy by Doc Savage.

Tugg was to lie low! That was the word. For the immediate future, he was to conduct himself as Prosper City's leading business man, and nothing else.

There was a catch to this.

"I will attempt to dispose of Doc Savage by other means," the Green Bell had advised. "If that fails it may be necessary for you to serve as a bait to draw Savage into a trap!"

The Green Bell had not upbraided Tugg for nearly turning traitor. But Tugg was not deceived. He was live bait. The minute Doc Savage was slain, that bait would no longer be needed.

Tugg shuddered, perspired freely. He was in the jam of his shady life!

A giant, silent bronze shadow dogged Tugg's footsteps until the fat man was ensconced behind the locked doors of his palatial home.

Doc made certain that Tugg showed no sign of immediate activity. Then he retraced his spectral way to Aunt Nora Boston's.

The place, from a distance, had all the aspects of a circus. The giant tents, brilliantly lighted from below, seemed many times their actual size.

Curious individuals were swarming the vicinity, although there was to be no food distribution to-night. The money payments of the night before had made that unnecessary. But they were greatly interested in the negotiations over the factories.

If Doc Savage was given control, they got jobs. If he was refused, there seemed nothing but hard times ahead. So they came to loiter and snap up the latest gossip.

Two of these loafers were arguing hotly about the Chief Clements slaying; suddenly, they fell silent. They gaped slightly; their eyes roved the night.

For upon the scene had come a fantastic note, a nebulous, wind-borne sound which might have been the song of some exotic bird, or the trilling of the night breeze. Up and down the scale, it chased a musical crescendo; yet it was without tune.

"What's that?" demanded a man. "Where'n blazes is it comin' from?"

No one knew—except Doc's four aids. Almost at once, they drifted casually into the darkness. They met a short distance away, where they were well concealed in the brush.

They gave no signal—Doc had, without a doubt, followed their departure closely. For Doc's strange sound, trilling in the murk, could have but one meaning—a meeting was desired.

Doc appeared like a wraith at Monk's elbow, causing that furry individual to all but jump out of his hirsute hide.

"What have you fellows been able to learn about that fake shot?" he demanded.

The four blinked owlishly. Doc had not been glimpsed around the house, but he seemed to know what had happened.

"I've been drifting around in the darkness, listening!" Doc explained. "I've heard a dozen different versions of what occurred."

"It was simple," Monk muttered. "It made us look like numskulls! A cartridge in an electric toaster! *Bang!* We all fog upstairs! And while we do that, somebody slips Tugg the word to keep his trap shut."

"What got Tugg in the notion of talkin', anyway?" pondered the gaunt Johnny, fumbling with his eyeglasses.

Doc told them about the machine-gun trick with which he had deceived Tugg into thinking his master was thirsting for his life.

"Now—you have no idea who talked to Tugg?" he finished.

Renny made rocky sounds by tapping his knuckles together.

"It's the darnedest thing I ever saw, Doc!" he rumbled. "We questioned everybody. It seems Tugg, being shy of friends because of his attitude toward you, was standing apart from everybody when the shell exploded in the toaster. Nobody knows who talked to 'im!"

"It could've been Collison McAlter!" Monk put in. "It could've been Ole Slater, Aunt Nora, Alice—anybody! I'm tellin' you, this Green Bell is slicker'n greased lightnin', as we used to say back home."

"And there's somethin' funny about Collison McAlter turnin' up at that factory this mornin'," added Long Tom, the electrical wizard. "It looked kinda like he might've been there with the hooded gang who came after the papers Jim Cash had hidden! He could've stayed behind!"

"Was there any proof of that?" Renny demanded of Doc.

"There was no proof either way," Doc replied. "Except, of course, Collison McAlter's word that he had come out to the plant when he found himself unable to sleep at home!"

"What gets me is this—what's behind this whole mess?" Renny boomed. "Is this Green Bell somebody who hates Prosper City —hates it so that he's tryin' to wipe it off the map?"

"Hate does not work like that," Doc pointed out. "Men hate other men, rather than such inanimate things as towns. You might dislike a town, but I don't think you'd try very hard to destroy it."

"I wouldn't!" Renny grinned. "But this Green Bell might. If you ask me, he's crazy!"

Doc shook his head. "Wrong!"

"Holy cow!" Renny exploded. "Have you got an idea who he is?"

"I have," Doc imparted dryly, "a faintest of suspicions!"

"Who?"

"I haven't enough on him to justify pointing the finger at him," Doc replied. "But as to why he is ruining Prosper City—that is as plain as the nose on your face. But, again, there's no proof as yet."

Long Tom shook a pale fist. "I'm all for divin' right into this thing! Doc, ain't there somethin' we can do?"

"That's why I called you out here!" Doc told them.

Grinning, the four aids of the bronze man drew a bit closer. They knew, from past experience, that the plans which Doc propounded had an uncanny way of working.

"Johnny," said Doc, "your profession is knowing the earth and what it's made out of! This job is in your line. I want you to get me a geologic map of this region!"

"Right!" echoed Johnny. "There's a firm of mining engineers right here in town that'll have 'em!"

"Get them to-night!" Doc directed. "I want the best—maps showing rock formations, coal veins, the different faults and fissures—all that stuff."

"Want charts of the mines?"

"Of course! Not only the late workings, but old ones as well!"

"O. K."

"Tell nobody about this. Not even Aunt Nora Boston!"

"Aunt Nora—sure! I won't tell her!" Johnny's voice sounded a bit queer. Did Doc suspect Aunt Nora?

Doc wheeled on Long Tom, the electrical expert.

"Long Tom, it's your job to work on that gonging noise with which the Green Bell summons his men over the radio! You know, of course, how he makes the noise?"

"Sure I do, but I ain't told anybody!" Long Tom chuckled grimly. "That noise simply comes from another radio station, hidden somewhere. It's on the wave length of the Prosper City station, and it's much the more powerful of the two. It simply blankets the Prosper City wave out almost completely."

"That's right."

"I learned from Aunt Nora that the United States government had radio inspectors in here, trying to find the interference," Long Tom continued. "They didn't get to first base! Once, they got a line on it. But they didn't find a thing."

"Where did they trace it to?"

Long Tom seemed reluctant to answer. "To Aunt Nora Boston's house—or at least, right in that vicinity!"

Doc's four men were uneasily silent. They liked Aunt Nora. They hated to see this evidence piling up against the motherly old lady.

"I don't like that Ole Slater!" Monk grumbled, to break the tension.

"You wouldn't!" snorted big-fisted Renny. "If you don't stop makin' eyes at his girl, he's liable to smear you!"

Doc said: "How about it, Long Tom? Can you find the secret radio station?"

"If it can be found—I can!"

This, Doc and the others knew, was not a boast. There was probably but one other living man knew more about electricity in all its branches than did Long Tom. And that other man was also in this group. It was Doc Savage.

"Go to it!" Doc advised him. "And the same thing I told Johnny goes for you! Don't tell Aunt Nora, Alice Cash—or anybody else!"

"Right!" Long Tom mumbled.

Doc now addressed the group as a whole. "What's your idea about the attitude of the police toward me?"

There was thoughtful silence.

"They're on the fence," decided Renny, the engineer. "Tugg's backing up helped things a lot."

"Tugg will return to his original story that he saw me shoot Chief Clements," Doc said with certainty.

Renny rumbled a humorless laugh. "The police won't be so ready to believe him. Even they can see Tugg is acting queerly. If that murder charge from New York was quashed, I believe you'd be safe in showing yourself, Doc."

"That's the way I sized it up," Doc agreed.

Monk's tufted brows crept together as he thought deeply. "Doc, I've been thinking about Judborn Tugg. I sure thought the Green Bell would croak Tugg. But he didn't. Don't you reckon that means that the Green Bell hopes to use Tugg to decoy you into a trap?"

"The idea occurred to me," Doc said wryly. "You can rest assured that I'm going to be very careful of Tugg. But here's a point you can check up on when this is all over—I think the Green Bell has another very good reason for not killing Tugg!"

This ended the conference. Doc's four aids would have liked very much to know what theory the bronze man did hold. But they knew it would do no good to ask questions.

Doc never put important theories into words until they were proven facts.

Monk and the others tramped back through the moonlight toward Aunt Nora's rambling house. Doc accompanied them part of the distance—they never did know exactly how far. Somewhere en route, the bronze giant faded silently from their midst. Shadows, soaking the undergrowth like puddled ink, had swallowed him.

Policemen eyed Doc's gang suspiciously when they appeared. Just a bit too late, it had dawned on the officers that these men might have gone to meet their remarkable chief. The fact that no mention was made of the incident was an omen.

One of the most powerful forces in existence was working in Doc's behalf—public opinion. The food and money he had distributed, the jobs he had promised, had put the working folk of Prosper City on his side.

This meant nine out of every ten men in town. Such a preponderance of sentiment could not help but sway the police.

For that matter, practically every officer had relatives who hoped to get jobs through Doc's great work.

Easing his gaunt length into one of the rented car fleet, the gaunt Johnny drove off in the direction of town. The geologist was going to locate one of the firm of mining engineers and get hold of maps showing the rock and mineral formation under Prosper City.

The flotilla of rented cars was parked along the road in front of the house. The yard lacked room for them. Flood lights in the yard did not reach the spot. Tall trees lifted near by. This combination made it rather gloomy around the machines.

Long Tom soon came up. Monk accompanied him, as a matter of safety. Long Tom unlocked the rear compartment of the roadster and stowed various packages of electrical equipment inside.

"I'm goin' back to the house to get a bite to eat," Long Tom declared. "Then I'll pull out "

The two men swung jauntily back past the flood-lighted circus tents.

Shadows covered the cars like black cloths. Little sound was about, except for talk from the near-by house.

Metal on metal made a tiny, mouselike squeak. This came again. The engine hood of Long Tom's roadster lifted.

The sheet-steel covering was raised only a moment. An arm—it might have been only a darker string of the night—deposited something atop the engine. It withdrew.

The hood now closed down. A wad of murk flowed stealthily away from the roadster.

Then things began happening. A flashlight spiked a blinding rod into the night. This waved, seemed to lick like a hungry, incandescent tongue. Then it fixed.

Impaled in the glare stood a somber figure—it might have been a black six-foot tube of flexible India rubber, except that it had arms and legs.

The breast of the weird form bore a bell in green. The eyes were the lenses of goggles—snakelike, with a green glitter.

The Green Bell himself! Only the sinister czar wore those green goggles to shield his eyes.

Chapter XVI
THE MAN WHO VANISHED

For ten or fifteen seconds there was a silence in the stricken dead. Night insects droned and buzzed. On the distant horizon, heat lightning jumped about, a gory blushing.

The flashlight beam in which the Green Bell was embedded held as steady as if cast in steel. It threw back a dull glow which faintly disclosed the big bronze man who held it.

Doc Savage had been watching his four aids—against just such an incident as this.

Slowly, the bronze man advanced on the sable figure of the Green Bell.

The darksome form suddenly lifted a clenched, black-gloved fist. The fist rapped against the bell design done in green on the mantle. And the bell rang! Dull, muted—but it rang!

Some sort of a small gong was mounted under the black cloth. A signal!

Near-by darkness came to rushing life. Dusky figures popped up like evil jinnies. Their arms waved, tentacle fashion, and yellow-red sparks leaped out of the ends. Gun sound convulsed the air.

Doc doused his flash. For all his sharpened senses, he had been unaware that the Green Bell's henchmen were standing by for an emergency.

Whipping right, then left, he evaded lead slugs which hunted him like whining, ravenous little animals. He headed straight for the spot where the Green Bell had stood.

A man besmocked in black, triggering a pair of pistols in wild aimlessness, got in Doc's path. The bronze giant, hardly pausing, snapped a casehardened hand to the fellow's spinal nerve center. The man dropped—marked by no wound, but absolutely incapable of further movement.

In learning this strange paralysis which he employed, Doc had delved deeply into the mysteries of chiropractic pressures and their effects on the muscular system.

Doc reached the spot where the black czar had stood. The nigrescent bird had flown. Doc felt disappointment, but no surprise.

The Green Bell had saved himself by having his men present. He had, while flaming guns harassed Doc, faded into the night from which he had come.

Dark-hooded forms whipped among the parked cars, hunting. Two of them bumped each other. Guns gulped thunder—each thought the other an enemy, so edged were their nerves.

Both sagged down, cursing, clawlike hands digging into their own flesh where bullets had torn.

Over toward the circus tents, bigfisted Renny raced to a flood light, picked it bodily out of its mounting, and turned the great calcium spray on the road.

The light ended the battle. The Green Bell's men were creatures of the night. Also, Renny, Monk, and the rest were charging from Aunt Nora's house. They were a fighting crew with which nothing less than a young army could cope.

The black-frocked men fled.

Doc haunted their retreat. Twice, he descended upon stragglers, to compress and knead his corded fingers, and leave his victims —limp and helpless—in his wake.

The light, as he had fully expected, showed no trace of a hooded figure with green goggles.

The czar sinister had managed his escape.

Doc Savage soon abandoned the pursuit of the fleeing black forms. He could not hope to corral all of them in the night.

Picking up the two he had just overcome, he carried them back to the parked cars. Three more of the darkly masked men lay there —the one Doc had paralyzed, and the two who had shot each other.

Doc's aids, police, and ex-service men swarmed the spot. With loud yells, hoods were torn off the Green Bell hirelings, and their faces revealed.

"Just bums from around town!" grunted Ole Slater, after eying the unveiled features.

"Here's two more!" Doc called from the darkness. Then he left the vicinity with great speed.

Policemen ran to the spot from which he had spoken. They found the two prisoners; nothing else. The officers were excited, but more by events of the last four or five minutes, than by the presence of Doc Savage.

The police made no effort to pursue Doc.

This was significant. There was a warrant out for Doc's arrest on the charge of murdering Chief Clements, but the police were rapidly getting in a frame of mind where they did not care much about serving it.

The prisoners were picked up and carried toward the house. A physician was summoned to patch up the pair who had shot each other. All five were in for a night of questioning.

No one paid the least attention to Long Tom's roadster. Certainly, no one lifted the hood. Whatever object the Green Bell had placed upon the engine, still reposed there.

In the house Monk bowed his great, sloping shoulders. Small kegs of muscle seemed to spring out on his gorilla frame.

"I know how Doc charmed these eggs," he said softly, little eyes boring the prisoners. "I can snap 'em out of it. I'm gonna do that. And, brothers, I'm gonna make 'em talk like phonographs!"

Renny blocked his huge fists and clanked them together. "Yeah! We'll make 'em talk!"

A policeman chuckled loudly. "You know, all of us guys are beginnin' to think alike!"

Monk made a homely grin. "Meanin' you're beginnin' to believe Doc Savage didn't murder Jim Cash or Chief Clements, or even the cop who was found hangin' in the vines?"

"Somethin' like that," the officer admitted.

This was just one policeman's opinion. But the same attitude seemed to be general.

Long Tom sighed. He would have liked to remain behind and take a hand at questioning the captives. The process of eliciting information was likely to be extremely rough. These prisoners probably did not know the identity of the Green Bell, but they might know other things.

For instance, could they swear Doc had not murdered Chief Clements and Jim Cash? And the bluecoat found slain and hanging in the vines?

"Sorry I can't attend the show!" Long Tom grumbled. "I've got a little errand to perform! It can't wait!"

The electrical wizard headed for the kitchen to finish his interrupted lunch. He had no idea how long he would be away, or how busy he would find himself. It was no simple task, this rigging of apparatus which would locate the Green Bell's secret radio station.

The mysterious transmitter was never on for more than half a minute. In that short space, it was very difficult to get accurate readings with an ordinary radio direction-finder.

Long Tom, however, had an intricate scheme which he intended to use.

He grinned as he ate. Things were looking up. Most of the town was on Doc's side. The police were approaching the point where they would ignore all charges, however heinous, faked against the remarkable bronze man. The Green Bell's agitators were afraid to open their mouths in public.

"We've got 'em on the run!" Long Tom chortled.

He did not know that the Green Bell had planted some mysterious object under the hood of his car.

The food consumed, Long Tom burdened himself with additional pieces of electrical equipment. He swung outdoors.

Around the cars, things were once more quiet and dark. Mosquitoes buzzed like small airplanes.

Long Tom swatted at one, chuckled: "Jersey canaries!" He was feeling very good.

He unlocked the rear compartment, leaned down to insert the articles he was carrying—and his jaw dropped.

A small slab of glass rested in front of his eyes. It was, he saw, one of the windshield wings which had been taken off the roadster.

The glass bore written words which glowed with an unearthly, electric blue. The script was machine perfect. There was a message of some length on the glass, yet it occupied little space.

The communication was from Doc, of course. The bronze man often left missives in this fashion—written on glass. He used a chalk of his own compounding, a chalk which left a mark invisible, not only to the naked eye, but also to all but the most powerful of microscopes.

When subjected to the glow of ultra-violet light—rays also invisible to the eye—the chalk marks glowed with this uncanny blue luminance.

A tiny ultra-violet lantern reposed on the compartment floor, its beam focused on the glass slab.

Long Tom read the message:

The Green Bell placed a chemical on the engine of your roadster. This, when heated by the motor, would have made a deadly gas.

The chemical has been removed.

Suppose you leave the impression you were slain by the gas, Long Tom. If the Green Bell believes you dead, you can work in peace.

Long Tom hastily switched off the ultra-violet lantern. The communication was unsigned, but there was no need for an appended name. Only one hand could write a script as perfect as that—Doc Savage's.

Reading of the note had taken only an instant. No onlooker would have dreamed Long Tom had done other than stow his burden in the compartment.

He got behind the wheel, started the motor, and drove off. He racked his brains. Too bad Doc had not suggested how Long Tom could fake his own death! But then, Doc usually left details of their respective jobs to his men. They were supposed to be the most astute in their individual professions.

Long Tom put a grin on his somewhat unhealthy face. He had it!

Prosper Creek ran along the south edge of Prosper City. This was not a large stream, but it had dug itself a deep ditch down through the centuries. A concern had installed a dam for a small hydro-electric plant. This backed the water up rather deeply.

A bridge spanned the creek where some of this back-water stood.

Long Tom zigzagged about town to shake off possible shadows, and finally headed for the bridge. He was certain no one was on his trail.

A few hundred yards from the bridge, he unloaded his equipment and concealed it in a weed patch. Then he rolled the roadster to the bridge, yanked the hand throttle open, and jumped out.

Motor thundering, the machine dived for the wooden railing of the bridge! It crashed the stringers! They gave. The car seemed to try to climb a steel beam which formed the bridge frame. The beam bent; metal screamed, rent!

The car rolled over and disappeared beneath the water.

After the roadster sank, bubbles came up with a loud gurgling and sobbing. It was as if the monster of rubber, iron, and frabric were a drowning, living thing.

A man, a resident of the neighborhood, came racing along the road, drawn by the crash sound. He peered down at the hideous sobbing in the water, lighted several matches and dropped them, then whirled and ran madly to call help.

Long Tom grinned and worked away from the vicinity. He gathered up his apparatus, such of it as he could carry.

He intended to locate two directional radio devices at widely separated points. These differed from the conventional apparatus in that the directional focusing was done automatically.

Compasslike, they would indicate the source of a radio wave. Long Tom intended simply to tune them in on the regular Prosper City broadcaster, and leave them. When the secret station came on, the indicators would swing to it, pulled by its stronger wave. An inked marker would show the exact direction.

In the distance, an ambulance siren wailed like a lost hound. Long Tom, listening, nodded. That would be an emergency crew coming to rescue his supposed body from the sunken roadster.

Not finding it, they would conclude it had been carried downstream by the slight current.

The Green Bell would believe the gas had overcome Long Tom at just the right moment for his car, running wild, to leap the bridge.

Chapter XVII
THE TOUCH THAT YELLOWED

Loud and blaring was the siren on the ambulance speeding to the spot where the car lay in water under the bridge. A police emergency truck followed it. This had an even noisier siren.

Many ears heard the uproar—among them, Doc Savage's. He was satisfied. The noise meant Long Tom had lost no time putting across his deception.

At the moment, Doc was loitering in the murk near the cars. Sounds from the house reached his sensitive ears. Howls of pain, curses, moans! The prisoners were being questioned.

Doc did not fancy the sounds. On occasion, he inflicted exquisite torture himself, but it was always of the type which did no lasting harm.

Too, administering physical pain was not the way to get information from hardened thugs such as these disciples of the Green Bell. Fist blows, the smash of gun barrels, they could understand. Men are less likely to fear what they can comprehend.

Doc's methods on the other hand, were so unusual that they impressed the average man, steeped in ignorance as he was, as smacking of the supernatural. And men fear what they cannot understand.

Leaving the darkness, Doc stalked boldly into the zone whitened by flood lights.

The bronze man wished to question the prisoners in person. But more important, he had plans—a trick to try. This trick required his presence in the house.

His appearance created a commotion equal to that of the recent fight. Policemen ran up. They did not flash guns, however. Nor did any handcuffs come out of pockets.

Questions volleyed.

Doc ignored them. A towering, metallic giant in the flood glare, he made for the house.

Collison McAlter jumped like a stricken man when he saw Doc, then sank in a chair.

"They'll arrest you!" he gulped. "Oh, why were you so reckless as to show yourself?"

Monk and Renny snorted in unison. They knew Doc's methods. The bronze man could, they were sure, escape from the police practically at will.

Aunt Nora Boston gave Doc a wide smile, and said warmly: "I think we can persuade the police to permit you to remain at liberty, Mr. Savage." She jabbed a plump hand at the prisoners. "Especially if those rats cough up the truth."

Charming Alice Cash also gave Doc a radiant smile. She was glad to have the bronze man in their midst again, and made no effort not to show it. Of late, she had seen very little of this strikingly handsome man of such amazing marvels.

Ole Slater grinned widely at Doc, but the grin was unnatural. He glanced covertly at Alice. Ole, it was plain to be seen, was getting more worried about losing his girl as each hour passed.

"Any luck?" Doc asked, indicating the captives.

Monk chuckled, pinched a hard-faced villain, and produced a lusty wail.

"A lot of that kind of music!" explained the homely fellow. "But nothin' that does us much good!"

Doc's weird golden eyes prowled the prisoners, appraising their faces and their nervous condition. He selected the weakest of the lot.

He said no word. He merely stood over the man and stared steadily. From his lips began to come the strange, mellow trilling note which was part of Doc. It seeped through the room, with nothing to show from whence it arose.

Doc had long ago learned this sound facilitated his efforts at hypnotism.

The man on the floor was a coward. He did not even wait to be mesmerized.

"Damn you! Damn them eyes!" He squirmed madly, gnashing the links of his handcuffs together. "What d'you wanta know? I'll spill! Only turn them glims the other way!"

Astounded expressions settled on the faces of those in the room. They had seen this man on the floor defy blows and threats of death. But he had succumbed to the mere stare of the bronze giant.

Monk and Renny showed no emotion. They had seen things like this happen before. Doc's presence seemed to have an uncanny effect upon evildoers—especially after they had come to know what a frightful foe he was.

"Who's the Green Bell?" Doc queried.

Collison McAlter shifted his feet nervously; his eyes roved to the doors, the windows. Aunt Nora shivered, put her hands to her plump cheeks. Alice Cash watched Doc, fascinated.

Ole Slater drew a revolver and seemed to be trying to watch every one present. Most of the Prosper City business men were there. Some one here, in this room, was the Green Bell.

Slater acted as if he were alert to seize the culprit, should his name be disclosed.

"I don't know who the Green Bell is!" groaned the man on the floor.

Doc had expected that. "Who killed Chief Clements?"

A minor convulsion seized the fellow as he made up his mind whether to answer to not.

"Judborn Tugg!" he wailed.

Several policemen charged for the door, yelling: "That settles it! We'll nail Tugg!"

"Who killed Jim Cash?" Doc demanded.

"I don't know nothin' about that!" moaned the prone man.

"And the policeman found hanging in the vines under Monk's window—who murdered him?"

"The Green Bell! The cop came upon the boss while he was plantin' the gun that Tugg used to kill Chief Clements! That was why he was croaked!"

Doc waved an arm which took in every individual present. "Do you think the Green Bell is one of these people?"

"Yeah! Sure, he must be!"

This had the effect of causing each person in the room to shrink slightly from his neighbor. They had, of course, suspected the Green Bell was one of them. But having it put into words in this way was a shock.

Doc now addressed the crowd: "Any questions you care to have answered?"

"Yes!" Ole Slater shouted shrilly. "What is behind all this horror? Why is the Green Bell tryin' to ruin Prosper City? Is he a madman who hates the town?"

Eyes rolled in the head of the man on the floor.

"I dunno!" he mumbled. "None of us knows what's behind it all!"

This was the extent of the information secured. The other four prisoners insisted sullenly that they knew no more than their companion.

"Which is probably the truth," Doc commented.

The bronze man now employed a small hypodermic needle upon each prisoner. This caused them to go into a trancelike sleep, from which only the application of another drug could arouse them.

The five were loaded into an ambulance which Doc called. To the ambulance driver, Doc gave secret directions, and a neat sum of money. The machine started off, ostensibly for a Prosper City hospital, where the men were to go into the prison ward.

The ambulance, however, never reached there. In fact, it was fully a year before the five prisoners were again seen. Then, it was in a distant city, and, had an old acquaintance hailed either of the five, they would not have been recognized.

The captives went into Doc's institution in upstate New York, where they were subjected to brain operations wiping out their past, and given training which fitted them to be honest citizens.

The policemen who had gone to arrest Judborn Tugg now returned. They were a disgusted lot.

"The bird flew the coop!" they explained. "There wasn't no sign of 'im!"

"Any of his clothing gone?" Doc asked.

"Didn't look like it! We'll spread a general alarm for 'im!"

"You're wasting your time!" Doc assured them. "Judborn Tugg is a man who likes flashy clothing. He would not have fled town without taking some."

"Then what became of 'im?"

Doc did not answer this, much to the puzzlement of the officers. Doc had an idea what had happened to Judborn Tugg. But that idea was part of the theory as to who the Green Bell was. Lacking proof, he was not yet ready to reveal it.

Johnny, the bony geologist, appeared. He carried a long, circular blue-print case. Catching Doc's eye, Johnny nodded —thereby affirming that he had secured the geologic survey maps of the region under and around Prosper City.

Doc received the maps, but did not immediately consult them.

Instead, he went upstairs. He secured, from where it had lain in Monk's room, the small segment of wood which was the chief remnant of the Green Bell's sonic device for producing insanity.

He worked over this perhaps half an hour. Then he carried it back downstairs, mounted a table, and made a speech.

"This"—he held up the bit of wood—"may lead us to the Green Bell. In fact, it is almost certain that it will!"

This pronouncement, coming without any previous dramatic build-up, was breath taking. The crowd surged close. Word was passed outside, and every one sought to get into the room.

As you all know, or, at least, have heard," Doc continued, "the Green Bell sought to drive me insane with a peculiar sonic device. The upshot of the attempt was that the device came into my hands!"

Monk, Renny, and Johnny swapped puzzled stares. What was the bronze man up to?

"We found that the box held finger prints of the person who made it—probably the Green Bell," Doc continued. "That they were the Green Bell's was made fairly certain by the fact that he sought to destroy them."

"Sought!" yelled a cop. "You mean that there's finger prints on that piece of wood? It's a hunk of the sonic box, ain't it?"

"It is!" Doc replied gravely. "And it bears proof which is almost certain to trap the Green Bell!"

Monk looked at Renny.

"That's the first lie I ever heard Doc tell!" he grinned.

"Lie?" Renny asked. "What was a lie?"

"When he said there were finger prints on that piece of wood. There ain't any! I examined it. Doc examined it. And there ain't a speck of a print."

"Doc didn't say there was a print on it!" Renny pointed out.

Monk scratched the top of his bullet head.

"Huh!" he snorted. "That's right—he didn't! But he sure gave the impression there was!"

"I guess he hopes the Green Bell will try to get the stick, and betray himself in the process," Renny hazarded.

This conversation had taken place in whispers which no one could overhear. In addition, both men had cupped palms over their mouths, so that, should the Green Bell be a lip reader, he could not eavesdrop by sight.

Doc Savage now waved every one away from the table on

which he stood. He was carrying his prize tenderly in a handkerchief.

"We must be careful that the Green Bell does not get this bit of wood!" he warned, and placed the piece on the table top.

The policeman promptly formed a circle around the table, keeping every one at a distance.

"Hm-m-m!" Monk breathed. "Doc's makin' it awful tough for the Green Bell to get that wood!"

"Bring a microscope!" Doc called. "Also a camera for taking finger print photos. You police have such devices handy, I presume."

"Huh!" Renny whispered to Monk. "D'you reckon there is a print on that thing?"

As if to answer him, the lights went out. Bulbs in the house, floodlamps on the grounds—all blotted simultaneously. The current had been shut off at the main switch, probably in the shed at the back of the house.

A stunned silence followed by a gush of blackness.

It was interrupted by a low hissing noise, a *clunk!* Neither sound was loud.

"The piece of wood!" a man bawled.

Excitement exploded in the room. Policemen yelled, drew their service weapons. Men elbowed their neighbors in their perturbation, and the neighbors, thinking it was the Green Bell seeking to escape with the wooden fragment, lashed out with fists. In a trice, a dozen fights were in progress.

Monk, Renny, and Johnny stood in the background. Whatever was going on, they did not think it had caught Doc napping.

Flashlights came out of pockets, spitting white funnels. The fighters discovered their opponents were friends, stopped swinging blows, and began profuse apologies.

"It's gone!" squawked a cop. "The chunk of wood is gone!"

Collison McAlter held up both his hands, shouting: "I want to submit to a search! And I think every one present should do the same!"

Ole Slater came elbowing through the crowd and agreed: "I second that suggestion!"

Aunt Nora Boston grumbled: "I'm agin' it!"

Alice Cash gasped in surprise: "Why, Aunt Nora!"

"Ain't no use searchin', child," said Aunt Nora. "This devil ain't fool enough to keep that thing on his person."

The hunt went forward, none the less. Even the police submitted.

Monk maneuvered over behind Doc, eyed the table, then asked: "How on earth did the guy get it? There was a ring of cops around the table!"

Doc pointed at a tiny cut in the table top.

"He simply tied a penknife to a thread, leaned over a cop's shoulder, and speared the piece of wood. Harpooned it, if you like."

Monk groaned. "He put over a fast one on you, Doc!"

The bronze man smiled slightly. "Not so you could notice, Monk!"

A loud shout came from the kitchen.

They dashed for the spot.

Aunt Nora Boston was crouched over the coal-burning kitchen range. Her jaw was slack, her eyes were bulging a little. She was peering into the firebox of the stove, from which she had removed a lid.

In the firebox, barely recognizable so charred had it become, lay the fragment of wood from the Green Bell's sonic device.

With it was a small pocketknife. This had had celluloid handles, but they were burned away.

"I was gonna put more wood on the fire," mumbled Aunt Nora. "And I seen this——"

"Recognize the knife from what is left?" Doc questioned.

Attractive Alice Cash answered the query. "I do! It is one I keep on my desk to sharpen pencils."

More inquiries followed, in which the police took a hand. But this got no results. Who had deposited the fragment and the knife in the stove?

Investigating, Doc learned what had happened to the lights. Some one had taken a fork from Aunt Nora's kitchen cabinet and jammed it across the terminals in the fuse box, causing the fuses to blow. There were no finger prints on the fork.

Monk had dogged Doc's footsteps. While the bronze man was installing new fuses, the homely chemist picked up the conversation which Aunt Nora's discovery had interrupted.

"You said the Green Bell didn't put a fast one over on you!" he whispered. "What d'you mean by that, Doc?"

Doc Savage surveyed the vicinity to make sure there were no eavesdroppers.

"There was no finger print on that bit of wood," he said.

"Sure! I know that!"

"But I soaked it in certain chemicals from your collection. Those chemicals were very powerful. If the skin is brought in contact with them, enough will be absorbed to affect the liver, causing an increased production of biliary pigment."

Monk blinked. "So what?"

"The biliary pigment will be absorbed in the blood, resulting in a yellow condition of the skin. In other words, the Green Bell, in touching that wooden fragment, merely contracted an excellent case of yellow jaundice."

Monk all but choked. "You mean—whoever picked up that wood will start turnin' yellow?"

"Exactly! All we have to do is set back, keep from getting killed, and wait for somebody to turn yellow."

"How long'll it take?"

"That is difficult to say. It depends on the individual. A day; perhaps a week. Not over that!"

Chapter XVIII
LULL

The rest of the night was uneventful. Dawn brought an airplane from New York—a small, speedy machine from Doc Savage's private hangar on the Hudson River.

The dapper Ham stepped out of it. He lost no time making his way to Aunt Nora Boston's home.

The only article of baggage which accompanied him was his slender, innocent-lolking black sword cane.

Monk observed Ham's arrival from within the house, and grinned from ear to ear. He had missed his usual diversion of insulting Ham.

Putting a black scowl on his homely face, Monk hurried out.

"Listen, shyster, you had orders to stay in New York!" he growled. "What's the idea of showin' up down here?"

Ham caught sight of pretty Alice Cash. He dressed Monk down with a cold look, swung over jauntily, and bowed to the young lady.

"You are more ravishing than ever!" he assured Alice.

Monk writhed mentally. He usually told pretty young women that Ham had a wife and thirteen children, all half-wits. But he had neglected to tell Alice the yarn. He'd better spill it in a hurry!

Ham guided Alice into the house, where Doc was studying the geology maps of Prosper City's vicinity.

"The murder charge against you in New York is all washed up!" Ham declared.

"How'd you work it?" Doc inquired.

"Simply by putting the fear of Old Nick into the four lying witnesses! I dug up some stuff in their past—burglary and blackmail. That did the trick! They broke down and confessed that they were hired to say they saw you kill Jim Cash!"

Alice Cash flinched at the mention of her brother's murder, and left the room hastily. Ham, glancing out of the window a moment later, saw Monk with an arm across her shoulder. Monk was an excellent comforter, especially if the grieved one was as good-looking as Alice was. Ham groaned.

"Who hired the four?" Doc asked.

"They didn't see the fellow's face. He wore one of those trick gowns with a green bell painted on it."

Doc nodded. "Rather thought it would be like that. What did you do with the four?"

Ham smiled fiercely and fiddled with his sword cane. "Got them out on bail when the cops arrested 'em for lodgin' that false charge; then grabbed 'em and sent 'em to our little place in upstate New York."

"Good work!"

After a glance about, Ham grunted: "I see everybody but Long Tom. Where's he?"

"Hiding out," Doc replied. "He has his apparatus all set to locate the Green Bell's secret radio station, once the thing goes into operation."

"I hope he finds it quick," Long Tom grinned. "I crave some action! That business in New York didn't get me warmed up!"

As the hours dragged, however, it seemed Ham was to see no action. The Green Bell and his hirelings made no hostile move. Judborn Tugg did not put in an appearance.

The day was marked with events of great interest for Prosper City, however. Practically all factories opened. The mines, as well!

Renny, with his vast fund of knowledge concerning engineering in all its branches, took active charge of this work. He organized crews, demoralized by the recent troubles and inactivity.

Since Doc intended to put the plants on a profitable basis, Renny's work was not easy. In the first place, a high wage scale was introduced in every department of each concern. This made economy of production a prime necessity.

Monk stationed his ex-service men guards over each plant, and made the rounds like a general, keeping things in form.

If he expected trouble, though, he was disappointed. Not a Green Bell agitator put in an appearance. Peace reigned. All was quiet.

"But it's kinda like the quiet of a guy who is aimin' his gun!" Monk muttered pessimistically.

Doc Savage set Ham to work clearing up the final legal details of the deal by which Prosper City's industries were being taken over, literally in the whole. When that was done, Doc visited the ramshackle old barn on the marsh.

He took particular notice that this was hardly more than three quarters of a mile from Aunt Nora Boston's home.

The bronze man did nothing while he was there, except drop a firecracker down the vertical pipe through which the Green Bell had addressed his men. He listened with great interest to the hollow reverberations as the cracker let loose, possibly two hundred and fifty feet below.

These sepulchral echoes seemed to rumble and gobble for fully a minute.

Leaving the spot, Doc visited the men who had suffered more than any others from the trouble in Prosper City—the poor souls who had been driven insane by the Green Bell's sonic machine.

He made a detailed examination of each case, using X rays, blood tests, spinal-fluid tests—almost every test known to medical science.

Late that afternoon, he made his announcement.

"Sections of the brain are merely in a quiescent state—a form of nerve paralysis induced by the disrupting force of the sonic vibrations."

"Will you put that in plain English?" Aunt Nora requested.

"They can be cured," Doc replied. "It'll take a little time. But there's not the slightest doubt."

Aunt Nora Boston sat down and cried.

"I never did tell you," she said moistly. "But one of the afflicted men is a nephew of mine."

While Doc was telephoning to New York, Chicago, Rochester, and other great medical centers, for specialists to take personal charge of the brain cures, Alice Cash offered her services.

"That's great!" Doc replied. "You can sort of look out for these cases."

"I've been watching your work," Alice told him thoughtfully. "I notice from the way you are organizing it that you are putting others in actual charge. Even Renny, the engineer, is serving merely as a supervisor. What does that mean?"

"Simply that we are going to step out as soon as the danger is past!"

"You mean that you are going to leave Prosper City?" Alice Cash sounded slightly stricken.

"You didn't expect us to remain here? Not, of course, that Prosper City isn't as nice a town as the average."

Alice flushed. "I—I was hoping you would."

Doc Savage saw how the wind was blowing. The young lady was more interested in him than he wished. Unwillingly, he had made another conquest, or was on the verge of making it.

This pained Doc. He did not care to hurt any one's feelings. So he did something that he rarely did. He took off an hour and explained his strange purpose in life—his life profession of going up and down the trails of the world, hunting trouble and peril, helping those in need of help, and administering punishment to wrongdoers.

He made it very clear to his beautiful listener that such a life precluded any feminine entanglements. When he finished, he believed he had painted such a picture of horror and danger that a female heart would quail at the thought of sharing them. He thought he had scared this gorgeous young woman off.

"What you need is a loving wife to attend to your needs," pretty Alice Cash said warmly. She did not say that she would like the job, but it was in her voice.

Doc mentally threw up his hands. What could you do in a case like that?

He got away as quickly and gracefully as he could, sought a

secluded spot, and went through the round of exercises which he had taken each day.

They were unlike anything else, those exercises. Doc's father had started him on them when he could hardly walk. They were solely responsible for his phenomenal physical and mental powers.

He made his muscles work against each other, straining until perspiration filmed his mighty bronze body. He juggled a number of a dozen figures in his head, multiplying, extracting square and cube roots.

He had an apparatus which made sound waves of frequencies so high and so low the ordinary human ear could not detect them. He listened intently to this—his proficiency along that line had already saved his life on this adventure.

He named several score of assorted odors after a quick olfactory test of small vials racked in a special case. He read pages of Braille print—writing of the blind. This whetted his sense of touch.

Many and varied other parts were in his routine. They filled an entire two hours at a terrific pace, with no time out for rest.

Monk and Ham came upon Doc as he finished.

Monk groaned. "Think of doin' that every day!"

Ham sneered audibly. "You, I suppose, don't take exercises?"

Monk flexed his hairy arms. "Some of these days I'm gonna have a workout on you! That's the one exercise I need!"

Unsheathing his sword cane, Ham flicked it. The fine blade twanged like a guitar string.

"Try it, and I'll do some sculpture work on you with this!" he promised.

The two glared at each other as if they had murder in their hearts.

"What's the trouble?" Doc questioned.

"This furry, lying dead beat!" Ham purpled and jabbed his sword at Monk. "He told Alice Cash that yarn about my wife and thirteen half-wit children! The missing link! I've never had a wife!"

At nine o'clock that night, there was to be a meeting at Aunt Nora Boston's. Heads of all plants in Prosper City—now actually in charge—were to attend.

At eight thirty, Alice Cash turned on Aunt Nora's radio.

Ten minutes later, the Green Bell's hideous clangor, squealing, and wailing, came from the instrument.

"I know it!" Monk yelled. "We're in for real trouble!"

From Doc Savage's actions, it seemed he had been waiting for just this. He raced upstairs to Long Tom's room. When he came back, he carried two small boxes. One was a radio transmitter, a tiny portable set. The other was a receiver.

Doc gave the receiver to Monk. "Keep tuned in on this! Clamp the headset on that knot of a head, and don't take it off for anything!"

The telephone rang. It was Long Tom.

"My equipment got the source of that secret radio wave!" he barked excitedly. "It came from Aunt Nora Boston's house!"

"It what?"

"From Aunt Nora's! I can't believe it! But it's a fact."

Doc hung up, faced Renny. "Where's Aunt Nora?"

"Dunno! Ain't seen her for a few minutes!"

The maps which Johnny had secured lay on a table. Doc seized them, carried them with him as he ran out of the house. He also bore the radio transmitter.

Doc consulted the charts, then headed due east, mounting the slope of the mountain. After covering a few hundred yards, he added stealth to his pace. He moved with the quiet of a windblown feather.

Blackened knots of buildings lurched up in the moonlight ahead. He eyed the maps once more, identifying the structures.

They were surface buildings of a coal mine—a mine which had been closed for several years, the veins below exhausted. For years, however, it had been the largest mine in Prosper City; at one time, it had led the nation in coal output.

Doc posted himself near by and waited. He was not disappointed.

A group of seven furtive figures crept up. They wore the hideous black gowns of the Green Bell. They disappeared into the maw of the mine.

Other men came, two of them, this time. Then three fellows arrived alone. Eight were in the next group.

The evil clan was gathering.

Doc waited until there came an interval of five minutes when no sinister men put in an appearance. Then he entered the black gullet of the mine.

The tunnel was exceedingly dry for an old working. It sloped downward. Doc sought a recess and used his flashlight on the maps. One of the charts showed every cranny of this particular abandoned mine.

When the tunnel branched, he turned left. The tunnel swept in a vast curve. Doc knew—the map showed it, too—that he was approaching a spot directly under Aunt Nora Boston's house.

He slackened his pace. The drift was long and straight—fully three hundred yards without a turn. A bullet could be fired the length of it without touching a wall.

He covered this direct lane.

Lights appeared ahead. A moment later, he was peering out into a great room. Pillars—coal left standing to support the roof —were a forest before his eyes.

In this forest, black-cowled men were clustered.

Chapter XIX
DEATH UNDERGROUND

Entering the underground cavern, Doc glided forward. There was not much chance of discovery. The Green Bell and his men thought themselves safe here.

The Green Bell was present—in person! He sat, cross-legged, as the dummy of sticks and fabric in the distant barn had sat. No doubt some of the masked men before him did not know there was a difference between this figure they were looking upon now, and the form in the dilapidated farm building.

The dummy in the barn! It was that which had given Doc his lead to this underground rendezvous. The pipe diving straight downward two hundred and fifty feet, from which the evil czar's voice had come! It could lead to nothing but a mine tunnel!

Geology maps of the region had shown that a sheet of hard rock underlay the swampy field. The presence of the rock, a great bowl holding water, accounted for the moist nature of the field itself.

And the map of this old mine showed a drift under the swamp.

The Green Bell had simply drilled a hole and forced his pipe upward, not a difficult task. Hydraulic jacks and a driving-head on the pipe would do the work.

The Green Bell was speaking.

"Are all of you here?" he boomed hollowly. "That is important, to-night! There must be no absentees! For on our work to-night depends success or failure!"

There was a general wagging of fingers as a count was made.

"Unmask!" commanded the Green Bell. "We must be certain!"

The black hoods came off, some a bit reluctantly. Flashlights furnished a glow sufficient to inspect the faces.

Doc surveyed them with interest. Three men were, he saw to his disgust, fairly prominent factory owners of Prosper City. It was these men who had objected most strenuously to his proposition to take over all plants.

Collison McAlter was not among them.

The Green Bell himself did not remove his hood. He stared, goggled green eyes malicious, glittering in the flash glare.

"All here!" he decided. "Now, we will get down to work!"

The Green Bell arose, strode through the ring of men, and vanished into the blacker reaches of the cavern. A chain rattled.

When the masked leader appeared again, he was leading a forlorn, manacled figure. Judborn Tugg! Tugg's face bore numerous bruises and cuts: dried crimson stains were on his clothing, his hair. His nose seemed to be damaged much more than it had been by Long Tom's blows. Most of his front teeth were missing.

Tugg had obviously been tortured.

"This worm!" intoned the Green Bell, kicking Tugg. "This worm was an unfaithful servant!"

Tugg blubbered: "I couldn't help it if——"

"Shut up! You would have betrayed me! That is regrettable. You were to be the mainstay of the industrial empire which I intend to build, with Prosper City as its center! You were to have been the apparent head of all my enterprises!"

The Green Bell's voice became a shrill tinkling, and he delivered another forceful kick.

"It was through you that I intended to buy all the factories and mines in Prosper City, once I had reduced the owners to a point where they would have to sell for a song!"

This information did not surprise Doc. He had surmised that such a scheme was behind the Prosper City trouble. This man, the

Green Bell, had money, a lust for more money—a scheming brain. The combination had launched him on this plan of forcing a whole city into bankruptcy, then buying its factories for a pittance.

"You were a fool to go against me!" the Green Bell snarled at Tugg. "I am powerful! I have millions, made by selling stocks short during the great depression! I will have more millions —billions!"

Tugg moaned. "Lemme go, won't you? I can't harm you! I've signed over every stick of my property to you!"

"Not to me!" The Green Bell turned, pointed a black-sheathed arm at one of the Prosper City business men, and said: "You, sir, may not know it, but you are now the owner of Tugg & Co. This —this gaudy worm signed his entire holdings over to you for a consideration of one dollar! Incidentally, I will now pay him the dollar!"

The Green Bell produced a bit of silver from his gown, using his left hand. He bent over and offered this to Tugg. His right hand remained out of sight in the robe.

Poor Tugg did not know what to do, except take the dollar. He reached for it.

Like a striking black cobra, the Green Bell whipped out a knife with the other hand. He ran the blade into Tugg's heart. The steel went in easily, as if it had been a hot wire making its way into grease.

Tugg emitted one piercing, lamblike bleat, then began to kick around convulsively on the floor.

The Green Bell put a foot on Tugg's squirming form and held it steady until all movements had ceased. Then he stepped back.

"You may wonder why I did not shoot him, and why I held him still!" he tolled monotonously. He leveled an arm. "Look! There is the explanation!"

To one side, a small tunnel penetrated. Evidently it had been drifted there long ago, in pursuit of some wisp of coal which had dribbled out.

"There is a room in that tunnel!" said the Green Bell. "It is only a few yards from this chamber. It holds the powerful radio set with which it has been my custom to summon you!"

Doc nodded slightly, where he was concealed in the gloom. This explained why the radio signals had apparently been traced to Aunt Nora Boston's! The room was directly under her house!

"Also, in that room are some thousands of quarts of nitroglycerin!" continued the Green Bell. "It is connected to electrical contacts rigged on a seismograph. Do you know what a seismograph is?"

"A jigger which wiggles when there's an earthquake!" some one muttered.

"That is an excellent description. The contacts are on the jigger which wiggles, as you call it. Any large shock in the earth near by will cause the explosive to detonate."

There was much uneasy squirming at this information.

"Do not worry!" boomed the voice of the robed man. "The seismograph is adjusted so no distant earthquake will operate it. Only a shock near by will close the contacts. Such a shock will be the explosion of a small quantity of nitro approximately half a mile from here, which I will arrange."

A hideous laugh gurgled from the lips of the cowled figure who had murdered Tugg so callously.

"Aunt Nora Boston's home is directly above this cache of explosive! Not many yards above it, either! The house and every one in it will be blown to bits!"

Doc Savage silently unlimbered the radio transmitter. The thing operated without noise, except for the faintest of clicking as he vibrated the key.

The radio waves, of course, would travel through the intervening earth and stone to Monk's portable receiver.

"Is this—necessary?" quavered one of the assembled men.

The Green Bell cursed. "Necessary! Of course it is! It's imperative that we get rid of Savage and the others at once! The devil is clever! To-morrow he will trap me!"

"To-morrow——"

"Exactly!"

"But how can he?"

"Shut up!" excitedly boomed the hooded leader.

Doc had finished transmitting, and was listening with great interest. He knew why the Green Bell was positive he would be trapped.

The fellow had found his skin was turning yellow! He had realized that Doc's maneuvering with the segment of the sonic box, the night before, had been a trick.

"I called you here to-night to warn you all to keep away from Aunt Nora Boston's house," said the Green Bell. "Now that the orders are given, you may go!"

As one man, the crowd whirled for the exit.

This took Doc somewhat by surprise. He was given no opportunity to circle the group, so as to remain in the cavern and disconnect the seismograph device. The only thing he could do was to retreat into the tunnel.

He sidled into it. Down the long, straight shaft he sped. Three hundred yards without a turn! He would have to cover that distance before the men behind him cast their flashlights down the passage. He ran as he had seldom run before.

He failed to make it.

A powerful flash scooted a white beam along the straight drift. A yell! "Savage—it's Savage! There he goes!"

The next instant, Doc seemed to become a bullet in a giant barrel of rock! Lifted by an irresistible force, he was hurled ahead. His eardrums threatened to cave!

Landing, he knotted himself like a circus tumbler. He was helpless to impede his progress. He was pushed from behind by a blast which might have been from a monster air gun!

Rock walls battered him! Dust, boulders, sprayed against him, past him! He crashed into the cross passage and dropped, almost unconscious. All of mother earth seemed to come down on his head!

One of the Green Bell's gang had forgotten the seismograph and the nitro, and had fired a bullet at Doc. The detonation had loosened the explosive.

Even now, the segments of Aunt Nora Boston's rambling, charming old home were probably floating around some hundreds of feet in the air. Any one in it would be dead.

Dead as those black-cowled men back there in the underground room! There was no possibility that any of them had survived. The sinister czar, who had chosen a green bell for his symbol, was dead—wiped out by his own death device.

His was a fate which had overtaken more than one enemy of Doc Savage.

Ten minutes later, Doc stumbled out of the abandoned mine. He did not feel like coming, even then. He was bruised, battered, damaged as he had seldom been in his life. But deadly gases were loose in the mine, and he had to get out.

Half an hour later, he encountered Monk.

The homely gorilla of a fellow stared at Doc's injuries.

"It looks like you caught yourself an earthquake," he suggested.

"How about the others?" Doc demanded.

"Them—they all got out, after you sent your radio warning, telling them to do so as quick as possible." Monk chuckled mirthfully. "Poor Ham! The overdressed shyster lost his sword cane in the rush. He was about to start back after it when the whole world blew up!"

"How did Aunt Nora take the loss of her house?"

"Swell! She said it was an old wreck that she'd been tryin' to sell for years, anyway!"

"She's a brick!" Doc said, absently fingering various aching muscles. "We'll have to put her in charge of charities here in Prosper City. Of course, we'll reimburse her for her house, and the money she spent on charity before we got on the job."

"She'd go for that," Monk agreed. "But you're forgettin' to tell me what happened down there under the ground."

Doc sketched briefly what had occurred.

"The Green Bell and every one of his followers is finished," he ended. "In a few days we can turn those factories back to their owners and clear out."

"You sound anxious to get away?" Monk said slyly, thinking of ravishingly pretty Alice Cash.

"Well, we should get back to New York," Doc told him. "Something may come up—it always does."

Doc's statement was only a guess, based on the past. He had no way of knowing what awaited them in New York, not being gifted with an inner sight. But it would be there—trouble, peril, mystery! These had always come to them.

"So the Green Bell found his hide was turnin' yellow?" Monk ruminated thoughtfully, as they moved through the night.

"There's no doubt of it!" Doc agreed. "And that persuaded him to rush his devilish plan to completion."

Monk grinned. "Ain't you gonna tell me who he was?"

"I didn't get a look at his face!" Doc said dryly.

"You mean we've cleaned this case up without knowin' who he was?"

"I think his identity will come out. It is pretty plain who he was."

"How d'you figure that?"

"Simply from the uncanny way the Green Bell had of knowing our every move. He was very close to us."

They had been striding down the road as they talked.

Pretty Alice Cash appeared. She showed relief at sight of Doc; then registered concern over his bruises.

"Have you seen Aunt Nora?" she asked, a moment later.

"She's around somewhere—I saw her a minute ago," Monk replied. "What'd you want with her? Important?"

"Well, not very," replied Alice. "I wanted to ask her if she had seen Ole Slater."

"Ain't Ole around?"

"No. And I'm curious. You see, Ole seemed a bit ill this evening, when I last saw him."

Monk gulped twice, swallowed, exploded: "What ailed him? Was he turnin' a funny color?"

"Ole Slater seemed to be turning yellow," Alice said. "It was the strangest thing!"

FORTRESS OF SOLITUDE

Contents

Chapter 1
THE STRANGE BLUE DOME

It was unfortunate that Doc Savage had never heard of John Sunlight. Doc Savage's life work was dedicated to attending to such men as John Sunlight, preferably before they managed to get too near their goal. But Doc Savage did not hear of John Sunlight in time.

It was also too bad that John Sunlight was destined to be the man who found the Strange Blue Dome.

It seemed from the first that John Sunlight had been put on this earth so that men could be afraid of him.

Russia was the first government to become afraid of him. It just happened that Russia was the first—John Sunlight wasn't a Russian. No one knew what he was, exactly. They did know that he was something horrible with a human body.

Serge Mafnoff wanted to give John Sunlight to a firing squad. Serge Mafnoff was the Russian official who captured John Sunlight and prosecuted him before the Soviet equivalent of a court.

"This thing known as John Sunlight," Serge Mafnoff said earnestly, "is incredible and shocking. We owe it to humanity to see that he is shot."

Serge Mafnoff was an honest, earnest, idealistic man. About John Sunlight, he was right.

John Sunlight took a silent vow to some day take revenge on Serge Mafnoff.

But the jury was soft. John Sunlight was accused of using blackmail on his superior officers in the army to force them to advance him in rank, and that might be only misdirected ambition. Serge Mafnoff knew it was more grim than that.

Anyway, John Sunlight didn't *look* the part. Not when he didn't wish, at least. He resembled a gentle poet, with his great shock of dark hair, his remarkably high forehead, his hollow burning eyes set in a starved face. His body was very long, very thin. His fingers, particularly, were so long and thin—the longest fingers being almost the length of an ordinary man's whole hand.

The jury didn't believe Serge Mafnoff when he told them that John Sunlight had the strength to seize any two of them and throttle them to death. And would, too, if he could thereby get the power to dominate a score of men's souls.

John Sunlight went to a Siberian prison camp.

He had never, as yet, heard of the Strange Blue Dome. But he was determined some day to pay off Serge Mafnoff.

The prison camp was located on the utter northern Siberian coast. Hundreds of miles of impassable ice and tundra lay south; to the north was the Arctic Ocean and the North Pole. Once each year, an ice-breaker rammed through to the prison colony with food and more prisoners.

No one had ever escaped the camp.

The ice-breaker took John Sunlight to the Siberian camp one August. It came back.

The next August, a year later, the ice-breaker sailed for the camp again. This time, it did not come back.

It was two months before the Soviets became excited and sent planes to see what had happened. They might have saved the gasoline the plane engines burned. For they found some piles of ashes where the prison camp had been, and nothing else.

They didn't even find an ash pile to hint what had become of convicts, ice-breaker, and ice-breaker crew.

Seven months later, John Sunlight stepped out on the bridge of the ice-breaker, and forty-six persons sank to their knees in craven terror. This pleased John Sunlight. He liked to break souls to do his bidding.

No one had been killed yet. The forty-six included the crew of the ice-breaker, and the convicts. For one of the queerest quirks of John Sunlight's weird nature was that he preferred to control a mind, rather than detach it from the owner's body with a bullet or a knife.

The ice-breaker had now been fast in the ice for four months. It looked very much as if they were all going to die.

None of them yet knew that the Strange Blue Dome existed.

Civan was John Sunlight's chief aid. Civan had helped in the prison camp break. It was he who emptied the powder from the guards' cartridges, working secretly over a period of days. Civan had fired the camp. Civan had a streak of sadism in his nature—he liked to destroy things. He had wanted to destroy the Soviet government. But he hadn't been in the prison camp for that. He had been there for destroying a man whose wife and money he coveted.

Civan was a bestial black ox to look at, but he did have a certain amount of brains. He had, however, absolutely no conscience. And so that strange and terrible thing, John Sunlight, had picked Civan to be his lieutenant.

Queerly, too, Civan feared John Sunlight infinitely more than anyone else. John Sunlight saw to that. Terror was the rope that John Sunlight kept around men's necks.

The ice-breaker drifted, trapped in the arctic ice. They shot a seal now and then. But they slowly starved, too.

Women are supposed to be more hardy than men.

So the two giantesses, Titania and Giantia—these were their vaudeville names—did not waste away. Their great muscles retained the strength to open horseshoes and bend silver rubles double. Giantia and Titania—their other name was Jeeves. They were Americans. They were great women, very blond. They were amazing women. They were a little queer, maybe, because all their lives men had been scared of them. They were such amazons.

They had gone to Russia with a vaudeville act, and had been accused of dabbling in a bit of profitable spy work on the side. They were quite guilty, so the United States government looked the other way when they were sent to Siberia.

Titania and Giantia were afraid of John Sunlight. They had never been scared of any other man. But they did not *worry* about John Sunlight.

Fifi—they worried more about Fifi, Titania and Giantia did. Fifi was their little sister, their tiny, cute, exquisitely beautiful sister. Fifi had been left in New York. Fifi was such a nitwitted little sweetykins, and they were bothered all the time they were in Siberian exile about how she would get along in big wicked New York. And they were still worrying about it.

It did look, though, as if they had troubles enough of their own.

Two months more, and they had surrendered themselves to all being dead in another month. But they didn't die.

Because they saw the Strange Blue Dome.

There was a fog, a low fog no more than twenty feet deep, and they could stand on the ice-breaker upper deck and look out over it. So they first saw only the top of the Strange Blue Dome.

"Blue whale off the bow!" the lookout squalled weakly.

Titania and Giantia galloped to the upper deck as if rushing on a vaudeville stage to bend iron bars and do handstands before an audience. Some of the others had to crawl—ten couldn't make it at all. John Sunlight came walking with slow, cold ominousness, like a devil in black, or a Frankenstein, or a Dracula. They shrank away from him, and did not forget to sink to their knees.

They looked at the Strange Blue Dome for a long time. And they became very puzzled. It was no whale, blue or otherwise.

It was no rock, either.

It was like nothing that should be. Its height must be all of a hundred feet, and there was a shimmering luminance to it that was eerie, even if they had not seen it standing, as if completely disembodied, above a gray carpet of fog. Generally, it resembled the perfectly spherical half of an opaque blue crystal ball—of incredible size, of course.

They stood and stared, breathing only when they had to.

The crushing of the ice-breaker brought them out of their awed trance. The ice-breaker hull caved in. Suddenly. There was no warning, just a great grinding and screaming of collapsing metal, a popping of pulled rivets, the feeble screams of the men who had been too weak to come on deck and were trapped.

"Get those men out!" John Sunlight ordered.

He did not want men to die. A dead man was a man he could not dominate.

Ten had been below decks. They got six out, but four had been crushed to death.

"Get the bodies out," John Sunlight directed, a spark of awful determination in the eyes that now burned like sparks in the hollows of his dark, poetic face.

They did it, shuddering all the while, for they knew what he meant. There had been no food for days and days, not even boiled shoes.

The ice was piling up against a stone island, and this had caused the ice-breaker to be crushed. They found that out soon.

The rocky island was as smooth as a great boulder, with no speck of soil anywhere, no chance of anything green growing. They crawled upon it in the fog, and it was more bleak and cold and inhospitable than they had believed anything could ever be, even after what they had been through.

They wanted to die, except for John Sunlight.

"Rest," he ordered. "Wait and rest."

He walked toward the Strange Blue Dome. It was now lost in the fog. John Sunlight went slowly, seeming to select and plan each step with care, for he was weaker than the others. He had taken less food than any of them, from the first, and the reason was that he did not want them to die. They were his, his toys, his tools, and he prized them as a carpenter values his best planes and saws, only infinitely more.

So he had given them most of his share of the food, to keep them alive, that he might dominate them. He was sustained now only by the power of the awful thing that was his mind.

This John Sunlight was a weird, terrible being.

At the outer edge of the bleak stone island—it seemed to be one great mass of solid gray rock—the wind had swept all snow away. But farther in, there was snow that got deeper, and was almost impassable to a man without snowshoes.

It was doubtful if a strong man of courage, well-fed, could have struggled through the snow to the side of the Strange Blue Dome.

But John Sunlight did so, and stood beside the fantastic thing and made a low growling sound.

Chapter 2
A MAN'S BLACK GHOST

It was still not too late, had Doc Savage known of John Sunlight. Doc Savage had the finest planes, and knowledge and courage and scientific skill. And he could have reached this arctic rock in time.

Doc Savage, combination of mental wizard, scientific genius, muscular phenomena, would not have been too late—yet.

For John Sunlight could find no way into the weird blue half ball. He looked first at the base of the thing, but the glasslike blue walls seemed to continue on down into the solid rock.

John Sunlight clawed at the glazed blue. It felt as hard and cold as steel. He put his face against it and tried to see through the blue substance, whatever it was. It seemed that he should be able to peer through it—the stuff had a certain transparent aspect. But he could see nothing.

Next, John Sunlight made a complete circle of the thing. He found no door, no window, no break of any kind.

The blue dome was not made of bricks, or even great blocks. It appeared to be one solid substance of a nature unknown. Not glass, and yet not metal either. Something mysterious.

It took a long time to satisfy John Sunlight that he could find no door.

He went back to the others.

"Get sledge hammers off the wrecked ice-breaker," he said coldly.

The sledge hammers were brought him. Titania and Giantia alone had the strength to fetch them.

John Sunlight took the heaviest sledge.

"Stay here." His eyes smoldered in the almost-black cups which his eye sockets had become. *"Stay here."*

He stood and gave each of them hypnotic attention in turn.

"None of you must ever go near that blue dome," he said with stark intensity.

He did not say what would happen if they disobeyed; did not voice a single threat. It was not his way to give physical threats; no one had ever heard him do so. Because it is easy to threaten a man's body, but difficult to explain how a terrible thing can happen to a mind. That kind of a threat would not sound convincing, or even anything but silly.

But they knew when they heard him. And he knew, too, that not one of them would go near the Strange Blue Dome. He had not exerted his hideous sway over them for months for nothing.

It took a longer time for John Sunlight to make his way back to the vast blue thing. He planted his feet wide, and raised the sledge hammer, and gathered all his great strength—his strength was more incredible than anyone could have imagined, even starved as he was—and hit the blue dome.

There was a single clear ringing note, as if a great bell had been tapped once, and the sound doubtless carried for miles, although it did not seem loud.

John Sunlight lowered the sledge hammer, examined the place where he had struck. He made his growling. It was a low and beastly growl, almost the only emotional sound he ever made. Too, the bestial growl was almost the only meaty, physical thing he ever did. Otherwise he seemed to be composed entirely of a frightful mind.

His sledge blow had not even nicked the mysterious blue substance of which the dome was composed.

John Sunlight hit again, again, and again——

He was still hitting when the Eskimo said something guttural.

It was a sinister indication of John Sunlight's mental control that he did not show surprise when the Eskimo grunted. He did not know what the Eskimo had said. He did not speak the Eskimo tongue. And an Eskimo was one of the last things he had expected to appear.

Particularly a well-fed, round butterball of an Eskimo with a happy smile, holding a large, frozen chunk of walrus meat.

John Sunlight smiled. He could smile when he wished.

"*How*, Eskimo," he said. "You fella savvy us fella plenty happy see you fella."

The Eskimo smiled from ear to ear.

Then he spoke in the best of English.

"How do you do," he said. "One of my brothers reported sighting you landing from a wrecked ship, and stated that he believed you were without food, so I brought you some walrus meat."

John Sunlight's bony, dark face did not change a particle. He was not a man who showed what he thought.

"You live close?" John Sunlight asked.

The Eskimo nodded and pointed.

"Over there, a few hundred yards," he said.

"How many Eskimos are in your camp?" inquired John Sunlight.

"An even dozen, including myself," replied the Eskimo.

John Sunlight leveled a rigid arm at the Strange Blue Dome.

"What is it?" he asked.

The Eskimo stared straight at the blue dome, and looked faintly puzzled.

"I do not see anything," he said.

John Sunlight gave a violent start—in spite of the fact that he rarely showed emotion. This was different. Insanity was the one thing he feared. Insanity—that would take away the incredible thing that was his mind.

He thought, for a horrible instant, that he was imagining all this; that no blue dome was there.

"You do not see a great blue dome?" John Sunlight asked tensely.

The Eskimo shook his head elaborately.

"I see nothing of the kind," he said.

John Sunlight took hold of his lip with teeth that were unnaturally huge and white, and gave him the aspect of a grinning skull when he showed them.

"What do you see?" he asked.

"Only snow," said the Eskimo calmly.

John Sunlight moved quickly then. He seized the Eskimo. The Eskimo was round and strong and well-fed, but he was no match for John Sunlight's mad strength.

John Sunlight hurled the Eskimo against the side of the blue dome. The Eskimo moaned and fell back to the snow, unconscious.

"That must have *felt* pretty hard, for something you couldn't *see*," John Sunlight snarled.

He then dragged the Eskimo back to the others, along with the large chunk of walrus meat. There was not enough walrus meat for everyone, so John Sunlight divided it among—not the weakest, this time—but the strongest. He wanted to make them stronger, so they could overcome the colony of Eskimos. They cooked up the walrus meat, and the weak sat back in shaking silence and watched the strong eat, although they were starving.

John Sunlight did not eat any himself. He was a strange man.

Meantime, the Eskimo regained consciousness. He rolled his little black grape eyes and said nothing.

He still had said nothing, even after John Sunlight had kicked in half of his ribs. He only lay silent, coughing a little scarlet when he could not help it.

The Eskimo had not even admitted that he could see the Strange Blue Dome.

They had saved rifles off the ice-breaker. They took those and went to capture the rest of the Eskimos.

The capture was easy enough. They merely walked in and presented the rifle snouts for the Eskimos' inspection, and the Eskimos, after first laughing heartily as if they thought it was one huge joke, realized it wasn't, and became silent and beady-eyed with wonder.

There were four igloos, very large and fashioned with picture-book perfection from blocks of frozen snow. Each igloo had a long tunnel for an entrance, and along these tunnels were smaller igloos used to store food. There were also other very small igloos scattered around, in which the dogs slept. There were not many dogs.

"What is that blue dome?" John Sunlight asked.

They stared at him wonderingly. "What blue dome?"

"Don't you *see* it?"

"No."

The Eskimos all talked like that, and it made John Sunlight more gaunt and grim, until finally, to satisfy himself of his own rationality, he broke down his order that no white person but himself should go near the Strange Blue Dome. He took Civan and Giantia and Titania and some of the others to the dome and made them feel of it, made them kick the sledge hammer out of the snow, pick it up and each strike a great ringing blow on the mysterious sides of the dome.

"You *see* it?" John Sunlight asked. "You *feel* it?"

"Dah, soodar," Civan said.

"Yes, sir," said Titania and Giantia, which was the same thing, only in English, not Russian.

John Sunlight thereafter felt much better, although there was no visible change in him. He knew now that he wasn't demented, or seeing something that wasn't there.

Two things were now possible: One, the Eskimos were lying for a reason; two, they were hypnotized. John Sunlight knew something of hypnotism, knew more than it was good for any man of his kind to know, and he soon satisfied himself the Eskimos were not hypnotized.

So the Eskimos were lying. Not lying—just not admitting anything. John Sunlight began breaking them, and he found that breaking an Eskimo was not as easy as doing the same thing to a white man or woman. The Eskimos had lived amid physical peril all their lives; their minds did not get afraid easily.

The Eskimos got no more food. Fuel for their blubber lamps was taken from them. So was their clothing, except for bearskin pants. Naturally, John Sunlight seized their weapons.

Six weeks passed. John Sunlight, all those off the ice-breaker, fared well, grew fat.

The Eskimos kept fat, too.

That was mysterious. It worried John Sunlight. The Eskimos got nothing to eat and thrived on it.

It was a human impossibility, and John Sunlight did not believe in magic. He wondered about it, and watched the Eskimos secretly, watched them a lot more than anyone imagined.

His spare time John Sunlight spent trying to get into the Strange Blue Dome. He swung the sledge hammer against the blue stuff for hours, and bored away with steel drills off the ice-breaker, and shot a lot of steel-jacketed, high-powered rifle bullets against the mysterious material. The results—well, he would have had better luck with a bank vault.

The Strange Blue Dome became a fabulously absorbing mystery to John Sunlight. He kept on, with almost demoniac persistence, trying to get into the thing.

If it had not been for the Eskimos staying so fat, he might never have succeeded.

One night an Eskimo crawled out of an igloo and faded away in the darkness. It was not really dark all the time, this being the six-month arctic night, but they called it night anyway, because it was time time when they slept.

The Eskimos had been making a fool of John Sunlight.

He had watched them days and days. They were eating; they must get food somewhere. He had not seen them get it, and the reason was simple—a long robe of white arctic rabbit. When an Eskimo crawled away, the white rabbit robe made him unnoticeable against the snow.

This time, the Eskimo accidentally got a brown hand out of the robe.

John Sunlight followed the Eskimo.

He watched the Eskimo go to the Strange Blue Dome, stand close beside it; saw a great portal swing open in the dome and watched the Eskimo step inside, to come out later with an armload of something. The blue portal closed behind the Eskimo.

John Sunlight caught the Eskimo, clubbed him senseless. The stuff the Eskimo was carrying looked like sassafras bark—food. Compressed, dehydrated food, no doubt of that. But strange food, such as John Sunlight had never heard of upon this earth.

John Sunlight stood thinking for a long time. He took the Eskimo's white rabbit-skin robe. He put it on. He stood against the blue dome where the Eskimo had stood.

And the portal opened.

John Sunlight walked into the mysterious Blue Dome.

It was now almost too late for Doc Savage, even had he known of John Sunlight, to prevent what was written on the pages of the book of fate.

John Sunlight vanished.

For a day, two days, a week, he was not heard of. Not for two weeks.

On the second week, he was still not heard of; but something incredible happened. Titania, Giantia, Civan, and some of the others saw an Eskimo turn into a black ghost.

The Eskimo who became a black ghost was the one who had vanished when John Sunlight disappeared and had not been seen or heard from, either.

It was night. That is, it was darker night, because there were clouds. Titania, Giantia, Civan and the others were wondering what they would do for food now that the supply taken from the Eskimo was running low, and they were standing on a small drift and discussing it, when they saw the Eskimo running toward them.

Screaming made them notice the Eskimo. He was shrieking —screeching and running. He came toward them.

Suddenly, the Eskimo stopped. He stood facing them, his arms fixed rigidly in a reaching-out-toward-them gesture. His mouth gaped a hole. Incredibly still, he stood. He might have been an old copper statue which was greased.

The next instant, he might have been made of black soot. The change occurred instantaneously. One instant, a copper man; the next, a black one.

Then smoke. Black smoke. Flying. Coming apart, swirling away in cold arctic wind; spreading, fading, going mysteriously into nothingness.

There was no question about it. The Eskimo had turned into a black smoke ghost, and the smoke had blown away.

Now it was too late for Doc Savage. And John Sunlight had not forgotten the score he had to settle with Serge Mafnoff.

Chapter 3
IS A DIPLOMAT DEAD?

Serge Mafnoff was an idealistic man, a fine citizen of the Soviet, and ambitious—all of these facts his superiors in the Russian government recognized. They kept a kindly eye on Serge Mafnoff, and shortly after he did his fine stroke of work by catching John Sunlight and sending him to Siberia, a reward was forthcoming.

Serge Mafnoff's reward was being appointed as an important diplomatic representative to the United States of America, with headquarters in New York City. It was a pleasant job, one an ambitious man would like; and Serge Mafnoff enjoyed it, and worked zealously, and his superiors smiled and nodded and remarked that here was a man who was worth promoting still again. Serge Mafnoff was very happy in New York City.

Then one evening he ran home in terror.

Actually ran. Dashed madly to the door of his uptown mansion, pitched inside, slammed the door. And stood with all his weight jammed against the door, as if holding it shut against something that pursued him.

His servants remarked on the way he panted while he was doing that. They told the police, later, how he had panted with a great sobbing fright.

It was interesting. And Serge Mafnoff had servants who liked to gossip. They gathered in the chauffeur's quarters over the garage, the most private place, and discussed it. They were concerned, too. They liked Serge Mafnoff.

Everyone liked Serge Mafnoff. He was quite a newspaper figure. A fine representative of the type and character of man the Soviet is trying to create, he was called.

Liking Serge Mafnoff made what happened that night infinitely more horrible to the servants.

The house of Serge Mafnoff in New York City was one long popular with residing diplomats, because it had an impressive dignity and a fashionable location and other things that were desirable for a diplomat.

It was made of gray stone and sat, unlike most New York houses, in quite a considerable yard of its own in which there was neatly tended shrubbery. There were two gates. From one gate a driveway led around to the rear, where there was plenty of lawn and landscaped shrubbery and the two-car garage with the chauffeur's quarters above.

The other gate admitted to a walk which led straight to the mansion door. The house itself was generally square; had two stories and an attic, part of which Serge Mafnoff had walled off and air-conditioned for his private study. Behind the house was a sloping park which slanted down, unbroken except for two boulevards, to the wide, teeming Hudson River and the inspiring Palisades beyond.

Serge Mafnoff screamed in his study.

Every servant in the great mansion heard the shriek, and each one of them jumped violently.

The cook cut the forefinger of her left hand to the bone with the butcher knife, so great was her start. The finger leaked a thread of crimson for some time thereafter—which turned out to be important.

The scream brought all the servants running upstairs. They piled into the study. They stopped. It was impossible to believe their eyes.

Impossible to comprehend that Serge Mafnoff could have become a black man.

Serge Mafnoff was all black. Not only his skin, his fingernails, his eyes, his teeth—his mouth was open in the most awful kind of a strangling grimace. All black. That evening he had put on pants and vest of a gray suit, and a robe the nationalistic red color of the Soviet: but these were now the hue of drawing ink.

A jet-black statue, standing.

The butler moaned. The chauffeur made a croaking noise. The cook's hand shook, and her cut finger showered red drops over the floor.

"Comrade Mafnoff!" shrieked the maid, who was a Communist.

The black statue turned to a writhing black ghost. Or so it

seemed to the servants. The whole man—they knew it was Serge Mafnoff, because the features of the all-black statue had been recognizable as his—appeared to turn into a cloud of sepia vapor.

A black ghost, it was like. It swirled and changed shape a little, then came swaying toward them, a ghostly, disembodied, unreal monstrosity.

Straight toward them, it floated.

The cook screeched and threw more crimson over the walls and floor. But the chauffeur snatched a pair of heavy pliers out of his hip pocket and hurled them at the black horror.

The pliers went through the thing and dented the plaster of the opposite wall.

Then, suddenly, impossibly, and before their eyes, the black thing silently vanished. It did not spread; it seemed to fade, disintegrate, go into nothingness.

"I killed it!" the chauffeur screamed.

Then the only sound in the room, for long moments, was the frightened rattling of the breath in their throats. The cook's hand dripped.

They were looking for some trace of Serge Mafnoff. Hurting their eyes with looking. And seeing nothing.

"I—I couldn't—have killed him," the chauffeur croaked.

"Ugh!" the butler said.

They were all primed for the next shriek. It came from downstairs, a man's voice in a long peal of imperative supplication and terror.

The cook barked out something hoarse, and fainted. She fell directly in the center of the door, just inside the attic den which was Serge Mafnoff's study.

The other servants left her lying there and raced downstairs to find out who had given that last scream, and what about.

There was a second bellow, just about the time all the servants, excepting the unconscious cook, reached the ground floor. This whoop was out in the back yard, and the whole neighborhood heard it.

Out into the back yard dashed the servants to investigate. They didn't know what they expected to find. Certainly it wasn't what they did find. Which was nothing.

Nothing at all. Only dark, cold night, and the gloomy clumps of shrubbery, which was evergreen and hence unaffected by the fact that the time was winter. Crouching black wads of bushes, and the sounds of the city—honking of automobile horns, a distant elevated, and the bawling of a steamship down on the Hudson.

They searched and searched.

Then they told the police about it. The police told the newspapers, who printed a great deal about the affair.

Doc Savage read the newspapers regularly.

Chapter 4
BRONZE MAN ATTACKED

Not everybody in the world had heard of Doc Savage.

But too many had. Doc Savage—Clark Savage, Jr.—had of late been trying to evade further publicity, and he had an understanding, finally, with the newspaper press associations, with some of the larger newspapers, and with most of the fact-story magazines extant. They weren't to print anything about him. They were to leave his name out of their headlines.

Now, if anyone heard of Doc Savage, it would be by word-of-mouth only. "Haven't you heard—Doc Savage has invented a cure for cancer, they say." The surgical and medical skill of Doc Savage was probably his greatest ability. "I hear that new wrestler from Czechoslovakia is a human Hercules, built something along the lines of Doc Savage."

The physical build of Doc Savage got attention wherever he appeared, for he was a giant, although so well proportioned that, seen from a distance, he resembled a man of ordinary proportions.

Talk, talk—there was always plenty of talk about Doc Savage. "I hear the Man of Bronze has invented an atom motor that could drive the *Queen Mary* across the Atlantic with a spoonful of coal." They called him the "Man of Bronze" because of the unusually deep-tan hue which tropical suns had given his skin. They—their talk—attributed fantastic inventions to him. Conversation made him a superman, a mental colossus.

Really, Doc Savage was a normal fellow who had been taken

over by scientists as a child and trained until early manhood, so that he was rather unusual but still human enough. He had missed the play-life of normal children, and so he was probably more subdued, conscious that he hadn't gotten everything out of life.

Talk, talk—it attributed all kinds of fantastic doings and powers to Doc Savage.

But it was only talk. Nobody, for instance, listening to it, could find out exactly where Doc Savage was at a given time. No enemy could listen to the gossip and get enough real information to lay a plan to kill the Man of Bronze.

His enemies were many. They had to be. Because his life work was an unusual one. That was why he had been scientifically trained; he had been prepared from childhood, in every possible way, to follow a career of righting wrongs and punishing evildoers, even in the far corners of the earth.

A strange career—his father's idea. His father who was no longer living. His father had located a fabulous source of gold in the Central American mountains, realized such a wealth should do good, and had trained his son, Clark Savage, Jr.—Doc Savage—to use the wealth to do good. Also to use it to right wrongs.

This was the real Doc Savage, who found it safer not to be too well-known.

Doc read the newspaper account of what had happened to Serge Mafnoff. The bronze man often spotted unusual wrongs that could stand righting, from reading the newspapers.

Doc Savage did not know, as yet, about the man waiting in the lobby downstairs, or the other men looking at books in a near-by bookstall.

Doc Savage was impressed by the Mafnoff thing.

He was so impressed that he did something which he only did in moments of great mental or physical stress; he made a strange, exotic trilling sound, a note that was created somehow in the throat, and which had a low quality of ventriloquism that made its vibrations seem to suffuse the entire surrounding atmosphere. The sound was often described as being as eerie as the song of some rare bird in a tropical jungle, or like the noise of a wind through an arctic ice wilderness.

There was nothing spooky or supernatural about this sound. Doc had acquired it as a habit in the Orient, where the Oriental wise men sometimes make such a sound deep in the throat—for the same reason, approximately, that the rest of us say, "Oh-h-h, I see. I see, I see-e-e," when understanding dawns.

Doc Savage had been seated at a great inlaid table in his reception room. He stood up quickly. Through the windows—this was the eighty-sixth floor of one of the city's tallest buildings—an inspiring view of Manhattan was visible.

Doc passed through a huge library crammed with scientific tomes, and entered a laboratory so advanced that scientists frequently came from abroad to study it. The bronze man picked up a microphone.

"In case you wish to get in touch with me," he said into the mike, "it is my intention to investigate the Serge Mafnoff story which is on the front pages of the newspapers this morning."

What he said was automatically recorded, could be played back at will. It also went out on the short-wave radio transmitter.

Doc Savage had five assistants in his strange work. Each of the assistants kept a short-wave radio tuned in on Doc's transmitter wave-length as much as possible.

The bronze man then rode his private speed elevator to the lobby.

He was instantly noticeable when he stepped out in the lobby. Not only because of his size. There was something compelling about his carriage, and also about his unusual flake gold eyes —calm eyes, fascinating, like pools of flake gold being continuously stirred.

The man waiting in the lobby noticed Doc instantly. The man had been loitering there for hours. He was a short man, blond, with a face that looked somehow starved. His story was that he was a process server lying in ambush for one of the skyscraper tenants. When he told that, he spoke with a pronounced Russian accent.

The instant he saw Doc Savage, this man stepped outside, hurried a dozen paces to the door of a small bookstore, entered —and walked right out again.

Several men who had been pretending to browse over books in the store, followed him. These men began getting in taxicabs.

Taxicabs always waited in a long string before the skyscraper, because it was a good stand. The bookstore loiterers took the first four cabs, and these pulled away from the curb. This left the fifth cab in the line as the next one up.

The fifth cab was the one they wanted Doc Savage to take. Driving this machine was a vicious-looking, black ox of a man.

Doc Savage had walked out of the building by now.

Having accomplished the job to which they had been assigned, the bookstore browsers and the fellow who had claimed to be a process server strolled away.

Doc got in the planted cab.

"Drive to the Hudson River water front," the bronze man directed quietly.

He had a voice which gave the impression of being infinitely controlled, a voice that could do some remarkable things if necessary.

The cab rolled among the high buildings, passed through the less presentable West Side tenement section, and neared the rumblingly busy street which ran along the Hudson. Here, it stopped for a traffic light.

The window between driver and passenger was open.

Doc Savage reached through this. He took the black oxlike man by the neck.

"That was an ambitious trick you tried to pull," the bronze man said quietly.

He squeezed the neck, trained fingers finding the proper nerve centers. The black ox fellow kicked around violently just before he became senseless.

Doc Savage got behind the wheel, shoving the unconscious passenger over to make room. He kept a sharp lookout around about while doing this, but saw no sign of more trouble. No cars following. As an afterthought, he got out and examined the taxicab.

The bronze man's powers of observation had been trained from childhood, and he still took almost two hours of complicated exercises each day, aimed at developing his faculties.

He had to notice little things—like a man wheeling suddenly and walking from a skyscraper lobby when the bronze man got out of an elevator—if he wanted to go on living.

He saw, under the cab floor, lashed to the chassis, a thick steel pipe which was closed at both ends.

Doc snatched the unconscious man out of the cab, carried him, and ran away from the machine. This was a one-way street. He kept in the middle, so as to stop any cars that might enter. But it was a little-used street, and no cars came.

He waited.

The explosion was terrific. Doc stood at a distance from the cab, but the blast jarred him off his feet anyway.

The cab came apart, flew up in the air, some of the parts going so high that they became small. A deep hole opened in the street itself. Fragments of pavement went bounding along the street. After the first slam of the concussion, there was a ringing of broken glass falling from windows all over the neighborhood.

Doc Savage went away from there in a hurry with his prisoner. He had a high honorary commission in the New York police force, but there was nothing in it that said he didn't have to answer questions.

It was obvious, of course, that the bomb under the cab was attached to a time-firing device which was probably switched on when the driver took his weight off the cushions.

No doubt the idea had been for the driver to stop somewhere and go in a store to get something, leaving Doc in the cab to be blown up.

Doc Savage carried the captive around the block, north two blocks along the Hudson water front, and reached a warehouse. The sign on this warehouse said:

HIDALGO TRADING COMPANY

It was an enormous brick building which appeared not to have been used for years. It was Doc Savage's Hudson River hangar and boathouse.

Doc carried the captive into the warehouse, closed the doors, put the man down on the floor and did things with his metallic fingers to the man's spinal nerve centers. The pressure which was keeping the fellow helpless could be relieved by these chiropractic manipulations.

Doc went through the man's clothing while he was reviving, found nothing except a flat automatic pistol. The dark ox of a fellow sat up. He batted lids over eyes that resembled peeled, hard-boiled pigeon eggs.

"Didn't I come to the end of the chain with a bang?" he muttered.

That was the first warning. In the case of this man, it was either one of two things: He was too stupid to be scared; or he had a brain that could control his nerves and make him wisecrack under circumstances such as this.

"Who are you?" Doc Savage asked calmly.

The man did not answer at once. He stared at the bronze man steadily. When he did speak, it was not to answer the question.

"They say no one has ever fought you successfully," he said slowly. "I begin to believe that—looking at you now."

Doc noticed the man's rather strong Russian accent.

"Atkooda vy pree-shlee?" Doc asked.

"Yes. I don't doubt that you would like to know where I come from," the man said. "But let's speak English."

He frowned at the giant bronze man, and could not keep a flicker of terror from his eyes. "You spoke that Russian with no accent at all," he muttered. "They say you can talk any language in the world."

Doc said, "We are not discussing what you have heard. The subject is—why did you try to kill me?"

The man shook his dark oxlike head. "We're discussing," he said, "whether I had better talk—or tough it out."

"Talk," Doc said.

"Threatening me?"

"No." Doc said quietly. "It is becoming apparent that you are not the type of man who can be frightened readily."

The remark—it was merely a statement of truth as far as Doc Savage was concerned—seemed to shock the prisoner. His big white teeth set in his lips, and unexpected horror jumped briefly into his eyes.

"You don't know John Sunlight," he croaked.

Doc watched him. "John Sunlight?"

The man swallowed several times and forced the terror out of his eyes.

"No, no—you misunderstood me," he said. "I said: 'You don't know, *so you lie.*' What I meant is that you are trying to kid me along, telling me I'm brave. It's a build-up."

Doc said, "Why did you——" and the man hit him. The fellow hit hard, and he was strong. But the bronze man got his shoulder up, and the fist hit that instead of his jaw. Then he fell on the man. They stormed around on the floor; the man began to scream in agony.

"Why did you try to kill me?" Doc repeated.

"My name is Civan," the man began.

Civan sat up on the floor, inched back a few feet from Doc Savage, and felt over his bruises, wincing as his fingers touched the places that hurt. Two or three times he peered at the bronze man, as though puzzled and trying to fathom where such incredible strength came from.

"I was the strongest man in my part of Russia," Civan said stupidly.

Doc said, "Why try to kill me?"

"The man with the long nose hired me to do it," Civan said.

"Who?"

"Eli Camel was the name he gave me," Civan said. "He was a tall man, bowlegged, as if he had ridden horses in his youth. He had a high forehead, a mouth with no lips. And there was his nose, of course. It was very long, and kind of loose on the end, like an anteater's nose."

Doc Savage had never heard of an Eli Camel who had a long nose. But then, he had never heard of many men who might want to kill him.

Voice unchanged, Doc said, "What did this Eli Camel want to kill me for?"

"He did not say," Civan said. "He just gave me twenty thousand dollars, and I agreed to get rid of you. Then he sailed for South America yesterday."

"What about those other men—the ones who saw to it that I took your taxicab?"

"I hired them."

"Who are they?"

Civan shook his head. "I won't tell you. They're not important. They're just men I hired to help me."

Doc Savage did not pursue that point.

"Eli Camel of the long nose, sailed for South America, you say?" Doc asked.

"Yesterday."

"What boat?"

"The *Amazon Maid*."

"That is all you know?" Doc asked.

"That's all."

Doc Savage went to the telephone. He knew there was a steamer on the South American run named the *Amazon Maid;* he knew what line owned her. He called their offices. When he explained who he was, he got service without delay.

"Yes," the steamship line official told him. "A man named Eli Camel sailed yesterday on the steamer *Amazon Maid* for South America."

"Radio the captain of the *Amazon Maid*," Doc Savage directed, "and learn if the sea is calm enough for me to land a seaplane alongside his vessel and be taken aboard."

"We'll do that."

"I'll call you for the information later," Doc said.

Civan stared at the bronze man. "You're going after Eli Camel?" Civan demanded.

"What does it sound like?" Doc asked quietly.

Doc Savage went next to a shortwave radio transmitter-receiver outfit—he had them scattered around at almost every convenient point, for himself and his associates used that means of communicating almost exclusively.

"Monk," Doc said into the microphone.

The answer came in a squeaky voice that might have belonged to a child or a midget.

"Yeah, Doc," it said.

Doc Savage spoke rapidly and in a calm voice, using remarkably few words to tell exactly what had happened, and to give Monk instructions.

"Hold on!" Monk squeaked. "Let me get this straight. You started out to investigate this Serge Mafnoff mystery?"

"Yes."

"And this guy Civan tried to kill you, and you've caught him, and he's in the warehouse hangar now, and you want me and Ham and Johnny to drop by and pick him up?"

"Exactly."

"Doc, do you think there's a connection between the Mafnoff thing and this attempt on your life?"

Doc Savage did not answer the question. That was one of the bronze man's peculiar habits—when he did not want to reply directly to a query, he simply acted as though no question had been asked.

"Pick up this Civan," Doc said, "then go on out and investigate the Mafnoff mystery."

"Um-m-m," Monk said. "Where'll you be, Doc?"

At that point, the other telephone—there were several lines into the place—rang, and Doc said, "A moment, Monk," and answered the other instrument, listened for a time, said an agreeable, "Thank you," and hung up.

"Monk," the bronze man said, "the line that owns the *Amazon Maid* just called and said the sea was calm enough for a plane to land alongside the steamer and be lifted aboard with a cargo boom."

"Oh!" Monk said. "So that's where you're going—to get that Eli Camel who hired this Civan."

Doc asked, "You will be here shortly, Monk?"

"Shorter than short," Monk said.

This terminated the radio conversation.

Doc Savage tied Civan securely with rope and left him lying in the middle of the hangar floor, lashed to a ring embedded in the concrete.

The bronze man walked to a seaplane. A number of aircraft stood in the hangar, including a small dirigible, but the ship he selected now was small, sturdy, and designed for landing on bad water, rather than for speed or maneuverability in the air.

He started the plane motor, taxied out on the river, fed the cylinders gas. The craft got up on the step, lifted into the air and went droning away and lost itself in the haze over the Atlantic Ocean.

Civan lay on the hangar floor and swore long strings of very bad Russian words.

Chapter 5
THE UNWILLING IDOL

Men do things because of love. Always. Without exception.

Some men love to work, so they work; others love the things money will buy, so they work to get the money. There are men who love to loaf, and loaf. Slaves did not love to be beaten, so they worked in order that they wouldn't get beatings.

Doc Savage's five assistants loved excitement and adventure, and that bound them to the bronze man.

"Monk" particularly. Monk's looks were deceptive. He was one of the world's greatest industrial chemists when he took time off from his adventuring to putter around with test tubes and retorts. He looked rather like something that had been dragged out of a jungle tree recently. Startling near as wide as he was tall, with arms longer than his legs, too much mouth, small eyes, a furry, coarse reddish hair, he looked like a large ape.

"You look," said Ham, "like something an expedition brought back."

"It don't worry me," Monk grinned.

"I'll bet it worried your mother," Ham grinned.

"Ham" was Brigadier General Theodore Marley Brooks, who practically supported the fanciest tailor in the city with his patronage, who carried an innocent-looking black cane which was really a sword-cane, and who was also admittedly one of the cleverest lawyers to come from Harvard.

"Listen," Monk said, "you keep on ridin' me, and I'll take you by the neck and shake a writ, a petition and a couple of torts out of you."

"Any time"—Ham glared—"you gossoon!"

If these two had ever spoken a civil word to each other, it was an accident.

They drove past Radio City, and picked up Major Thomas J. "Long Tom" Roberts, who had been hired as consultant on an intricate problem having to do with television. They found a group of eminent electrical engineers staring at Long Tom Roberts in amazement.

No one would stare at Long Tom because of his looks. He was a scrawny fellow with complexion ranging between that of a fish belly and an uncooked mushroom. So they must be admiring his brains. They were. Long Tom had just pulled an electrical rabbit out of a hat.

Monk, Ham and Long Tom arrived at the warehouse on the Hudson water front, drove their car inside, got out and listened in amazement to Civan's swearing. None of them understood Russian. But they could tell that Civan was doing some very good work with words that were unlikely to be in the Russian dictionaries.

When Civan ran dry, they read a newspaper account of how

Serge Mafnoff, the diplomat, had apparently turned into a black ghost and vanished.

"Very mysterious," Long Tom commented.

"I believe I'm going to like looking into it," Ham remarked.

"Then I won't like it," Monk said contrarily.

First, they settled the question of what to do with Civan.

"Drown him," Monk suggested. "Tie Ham to him for a weight. Throw 'em in the river."

"That's very funny," Ham sneered. "I'll bet I come nearer solving this mystery than you do."

"You see what I mean," Monk told Long Tom. "Ham's opinion of himself is heavy enough to hold them both under water."

They compromised by taking a hypodermic needle from an equipment case in the warehouse hangar, and injecting a harmless chemical concoction in both of Civan's legs and both his arms. They waited several minutes until the chemical took effect.

Thereafter, Civan could not move his arms or legs. He could only talk, and he did so, giving detailed opinions of them. Monk picked Civan up and sat him in various places, and Civan remained there; he could not stir. He sat stiffly, resembling an ugly image made out of dark meat.

"Kind of like an unwilling idol," Monk commented. "Only a little noisy."

They loaded Civan in their car and drove uptown to the home of Serge Mafnoff, vanished diplomat. Their credentials got them through the ring of police guards around the place.

"How much have you learned?" they asked the police.

"Are you gonna start that, too?" the cop demanded sourly.

"Then we are to take it you're mystified?"

"Look around," the cop invited. "We're always willing to learn. We'll watch."

They questioned the servants. They got a bloodcurdling, hair-curling description of the black ghost which Serge Mafnoff had become. Nothing else.

They pulled on rubber shoes and entered the attic study where the mystery had happened. The room was about thirty feet long, a little over half as wide, with a large gable window at each end, and small doors on each side. These doors admitted to the unused part of the attic, windowless and dark.

"There's been rats and mice running around here." Monk poked a flashlight beam over the rafters and sills in the unused part of the attic. "You can see their tracks in the dust."

"Yes," the cop said. "We found mouse and rat tracks, too."

"Your tone," Monk said sourly, "insinuates that I'm not gonna find anything you haven't."

The cop grinned. "I've always heard Monk Mayfair was a whiz," he said. "I'm waiting around to see a whiz working."

Monk did nothing to justify the cop's expectations in the attic study. In fact, they succeeded in confusing the issue a trifle. This happened when Monk put the pliers—the same pliers the chauffeur had thrown through the black ghost of Serge Mafnoff—under a microscope.

"Huh!" Monk squinted at the pliers. "That's strange." He took a file and rasped a nick in the pliers, then looked through the microscope at them again. "Yep," he decided. "I was right."

"Right about what?" Long Tom asked.

"The metal of these pliers," Monk said, "is strangely crystallized."

The cop said, "What do you mean—crystallized?"

Monk addressed the chauffeur, asking, "Have you been in the habit of using these pliers regularly?"

"Sure," the chauffeur said. "They're my favorite pliers."

"Do any hammering with 'em?" Monk inquired.

"Of course."

"Look," Monk said.

He tapped the pliers with his file, and they broke into several pieces. It was as though they were as brittle as glass.

"Why, that's funny!" the chauffeur gulped.

They turned up nothing else in the attic study, so they shifted attention to the scream which had been heard behind the house. First, they gave the back yard and the alley a thorough search. But all they got out of this was a good deal of exercise at squatting and peering.

"Blast it!" Monk complained.

The cop said, "I'm still waitin' for you guys to do somethin' to live up to your reputations."

When they stood inside the house later, and the cop was not with them, Monk confided to Ham, "That cop is gettin' in my hair, goin' around makin' cracks. He's beginnin' to think I'm stupid."

"The cop probably can't help it," Ham said, "after looking at you?"

"I'm gonna show 'im up!" Monk squeaked. "He can't make a monkey out of me!"

"If he'd put you in a tree," Ham said unkindly, "I'd hate to try to tell the difference."

Monk grumbled, and stalked around peering in unlikely places for clues. He was in the kitchen when the cop came up to him.

"Look," the cop said, "I'm gonna have to help you out a little, whiz."

"You don't need to bother———"

"We found this," the cop interrupted, "in the back yard."

The article the policeman presented was a novelty pencil, a combination of pencil and tiny flashlight, and the clip which was designed to hold it in the pocket had been broken off close to the barrel. The clip had not come unsoldered; it had broken off.

"None of Serge Mafnoff's servants admit owning this," the cop explained. "And it didn't belong to Mafnoff."

Monk took the pencil with bad grace. "I'll examine it for fingerprints."

"We've already done that," the cop said, "and found none."

"I'll do it scientifically," Monk said.

Monk had little confidence in the pencil as a clue; he carried it carelessly as he went back and joined the others, and he was thoroughly astounded when Civan gave a violent croak, pointed his popping eyes at the pencil.

They had set Civan on the floor, where he'd remained helpless, but occasionally quite noisy.

"That pencil!" Civan ejaculated. "Where did you find it?"

"The cops found it in the back yard," Monk replied. "What about it?"

Civan said, "If I wasn't in this too deep to help myself, I wouldn't tell you. But I saw Eli Camel with a pencil something like that. Hold it closer."

"Eli Camel was the man who hired you to kill Doc, eh?" Monk asked, and held the pencil close to Civan's eyes.

"Yes," Civan said. "That's Eli Camel's pencil."

Monk exploded, "Then Eli Camel was probably the man who screamed in the back yard here."

"Right," Civan agreed. "And now he's on the steamer *Amazon Maid* bound for South America."

Monk squatted in front of Civan and asked the man quite a number of questions, but added nothing to the plain fact that

Civan knew this pencil had belonged to Eli Camel, the mysterious man with the long nose.

Monk was much pleased; he permitted himself to gloat. "Now I'll show that cop I'm not as dumb as I look," he chortled. He went looking for the cop.

Monk found the cop gaping in admiration at Ham.

Ham was saying, "The man you want is named Eli Camel. He is tall, bowlegged, has a high forehead, a long nose. And he is on the steamer *Amazon Maid* headed for South America."

"You learned all that?" the cop gasped.

"You bet," Ham said.

"Amazing!" the cop exclaimed delightedly.

The cop then looked at Monk and sniffed.

"If you had lived up to your reputation, short-and-hairy," he said, "you'd have dug up something important, like Mr. Ham Brooks, here."

Monk glared at Ham.

"Glory hog!" Monk howled. "You knew I was tryin' to impress this cop!"

This was the beginning of a wrangle of some duration between Monk and Ham.

Seven other policemen were guarding the Serge Mafnoff diplomatic residence, the guarding consisting of turning back curious people who had read the newspaper stories and wanted to have a look at the house, and possibly play amateur detective.

Two officers stood at one end of the street, two at the other end; one was stationed at the northern extremity of the alley, one at the southern extremity, and the seventh watchman roved over the grounds.

They were surprised when two large touring cars rolled up, stopped, and a group of men alighted. The newcomers wore plain blue suits, and had rather grim faces. Their spokesman confronted the cops.

"We're special plain-clothes men from the district attorney's office," he growled. "We're to take over here."

"But——"

"The D. A. isn't satisfied with the progress you've been making on this," the newcomer snapped.

There was never a great deal of love lost between the regular police and special detective squads. In this case, the uniformed cops were secretly enthusiastic about the idea of turning the Serge

Mafnoff case over to specials. They were glad to pass the buck. The case was a lemon, utterly baffling.

"Luck be with you," the uniformed cops said, and betook themselves away.

The leader of the "special plainclothes men from the district attorney's office" beckoned his men together. His whisper was a hasty hissing.

"Them cops will find out we lied to 'em," he said. "We've got to move fast."

"Can't move too fast to suit me," a man muttered.

"Get Civan," the leader snapped. "Rescue him. That's the most important. Then wipe out these three Doc Savage aids."

"Rescue Civan," a man repeated, "then croak the Savage helpers."

Now that they all understood, they separated, quickly taking up positions at various points around the grounds of the Serge Mafnoff residence.

Inside the house, Monk was still lambasting the dapper lawyer, Ham, but the homely chemist was beginning to run out of breath.

"You know what a lawyer is?" Monk yelled.

"I'm not interested," Ham said.

"A lawyer," Monk roared, "is a guy who persuades his client to strip for a fight, then runs off with the client's clothes!"

Monk always bellowed when he got excited. Normally, his voice was a mouse among voices, but when he became agitated, or got in a fight, his howling was something remarkable.

Monk stopped for breath.

And all light disappeared.

Chapter 6
THE GRIM BLACK WORLD

All light disappeared. Nothing else quite described it, although it might have been said that the Serge Mafnoff house and its immediate surroundings abruptly and inexplicably became trapped in intense blackness. One moment it was a sunlight day, moderately bright; the next instant everything was blacker than black.

Ham's first thought was that Monk had hauled off and knocked him cold, and that the blackness was unconsciousness.

"You hairy hooligan!" he yelled.

He heard his own voice, so he knew he wasn't senseless.

"Has something grabbed you?" Monk demanded.

"Shut up," Ham said, embarrassed. "Can you see anything?"

"No." Monk said. "That is, I can see black."

They could all see black, and nothing else. They lifted their hands before their eyes, and discerned not the slightest vestige of their presence. Their first involuntary impulse was to try to feel of the blackness, for it was so intense that it seemed solid; but it wasn't, for their fingers touched nothing more tangible than air.

Then their eyes began stinging.

"It's some kind of black gas!" yelled Long Tom, the electrical wizard.

But that was wrong, because they smelled nothing and tasted nothing.

Monk let out a frightened howl. He had remembered something —remembered the way they had been told that Serge Mafnoff had turned into a black ghost of a figure.

"Maybe we've turned into them black ghosts!" Monk shouted.

The terror of that held them spellbound—until Civan laughed. It was an ugly, delighted, much-relieved laugh that tore across Civan's lips.

That laugh was the wrong thing for Civan to do. Probably he couldn't help it. But it shocked Monk, Ham and Long Tom back to a grip on common sense.

"Grab that guy!" Long Tom yelled.

Monk sprang upon Civan. "I got 'im!"

Ham said, "We better lock the door. I don't know what this is about, but I——"

Ham never would have spoken another word, then, except that he wore a bulletproof undergarment of alloy chain mesh. Doc Savage and all his men wore them habitually, for they were light enough not to be uncomfortable. They were also knifeproof.

A knife blade struck Ham's chest, skidded on the chain mesh, ruining his expensive coat and vest. Ham grabbed the knife-wielder's wrist, held it tightly, twisted and turned. An arm broke. The attacker started screaming, and kept screaming almost continuously.

Fighting was suddenly all through the room. Fist blows, the *gr-r-it!* of knife blades striking chain mail, and shots. The shots were deafening.

A voice crashed out in Mayan.

"Gas masks," it ordered. "Put them on!"

It was Doc Savage's voice. Mayan was the little-known language which Doc and his men spoke—almost no one in the civilized world spoke it besides themselves—when they wished to communicate without being understood.

There was no time to be astonished that Doc Savage had turned up in the middle of this weird, black mêlée. He had a habit of appearing unexpectedly, anyway.

The gas masks they carried were simple: Gas-tight goggles, spring-wire nose clips, and breath filters something like over-grown police whistles, which they held in their mouths. They were effective enough, providing you didn't snort off a nose clip, or get a filter knocked out of your mouth or down your throat. The goggles were nonshatterable, however.

Doc Savage called, "Where is Civan?" in Mayan.

Monk took out his breath filter long enough to say, also in Mayan, "Here."

Doc went toward Monk's voice—and straight into violent turmoil.

The assailants, apparently every one of them in the room, had charged toward Monk's voice. Probably because it was so distinctive. When Monk said something in a fight, there was no doubt about who said it.

Monk barked painfully—hit or kicked. His breath filter clinked against a wall. Monk fell down. He felt a powerful wrench on Civan, so Monk let Civan go. He thought Doc had taken the man. Monk was plenty willing to turn him loose; he wanted to fight.

There was no more shooting. But there was everything else. Blows. Furniture breaking. Someone tore the rug up with a ripping sound and plunged with it, upsetting people.

Doc Savage broke anaesthetic gas grenades. The stuff was extremely potent and abrupt; it would make a man unconscious, almost invariably, in less than a minute. But it didn't this time. It had absolutely no effect, except that Monk stopped howling and hitting and went to sleep, falling heavily.

The assailants wore gas masks, evidently.

They wore more than that, Doc began to have an ugly suspicion. His fight efforts were too futile. His senses, his muscles, were trained. He should be able to fight in the dark as well as the next man.

The attackers apparently could see in the blackness! And Doc couldn't. Nor his men.

Doc Savage plucked the breath filter from his lips and ordered, "Get into the next room, quick!" without taking gas-charged air into his lungs. He put the filter back.

He got down, felt, and found Monk. He dragged Monk to the door of the next room.

Long Tom and Ham were already in the next room. Doc joined them. They banged the door, and Doc found a key and turned it.

"Upstairs," he said taking the filter out of his mouth briefly.

They rushed across the room, through a door, found the stairs. Up these, they went. Behind them, there was a crashing as the locked door was caved in.

At the top of the first flight of stairs, Doc said, "Go on."

His men went on.

Doc flipped a small high-explosive grenade down the stairs. He wore a padded vest which was mostly pockets to contain the gadgets.

Came a crack of an explosion. Crashing and splintering was mixed in with the blast. And the lower half of the stairs came to pieces and fell down.

A considerable number of bullets came up the stairway during the next three or four minutes. Then the strange attackers went away.

After a while, it was suddenly daylight again.

Daylight brought stillness. It just had to. What had happened was so eerie, so impossible, that it left an aftermath of shocked awe.

Sunshine slanted in through the windows. Somewhere out in the shrubbery, a bird emitted a frightened cry. In the distance, city traffic still rumbled, and farther away there was a ghostly, undulating whining noise. Police sirens.

The walls of the room in which Doc Savage stood were papered blue, the ceiling was cream, the carpet was very dark blue and the furniture upholstered in plush. Monk lay on the floor at Doc's feet and snored. Around about was some debris which had flown up from the blasted stairs.

Doc held a long, thin, telescoping periscope at the door, and saw no one was now at the foot of the stairs. Lower half of the stairway was a complete wreck, scalable only with a ladder.

Long Tom and Ham were peering cautiously around an upper landing, where they had taken shelter. They came down.

"I thought you had Civan!" Ham exclaimed.

Doc Savage shook his head slightly. "Our own lives were more important."

"But—"

"They could see in that blackness," the bronze man said. "They concentrated on rescuing Civan. Then they were going to turn their attention to getting rid of us. We got away just as they started the last."

The tension of shocked awe subsided. Ham and Long Tom began to think of rational questions.

Ham pointed at Monk. "Is he hurt?"

Considering how the two quarreled, Ham's anxiety over Monk was surprising.

"He got some of the anaesthetic gas," Doc explained.

"Oh!"

Ham felt of his own person for damage. He groaned at the rip in his expensive suit. "You haven't had time to go to the *Amazon Maid,* Doc."

The bronze man shook his head slightly. "The *Amazon Maid* story was a gag."

"Gag?"

"To send us off on the wrong trail."

"How did you figure that out?" Ham demanded.

"Civan," Doc said, "was too eager to explain about a long-nosed man named Eli Camel, and the *Amazon Maid*. Moreover, his tongue slipped once—he mentioned someone named John Sunlight."

"John Sunlight?"

"The unknown quantity, so far." Doc Savage started mounting the stairs toward the attic. He explained. "Instead of flying to the *Amazon Maid*, I watched this place from a house across the street, to see what would happen."

Doc Savage reached the attic, looked out of the windows. They gave the best available view of the neighborhood. There was no sign of their late assailants; they had fled successfully.

They brought Monk up to the attic, administered a stimulant, and when the fogging effects of the anaesthetic gas had been knocked out of the homely chemist's brain, he sat up and made noises, then asked a question—the question uppermost in the minds of Ham and Long Tom.

"What was the *black?*" Monk demanded.

They all looked at Doc Savage; if there was to be an explanation, it would have to come from the bronze man. Monk, Ham and Long Tom were utterly at a loss.

Then they stared in amazement at the bronze man. His face —they had never seen quite such an expression on his face before. It was something stark. Queer. They could not, at first, tell what it was; then they knew that the bronze man was feeling an utter horror.

"Doc!" Monk gasped. "What is it?"

Doc Savage seemed to get hold of himself with visible effort. Then he did a strange thing; he held both hands in front of him and made them into tense, metallic fists. He looked at the fists. They trembled a little from strain.

Finally he put the fists down against his sides and let out a long breath.

"It cannot be anything but what I think it is," he said.

His voice had a hollowness. Such a macabre quality that the others were too startled to put questions. They had never before seen the bronze man this disturbed.

They knew, now, that he would not answer questions.

They watched him pick up the fragments of the pliers which

had broken in such a brittle way when Monk tapped them with the file.

"Microscope?" Doc asked.

Monk's pocket magnifier had remained miraculously unbroken. He handed it over, and Doc examined the bits of shattered steel.

"Crystallized," he said. Which also seemed to be what he had expected.

Next, he gave attention to the unused part of the attic, the portion that was dark and windowless.

"Just mouse and rat tracks in there," Monk volunteered.

The bronze man examined the "mouse" tracks closely, and gave the homely chemist a shock.

"Some of the rat tracks," Doc pointed out, "are impressed in the wood."

"Huh?"

"They were probably made by small pieces of metal driven into the underside of boards, the boards having been laid on the rafters. Probably the metal bits were to disguise the fact that boards had been laid on the rafters for someone to stand upon."

Monk swallowed as he digested this. "You mean—somebody hid in there?"

"Apparently."

Doc Savage went next to the entrance of the attic study, where his interest centered on the crimson stains, now dried, left by the Mafnoff cook, who had fainted, they understood, when the shriek was heard downstairs.

There were two sets of the dark stains.

"Two stains," Doc remarked, "indicate the cook might have been moved while unconscious."

Monk eyed the stains, one in front of the door, the other to one side, until Doc's meaning dawned on him.

"Hey!" Monk exploded. "Somebody was hiding in the attic. The scream downstairs drew the servants away. Whoever was in the attic fled, moving the unconscious cook out of the way."

Ham said, "But why go to all of the trouble of moving the cook?"

"Perhaps the one who fled was carrying a heavy burden," Doc said slowly.

They could not get him to elaborate on this remark.

Chapter 7
BIG WOMEN

The police came; so there naturally had to be extensive explanations, with much of the explaining devoted to making the police comprehend that the whole chain of events had happened. If there had been a shooting or a stabbing, the police would have accepted the fact that a crime had been committed. But this case was unusual. It was incredible. A noted diplomat, Serge Mafnoff, had vanished under—since he had apparently turned into black smoke—impossible-to-believe circumstances. A stranger with a Russian accent—that was Civan—had come to Doc Savage and tried to kill him.

"Wait a miute," the police captain said. "Why'd they try to kill you?"

"That can be part of the mystery," Doc said.

The attack on the Serge Mafnoff home to rescue Civan—the police could grasp that. But they couldn't grasp the strange blackness that had clamped down on the neighborhood; it was as bad as Serge Mafnoff turning into black smoke. It was impossible, it couldn't have happened, and there must be a catch somewhere.

Doc Savage left the representatives of the law with their headache. The bronze man, Monk, Ham and Long Tom went to their cars. They had two machines—one that Doc had driven, and the automobile used by his three men.

All three associates, it developed, wanted to ride with Doc and discuss the mystery.

"But someone has to drive the other car," Doc reminded.

"Let the gossoon do it," Ham suggested, pointing at Monk.

"We'll draw lots," Monk said promptly, which was wasted effort, because when they drew, Monk lost anyway.

Monk seated himself grumblingly at the wheel of the second car, and drove all alone in the wake of Doc Savage's machine.

192

Because the mystery they were embroiled in was so fantastic so far that it completely confused him, Monk decided to keep his mind off it by thinking about something else. He thought about Ham. He tried to dope out a new insult to throw at Ham.

Ham was proud of his Harvard background, his membership in certain exclusive clubs. He often boasted to Monk that he was one of the Four Hundred.

"Four hundred!" Monk snorted. "He comes nearer bein' one of the fifty-seven varieties."

Thinking up verbal spears to stick in Ham was always an absorbing pastime with Monk. He grew completely occupied with the avocation. He paid no great attention to following the others; they were all enroute back to headquarters, anyway.

Monk fell behind and entirely lost sight of the other machine containing Doc, Long Tom and Ham.

On a very deserted street, a shabby old sedan suddenly cut in front of Monk's car, and the result was a resounding crash. Both machines came to a stop.

Monk craned his neck.

"Blast women drivers!" he grumbled. "Er—that is"—he took another look to see if the woman was pretty, and she wasn't—"yeah, blast 'em!"

Monk's car was one of Doc Savage's special machines, body of armor steel, wheels of puncture-proof sponge rubber, and it had not been damaged. The other car had not fared so well.

Not one woman, but two got out of the other car. They came striding toward Monk's machine, looking apologetic.

"Gosh!" Monk said.

He was seeing two of the biggest women he had ever glimpsed in his life. Not fat women—big! Two Herculean females, not badly proportioned, but built with at least a triple or quadruple measure of everything.

"Woe is me!" Monk gasped, and hurriedly rolled up the bulletproof glass car windows.

However, when he heard the two feminine titans saying how sorry they were, he rolled down one window.

"We're awfully sorry," one female tower said.

"You bet we are," the other added.

Their voices were distinctly feminine, but as might be expected, had tremendous volume.

"Well," Monk said, "of course your car suffered the most—"

One big woman reached suddenly and got Monk by the hair. She held him.

"Search 'im, Giantia," she said.

The other female tower went through Monk's pockets, slapped the places where men generally carry guns. Monk's squawking and writhing didn't seem to bother her.

"Nothin' on 'im, Titania," she said.

Giantia released Monk's hair, simultaneously giving him a shove in the face. This skidded Monk over to the middle of the seat. One giantess got in on Monk's left, the other on his right, and they closed the car doors.

Monk howled, "Now, look here—"

Both big women put their arms around Monk, but they weren't hugging, exactly. They were squeezing. Monk heard his joints cracking, felt his breath whistle between his teeth and thought his eyes were going to pop out. When they released him the argument was all squeezed out.

"We used to wrassle a bear in one of our acts," Giantia said. "So we know how to handle you."

Titania looked at Monk speculatively.

"Only you're more like a baboon," she decided.

Monk felt of his neck tenderly.

"I can see I'm gonna like you two," he muttered.

Giantia started the engine, backed up, turned and drove away. It was evident to Monk that the two remarkable big girls intended leaving their own wrecked machine and taking him somewhere.

"What's the idea?" he asked fearfully.

Giantia said, "We're gonna make you tell us where we can find John Sunlight."

"John Sunlight?" Monk questioned. "What's that? Some guy's name?"

"Don't kid us," Giantia thundered.

"No," Titania rumbled, "don't kid us. We saw you goin' around takin' care of Civan. We know you're one of his pals."

"But——"

"Shut up," Giantia roared. "We'll tell you when to talk. And you'll talk then, plenty."

"I bet," Titania boomed, "that he knows John Sunlight grabbed our little sister Fifi and is holdin' her to make us keep our mouths shut."

"Sure," exclaimed Giantia. "I bet he knows it all. I bet he knows about the Strange Blue Dome, an' everything. Betcha he knows we only promised to throw in with John Sunlight's an' help him so we could get back to New York an' take care of little Fifi."

Monk started off to do some roaring of his own.

"Fifi be danged—"

He got a slap that made his ears sound as though they contained steamboat whistles.

"Don't you talk that way about our Fifi!" Giantia thundered.

"Dad blast my kind of luck!" Monk grumbled.

As a driver, Giantia belonged decidedly to the Barney Oldfield school. When the speedometer needle got below fifty, it seemed to bother her. Monk was confronted with amazement as he watched speed cop after speed cop let them go by, with never an attempt to halt them, or even to follow. Then he remembered that the car carried the special Doc Savage plates which entitled the machine to make its own speed laws.

The destination seemed to be no particular place—just any remote spot where there was a thick growth of concealing trees. Monk began to have a grim suspicion that they were seeking a locality where his screams of agony would not be heard.

"There has been a little mistake," he ventured uneasily.

"Your mistake," Titania said, "was in being born."

"Judgin' from his looks," Giantia added, "there was a mistake somewhere."

Monk squirmed and debated mentally over the things he could do. Jumping out of the car was certainly not one of them, since the machine was now doing seventy-five.

"I'm one of Doc Savage's crew," Monk explained earnestly.

The two giantesses were puzzled, but not impressed.

"Doc Savage—never heard of him," Titania said.

Monk swallowed this pill of surprise. Persons who had not heard of Doc Savage, at least through rumor, were becoming scarce.

"Who is he?" Giantia demanded.

There was a subject on which Monk could wax eloquent. He had a sincere admiration for the bronze man—which very fact probably saved him a great deal of grief on the present occasion. His sincerity was expressed in his voice so effectively that Giantia and Titania were impressed. They stopped the car.

"Now tell us that again," Giantia ordered.

"Doc Savage," Monk said, "is a man whose business is

shooting other people's troubles. He was trained from childhood for the job. I know it sounds queer. But it's a fact."

Monk waved eloquent. He had a bill of goods to sell, and he suspected it was rather imperative that he sell it. Ham, the silver-tongued lawyer-orator, could have taken lessons from Monk's speech to the two Herculean women. Monk left out very little. Doc's scientific training, physical ability, his five assistants —Monk touched on it all with an earnestness that was completely effective.

"Strong man, eh?" Titania muttered, with an unmistakable gleam of interest.

"Yep," Monk said.

"How big did you say?" Titania asked.

"Bigger than you are," Monk assured her.

Titania sighed. "You know," she remarked, "I've never met a man I could fall—er—that is, a fellow who is as big as I am."

Monk took a deep breath.

"Doc," he said, "has never been able to find a girl quite his own equal either."

Doc would probably exile him for that remark, if the bronze man ever found out about it.

Titania and Giantia were obviously intrigued. They exchanged glances which Monk had no trouble reading correctly.

"Maybe," Titania said thoughtfully, "this Doc Savage is the man to rescue Fifi from John Sunlight."

"He sure is!" Monk exlaimed quickly.

"We know all about this John Sunlight and the Strange Blue Dome, and everything," Giantia said.

"Doc will sure be glad to get the information," Monk declared earnestly.

Giantia stopped the car, turned it around, and headed back toward New York City.

"You tell us where to go," she ordered Monk.

Monk was expecting a sensation when he ushered Giantia and Titania into the presence of Doc Savage, Ham and Long Tom. He was not disappointed. Ham sprang up and dropped the sword cane.

"What's this?" Ham gasped.

"Little present I brought you," Monk explained. He felt of his neck, which still ached. Then an idea hit him. He nudged Giantia and Titania, called their attention to Ham.

"When we rescue Fifi," Monk said, "you want to watch this shyster, Ham. He's a lady-killer from way back."

Giantia strode to the astonished Ham, gave him a shove, and Ham sailed back and fell over a chair.

"That," Giantia said, "is just a sample of what you'll get if you make one single sheep eye at Fifi."

"Wuh—wuh——" was the best the astounded Ham could do.

Giantia and Titania suddenly lost interest in Ham. They were looking at the Man of Bronze. They stared, not exactly with their mouths open, but with almost its equivalent.

Doc Savage wore tan trousers and a matching tan shirt which was open at the neck, and the effect of his metallic figure seemed unusually striking. His vitality, strength, size, and the quality of unbounded power which was somehow a part of his personality, were impressive.

Giantia glanced at Monk.

"You ain't the liar I thought you was," she said.

Monk performed introductions—Ham retreated to the other side of the reception room and acknowledged the introduction from that safe distance—and Titania and Giantia were left with nothing to do but stare at Doc Savage, which they proceeded to do with enthusiasm.

"Your accent indicates you have been speaking Russian recently," Doc Savage said.

There were some slight indications that already Giantia and Titania were beginning to make him uncomfortable. Women made Doc uncomfortable rather easily.

Monk said, "Doc, these two young women know all about this infernal mystery. They know all about Civan, and some guy named John Moonbeam——"

"John Sunlight," Titania interrupted.

"Suppose they tell us about it," Doc suggested.

Titania nodded. "It's a long story. It began in Russia where——"

"—where we got mixed up in a spy racket, were caught, and sent to Siberia," interposed Giantia, who seemed anxious to do any talking that was to be done to Doc Savage. "We were sent to Siberian exile, where we——"

"—we met John Sunlight," put in Titania, who seemed to have the same idea about monopolizing any talk with the bronze man. "John Sunlight organized an escape from the Siberian prison camp aboard——"

"—aboard an ice-breaker," interpolated Giantia. "And——"

"Shut up, Giantia!" said Titania. "I'm telling it."

"Shut up yourself," ordered Giantia. "I can tell it as well——"

Doc put in quietly, "Perhaps if we closed the windows, there would be less noise to interfere."

Since the headquarters was located on the eighty-sixth floor, there was ordinarliy not enough noise to interfere in the least with a casual conversation, but just now there was an unusual amount of uproar. Doc Savage stood for a moment at the window listening. His interest was caught.

A plane was flying slowly over New York City at an altitude of at least two thousand feet. It was a ballyhoo plane—one of the type that had a great aerial loud-speaker, or probably a battery of them, mounted in the cabin, their openings downward. Such a plane could fly a mile in the air and someone speaking into a microphone aboard it could make words heard by the entire city.

A ballyhoo plane over New York City was an unusual sight. There was an antinoise ordinance against them.

This one was talking.

"This is Fifi," it kept saying over and over. *"Giantia and Titania, please do not tell Doc Savage anything."*

It was a woman's voice.

Chapter 8
QUEST FOR FIFI

The idea of a ballyhoo plane flying over the city, warning someone not to talk to Doc Savage, was preposterously fantastic. Yet effective, too. More effective than newspaper advertisements, or any other quick way of giving warning.

Doc whipped the double soundproof windows shut. But he was too late.

"What was that?" Titania shouted. She flung the windows open again.

Giantia jumped to the window, too. The two big women listened.

"This is Fifi," said the voice from the sky. *"Giantia and Titania, please do not tell Doc Savage anything."*

Giantia and Titania stared at the ballyhoo plane with stark intensity, and horror came over their faces.

"Fifi!" Titania gulped. "Fifi's voice!"

"John Sunlight has her in that plane!" moaned Giantia.

They stood there, listening as if hypnotized, until the plane reached the far side of the city and banked around and came back. The ballyhoo craft was sweeping back and forth, covering the entire metropolis.

Doc said, "Go ahead with the story of John Sunlight."

Giantia and Titania looked at him with their lips tight.

"We can't tell you anything now," Giantia said hoarsely.

"John Sunlight would kill Fifi," Titania added.

It was plain they had no intention of continuing with any story. Fears for their little sister's safety had silenced them completely.

Doc turned to Monk. "How much did they tell you before you got here?"

Monk scratched his bullet of a head.

"Not much, Doc," the homely chemist admitted. "They did say somethin' about a thing they called the Strange Blue Dome."

"The what?" Doc's face became frozen metal.

"The Strange Blue Dome," Monk explained. "Or so they called——"

The homely chemist stopped speaking, swallowed. For Doc Savage had spun, and flung into the library.

The bronze man snapped the library door shut behind him, then did nothing more exciting than stride to one of the great windows and stand stiffly, staring into the hazy northern sky. Doc's sinew-cabled arms were down, as rigid as bars, at his sides, and his powerful hands worked slowly, clenching and unclenching.

He was doing something that none of his men had ever seen him do before. He was taking time out to get control of himself.

Had his men seen, they might have guessed the reason. They were clever men, each one a headliner in his chosen profession. Probably they would have realized that Doc Savage knew more about the Strange Blue Dome than any of them dreamed he knew.

Monk, Ham, Long Tom—none of Doc's men had ever heard of any such thing as the Strange Blue Dome.

But Doc knew of it, obviously. Knew so much about it that he was shocked more profoundly than his men had ever seen him shocked before, by the mere mention of the Strange Blue Dome in connection with this mystery.

Strangest of all, Doc Savage seemed to be blaming himself for what was happening.

Doc went back into the other room.

"Ham," he said, "you and Long Tom watch these two women, Giantia and Titania."

Ham had no liking for that task. He gulped a hasty, "But——"

"Monk and myself are going after that ballyhoo plane," Doc said.

"Aw—O.K.," Ham grumbled.

Monk grinned derisively at Ham, touched his hand to his forehead in a boy-am-I-laughing-at-you gesture. Then Monk followed Doc Savage into the big laboratory. They wended through long tables laden with intricate glass and metal devices. Many cabinets stood filled with chemicals.

Doc opened a wall panel, disclosing a steel barrel several feet in diameter. There was a door in this, which he opened. He stepped through into a bullet-shaped car which was well-padded, and traveled through the steel barrel, driven by compressed air. When Monk got in, there was little room to spare.

Closing hatches, Doc pulled levers which tripped the air pressure on. There was a shock, a whining noise, and the vibration of great speed. Then they were jammed against the lower end of the cartridgelike car as air cushioned it to a stop. Holding devices clicked and a red light came on.

Doc and Monk stepped out in the bronze man's Hudson River water-front hangar boathouse.

Monk ran for the plane which stood nearest the water, sprang in, got the propeller turning over.

"Hey, Doc!" he yelled. "Ain't you comin'?"

Doc Savage said, "You go after the ballyhoo plane alone, Monk."

Monk didn't understand why Doc wanted to remain behind. But he was not displeased. The prospect of chasing the ballyhoo plane, maybe an aerial dogfight, intrigued Monk.

"Keep your radio cut in," Doc called.

Monk's arm shot up to acknowledge that. He gunned the plane down into the water. The craft was an amphibian. When it got close to the big doors, it cut a photo-electric-cell-and-beam device, which caused the doors to open.

Monk's plane scudded across the river, and was in the air about the time the hangar doors were closing.

Doc Savage was already in a car in the hangar. He kept a car in the hangar for emergency use, and it was one of his fully equipped machines.

The car had, among many other gadgets, a very good radio direction-finder. A finder that could cover the entire band of either wave-lengths. Doc turned the tuning dial slowly, changed wave coils, kept on tuning. Carrier wave after carrier wave was picked up as a violent hissing.

Finally Doc picked up a transmitter which seemed to be sending nothing but—at intervals of two or three minutes—an apparently meaningless combination of dots and dashes.

The bronze man took a careful bearing on that station.

He started the car, drove furiously, covered about half a mile, and took a second bearing on the transmitter which was sending dot-and-dash combinations.

Doc watched the ballyhoo plane as he took this second radio bearing. The plane was a distant bumblebee against the sky. Another bumblebee—Monk's ship—was wheeling around it.

The ballyhoo plane changed its course in obedience to the dot-and-dash signal on which Doc was taking bearings.

The bronze man made his small, characteristic trilling sound briefly. It had a satisfied quality. His surmise had been correct —his suspicion that grew out of the fact that Fifi's voice, from the ballyhoo plane, *was repeating the same words over and over.*

Doc drew bearing lines on a scale map of New York City. The lines crossed in the section immediately below Forty-second street. He drove for the spot.

Only at street intersections could Doc Savage see Monk's plane and the ballyhoo ship. At other times, high buildings hid both craft.

Time after time, Monk flew around the loud-speaker ship. Doc was anxious about that, at first. But Monk was cautious; he did not get too close to the strange craft. This jockeying went on for minutes. Then it appeared that Monk had surrendered caution, and was flying very near the other ship. Monk's plane was on the opposite side; it seemed to blend with the ballyhoo craft, and then——

A splattering volley of dots and dashes came from the radio transmitter which Doc was tracking down with the direction-finder.

Instantly, the ballyhoo ship exploded. Doc saw the flash, a flash that jumped in all directions; it was like looking at a distant mirror which had unexpectedly reflected sunlight into his eyes. The flash faded; Doc watched the smoke. It might have been from an Archie shell. Then came the blast sound, a distinct concussion, despite the distance. And echoes followed, bouncing around among the skyscrapers like thunder.

Then Monk's plane appeared. It had been safely beyond the other ship; only the distance had made it seem close.

Doc turned the radio to Monk's wave length.

"Damaged any, Monk?" he asked of his own transmitter mike.

"Startled out of six years' growth," Monk's voice stated shakily. "You know what, Doc?"

"There was no one in the plane," Doc said. "It was being flown by a radio robot. The girl's voice was coming off a record that was being repeated. And they exploded a bomb in the plane with radio control."

"You must be a crystal gazer!" Monk said.

His distant plane spun down in the sky and swooped in toward the Hudson River.

Doc Savage reached the spot where, as closely as he could judge, the radio-control transmitter had operated. He tried to tune it in again. It had been shut off. That was not so good; the plane might have been controlled from any building within a block.

Doc Savage made a quick survey of surrounding buildings, their height, their position with reference to the spot where the plane had blown up in the sky—a smudge of dark smoke still marked that point.

One tall building—it had to be that one. It was the only roof that offered a view of the spot where the plane had exploded.

Doc Savage drove away two blocks, parked, and got his make-up case from under the rear seat.

The bronze man, getting out of the car some minutes later, was a large dark-skinned man with artistically long black hair, nostrils with an almost negroid flare—the celluloid nostril inserts did not hamper breathing and added a remarkable touch—and a nervous habit of twitching his lips.

Doc carried a leather tool bag which was worn.

He walked into the lobby of the building he suspected, saw no one there, entered an elevator when it arrived, and said, "Top floor."

From the top-floor corridor, a door gave into a flight of stairs that led up to the roof. The door to the stairway was open, and a man lounged there, obviously a guard. He was a thin dark man.

The lookout stared at Doc narrowly.

The bronze man walked up to the fellow, dangling his worn tool bag prominently.

"Have you noticed any peculiar smells?" Doc asked.

The other scowled.

"You've got me there, buddy," he said. "Smells."

Doc said, "I am making a building inspection."

"So what?"

"You don't understand," Doc explained patiently. "There is a chemical firm on a lower floor of this building, and it is possible that a leakage of chemicals occurred. The chemicals form a gas, and it might have risen to the upper floors, following the elevator shafts. In such a case, it would be noticed here, or on the roof. Have you noticed anything?"

"Not a thing," the man said sourly.

He spoke with a strong Russian accent.

"Very well," Doc said. "The gas may not have reached this high yet. Or there may not even be any gas at all as yet."

The bronze man then walked, swinging his tool bag and whistling, to the stairway, opened the door, stepped through and left the door ajar a crack. He made tramping sounds with his feet so that it would appear he had gone on down the stairs.

Out of the bag he took a gas mask, which he donned. Then he took a gallon jug of villainously colored liquid from the bag and poured it on the floor.

He waited fifteen minutes, approximately. There was a strong draft up the stairs and through the door, and through the stairs that led up to the roof. The liquid Doc had poured on the floor slowly turned into gas and was swept up to the roof.

After the fifteen minutes were up, he went investigating.

There was one man asleep in the top-floor hallway.

There were six men and a girl asleep on the roof.

The girl was very small, very pretty—if you liked the kewpie-doll type.

Chapter 9
LOST WOMEN

Doc Savage had a way, as those who knew him put it, of walking up and taking death by the beard. And not only getting away with it, but in unexpected fashions all his own, of leaving the old man with the whiskers and scythe wondering just whether he had been treated with disrespect.

But Doc's working methods were not as reckless as they appeared. He knew this strange trade which he followed; he had received years of training for it, and he carried with himself always an astounding number of scientific gadgets calculated to cope with emergencies.

Whenever possible, he tried not to do what was expected of him.

There was a portable radio transmitter of some power standing on the roof. In a case beside it was the additional mechanism necessary to make an ordinary radio into a plane-control.

Doc freed Fifi—she was bound and gagged—and left rope and gag lying on the roof.

Doc carried the men from the roof to the top-floor hallway, and put all seven of them in the freight elevator, which operated automatically and thus did not have an operator.

Next, Doc carried Fifi down and put her with the others. He had no doubt that he was carrying Fifi.

He locked the door leading to the roof, then sealed it with a bit of chewing gum. Not ordinary gum, exactly. This would turn white when he touched it with a drop of chemical; and if it didn't turn white, he would know it was different gum.

Fifi had the cutest form of any small girl Doc had ever seen. Short girls are usually spread out a bit.

The bronze man got down to the alley, got his car around there, got his passengers loaded into it without attracting anyone's attention. He drove toward his headquarters.

Fifi slipped over and her head rested against his shoulder. She was the type of little thing that could look delicious when she was sleeping.

Doc's car traveled quietly, and did not take long to reach the high building which housed his headquarters. The machine rolled into the private basement garage.

He loaded in seven prisoners into the speed elevator. Then he put Fifi in.

Fifi seemed, if anything, smaller and more exquisitely pretty. She looked like trouble. She looked like nothing else but trouble.

Doc piloted the elevator and his load up to the eighty-sixth floor and got out. He began unloading.

Neither Ham nor Long Tom came out to help him.

Suddenly concerned, Doc Savage hurried to the door, opened it and went into the reception room. He stopped, stared about in astonishment.

Two thoroughly angry bulls might have put the place in the shambles he saw before him. Two bulls—it was hardly likely one could have done as thorough a job.

Ham and Long Tom were skinned, lacerated, contused. They had black eyes, were minus some hair, and their noses leaked crimson. Another expensive suit had been ruined for Ham.

The two were also bound and gagged.

Doc untied them.

"Titania!" Ham yelled.

"Giantia!" Long Tom shouted.

"They got away!" they groaned in chorus.

Doc Savage's metallic features did not change expression, which was a tribute to his self-control.

Titania and Giantia had been going to tell everything about John Sunlight, the instant they knew their sister Fifi was safe. Well, Fifi was safe; she would have no more than a slight headache when she recovered.

"How did it happen?" Doc asked quietly.

"They saw that plane explode—the plane Monk was after," Long Tom muttered.

"And they went wild," Ham added ruefully. "You never saw such a performance. They landed on us before we knew what'd happened. Insisted we had gotten Fifi killed. They thought she was in the plane, you know. Well—that is—anyhow, they got the best of us."

"They left," Long Tom explained, "swearing they were going to join John Sunlight and help him get you, to pay you back for causing Fifi's death in the plane."

Ham stood up, felt of himself, ran to a mirror and got a good look at the damage which had been done to his garments. He made a croaking noise. He loved his clothes as if they were his children.

Another hideous thought hit Ham. Monk—if Monk heard of this, the homely ape would have the time of his life kidding Ham. And he was certain to hear of it. Ham's groan was so loud it sounded like a honking.

Doc Savage said nothing more on the subject of the two giantesses escaping. He never criticized his crew for errors or shortcomings. The bronze man made mistakes himself.

Mistakes—his metallic face settled into the grimmest of lines. Mistake! This whole thing was the result of a mistake he had made. A horrible error. He had not told them that as yet, but the fact had taken shape in his own mind, and was there whenever his thoughts relaxed, to torment him like a spike-tailed devil.

In grave silence, the bronze man carried the captives into the laboratory. Ham and Long Tom helped him.

Before the job was done, Monk put in an appearance with an aviator's helmet and goggles perched on his bullet head. He listened as Long Tom told what had happened. Then Monk looked at Ham and roared with mirth.

"You look like an accident goin' someplace t' happen!" Monk howled.

"At least," Ham said unkindly, "I don't look and act like something six months out of a jungle."

Monk scowled. "Listen, shyster, my ancestors came here on the *Mayflower*."

"It's a good thing," Ham sneered. "The country has immigration laws now."

They did not notice Doc Savage closing the laboratory door. And later, when they tried the door, it was locked, and although they called out, the bronze man returned no answer from within.

They sat down in the reception room to wait, puzzled.

Doc Savage preferred to work alone whenever possible. This did not grow out of an overconfidence in his own ability, nor did it mean that his aids were inefficient. They were not; they were highly intelligent, if unusual fellows, and of enormous assistance at times. But Doc still liked to work alone when he could. There were things that one man could do better.

It takes an army to fight an army. But sending one scout out to locate the enemy is the sensible way.

The effects of the gas would wear off shortly, if the prisoners were left alone. But Doc did not leave them alone.

He gave each one of them, Fifi included, a treatment with truth serum.

Truth serum, at the best—and Doc Savage had done considerable work toward developing the stuff, as had Monk—was not always dependable. It functioned by causing the patient to lapse into a coma, so that the mind exercised no conscious control over the will. When the subject heard a question, but insistently, the impulse was to answer it, and the dulled will power was unlikely to interfere.

Fifi was the type of character most susceptible to truth serum, so Doc began his questioning with her.

Fifi knew absolutely nothing of value.

Doc went to work on the others.

He kept questioning them for almost an hour——

And when the bronze man unlocked the laboratory door, there was an expression on his face which shocked his men. It was a stricken look—one of such intensity that it was startling, for Doc Savage so rarely showed his emotions.

"Doc!" Ham gasped. "What——"

The bronze man shook his head.

"We haven't much time," he said. "You might help me."

They carried the men prisoners out, one at a time, and put them in the speed elevator.

Monk maneuvered himself into carrying Fifi.

"Not a bad little number," he said admiringly.

"Keep her here," Doc said.

Monk burst out in a big wreath of grins.

Ham complained, "That ugly clunk is havin' all the luck——"

Doc said, "Ham, you and Long Tom stay here. Be ready for a call."

They nodded, puzzled. The strangely set expression on his face deterred them from asking questions.

Doc Savage got a larger make-up box out of the laboratory. He took also two equipment cases.

Then he lowered the prisoners to the basement garage, loaded them in the car, drove back to the building where he had captured them, and managed to return them to the roof, still without being noticed.

The prisoners lay limp and snored where he placed them. He put the thin dark one at the foot of the roof stairs. He scattered the others over the roof, near the radio plane-control, where he had found them.

He emptied another bottle of chemical on the roof. At once, the air became filled with a reeking odor which certainly smelled like a chemical vapor potent enough to overcome men.

Doc Savage then left the roof.

Chapter 10
WAR LORDS

The first John Sunlight man to sit erect on the roof looked around himself in a dazed way. His next act was an impulsive glance at his wrists, as though he expected to find handcuffs there. He began shaking his head.

"Hey!" he yelled. He shook the limp form nearest to him.

The shaken man groaned.

Doc Savage's skill with drugs was highly developed; he had calculated the combined dosages, in proportion to the bodily resistance of the men, so closely that they were all reviving at approximately the same time.

Half an hour saw them all on their feet, stumbling around, asking each other foolish questions. Then the man came crawling up from the stairs.

"Gas!" this man gasped. "Gas that came from a chemical firm downstairs. The fumes musta got us!"

"How'd you know that?"

"There was an inspector come around just before I keeled over."

A man rubbed his forehead bewilderedly. "I kinda feel as if

somethin' happened to me when I was unconscious," he mumbled.

"What?"

The man tried to think, gave it up finally. "Nothin', I guess," he said.

Which was as near as any of them came to imagining that they had been taken to Doc Savage's headquarters, had talked under the effects of truth serum, and had been returned.

"Where's the girl?" one yelled suddenly.

She wasn't there, obviously.

"She must 'a' failed to get as much gas as we did, and crawled off," one man decided.

They saw the ropes and gag lying where the girl had been. But no girl. There was a furious rush in search of the girl, and when it netted them nothing, they were uneasy.

"John Sunlight ain't gonna like this," seemed to be a general consensus.

They conferred, holding their heads, which ached splittingly, and decided there was nothing to do now but take their radio outfit and leave. They did this. Their cars were parked in a near-by side street.

They drove north for over an hour along the bank of the Hudson River, then parked their cars at a wharf near the water's edge.

There was a speedboat tied to the wharf. Into this, they climbed. It carried them out on the river, and toward an island.

The island was mostly stone, although there was enough soil to support a few trees. The island was crowned by a house.

Crowned—there was no other word for it. Nothing else quite described how the house sat on the peak of the island, or described the house itself. The structure was like a crown, round, with four ornamental spires, one at each corner, and windows which, due to the reflections of afternoon sun from their colored glass, resembled jewels.

Of course the house could have been called a fortress, too. But not at first glance. The machine guns mounted inside the windows were not visible at any first glance.

The house might have been termed a spot for a quick get-away, as well. But to realize this, it was first necessary to know that the big boathouse on the south held a fast plane, as well as a hundred-mile-an-hour speedboat.

John Sunlight did not believe in taking chances.

John Sunlight sat on a deep chair which was covered with a rich purple velvet cloth. He wore a matching set of purple velvet pajamas and purple velvet robe, and on the forefinger of his right hand was a ring with a purple jewel.

John Sunlight had very few changeable habits, but one of them was his fondness for one color at one time, and perhaps a different one later. Just now he was experiencing a yen for purple, particularly the regal shade of the color.

The man could go in for colors like a male movie star, and still be dangerous.

He did not look dangerous as he listened to his men tell him they had been gassed on the building roof, and had awakened to find the girl, Fifi, gone, and that nothing else had happened to them—except that they hadn't succeeded in blowing up anybody with the bomb plane.

John Sunlight never looked dangerous.

"That is too bad," he said.

He resembled, with his thin aesthetic face, a dreamer of a poet who had listened to an editor turn down one of his rhymes.

"Too bad," he said. "You will have to be punished."

The terrified uneasiness which jumped over the faces of the gas victims at this was a tribute to the grisly qualities of the innocent-looking, tall, thin man before them. There was something hypnotic about it. He had not touched them, had not ordered them shot or even beaten.

"Put them each in a separate dark room of the basement," John Sunlight said. "After they have been there forty-eight hours, I will talk to them."

One of the men made a croaking sound. John Sunlight had done that to him once before, put him in darkness for a long time, then came and talked to him. And the talk of John Sunlight, spoken quietly and steadily, had contained such a combination of horrors and obscenities, ghastly implications and frightful verbal statements, that the man remembered he had been a gibbering wreck of terror for many hours afterward.

An impartial observer would have called John Sunlight's method a form of hypnotism.

The horrified gas victims were led away.

John Sunlight was thorough. Attention to details, he had long ago learned, is important. Overlook a seed, and it may grow into a great tree of thorns.

He consulted a Manhattan directory.

"Why," he said mildly, "there is no chemical firm registered as being in that building!"

He got on the telephone. He could speak English with almost no accent at all, so he made out fairly well with a deception that he was a Federal agent.

"Yes, do," he said.

Soon a voice said, "This is the Eureka Products Chemical House."

"What address?" John Sunlight asked.

The address given was the proper one.

"Did you have an accident there today?" John Sunlight inquired.

"Why, yes," the other said. "Some gas got loose in the plant, but as far as we can tell, it did no damage. We were afraid that it would rise to the upper floors, and cause people to become unconscious. However, the gas is harmless, unless one has a very weak heart."

"Thank you," John Sunlight said.

"Thank *you*," said the voice.

The voice was Long Tom. His thanks *were* sincere. He was still a little breathless from rushing around, warning the telephone people that there was a chemical firm in the building, in case anyone asked, and using his electrical skill to get a telephone connection in the building in a hurry. He hoped he had fooled John Sunlight.

He had.

John Sunlight was deceived, but he did not put the telephone aside at once, because he had another call to make.

"Hello, Baron," he said pleasantly, "I wonder if you could arrange to hold an immmediate consultation with me?"

The "Baron" was silent, cautiously considering.

"Is it dangerous?" he demanded.

"It is to avoid danger," said John Sunlight, "that I wish to see you. This is very important, Baron. One of my men will call for you immediately in a car."

Again, the Baron thought it over.

"All right," he said finally, in a tone that said he doubted very much if it would be all right.

This Baron was one of John Sunlight's "contacts." John Sunlight had many contacts, more than anyone would have believed. He was not a young man, and he had worked all his evil life toward one hideous goal; and he had made his arrangements as he went along, always with an eye to the future. John Sunlight's idea about his destiny on this unfortunate earth was far from being as changeable as his fancy for colors.

The Baron was a representative of a Balkan country. The secret representative. His position at home was high, but the work he did was of the lowest kind. He was the head of his nation's spy system; he also personally handled the purchase of information, or anything that would be of value to his vicious little government.

This Baron Karl—he was known as Baron Karl for short—was bosom buddy to the prime minister of his government, and the prime minister was as blood-thirsty and intolerant a tyrant as ever seized life-and-death control over an unsuspecting population. The prime minister had his eyes on his neighboring Balkan country, and he would willingly give the lives of a few hundred thousand of his soldiers to grab the other country.

The only redeeming feature about the situation was that the other Balkan nation was ruled by as vicious a rascal as either the prime minister of Baron Karl, who dominated the neighboring "democracy." The ruler was known to the world as the "playboy prince" because of his hilarious career. But what the world didn't know was that he was a bloodthirsty, power-hungry kind of weasel, and the first throat he wanted to cut was the neighboring "democracy" of the prime minister and Baron Karl.

Fortunately, the two countries, armed to the teeth, had so far been too evenly matched for either to risk a war.

But if anything gave either a balance of power, there would be a war at the drop of a hat.

No one knew that the so-called playboy prince had landed in New York yesterday. He was traveling incognito. Very much incognito.

This playboy prince was the next man John Sunlight called.

"I'll have my car call for you in about an hour," John Sunlight said.

John Sunlight made several other telephone calls and appointments. Each of these was to a representative of a government which wanted above all things to have the power to whip somebody else in a war.

Baron Karl arrived at six o'clock. It was getting dark around the island.

Chapter 11
ARCTIC RENDEZVOUS

Baron Karl was a smooth customer. He even wore a monocle. And, of course, the best of clothes. He was quite a hand with the chorus girls.

In the "revolution" in his country, it was rumored he had personally shot to death some fifty or so political enemies, having them brought, one at a time, to a dark little room under the castle. When he wished, he could look and act like a candy salesman. But when he relaxed, and was his normal self, he was so much like something made out of snake flesh that even his boss, the prime minister, didn't like to be around him socially.

Baron Karl sat with military erectness in the stern of the motorboat which brought him out to the island, and made rather a distinguished figure. He gave the island and its castlelike house a glance of approval. It looked like a safe place. As a matter of fact, his own castle in his native land was along the same order.

"Sometimes I think," he remarked, "that this John Sunlight is destined to be history's greatest evil genius."

He thought along that line while he was being led up to the castle. Like all evil men, he liked to think that other persons were worse than himself—and in the case of John Sunlight, he was eminently correct. Baron Karl was only a menace to a pair of small Balkan nations, whereas John Sunlight was a menace to practically all humanity.

Baron Karl made a little speech when he met John Sunlight. "I salute again," he said, "the man who has inherited the qualities of the Erinyes, the Eumenides, of Titan, and of Friar Rush, with a touch of Dracula and Frankenstein."

"Those were very bad people," John Sunlight said dryly.

Baron Karl peered sharply at the other, a little apprehensive lest he had angered John Sunlight. He was afraid of the man.

"Let us call you a genius," he said, "and I say that sincerely. Er—may I sit down?"

He sat in a comfortable chair, crossed his legs, and dropped his candy salesman manner. He was ready to get down to business.

"What do you want?" he asked.

John Sunlight was blunt. "I wish to make an appointment to meet you at a point north of Hudson Bay in exactly five days," he said.

The stooge for one of Europe's worse tyrants looked startled. "Hudson Bay—you don't mean the Hudson Bay in Canada?"

"Yes. Our meeting place is near the Arctic Circle."

"You're crazy!" Baron Karl exclaimed. "Why, it's still winter up there. It's cold."

"Only about fifty below zero," John Sunlight said.

The other shook his head. "Meet you in the arctic? Not me! Particularly not unless you explain why."

John Sunlight did not lift his voice.

He said, "This is very, very important. On your meeting with me in the arctic will depend the future of your country."

"That is big talk," the European agent said dryly.

"Fail to meet me, and your country"—John Sunlight held up five fingers of one hand—"won't last that many months."

Baron Karl sat quite still and thought of the things he knew about John Sunlight, and of the whispers he had heard about the strange, terrible man. Baron Karl was given to quick, impulsive decisions. He stood up.

"I'll meet you in the arctic," he said. "Although I'm mystified."

Royalty visited John Sunlight's island in the Hudson at ten o'clock that night, which was two hours after Baron Karl had departed in an extremely puzzled state of mind.

Royalty was the playboy prince who had come dashing to America in secrecy and much haste.

The prince sat in the launch and pouted as the boat ran toward the island. He was a large young man, and his personal opinion was that he was handsome. The newspapers called him "dashing." What they meant was that the things he did were dashing. Or sappy. It depended on how you looked at such things as drunken chorus girls bathing in champagne tubs on the royal table.

He had a mouth made for pouting, large wet-calf eyes, and in a few years, if he kept putting on weight, he would look like a large brown worm.

"My cabinet," he told John Sunlight peevishly, "advised me to come, as your message requested."

He'd filled his cabinet with the coldest, cleverest rogues in his country, and he had gumption enough to take their advice.

"One week from today," John Sunlight said, "I want to meet you at a rendezvous near the Arctic Circle, north of Hudson Bay."

The prince didn't like cold weather. He refused.

Then he listened to John Sunlight assure him that, if he didn't keep the appointment, his country wouldn't last—John Sunlight held up five fingers—that many months. The prince thought of what his cabinet advisers had told him about this weird man before him, and remembered that they had assured him that if John Sunlight said a thing was important, it was assuredly important.

"How do I get there?" he asked grumpily.

"By plane—secretly."

That was all, and the prince left. He was mad at himself, because he was royalty, and here he was taking orders from a man who had no royal blood whatever. He was taking the orders simply because he had heard enough about the man to make him afraid not to do as he was told.

He was puzzled. He had no idea why John Sunlight wanted him in the arctic.

As a matter of fact, the prince was not the only one who was puzzled. Andrew Blodgett "Monk" Mayfair was also baffled. And so was Theodore Marley "Ham" Brooks.

The two remarkable friends were stationed behind a bush on a cliff which formed a bank of the Hudson River opposite John Sunlight's island. Monk and Ham were behind the bush because they had received a radioed request from Doc Savage to appear there. They knew nothing more than that.

Monk and Ham had not seen Doc Savage since he had left headquarters with seven unconscious members of John Sunlight's gang. They did not know that Doc had taken the seven sleepers back to the same roof-top off which he had collected them. All they did know was that Long Tom had been left back at headquarters to watch Fifi. They weren't too happy about that. Fifi was pretty.

Monk had been prowling around, taking a brief look at their surroundings. The brush was thick, the night fairly dark, and Monk's mind was on Fifi.

When Monk came back to Ham, he grumbled, "I almost lost my way."

"You never had a way," Ham said unkindly.

Monk continued to think of exquisite Fifi being guarded by Long Tom.

"Thank heavens, Long Tom ain't got a way with 'im, either," the homely chemist said heartily.

Starting to sit down in the darkness, without having his mind on it, Monk had a rock roll under his feet, and he fell heavily.

O-o-o!" he croaked. "I lit on my crazy bone!"

"Oh, dear," Ham said solicitously. "Your whole skeleton must hurt."

Monk was feeling around for a stone, entering vague ideas of seeing whether it would bounce off Ham, when the shadow of a boulder beside them seemed to grow much larger. There was no perceptible sound; the boulder shadow just seemed to grow mysteriously.

"Doc!" Monk gasped.

Doc Savage's quiet, controlled voice came from the shadow which had grown.

"Did you bring equipment cases?"

"I'm sitting on them," Ham said. "Doc—where have you been? What became of the seven unconscious men? What——"

Doc said, "The seven revived on the roof, under circumstances which made them think the whole thing was an accident. They are now on that island you can see yonder. Fortunately, they did not see me following them."

"Oh! Then——"

"John Sunlight is on the island," Doc Savage interposed gravely. "It is up to us to raid the place and seize him."

They picked up the equipment cases—these were of metal, waterproof, shockproof, with handles for convenient carrying —and crept down the face of the cliff to the edge of the Hudson River.

Doc Savage stopped and gave a solemn warning.

"John Sunlight," the bronze man said, "is probably as complete a fiend as we ever met. He is extremely clever."

Monk spoke for himself and Ham. "We don't scare easy," he said.

Doc knew that. But he wanted to impress on them the need for caution—and success.

"Baron Karl does not scare easily, either," Doc said. "Baron Karl is the representative of a small war-hungry European government. Neither does the playboy prince scare readily."

"I've heard of them two guys," Monk admitted.

"They were enough afraid of John Sunlight that they came from Europe to see him, the moment he demanded it," Doc Savage said.

Monk peered in astonishment at Doc Savage.

"How come you know so much about what's been happenin' on that island, Doc?" he muttered.

Chapter 12
ISLAND RAID

Monk's problem was solved shortly. Doc Savage opened one of the equipment cases they had brought, extracted diving "lungs" and they donned these. The devices—nose clips, breathing tube that ran to a chemical purifier pack—would enable them to remain under water for hours, if necessary.

They weighted themselves by carrying a rock under one arm, an equipment case under the other, and waded into the river.

Doc wore a luminous wrist compass. He consulted this until they reached the island, then turned the luminous compass face against his wrist, so it would not betray his presence in the darkness.

They climbed silently from the water and crouched in a river-worn pocket in the stone. Above them was a low cliff, standing limned in the faintest of light only at intervals, when it was touched by the beam from a distant navigation blinker far up the river. The castlelike house must be beyond that.

There was a faint click as Doc opened an equipment case again, then other clicks, and Monk and Ham found telephone headsets thrust into their hands. They put on their headsets.

"Civan," they heard a voice saying, "you recall what Serge Mafnoff meant to me?"

There was something about that voice that caused Monk and Ham to shove out their jaws, although they had never heard it before.

"Serge Mafnoff was your greatest enemy," Civan's voice said.

"Exactly," said that other voice, the hideous one. "And now I have another greatest enemy."

"Who?" Civan asked.

"Doc Savage," the other growled. "Civan, there is nothing I would rather do than stay in the neighborhood of New York and fight this Doc Savage to the finish. But it is not wise. I have other plans, and I do not want them ruined. Doc Savage might ruin them. Therefore, we are fleeing to the arctic."

"Yes, sir," Civan said.

"I have made appointments with the men I wish to do business with," the other explained. "They will appear in the arctic, one by one."

"I see," Civan said dutifully.

Monk and Ham bent close to Doc Savage, and Monk said, "Doc, who is Civan talking to?"

"John Sunlight," Doc Savage said.

"How——"

Doc explained quietly. "I managed to creep close to the walls and fasten supersensitive contact microphones to several of the windows. I did that as soon as I had trailed the men who thought they were gassed on the roof. It was impossible to get inside the house. He has every inch of the place under guard. For that matter, he was the entire surrounding river guarded by photo-electric-eye arrangements mounted in buoys. It would be impossible to approach unobserved in a boat."

Monk growled, "Ain't we wastin' time here?"

He never liked to put off a fight.

There was a guard at the head of the stairway that led up the last sheer few yards of rock to the castle front door. He was a dark man. He leaned on a rifle, and he was preoccupied with thoughts of the months he had spent on the ice-breaker in the arctic. He was recollecting some of the things they had eaten, and it had made him a little sick at the stomach.

"*Beregeeles!*" a voice ripped from a window. "Take care, fool! Don't you see that fire!"

The guard came to life with a start, saw a lurid-red glow of flames a few yards down the trail, and raced to the spot. The fire was not much. The guard pointed a flashlight beam, saw a smouldering cigarette stub at the base of the burned wedge. He fell to stamping out the flames.

"Somebody threw a cigarette into the brush!" he shouted reassuredly.

By that time, Doc Savage, Monk and Ham were inside the castlelike house. Doc had started the fire, but not with a cigarette. The cigarette was just trimming.

Doc went ahead. He whipped across a reception hall that was as large as some schoolrooms. Knocking open the door with quick silence, he went through.

John Sunlight was not inside.

Civan, however, was.

Civan ogled Doc Savage, let out a howl, and dived backward for a door. Probably Civan had never seen a figure quite like the one the bronze man presented. Doc Savage wore a bulletproof helmet gas-protector, a transparent globe of a thing made of tough glasslike composition, holding the bronze man's entire head. The rest of Doc's great form was enveloped in a coverall garment of bulletproof chain mesh, there even being mesh gauntlets.

Civan got through his door, got the door shut just as Doc hit it. The panel was dark, old oak, studded with iron, and it held.

Doc dropped a hand grenade against the door, got back. The grenade let loose. Rock and wood fragments hit his armor grittingly. He went through the smoke, found the door and part of the stone frame demolished.

The bronze man had a stout canvas sack slung from a shoulder by a strap. From it, he began taking gas bombs. He broke these on the floor.

The bombs contained a gas that would take effect through the skin pores. Only protection against it was an airtight suit—a garment such as the rubberized lining of Doc's alloy mesh armor.

Doc reached another door, this one also closed. He reached into the canvas sack and brought out an object resembling a small metal apple equipped with a vacuum suction cup. He stuck that against the door.

The device was one of the supersensitive contact microphones, and a wire ran from it to an amplifier in the canvas sack; and from the amplifier, wires ran to a headset which Doc wore inside the helmet.

The mike picked up voices beyond the door.

John Sunshine said, "Don't fight them, you fool! Get the men out."

"Yes sir," Civan barked.

Doc Savage threw small switches quickly, disconnecting his headset from the sonic amplifier and connecting it to a tiny microwave radio "transceiver" that had half the bulk of an ordinary shoe box. He spoke into a tiny mike mounted inside the transparent helmet.

"Monk! Ham!"

The two acknowledged over their own transmitter almost instantly.

"Get out of the place!" Doc ordered.

Monk howled, "But Doc, we've just started——"

"Out!" the bronze man rapped.

He retreated himself, and overtook Monk and Ham at the outer door. They went—as fast as they could in the darkness—down the path.

Behind them, the castle jumped off the top of the island.

More properly, most of the island tip went up, and took the castle with it. The blast seemed to knock the rocky earth down a foot, shove it sidewise—or maybe it was the impact of air against them that made the earth seem to shift.

Amid the castle sections, sheet flame stood or lunged. The flame sheets seemed to shove the walls and rooms apart, push them outward. The debris came showering down the steep slope, making a shuddering rumble.

Doc seized Monk and Ham, yanked them down in the narrow trench that was the path. They lay flat. Boulders flooded over them like water, and bounced on to land with splashing violence in the river. Smaller stones and earth settled on them until they were almost covered.

Toward the end of the holocaust, Monk made a remark.

"That John Sunlight," Monk muttered, "must like to destroy things."

With that comment, and without having seen John Sunlight as

yet, Monk drew as true a word picture of the man's character as probably could have been drawn.

Doc said, "Down to the boathouse!"

They started leaping and sliding for the boathouse at the water edge.

It was then that the night suddenly got darker. Everything went intensely black. It had been a dark night without stars, but there were lights from distant houses, and lights on the river. Now these vanished.

Monk got out a flashlight—he and Ham both carried the canvas knapsacks—and thumbed the light switch, but nothing happened.

"My flashlight's broke!" Monk barked. "Ham, use yours——"

Ham said, "I'm trying, but it won't light——"

"The lights will do no good," Doc Savage said quietly.

They knew then; they had half guessed it anyway. The *black!* The eerie, incredible, impossible darkness that had enveloped Serge Mafnoff's mansion. It was here now.

They stood silently, gripped by awe in spite of themselves. And in that quiet, they were aware of a faint hissing in their radio headsets, a low windy noise, something close to static, but still different.

Doc Savage removed his transparent helmet. The thing would keep out sound as well as bullets. He listened.

From the river came another noise. This one might have been steam rushing. But it was a silenced airplane motor.

Monk and Ham took off their helmets, listened also.

"Doc!" Monk exploded. "That motor—that silencer——"

The homely chemist fell silent.

"Go ahead and say it," Doc suggested.

"It sounds like the type of silencer you use on your planes!" Monk exploded.

Doc Savage, instead of answering, made for a brief interval the small, exotic trilling sound that was his peculiar habit when mentally disturbed. The trilling was low, indescribably vague.

After that, they went down to the boathouse, and they could tell that it had contained a plane—probably the plane they had heard take off from the river.

The lights of distant houses, the lights on the river, were suddenly visible. The *black* had gone away.

CHAPTER 13
ADONIS AND BEAUTY

Doc Savage's trained eyes picked up the stabilizer light of a plane, far away in the sky. It was soon lost.

And as thoroughly as that airplane light vanished, so did all trace of John Sunlight, Civan, Giantia, Titania and all the rest of the Siberian convicts.

The island was a wreck; at least, the top part of it was. People who had heard the explosion came from miles up and down the river, and some of them put out in boats to investigate, while the others maneuvered their automobile headlights around so that they pointed at the island.

Doc Savage and his two men put on their hoods, and waded down the bottom of the river half a mile, came out unobserved, and went on back to their skyscraper headquarters.

Long Tom had been doing some investigating in their absence. This was at Doc Savage's suggestion.

"I've been talking to Moscow on the telephone," Long Tom said, "and I have learned——"

"Moscow—Russia?" Monk demanded.

"Of course," Long Tom said. "The Soviet officials furnished me with descriptions of the convicts who disappeared from that Siberian camp. There is no doubt but that John Sunlight's men are the same crowd."

"Well," Monk said sadly, "they got away from us."

"Where did they go?"

Monk looked at Doc Savage. The homely chemist had been told by Doc that John Sunlight had made appointments in the arctic with at least two men—Baron Karl and the young European ruler known as the playboy prince.

"Where was that meeting to be, Doc?" Monk asked.

The bronze man shook his head.

"I never did hear the exact spot," Doc Savage said quietly.

The calmness of his tone belied the importance of his words.

"You mean," Monk exploded, "that we're completely at a loss as to where John Sunlight went?"

"Yes," Doc agreed.

Monk groaned. "Blast it! Then we're stymied! We're out of luck!"

At this juncture, there was a plaintive feminine appeal from the library.

"What about poor little me?" was this helpless inquiry.

Long Tom made a face. "Ugh!"

"Whatcha mean—ugh?" Monk demanded.

"That's little honey lambkins," Long Tom explained. He made another face. "Fifi."

"You don't like Fifi?" Monk asked incredulously.

"Listen," Long Tom said sourly, "all the time you guys were gone, I kept trying to add things up so this mess would make sense. Every time I came to Fifi, I added a zero."

"No appreciation of feminine pulchritude," Monk declared, and started in to comfort Fifi.

Ham put his hands in his pockets.

"It seems strange," he said unkindly, "that our friend here, the homely gossoon, should drop everything and go comfort Fifi."

Monk stopped, scowled, and pointed at Ham's pocketed hands.

"It ain't any stranger," he sneered, "than the sight of a lawyer with his hands in his own pockets."

Monk then stalked on in to comfort Fifi.

Ham, glaring, hurried to help with the job.

Doc Savage seated himself at the great inlaid table in the reception room, with three telephones close at hand. He called the central telephone office, and placed, in quick succession, a series of transatlantic telephone calls.

At last as the world knew, Doc Savage worked at his strange career of righting wrongs and punishing evildoers, aided only by his five associates, of which Monk, Ham and Long Tom were three.

The two remaining members of the group of five were Major John "Renny" Renwick, the engineer, and William Harper "Johnny" Littlejohn, the archaeologist and geologist. These two were at present not in America.

Renny was in France, serving as consultant in the construction of a number of new flying fields designed for high-speed modern transport planes. Johnny was in Egypt, opening up another Pharaoh's tomb which had just been discovered.

Doc Savage consulted Renny and Johnny by long-distance telephone, and requested they make inquiries about the past of a man known as John Sunlight.

Next, Doc contacted the foreign representatives of a famous world-wide private detective agency. Doc had organized this agency. Its real work was to gather information for the bronze man. When not doing that, the agency did a very profitable business along regular private detective lines.

Doc put the private detectives to learning what they could about John Sunlight.

"John Sunlight is working on some kind of a plan," Doc explained. "If I can learn enough about his character, I may be able to guess the nature of his plan."

There was a lapse of time while Renny, Johnny and the private detectives worked.

Doc trusted his private detectives implicitly. And for a strange reason. Doc trusted each private agent because each one had once been a vicious criminal.

Whenever Doc Savage captured a crook, he sent the fellow to a strange institution in upstate New York, a place Monk and the rest called the "college." At the college, the crook underwent a delicate brain operation which wiped out all memory of the past, after which the patient was trained, taught to hate crime and criminals. The private detectives were all graduates of the college.

Reports began coming in from Europe by transatlantic telephone.

John Sunlight, it seemed, was more rumor than man. An evil rumor, a name that was whispered from mouth to mouth in the circles of international intrigue. The agents had found men who feared him, and would not talk. Many of those. But here and there they had unearthed a scrap of real information.

"You say," Doc Savage said, "that John Sunlight has always been hungry for power?"

"And money," the European agents explained. "It seems that he always believed that if he had money, he could get the power."

All the reports seemed to agree on that angle.

Renny and Johnny, having made inquiries of their own—they both had high government contacts in the countries in which they were working—verified the point about John Sunlight being hungry for power over men.

"That," Doc Savage said, "helps a great deal."

Long Tom, frowning at Doc in the New York headquarters could not see where the bronze man had learned much of value. Monk and Ham were interested in Fifi, but they could not see where Doc had learned so much, either.

Doc, however, seemed satisfied.

"Now," he said, "we find a king."

"A king?" Long Tom exploded.

"A king incognito."

The playboy prince of European royalty—the newspapers called him the "former playboy prince" because he was now a king—would have greatly enjoyed his incognito visit in New York, except for one thing.

He did not relish having to fly into the arctic to keep an appointment with John Sunlight.

Tomorrow he would have to take off by plane for the arctic, and in the meantime, he intended to enjoy himself. His idea of enjoyment was a series of night clubs, where he spent money furiously and drank himself loop-legged. He made a thoroughly disgusting spectacle of himself, and managed to indulge in repeated fights. That is, he started repeated fights. It was up to his bodyguards to finish them.

He'd brought his bodyguards from home. Two of them. They were big men, one a little larger than the other. They were obviously tough. Their hides seemed to be made of the same stuff as well-worn riding boots. They had enormous, scarred fists, and their faces were somewhat like the wax casts in museums labeled, "Head of a Prehistoric Cro-Magnon Man."

The fight in the Wacky Club was about typical of several the roistering prince started. Except that one small thing happened which was different, and queer.

It began when the prince spanked a showgirl. He liked to spank them. He thought it great fun. But in this case, he got hold of some young fellow's girlfriend. The prince was too intoxicated to notice the difference, and wouldn't have cared, anyway.

The girl's boy-friend knocked the prince over a table. The two hideous bodyguards sprang onto the boy-friend, knocked him down, began kicking him horribly. Someone unshaped a chair over one bodyguard's head, but it didn't seem to bother the fellow.

There was quite a bit of hullabaloo, before the night-club attendants dragged the boy-friend out and got things quieted down, taking pains that the police were not called.

When the prince revived, he at once demanded a drink.

He was handed a drink instantly. One of the waiters in the night club did the handling, and the prince gulped the drink down at one swallow. Then the prince got up and cursed his bodyguards and threw bottles at them, and they took the abuse with stupid patience, because this mouthing, drunken fool was their king.

So far, there had been nothing particularly queer about the incident.

The queer thing happened when the waiter drifted over and tapped on a door which gave into a private dining room. The door opened a crack.

"I gave 'im the stuff in his drink," the waiter said.

A bank note promptly came through the door. It was a fifty-dollar bill. The waiter picked it up and went away, well satisfied.

The private room had a window that opened into an alleyway.

The prince was staying, naturally in the city's most flamboyant hotel. He had the finest suite, and he had ruined most of the furniture in his wild orgies, and the hotel management was going to be heartily glad when he was gone, even if he had promised to pay for the ruined furniture.

The following morning, the prince awakened feeling badly. His conscience wasn't bothering him. It was his body. It ached, and judging from the taste, a cat had slept in his mouth.

He snatched a water carafe and smashed it against the door.

"Adonis!" he snarled.

"Adonis" was one of the two evil-faced bodyguards.

The fellow appeared, shuffling and kotowing at every other step.

"Shut the damn windows!" the prince screamed. "The room is full of fog!"

The bodyguard shut the window, then stood looking uneasy and changing feet.

"May this humble one speak, sire," he asked fearfully.

"Speak about what?"

"There is no fog in this room, sire," the bodyguard got around to explaining.

The prince did some cursing, and threw a telephone at the bodyguard. Then he got a little frightened, for it became obvious that there was really no fog. He could hardly see; the objects before him were discernible only as hazy presences.

He called a doctor.

"You must have got hold of some bad liquor," the doctor said. "Your eyesight is temporarily impaired."

"You blasted fool," the prince said. "Do something."

The doctor explained stiffly that he could do nothing; it would just have to wear off.

The prince broke up some furniture, smashed a few pictures, and became resigned, if not pleased.

"Beauty!" he howled.

"Beauty" was the other bodyguard.

The prince heard someone approach, and there was a rather unpleasant gurgling noise.

"Talk up, you fool!" the prince yelled.

The voice of Adonis said, "May this lowly one advise you of an unfortunate fact."

"Eh?"

"Beauty had his throat hurt last night," Adonis said fawningly, "and now it seems he cannot talk. But he is here and ready to serve you, sire."

The prince was delighted; he had that kind of a mind. He roared mirthfully, and forgot for a few seconds his own lack of eyesight.

Then he fell to whining and complaining and swearing.

"I've got to take off for the arctic today," he grumbled. "And here I cannot see!"

"Sire, you cannot go," Adonis said.

The idea of a vassal bodyguard telling him what he could not do enraged the prince.

"Get my clothes on me!" he snarled.

They got his clothes on him. Then they led him down to a taxicab, and the prince told the driver where to go.

"Newark Airport!" the prince ordered.

The cab drove for a long time—but it did not go to Newark Airport. It went, instead, to a smaller field on Long Island.

The cab went to the other field principally because Beauty sat in the front seat—and Beauty was holding a large pistol against the ribs of the taxi driver.

The prince got out of the cab cursing the fact that he could not see.

"Is the plane I ordered here?" he yelled peevishly.

"Yes, sir," said a crisp voice.

"Who're you?"

"I'm the pilot," the crisp voice said.

"You have plenty of fuel?"

"Yes, sir."

"Get me in the cabin then. And take off."

"Where do you wish to fly to?" the crisp voice asked.

The prince said, "I'll tell you that, you fool. It's a latitude-and-longitude figure."

"Very well, sir," the voice said.

No doubt the peevish prince would have been rather astounded had he known that the crisp voice he was hearing came from the hideous lips of the fellow he had been calling Adonis.

They got in the plane, and it took off.

The prince was spared further surprise by not realizing the plane was being flown by the creature who had been making the croaking noises, the one he had called Beauty.

As a matter of fact, only the prince, Adonis and Beauty were in the plane as it flew northward.

The prince was a complaining, quarrelsome passenger, and when he was not abusing Adonis, he insisted on drinking, or howling obscene tunes at the top of his lungs.

Later, Adonis went forward to see how Beauty was making out with the flying.

"Doc," Monk, who was Beauty said, "I don't envy you the job of takin' care of that thing back there."

"He has given me the latitude and longitude of the place where we are to go," Doc, who was Adonis, said, and wrote the figures on the chart board. "Think you can find the spot, Monk?"

"Swell!" said Monk in a squeaky voice. "Now I'm in favor of dumpin' 'im overboard."

"No. We'll continue to be his bodyguards."

Mention of the word "bodyguards" seemed to arouse a bit of musing recollection in Monk's mind.

"Doc, I guess the two real bodyguards are arrivin' at our college about now," he said thoughtfully. Then he grinned. "I'll never forget what a job we had knockin' 'em senseless when we called 'em to the door of the prince's suite last night."

"The chemical we had the night-club waiter put in the prince's drink had exactly the effect we hoped for," Doc said. "There is not much chance of his recognizing us."

"I don't think he'd recognize us anyway, considerin' how we're disguised to look exactly like Adonis and Beauty."

"Probably not."

Monk flew in silence for a while. Then he sighed.

"What burns me up," he complained, "is the idea of Long Tom and Ham followin' in another plane—with Fifi."

"Fifi will be left in some little town upstate," Doc assured Monk. "She will be safe there."

Later, a plane piloted by Long Tom, with Ham and Fifi as passengers, was circling a tiny landing field near a small town in Vermont.

Ham had been making headway with Fifi.

"Landing!" Fifi exclaimed. She gave Ham's arm a squeeze. "You didn't tell me we were going to stop anywhere."

Ham took off and put on the natty aviator's helmet which he wore.

"Er—I—we——" he said. "Well—it's not my idea."

"Aw—tell her we're leavin' her at a little hotel here!" Long Tom snapped.

"Oh, but I don't want to be left!" Fifi gasped.

She gave Ham her most toe-curling look.

" You don't want to leave Fifi, do you?"

"Er—it may be too dangerous up north," Ham said weakly.

"But you're going!" Fifi pointed out.

"That's different," Ham said.

"Aw—throw her out!" Long Tom flung in disgust.

Ham patted Fifi's arm, scowled at Long Tom. Ham enjoyed having kewpie-doll girls hanging onto him.

The plane landed.

And Fifi changed her tactics. She showed an unexpected bullheaded streak.

Fifi screamed, "Listen, you two! I'm going along! I want to help my sisters! Now get this: You leave me behind and I'll tell John Sunlight what you're doing——"

Long Tom glared at her. "You want me to fan your skirts with a frying pan?"

Fifi glared right back at him.

"I'll trade John Sunlight information about you for the release of my two sisters!" she shouted.

"You don't know where John Sunlight is!" Long Tom yelled.

"I'll advertise in the newspapers!" Fifi screamed. "I'll broadcast on the radio!"

"Women and trouble!" Long Tom groaned.

He tuned on the short-wave radio and contacted Doc Savage.

"Doc," he said, "Fifi has turned cocklebur."

"How is that?" Doc asked.

"The nitwit says if we don't take her along, she'll trade information about us to John Sunlight for her sisters' freedom."

"That is bad."

"It's terrific," Long Tom said sourly.

"Bring her with you," Doc said reluctantly.

As Doc Savage made the decision, Monk groaned.

"That burns me up!" Monk complained. "The idea of Ham followin' in that plane—with Fifi."

"If we understood women, we might have argued her out of it," Doc said.

"Huh!" Monk said disgustedly. "That Ham understands 'em too well."

Chapter 14
SPOT IN THE ARCTIC

There is something completely monotonous about riding in an airplane. Certainly it is fully as uneventful as a train ride across a Nebraska prairie, despite even the mental pastime in which the most seasoned air traveler finds himself engaging—the pastime being to pick out possible landing fields on the earth below.

In the case of the prince's plane flown by Doc and Monk—they managed to go on playing the parts of Adonis and Beauty—air travel became doubly monotonous because, from the time they left New York City's cloud-tickling spires behind, there was a blanket of haze over the earth that, at the height they were flying, made the wooded hills and rivers an unending gray blur which might have been anything.

The prince was as peevish as an ugly baby, and seemed satisfied only when they gave him his bottle—not milk—or if not satisfied then, he at least occupied himself only with thinking up loud, profane opinions of the kind of scheme that would let him, a king, get in a shape where, when he put his hands before his eyes, all he saw was a dark blur that might have been his hand or, as he expressed it, a dirty buzzard. Just why he referred to a dirty buzzard in that connection was obscure, unless it was simply he subconsciously connected the hands with something they had done in the past.

The plane seemed slow. Doc Savage and Monk were accustomed to the specially designed speed ships which the bronze man used. This was an ordinary type of craft, and comparatively clumsy, and conceivably not nearly as safe; but they had not thought it wise to substitute one of their own, because such a ship would have been distinctive enough to attract suspicion.

It began to get colder.

They stopped twice and refueled, and it was very chilly, and there was snow on the ground at the last halt, where they took plane skis out of the cabin and fastened them to the landing gear. Hereafter, landings would have to be made on snow.

They flew on for hours, and Doc Savage knew they must be getting near the arctic rendezvous with John Sunlight.

Doc contacted Long Tom and Ham by radio.

The prince sat back in the cabin, but could not hear because the plane was so noisy.

"Long Tom," Doc said, "what is your position now?"

There was a "scrambler" here in Doc's plane, and another one in Long Tom's ship; one scrambler mixed up the voice until it was an unintelligible gobble, and the other unmixed it and made it understandable. That was so John Sunlight could not comprehend, in case he did tune in on them.

Long Tom's position proved to be approximately one thousand miles southward.

"Stay back about a hundred miles," Doc directed, "once you draw near the rendezvous. Land and wait for some word from us."

"O. K.," Long Tom said. "Maybe once we get down on the snow, Fifi will cool off."

"Fifi? What is wrong with Fifi?"

"Listen, Doc, that Fifi is a pain," Long Tom complained. "All she does is cuddle up against Ham and wail, 'Poor little me!' "

Monk heard that, and he was so indignant he forgot himself and snatched the microphone out of Doc's hands.

"Did you say Fifi is cuddlin' up to Ham?" he howled.

"Yes. And——"

"You tell Ham to cut that out!" Monk squalled wrathfully.

Long Tom evidently conveyed the order to Ham, because he came back to the mike in a moment with an answer.

"Ham says," Long Tom explained, "for you to go jump in a snowbank."

Monk collapsed and made strangling noises, opening and closing his hands as though he had his fingers around the neck of his favorite enemy. His agitation must have been considerable, because he came to the point of criticizing a Doc Savage tactic, something he rarely did—not because Doc couldn't take it, but because the bronze man's judgment was usually first-rate.

"Doc," Monk said, "why the dickens didn't we leave Fifi in New York?"

The bronze man had explained that before, but he expounded it again for Monk's benefit.

"Fifi," he said, "is our hold over her two freak sisters, Giantia and Titania, who are probably with John Sunlight."

Monk subsided, since only the future would show whether Fifi would be of any value.

The prince grew worse. They hadn't thought that possible, but the prince demonstrated that it was. He howled and roared.

Doc Savage was kept very busy. Doc had to be the pilot as well as Adonis, the bodyguard. Monk had to be only Beauty, the other bodyguard, but that grew complicated when the prince began to express an insane desire to choke Beauty and see if that would bring back his voice.

Monk could not afford to have Beauty's voice brought back, because he could not speak Beauty's language.

"Where's that Beauty!" the prince screamed. "I'll beat a voice back into him."

Doc Savage said, using the imaginary pilot's voice, "I think we are approaching the landing place."

The prince jammed his face against the cold plane windows and swore at his inability to see.

"What is it like?"

Doc Savage scrutinized the terrain through the plane window. He saw an expanse which appeared to be nothing but pack ice covered by snow. A cold, white waste across which swirling ghosts of snow were carried by the wind.

Doc described what he saw.

"You fool!" the prince screeched. "This can't be the place."

"We are within fifteen minutes flying of the spot to which you have directed us," the bronze man explained. "I have checked the latitude-and-longitude figures carefully."

"Call me," the prince snarled, "when you reach the spot. I want you to describe what you see!"

Doc went back to the cockpit. Monk flew on. Monk had drawn a black dot on the chart, to mark the latitude and longitude of their goal, and a red line to indicate their progress. The red line had about reached the black dot, and Monk was wondering.

"This territory is all unexplored," he remarked. "Has been, for the last thousand miles."

Doc did not comment on that.

Monk had evidently been thinking about their chances of getting back, in case they had engine trouble, for he continued.

"This is about the most remote corner of the earth," he grumbled. "They talk about the polar seas being explored, but believe you me, that's an exaggeration. Nobody is supposed to have ever been within a thousand miles of this point."

Doc Savage was silent. His strange flake gold eyes were focused ahead rather intently.

"There," he said, and pointed.

Monk grabbed a pair of binoculars, knowing very well that his own vision was not equal to the bronze man's trained eyes. Monk focused the glasses, peered into the misty grayness that was the perpetual arctic daytime.

"Blazes!" he croaked.

He stood up and leaned forward in an effort to see more of the strange object he had sighted.

"What—what is that?" he gasped.

Doc said nothing. And in a moment, Monk emitted an astounded gasp, and sagged back on the cockpit seat.

"The Strange Blue Dome!"

For miles and miles in all directions the white waste looked absolutely barren—except directly ahead, where there was obviously an island.

The island seemed to be solid stone, with no bit of soil and no vegetation. Just a high, bald knob of stone. A mass of rock rearing up from the floor of the Arctic Ocean. It must be as solid as Gibraltar, for it stood firm against the ice pack. The ice had piled up against the island, and for leagues it was broken in great bergs. The floes had squeezed and piled one on top of the other, and the ice had lumped up in masses that were sometimes as large as factory buildings.

The Strange Blue Dome stood, a weird-looking thing, on the rock island.

It was like half a blue agate marble.

Like a marble that some fabulous titan had lost here in this unknown part of the globe, to become buried in stone and surrounded by fantastic ice.

It was strange.

Lying where it did, it should logically have been about the most completely lost thing upon the earth.

"Uh—I—well," Monk said. "Uh—that is—hmmm!"

He fell silent.

Then he looked at Doc Savage—stared at the bronze man's face at close range. And suddenly, he knew! He was positive. Doc Savage, not even Doc, could maintain composure in the face of such an incredible discovery as that queer blue thing yonder —unless Doc had known it was there.

"Doc," Monk said.

The bronze man did not seem to hear.

"Doc!"

The bronze man's eyes left the blue mystery.

"Doc," Monk said, "what is that thing?"

The bronze man was silent and grim-faced.

Monk suddenly seized Doc Savage tightly with both hands, and all the puzzled amazement came out of him in a shouted demand.

"You know what the blue thing is!" Monk bellowed. "What is it, Doc?"

Doc never answered.

Because the prince shoved his head into the pilot's compartment.

"I heard you!" he said loudly.

Chapter 15
HALF A BLUE BALL

There was—Monk was a long time forgetting that moment—an interval when it seemed certain that their hoax was discovered, that all their careful planning had gone for nothing. Then:

"I sometimes talk to myself," Doc Savage said quietly in the pilot's voice.

Monk held his breath.

"Oh," the prince said. "I could only get a voice. The damned plane makes so much noise."

Monk began breathing again. It was all right. The prince was too stupidly drunk to fool them.

"What do you see below?" the prince demanded.

"There is a rocky island," Doc said quietly enough. "And on the island is a strange-looking blue dome."

"A blue dome?"

"It seems a very queer thing to find in the arctic," Doc said.

The prince announced in a profane, inebriated voice that he didn't like queer things, and the thing he liked least of all was the fact that he had come here without knowing why he was doing it.

"Land!" he ordered.

"Very well," Doc said.

Monk itched to ask a legion of questions, but the prince stood close, and he dared not speak.

Completely flabbergasted, Monk examined the blue half-sphere. The plane was dropping now. The ice waste, the solid rock island, the blue mystery, seemed to swell as they came upward. The berg pinnacles appeared to grow. It was startling. The pack ice was even more formidable than it had appeared from a great height.

It occurred to Monk again that this was as inaccessible a spot, probably, as existed on earth.

"You had better get back in the cabin," Doc told the prince, "and fasten your safety belt. Have your bodyguards help you."

Monk helped the prince back into the cabin, doing his best to seem like two men. Handling the prince was about like handling a warm worm, Monk thought.

Then Monk went back to the cockpit and stood by for the next move in their plan.

He watched the island. Snow covered most of it, and in places there was ice; obviously it was no spot for a landing, except along the southern edge, where there was a level area where the snow looked deep and level—a smooth white stretch which terminated against a ridge of high, broken pack ice that had jammed up against the island.

The plane leveled, skimmed the gleaming ice fangs, swung past the blue dome—Monk was made breathless by the queer shimmering luster of the thing—then the craft dipped for the level area of snow.

There would be no room to spare. But the less room the better, for what they had in mind.

The plane skis touched. The craft landed fast. Too fast. Doc knew that; he deliberately had too much speed.

"Monk!" he rapped.

Monk knew what to do. He jerked his fascinated gaze off the blue dome, dashed back to the rear, then came rushing forward again, doubled low so he could not be seen from outside. He had a bundle—a strange man-shaped bundle.

Monk slapped the bundle in the spare pilot's cockpit seat.

The plane slid on across the clearing. It climbed up the side of an ice pinnacle, moving slowly now. It slid sidewise, turning. One ski runner snagged. The plane went over, a wing buckling.

The craft dropped down behind an ice ridge, somewhat of a wreck.

Monk snatched the prince, dragged him out of the door. He pulled behind him one of Doc's equipment cases of metal.

Doc wrenched at a tab overhead in the pilot's cockpit. He tore the tab off. Gasoline burst through from the tanks in a flood that soaked the cabin.

Standing in the plane door, Doc struck a match, tossed it. With a low *whoop*, flames enveloped the plane interior. Doc bounded backward, but not before he was singed enough to make it convincing—the fur burned off around his parka hood, his bearskin trousers scorched and smoking.

Doc gestured at the case.

Monk let the prince drop in the snow, carried the equipment case to a snowdrift near by, made a hole with great haste, and buried the box. Monk used his hands to scoop great banks of snow over the case, then went back to Doc.

"Our next egg," Monk whispered, "is all planted."

Fire devoured the plane with roaring greed. In the cockpit particularly, it burned and blackened the long bundle which Doc had left there—a fake thing made of beefsteak, imitation bones of composition, enclosed in a pilot's flying suit.

They had to have some way to account for no pilot getting out of the plane.

The prince showed further that he was a spineless, cruel fool. The roaring flames scared him, and he ran away, or tried to, clawing at an ice ridge and slipping back, screaming all the while.

"Adonis!" he screeched. "Beauty!" Then: "Where's the pilot?" he wanted to know.

"The pilot did not get out," Doc said, using the voice of the bestial Adonis.

"It serves the clumsy so-and-so right!" the prince gritted. "I hope he burns to death."

A moment later, Civan appeared.

Giantia and Titania were with Civan. So were some others. But no John Sunlight.

Their coming gave Monk a vast start; he had no idea from whence they came.

They came in haste, plowing in the snow, slipping on ice where it was bare. They had guns, big revolvers with mechanisms that would not freeze and become useless in this cold, as automatics sometimes did. The guns went back into clothing when Civan recognized the prince, and gave the word.

They got the odor coming out of the burning plane. There were also faint cries for help coming from the plane now.

"The pilot's burning to death!" Civan bawled.

"Let him burn!" the prince snarled.

After a while, the low, awful cries that seemed to come from the plane were no longer audible.

Doc Savage was a skilled ventriloquist, and he had done a very good job putting the cries for help into the plane; but he did not believe in pushing his luck too far, and anyway, it was about time they thought the pilot had burned to death.

Civan looked over the damage. —

"Kakoi srahm!" he said. "What a shame! It was a good plane."

He gave Adonis and Beauty a close inspection. They did not look at all like Doc Savage and Monk Mayfair to Civan. They looked like two tough lads with whom it might be a good idea not to be found alone.

"Who are these cookies?" asked Civan, who could speak American slang with a Russian accent.

Adonis and Beauty were not supposed to be able to speak any English, and they murdered their mother tongue when they spoke it. They merely glared at Civan and made ugly noises.

"They are my bodyguards," said the prince sharply. "Take me to John Sunlight!"

Civan turned and walked back the way he had come. The fact that he slipped almost at once and fell flat on his back did not improve his dignity, but seemed to do no harm to his disposition. It developed that progress on the ice was likely to be a succession of spills, none of them expected. The prince cursed every time he fell down, and struck his bodyguards.

"Oh, boy!" Monk said. "What can that blue thing be, anyway?"

Monk did not say this out loud, but Doc Savage was lip reader enough to catch the words, even though Monk's lips looked stuffy and unnatural because of an injected chemical which produced a harmless form of swelling, and was infinitely better than internal padding of paraffin or some other substance which might be discovered.

The bronze man did not explain about the blue dome.

John Sunlight had covered his planes with white tents. That was why they had not been discernible from the air. There was a wind of some force blowing, and the air was full of driving snow, and that had helped make the tents invisible.

The men seemed to be camped in white tents, fully a quarter mile from the weird blue edifice.

Covered planes, white house-tents, and igloos were located on the south side of the level, natural landing field in the arctic pack ice.

The prince was conducted into one of the tents. Civan made an effort to prevent the two hideous bodyguards from sticking with the prince, but he got a shove that sat him down in the snow for his pains.

"They cannot understand English!" the prince said indignantly.

John Sunlight sat in the largest of the white tents. He had caused a block of ice-hard snow to be cut and brought into the tent, and he had a polar bearskin over this to make a seat.

Doc and Monk stared at John Sunlight in astonishment. The prince would have stared, too, only he couldn't see.

John Sunlight wore light duck trousers and a white silk shirt which was open at the neck. Tropical attire! And yet it must be thirty below zero outside. A warm day in the arctic for this season. But still thirty below.

John Sunlight was not unaware of the effect. He liked effects. Probably his whole weird, macabre life was devoted to getting them.

"Sit down," he said politely. "And do only one thing—do not ask questions about the blue dome."

Then the placidity left his dark poetic face and burning eyes, for he could see that something was wrong with the prince's eyesight.

"Your eyes!" he rasped. "What is it?"

The prince said a great deal that was uncomplimentary about the brand of liquor served in New York.

"How long will you be blind?" John Sunlight demanded.

"About twenty-four hours more, the doctor thought," the prince explained.

John Sunlight was not pleased, but there was nothing he could do about that.

"You will have to wait," he said grimly, "until your vision has returned."

"Wait? Wait for what?"

"My demonstration."

The prince was befuddled. Why he had come to the arctic was still a complete mystery to him, and he had come only because his ministers at home had told him anything in which John Sunlight was involved would be important.

"Demonstration?" the prince repeated. "What kind of a demonstration?"

"You must see it to appreciate its value," John Sunlight said.

"See what?"

"The thing," John Sunlight said, "for which you and your government are going to pay me ten million dollars."

Chapter 16
SNOW TRICKS

That was all the satisfaction the prince got. He yelled and swore, and John Sunlight gave him liquor to quiet him. Usually John Sunlight could quiet men without using outside means, either liquor or a club, but in this case the prince couldn't see John Sunlight.

You had to see John Sunlight to appreciate him.

The prince was shoved into a tent, Doc and Monk were shoved in with him. This was not to their liking, and they started to come right out of the tent.

A guard put the muzzle of a rifle close to their noses and waggled it.

"In the tent you stay," he growled. "And if you go near the Strange Blue Dome, you'll get plenty dead. Savvy?"

Doc and Monk sat down on polar bearskins. There seemed to be nothing else to do for the time being, and it was bitterly cold.

The prince howled and sang, and swore for a while, then fell over in a stupor, and they rolled him up in more bearskins.

Doc and Monk began talking with their hands.

"This is insane business," Monk fingered.

"Not so crazy," Doc replied. "John Sunlight feels safe this far from New York City."

They were skilled in use of the finger alphabetic system used by deaf-and-dumb persons.

"But what's he doing here?" Monk demanded.

"Making arrangements to sell something to various European nations, it would appear," Doc responded.

"Doc, that blue dome——"

Monk did not go any farther into this at the moment because there was an interruption. Giantia and Titania came into the tent. One carried a kettle of what seemed to be hot stew, and the other

240

had cups and a pot of hot coffee. Steam from the warm food boiled around the two big women.

"Cooks!" Giantia grumbled.

"Here!" Titania snapped, and shoved the food at Doc and Monk.

Evidently the large ladies were not satisfied with their lot.

They looked Monk and Doc over with distaste, but no fear. The two big women seemed to have infinite confidence in their own ability to handle any situation. No normal women could have looked at Doc and Monk—in the kind of disguises they now wore—without feeling frightened.

Suddenly, Doc straightened, looked interested in something outside, and cupped hands to his ears. His pantomime was plain; he meant that he had heard something outside, very faint, and he was listening.

It was perfectly natural that Titania and Giantia should also listen.

There was, at the moment, a lull in the arctic wind.

A voice drifted to them. It was a voice that could be unmistakably identified as belonging to John Sunlight.

"Giantia and Titania," this John Sunlight voice said, "are fools. They do not know their sister, Fifi, is safe and in the hands of Doc Savage's men."

There was a mumbling answer, no words distinguishable. Both voices seemed far away, reaching the tent only through some freak of the lulling wind.

But Giantia and Titania were staring at each other with the most stark shock that Monk had ever seen.

"Fifi—alive!" Giantia croaked. "But she was in that ballyhoo plane. Doc Savage blew her and the plane to bits."

Titania said, "I——" then went silent, for the John Sunlight voice was going on.

"As long as the two fool women think Doc Savage got their sister killed," the voice said, "they will work with me. They may be useful."

The voice cackled delightedly.

"I've even made them think," it ended, "that Doc Savage blew up that ballyhoo plane. They don't know there was a radio-controlled bomb in the plane, and that Fifi wasn't even in it—that her voice was coming off a phonograph record."

That was the end of the John Sunlight voice, for the arctic wind had started to blow again with whining chill.

Giantia and Titania stood and stared at each other in incredulous amazement. Delight—it had soaked in that Fifi was alive—leaped over their faces, and Titania opened her mouth, doubtless to emit a yell of joy. But Giantia stopped her by clapping a hand over her mouth.

"Fool!" Giantia hissed. "Do you want him to know we've learned the truth?"

Titania subsided. She assumed an expression of grim purpose.

"I'm gonna break John Sunlight's back with my two hands!" she gritted.

Giantia shook her head warningly. "Sh-h-h. Too risky. I don't think we could get away with it."

"Then what'll we do?"

"I don't know," Giantia said. "We'll think it over. But one thing sure—we'll do something."

The two huge women stumbled out of the tent.

Monk waited until they must be well away. Then rolled over close to Doc Savage.

"Doc," Monk breathed, "that was as nice a job of voice imitation and ventriloquism as I ever saw."

"It should do no harm, at least," Doc admitted. Which was probably as close as he ever came to admitting that he considered he had done a difficult piece of work rather well.

Monk still had the Strange Blue Dome on his mind.

But again he was sidetracked off that subject. He listened. Then he threw a quick glance at Doc Savage, half suspecting the bronze man might be imitating this new sound. But obviously he wasn't.

"A plane!" Monk muttered.

Then abrupt anxiety seized him.

"Maybe it's Ham and Long Tom!" he croaked. "Maybe they misunderstood instructions and have come on here!"

The arriving plane did not carry Ham, Long Tom and Fifi.

It carried Porto Novyi—that was the man's name, although his name wasn't important, since this was the only time he stood out particularly in the grim scheme of things. The rest of the time, he was just another harpy in the pack of soul-snatchers. Porto Novyi was a squat, wide man who had not been a Siberian convict, and had not been on the ice-breaker. He was a free-lance pilot, a swashbuckling daredevil who fought in wars for hire, or did any other kind of flying that paid well.

Neither laws nor human rights meant much to Porto Novyi. He was scared of only one man in the world, and that was John Sunlight. There was probably not a living person he would not have double-crossed for money—except John Sunlight.

The plane swung down and landed. It was a slim ship of remarkably advanced streamlining. It was painted a color which camouflaged it against the sky; it could hardly be seen from the earth when it flew at any considerable height. Moreover, the two motors were scientifically silenced.

Flying two miles up in the sky, this plane could be a ghost.

Porto Novyi bounded out of the plane. He was excited. He ran, a roly-poly figure in flying furs, to the tent occupied by John Sunlight. He even neglected to give the blue dome thing his accustomed number of puzzled looks.

John Sunlight looked sharply at the pilot.

"Did something happen to Baron Karl?" John Sunlight demanded.

The aviator shook his head.

"I took Baron Karl to a Montreal airport," he said.

John Sunlight still looked concerned. Baron Karl had been here to the arctic rendezvous, and John Sunlight had put on a demonstration of what he had to sell, and everything had gone off well.

Baron Karl had seemed satisfied. Enthusiastic, in fact. That was important. John Sunlight needed ten million dollars from Baron Karl's government. He needed, of course, infinitely more money than that—for what he had in mind. But ten million of it was to come from Baron Karl's government, and it was imperative that nothing should interfere with that.

Baron Karl had promised to buy what John Sunlight had to sell.

So it was very essential that Baron Karl remain satisfied.

"I landed Baron Karl at Montreal," the pilot repeated. "He was enthusiastic about your proposition."

John Sunlight frowned. "Then what," he demanded, "are you worried about?"

"A plane," the flier growled.

"Plane? What's wrong with that ship you're flying? It's the best——"

"I don't mean that one," he growled.

"You——"

"I refer to the plane," the flier said, "which is resting on the snow about a hundred miles south of here."

John Sunlight looked dumfounded.

"But I know of no such plane!" he exclaimed.

"That's what I was afraid of," the pilot agreed.

John Sunlight got up and took a quick turn around the tent, his feet causing the frozen snow under the tent floor to make squeaking noises. It was bitterly cold, and he had been putting on a show, going around in light trousers and thin silk shirt, pretending not even to notice the chill.

But now he forgot himself and gave a violent shiver. He shook, in fact, until he all but fell down. Then he got control of himself and glowered. It always aggravated him to have his control on himself slip.

"It will be dark soon," he said. "Judging from the clouds it is going to be as dark as night before long."

Porto Novyi looked up through the misty grayness at the dark clouds gathering on the southern horizon and climbing up into the sky like stalking animals.

"As dark as night," the pilot agreed.

"We'll drop some men off by parachute," John Sunlight said, "and have a look at that mysterious plane. You marked the location exactly, did you?"

"I can take off blindfolded and find that plane," the flier said, "because it's standing beside an open lead in the ice, the only open water I saw for a thousand miles."

Chapter 17
DELILAH

Long Tom and Ham were finding it comfortable waiting beside the open lead in the ice.

The open "lead" meant open water—a crack where the ice pack had spread apart, leaving a narrow, salty lake which had not frozen. Long Tom and Ham had landed on this water, after first looking it over to make sure there were no floating ice blocks. It was the only suitable landing place they had been able to find. So they had come down, although the spot was too close to a direct line to the southward for their liking.

Their plane was a type that could land on water, snow, or earth.

The cabin was snug, and readily kept warm. Moreover, they wore special arctic gear which Doc Savage had developed —garments that were chemically heated.

The plane stood on the ice. They had driven it up there with the motors, and it was poised for a quick take-off, should the ice lead threaten to close, or should they get a call from Doc Savage.

Fifi was pouting. She had turned out to be consistent with her pouting, and it aggravated Long Tom, although Ham didn't seem to mind. Ham, indeed, seemed to enjoy listening to Fifi's complaining.

Just now, Long Tom was listening to Ham tell Fifi what a sweet, pretty, brave, patient little creature she was.

"Ahr-r-r!" Long Tom said disgustedly.

He got out of the plane. Wind caught his clothes and shook them, and the snow particles stung his face. He walked around the plane, to make sure that no light was showing from the shaded windows.

It was intensely dark; the clouds that had been hunched in the south, now turned the whole sky black. The small waves in the open lead made slapping noises. From time to time, there was a long rumbling grunt as the ice floes cracked; sometimes the ice made gunshot reports, a characteristic of freezing floes.

Long Tom felt along the side of the plane for a wire. He found it. But an instant before, just as he came near the wire, there was a whining sound inside the plane.

The wire was spread in a huge circle around the plane, in the same fashion that cowboys spread a rope around their bedrolls when they bed down on the range, thinking to keep away the snakes. But this wire was more efficient.

The wire was a capacity burglar alarm; if anyone came near it carrying a rifle or some piece of metal of like size, a delicately balanced electrical field around the wire was disturbed, and carefully adjusted apparatus in the plane would give an alarm.

Satsified the alarm was operating—the machine pistol Long Tom carried in an armpit holster was metal enough to set it off —the feeble-looking electrical wizard climbed back into the plane. The capacity alarm was his pet; he had an infinite amount of confidence in the thing.

They were just deciding to go to sleep when the buzzer whined again.

Ham and Long Tom went into action as if a starting gun had fired. Ham sailed into the cockpit, grabbed switches. The big motors—chemical heaters had kept them warm—exploded into life.

Long Tom landed spread-legged in the center of the cabin, knocked another switch. This ignited flares. The flares had been planted in the ice near the plane; they were high on light, collapsible rods, and reflectors threw the light away from the plane, kept it from blinding those in the craft.

A glare as white as the sun spread hundreds of yards in all directions from the plane.

The white blaze disclosed three fur-clad figures. They were about seventy-five yards distant. Friends? No. That was soon settled. Down they went; their rifles came up, and jacketed bullets began hitting the plane.

The lead slugs made big drumstick noises, but did not come into the plane, because its cabin was alloy-armored.

"Take off!" Long Tom yelled.

Ham barked, "There's only three of——"

"Take off!" Long Tom roared. "I don't like this!"

Ham fed the engines gas.

Long Tom picked his machine pistol out of its holster, used the muzzle to prod open the lid of a firing port in the plane cabin. He latched the pistol in single-fire position. He shot. The gun noise was not big, but the sound its bullet made was astounding. The slug was high-explosive. A cloud of ice flew up in front of the three riflemen.

Long Tom shot again, this time at one of the men. This second bullet was a "mercy" slug; it would cause unconsciousness without doing much damage. But apparently he missed with that one.

The third shot, he put in front of the trio. This bullet hit and became a cloud of black smoke.

That was how the supermachine pistol charge alternated—one explosive, one mercy, one smoke barrage.

The plane tore its runners loose from the ice, wallowed forward like a duck, splashed into the water.

"We'll lay 'em out from the air!" Long Tom yelled. "But first, we gotta find out what this means!"

The plane scudded along the lead. The water was black, heaving, ominous in the light. But it was good enough for a take-off.

Good-enough water, but the plane never made it. The reason it didn't was a bomb. A bomb that fell from a plane which came down in a silent dive. The bomb was almost a direct hit.

A geyser of water climbed, the plane almost in the middle of it. The plane wings folded downward like a sick bird. Then the plane seemed to complete a convulsive jump, and fell over on its back.

Porto Novyi, war pilot for money, was good at his trade.

Water gushed into the plane cabin. The bomb had opened a rip in the side.

"Help!" Fifi screeched. "Help! Help!" And she went off into senseless, hysterical shrieking.

Ham and Long Tom fought to get the girl to the plane door, to get the door open. The door on that side had jammed. They tried the other. Water pressed against it; then they got it open and water jumped in with a great gurgling whoop, and mauled them around in the cabin.

They fought back to the door, hung to its edge, pulled themselves—and Fifi—outside. The plane was under, sinking. The water felt incredibly cold, for they had been warm and comfortable in the plane. It chopped at them like a million knives, that water.

It seemed frozen ages before they got to the surface.

The three men with rifles were standing on the edge of the ice. One lifted a rifle, and the bullet, hitting the water beside Long Tom's head, sounded as though a firecracker had gone off.

"Hold it!" one of the riflemen shouted. "Savage isn't there!"

No more bullets hit. The men with the rifles gestured, shouted.

There was nothing to do but for Long Tom and Ham to swim to the men, hauling Fifi. She screamed and tried to climb on top of them. She fought them madly.

Overhead, the plane came diving back. Its superbly silenced motor made a noise only a little greater than the wind. Satisfied, the pilot made another circle, then came down in a landing glide toward the open lead of water. That plane, too, was equipped to land on ice, snow, water, or earth.

"Come out!"

The rifleman who gave that order was Civan.

Climbing out of water onto slick ice was hard work. Long Tom and Ham, knowing how it was done, threw their arms up on the ice, and waited for the quick cold to freeze the fur of their garments to the ice. Then they got themselves out and dragged Fifi onto the ice.

Fifi kicked and struck at them, cried at the top of her voice.

"Stop that!" Long Tom gritted.

She paid them no attention.

"You little idiot!" Long Tom hissed. "You made us bring you along!"

She kept on squealing.

Civan growled an order. One of the two riflemen went away and came back shortly dragging three parachutes—obviously chutes by which the men had descended quietly from the plane.

The plane taxied up. A man out on the nose kept it from bumping the ice too hard, using a boat hook.

Porto Novyi, the pilot, put his dark, unpleasant face out of the cockpit windows.

"Are those flares about burned out?" he demanded.

"Just about."

Porto Novyi turned on his plane landing lights, and thereafter these illuminated the scene.

"Question them," Porto Novyi ordered.

"I'm running this!" Civan said.

Civan jabbed his rifle at Ham and Long Tom.

"Strip to your underwear!" he gritted.

Ham was cold, but he suddenly got much colder.

"We'll freeze!" he gasped. "You can't——"

"I'd love to see you freeze!" Civan snarled. "We'd all love to see you freeze. Strip!"

Ham and Long Tom got their soaked fur garments off, after which they knew they would freeze to death in, at the most, half an hour.

"Where is Doc Savage?" Civan demanded.

That, obviously, was a question that Long Tom and Ham could not afford to answer. They were actors enough not to glance at each other, not to give any sign that they were making up a story.

Turning slowly, Ham stood shivering and looking at the dark, squirming water of the lead. He did nothing but that for a moment. Then, suddenly, he fell to his knees and broke into realistic sobs.

"Don't take it so hard," Long Tom said miserably.

"I kuk-can't huh-help it," Ham sobbed.

"What the hell is this?" Civan snarled.

"Doc Savage was in that plane," Long Tom gulped. "He was killed by the bomb."

This was an out and out untruth, but under the circumstances Long Tom did not feel like letting a lack of veracity trouble him.

"Doc Savage—dead?" Civan began to grin.

"Yuh-yes," Ham sobbed. Suddenly Ham sprang to his feet, and gave every indication of intending to spring upon Civan and the others in a grief-crazed rage. "You killed Doc!" he shrieked.

It was good acting, and Civan was convinced.

"All right," he said. "We might as well shoot them and finish off all the blasted trouble they've caused."

Long Tom, suddenly relieved, said, "Thanks."

"Thanks?" Civan was startled. "What for?"

"For shooting us," Long Tom said grimly. "I wouldn't care about being left to freeze to death. I figured that was about your caliber—so thanks for the shooting."

"Go ahead," Civan ordered. "Shoot them!"

Fifi screamed then. All her other screams were mere kitten mewings compared to this one. If there were polar bears within miles, they must have started running.

"No!" she screeched. "You—they lied to you! Doc Savage wasn't in the plane!"

Long Tom yelled, "Shut up——"

But Fifi was scared; she didn't see the slightest chance of going on living. She didn't know that Ham and Long Tom were gathered to leap backward into the water, and that they had other plans if that was successful.

"I can tell you where Doc Savage is!" Fifi screeched.

"Where?" Civan demanded.

Fifi was not too scared to bargain.

"You take me to John Sunlight," she gasped cunningly, *"and I'll show him Doc Savage."*

Civan said, "Take her in the plane!"

They boosted the cute little Delilah into the plane. Civan and the other two riflemen climbed into the craft.

"Hey!" Long Tom squalled. "You said you wouldn't leave us to freeze and——"

"I change my mind sometimes," Civan shouted at them.

Long Tom and Ham stood, in thin cotton underwear and woolen socks, on the ice, and watched the plane scud down the lead and take the air. The craft, once it was off, cut its lights; so that there was only the hissing of engine exhaust to mark its presence. Then that sound left, and there remained nothing but darkness and intense cold, the noise of waves slopping the ice, and the chill whining of the arctic wind that blew interminably, carrying a fine fog of snow particles that hit their naked skin and felt like needles.

In that chill darkness, in this lost waste, there was one thing that stood out with the staring certainty of death: The nearest civilization was thousands and thousands of miles to the south, and they were two practically naked men left alone.

"Swell!" Long Tom said.

"It could be worse," Ham admitted. "Say, if you hadn't given him that speech about not leaving us to freeze, I don't think he would have done this."

"Contrary, isn't he?" Long Tom remarked. He had a little difficulty with his speech, because his teeth insisted on hitting together.

"Let's get busy," Ham croaked, "before our teeth get knocked flat."

They walked, judging their directions carefully in the darkness, until they reached a drift of snow. They kicked into the drift, scooped with their hands, searched.

Hidden in the drift was the cache of equipment they had placed there against possible emergencies. Taking a leaf out of Doc Savage's book, they had overlooked no bets. They found the cache.

There was clothing, food, a tent, rifles, a sled. The sled could be covered with the tent, thus converting it into a boat with which they could cross open leads. There was a compass, sextant, for finding their way to a destination.

They dressed, then ran and jumped until their circulation was restored.

Best of all, there was a portable short-wave radio with which they could contact help.

The plane came back while they were setting up the radio. It dived, dropped a flare. The flare swung from a parachute, and stayed in the air a long time, and when it hit the ice, the plane dropped another one. The plane also dropped a few bombs, and sent down many bullets.

Long Tom and Ham eventually had to throw away their rifles and hold up their arms. Otherwise, they would have died.

The plane landed on the lead, and Civan came to confront them and cackle pleasantly.

"I got to thinking," Civan growled, "about the reputation this Doc Savage crowd has got. They didn't get that rep for nothing, I thinks. So we came back. Lucky for us, eh?"

Long Tom and Ham were loaded into the plane and tied hand and foot.

"You see," Civan explained, "we contacted John Sunlight by radio, and he says to keep you alive. We may be able to use you as hostages to keep this Doc Savage off our neck, if worse comes to worse."

Fifi whimpered in the cabin.

"I wonder if we shouldn't just shoot you and put you out of your misery?" Civan growled.

"But I'm going to show Doc Savage to you!" Fifi wailed.

One of the bullets Ham and Long Tom had fired up at the plane had damaged the wiring of one motor. It could be repaired, but it would take a little time.

Porto Novyi, the pilot, set about making the repairs.

Chapter 18
THE POISONED SEAL

John Sunlight, having contacted Civan and the plane by radio, knew about the delay caused by the necessary motor repairs. He said pleasantly enough that he didn't mind. But he did. He spoke pleasantly, because he considered that his expedition had done a very nice piece of work. Wasn't Fifi going to show them where Doc Savage could be found?

Of course, the silly little fool of a girl wouldn't tell anybody but John Sunlight. She probably thought she could save herself in that fashion.

Fifi did not know John Sunlight very well.

John Sunlight took a walk over to the tent wherein slept the prince. He kicked the prince in the ribs, got him awake.

"Can you use your eyes yet?" John Sunlight demanded.

The prince did not relish being kicked in the ribs.

"I can see much better!" he snarled.

John Sunlight was pleased.

"In half an hour," he said, "I shall make my demonstration for you."

"You mean," the prince gritted, "that you'll show me why I made this crazy trip up here?"

"Exactly."

John Sunlight then walked out of the tent.

The prince, still rankling over being kicked in the ribs, rushed over and kicked Monk—Beauty—several times to relieve his feelings.

"I'll kick your voice back into you!" he roared.

He had no success, but he felt better.

"Get out of here!" he screamed. "I hate the sight of your ugly faces!"

Doc and Monk did not like the sight of the prince's face any

better by now, and they were very willing to get out of the tent
—providing the guard outside would let them. They scrambled
out through the tent door—and confronted John Sunlight.

John Sunlight stood, a tall dark tower of a figure; he had given
up his show of not feeling the cold, and had donned dark clothing
and a black cape and an aviator's black helmet. He presented a
picture that was not in any sense pleasant. He showed his teeth.

"Your master treats you roughly," he said.

He spoke these words in the tongue which Adonis and Beauty
were supposed to use.

Doc replied. He spoke the tongue fluently, as he spoke many
others.

"Our lot is not a bad one," Doc replied in the language. He used
the illiterate form of the tongue, as Adonis might be expected to
do.

"You have been with his highness long?" John Sunlight asked.

"A long time," Doc replied promptly.

He didn't know whether that was the correct answer; there had
been no time to check on all details of the prince's two
bodyguards.

"Where were you born?" John Sunlight asked.

Doc immediately named a small mountain town in the prince's
native land.

"I have heard of the place," John Sunlight said. Then he added,
"Well, you will be out of the cold weather before long. Your
master will probably start back at dawn. I shall send you all in one
of my planes."

He walked away.

Monk breathed, "Doc, we could grab him now——"

"No," the bronze man whispered. "We have to learn exactly
what he is doing. We have to be sure. We suspect the truth, but we
are not sure."

"O. K.," Monk said. "But this prince is gonna get strangled if I
hafta bodyguard 'im much longer!"

Doc said, "We had better make a try for that equipment case."

"Want me to help——"

"You go get it," Doc said. "I will stay here and try to alibi your
absence, in case you are missed."

Doc Savage watched Monk move away. The homely chemist
was lost in the blackness of the brooding dark clouds almost at
once, and the drifting snow covered his footprints.

There was no sign of the guard who had been watching the tent, and Doc wondered about what had become of the fellow. That mystery was not long being clarified.

There was a sudden, frightened outcry from a near-by igloo. There was genuine horror in the voice. It was the guard.

The fellow had evidently gotten cold, crawled into an igloo to keep warm, and dozed off. John Sunlight had found him missing, and put men hunting for him.

Another guard appeared shortly. He had an electric lantern, and he was too concerned over the failure of the other guard not staying on the job to order Doc back in the tent.

"The poor fool," the new guard muttered. "He should have known better."

Evidently, he referred to the other guard.

Monk would be coming back soon. Something had to be done about that.

Doc began to sing. There was not much music in his singing, but there was volume—and sense, if one understood ancient Mayan, the language which he and his men used for private conversation. Over and over, he told Monk to be careful, to wait until a propitious moment to show himself.

Doc allowed plenty of time—time enough that he knew Monk was lying low, out in the darkness.

Then the bronze man took a coin out of his pocket and began to play with it. He tossed it high, and caught it, cackling like the half-witted oaf he resembled in his disguise.

Directly what looked like the inevitable happened. The coin flew over, hit the side of the tent, and skidded down into the snow.

Doc gasped, ran to look for the coin. The guard watched idly. When Doc beckoned him to help, the man came over on that side of the tent and began kicking around in the snow.

"Monk—your chance!" Doc called in Mayan.

He made it sound as if he were saying something disgusted about losing the coin.

When Doc found the coin and entered the tent, Monk was inside, looking innocent. The guard, thanks to the diversion, had not seen him return.

The prince apparently had rolled up in his blankets again and gone back to sleep. He must be a physical wreck. It was not hard to believe. Doc shook him gently, and the dissolute fellow snored. He was asleep.

"Where is the case, Monk?" Doc breathed.

"It's cached in a snowbank about forty feet from the tent," Monk whispered. "If you could follow my tracks, you can find——"

"All right," Doc said. "You hold the fort down for a while now."

"But how you gonna leave? The guard——"

Doc used a sharp knife—he and Monk had not been searched—and opened a slit in the rear of the tent. He opened it close to the floor, and after he crawled out, tied the canvas together again with a spare four inches of shoestring. Monk, inside, placed bearskin sleeping covers against the spot, and it was temporarily unnoticeable.

Doc faded away quickly in the darkness, keeping low. He circled, and found, not without some difficulty, Monk's tracks. The wind was filling them rapidly.

It was only by bending low and watching the reflection of the tent guard's electric lantern that Doc was able to locate Monk's footprints at all. Once he had found them, he managed to help along the business of following the prints by utilizing the sense of touch.

Later, the bronze man located the equipment case which Monk had buried. Carrying it, Doc retreated a short distance, then opened the case.

Principal item in the equipment box was a portable short-wave radio outfit.

Doc spent ten minutes in a futile effort to contact Ham and Long Tom.

He was worried enough over that, after he had checked the radio and was sure it was putting out a signal, to make his strange, low trilling sound. He made it unconsciously, and the instant he realized what he was doing, he stopped. The exotic note had an unusual carrying power; he listened, but it was evident no one had heard.

Probably everyone but John Sunlight would have been astounded at what Doc Savage did next, and what happened as a result.

Doc concealed about his person such articles of equipment as he might need. There was nothing astounding about that, nor about the fact that he concealed the radio outfit in the snow again.

Next, the bronze man moved off in the darkness, crawling much of the time, and came to an igloo. It was an Eskimo *igloovegak*—an igloo. Doc found the long tunnel that was part of the igloo entrance, crept in, and moved past small food-storage igloos—called *suksos*—into the bigger room of ice-blocks where the Eskimos lived.

There were animal skins on the floor, the walls and ceiling had been darkened by blubber lamp soot, and around the smoke vent in the ceiling a swelling of frost had gathered. Almost circling the interior of the igloo was the ice-block shelf which served the same purpose for the Eskimos as the studio couch serves New York apartment dwellers.

A blubber lamp burned in the center of the igloo, giving off a dark worm of smoke. There were sleeping forms around the shelf.

Doc went to one of the sleepers, touched him.

"Aput," the bronze man said. "Do not be alarmed—I am Doc Savage."

Aput opened his eyes. He was a sturdy man whose face was rutted by the years. He stared at Doc Savage unbelievingly.

"Doc Savage!" Aput muttered. "You do not look—but it is your voice."

Aput was one of the group of Eskimos whom John Sunlight had found living on the rocky island of the Strange Blue Dome. Aput was one of those who had first looked John Sunlight in the eye and insisted they could not see any weird blue dome; that it didn't even exist. That had been, of course, a clever trick to further bewilder and confuse John Sunlight.

Aput was a venerable man, still a great hunter in spite of his years, and a man who was looked to for advice and leadership. He was not, correctly speaking, the chief, because this little group of Eskimos had no chief.

The Eskimo word *angakoeet* better described Aput's position among his people. *Angakoeet* was the vernacular for "medicine man," which meant that Aput was a combined oracle and father-confessor, the man who had the most influence.

Aput knew Doc Savage very well—obviously. It was several moments before Aput recovered from his astonishment at seeing the bronze man.

"Chimo!" Aput muttered fervently. "Welcome!"

"Thank you," Doc Savage said quietly in the Eskimo tongue.

"It moves me deeply to hear you make me welcome when it is plain that I have caused you much sorrow and trouble."

Aput shrugged, and got out of his sleeping skins, took Doc Savage's hand and shook it.

"We have been hoping you would come," he said. "*Elarle!* Indeed, yes!"

Doc saw that Aput had nothing to wear but a sealskin singlet.

"Your clothing?" the bronze man asked.

"This John Sunlight," Aput said, "took away our clothing long ago. It is to prevent our escaping. They count each bearskin and sealskin daily, so that we will not be able to make any of them into garments. We are given clothing to go out to hunt, and armed men go along; and after the hunting, our clothing is taken away again."

Doc Savage was grimly silent.

"When did Sunlight come?"

"*Akkane,*" Aput replied.

The word *akkane* meant last year.

"They were on a great boat, a boat as big as a hundred *umiaks*," Aput continued. "It was crushed in the ice. They come ashore. We take them food. But this strange dark one, called John Sunlight, got to want only to enter the Strange Blue Dome."

"That was bad," Doc said.

"Very bad," Aput agreed. "John Sunlight tried to starve us into telling him what the Strange Blue Dome was. We pretended to be very ignorant Eskimos."

"That was good," Doc said.

Aput smiled wryly. "We were doing as you told us. We were doing the thing for which you brought us here. We were following your orders not to allow anyone to enter the Strange Blue Dome."

"And to take care of what was inside the dome," Doc said.

Aput nodded. "Yes. But we failed. For John Sunlight watched one of us, and saw that the secret door opened when we came near it with the white rabbit cape. He seemed to guess how it operated——"

"John Sunlight," Doc said, "is clever enough to know all about magnetically operated relays and door-openers, particularly since he would have little difficulty finding the tiny, permanent magnets sewed in the lining of the white rabbit cape."

Aput was silent a moment. His face clouded with grim memory.

"This John Sunlight got into the Strange Blue Dome," he said, "and thereafter weird and horrible things began to happen." Aput closed his eyes and shuddered. "There was the time one of my people turned into a black ghost of smoke and blew away."

"That happened to an Eskimo here?" Doc asked.

"Yes," Aput said, and shuddered again.

Doc Savage's metallic features went grave.

"John Sunlight was making a test," he decided.

"Test?" Aput was puzzled.

"You do not understand, Aput," Doc said quietly. "There are many mysterious and terrible things in that Strange Blue Dome. You would not understand them." The bronze man shook his head slowly. "Few people in the world would understand many of them. So it is too bad that a man with John Sunlight's type of mind had to discover the dome."

Aput's curiosity was sharpened.

"What were those things in the dome that you told us never to touch?" he asked.

"Things that the world was better off without," Doc said.

"I do not understand," Aput said.

Doc Savage patted the old medicine man's shoulder.

"If you found a seal that was poison, Aput," Doc said, "what would you do with it?"

Aput answered promptly.

"I would bury the poisoned seal," he said, "where none would ever find it."

Doc made a short, grim sound.

"That was my idea, too," he said.

He went on—he spoke quickly, for time was getting short—and advised Aput how to help when the fight against John Sunlight started. Aput said he would spread the word among his people to be ready.

Chapter 19
DEMONSTRATION

When Doc Savage—his Adonis disguise was holding up very well in the cold—crawled back into the prince's tent, he had hardly replaced the slitted canvas when there was a commotion outside. It meant that John Sunlight's men had come for the prince.

"Monk!" Doc breathed. "Ham and Long Tom did not answer my radio call."

Monk's mouth fell open.

"But what on earth could 'a' happened to 'em?" he gulped.

There was no time to discuss that, because a swarthy head shoved into the tent and said, "John Sunlight wants the prince."

The prince was still in his drunken sleep.

Monk winked slightly at the others, then gave the prince a terrific kick on the part of the anatomy most generally kicked. Monk sprang back, looked quite innocent as the prince awoke and turned the adjacent arctic air blue with profanity. Monk had been aching to kick the besotted prince.

They were not taken to a tent. Their escort led them to an igloo, a large one, made expertly of snow blocks well-frozen. Actually, there was one large igloo, and three more built against it, like a cluster of grapes with one big grape.

John Sunlight lost no time in getting down to business.

"I am going to tell you a story," he said.

The prince blinked stupidly. "Story?"

"It concerns an amazing man," John Sunlight said. "This man was——"

"Do I have to listen to your bragging?" the prince asked impolitely.

John Sunlight frowned, and looked as though he had made a

mental note to raise his price to the prince an extra million dollars for that crack.

"This is not the story of myself," John Sunlight said coldly. "No one will ever know that story. This is another tale, a brief synopsis of the fantastic life of one human being. It is a story which illustrates to what extent a human mind can be developed."

"I'm not very interested," the prince said.

John Sunlight ignored the interruption.

"This man," he said, "was taken from the cradle, literally, and put into the hands of scientists, who were ordered to train the child. They did so. And the child grew into a young man who possessed a fantastic brain. People sometimes call him superhuman. But he is not that—he is only a scientific product."

"Humph!" the prince grunted. "About that demonstration——"

"This scientifically trained young man," John Sunlight continued, "dedicated himself to a strange career. A career of aiding mankind and of increasing his own knowledge that he might help the human race. In other words, this young man continued to study—study—study——"

The prince shook his flabby shoulders impatiently.

"It sounds damned dry and uninteresting to me," he said.

John Sunlight's dark, poetic face remained composed.

"Study," he said. "Study—study—that was the young man's occupation in every spare moment. The most intense kind of study. Study that demanded solitude, no interruptions."

The prince shrugged, lit a cigarette.

"Solitude," said John Sunlight, "was what this unusual young man had to have. So he came here into the arctic, and found this island."

The prince abruptly became interested. "Here?" he said.

"Yes."

"Say, who is this—this scientific marvel you're talking about?"

"Doc Savage," John Sunlight said.

The prince started violently. "Doc Savage!"

"You seem to have heard of him," John Sunlight said dryly.

As a matter of fact, the prince had heard of Doc Savage—and so had the rogues who composed his cabinet in his native land. A number of times they had discussed Doc Savage, and the possibility of the Man of Bronze appearing in their nation to attempt to remedy certain cruel malpractice on the part of the prince and his government.

Doc Savage had a habit of doing such things, they'd heard. And that was why a strict censorship had been clapped down on news that left the country. They didn't want the mysterious, almost legendary Man of Bronze to learn too much about the succession of political assassinations in the land.

"I have heard of Doc Savage," the prince admitted. "Er —faintly."

John Sunlight smiled wolfishly. "I imagined you had."

The prince swallowed uneasily. "Doc Savage—you mean—" He scratched his head, worked his loose mouth around in several shapes, then got an inkling of the truth. "You mean that Doc Savage—he constructed that blue dome?"

"The blue dome," John Sunlight said, "is the Fortress of Solitude."

"Fortress of—huh?"

"The Fortress of Solitude," John Sunlight said, "is the place which Doc Savage created so that he would have a place to do his studying in solitude."

The prince gulped and muttered, "That—it all seems fantastic."

John Sunlight nodded. "You must understand that Doc Savage is something of a fantastic person, a man who is many generations ahead of the day in scientific knowledge. This place here—this Fortress of Solitude—was unknown to the world. It was built by Eskimos under Doc Savage's direction, with materials brought in by a huge transport plane. The construction took a long time."

At this point, Monk Mayfair realized his mouth was hanging open, and he closed it. This story that John Sunlight was telling might sound fantastic to the prince; Monk, however, knew it was true. He had known the Fortress of Solitude existed. He had not known where it lay, or exactly what it was.

Doc Savage had never told. The bronze man simply disappeared from his usual haunts, sometimes for months at a time, and during these absences, it was absolutely impossible to get in touch with him.

When Doc came back from these absences, he explained simply that he had been at his Fortress of Solitude—and usually, too, he brought back some new invention, or the solution of some complicated problem of science or surgery.

The Fortress of Solitude!

Monk knew it must be a marvelous place. A great laboratory, probably. Monk, who was something of a chemical wizard himself, had often wished he could see what kind of a chemical laboratory Doc kept in the Fortress. It must be amazingly complete, undoubtedly the finest in existence.

An interruption shocked Monk out of his reverie. A plane! There was a plane circling in the arctic gloom overhead.

A man put his head into the big igloo.

"Civan and the others are arriving in the plane," he announced.

John Sunlight gathered his dark-red cape around him. He had worn black earlier in the evening, but now he had changed colors again, and wore an impressive, bloody-red ensemble. It gave him the aspect of a satanic alchemist. He was probably aware of that.

"Bring Civan and the others here," he ordered, "as soon as they land."

He laughed then. A laugh that was a quick, ugly report.

"I want everyone in the plane here for my demonstration," he added.

The messenger went away.

"Now," John Sunlight continued, "I shall finish my story of Doc Savage and the Fortress of Solitude—which the bronze man thought no one would ever discover."

The prince licked his lips uneasily. He was learning for the first time that he was involved in something that concerned Doc Savage, and the idea was giving him a worse case of the jitters than he had ever gotten out of a bottle.

"For some time now," John Sunlight said, "Doc Savage has been following his unusual career. And in the course of it, he has captured a number of amazing inventions."

The prince's mouth fell open.

"Inventions," said John Sunlight, "which Doc Savage considered a menace to the world. Among these is the machine which through creation of an unusual type of concentrated magnetic field, stops atomic motion entirely."

Monk took a deep breath. A great many things were coming clear to the homely chemist.

John Sunlight said, "I'll explain about atoms." He took a one-cent piece out of a pocket. "This coin, for instance, is made of copper. And copper is made up of molecules. The molecules are in turn composed of atoms. And each atom is a nuclea of electrons. Just what the electrons are composed of is a matter about which science is not certain, but it is believed they are electrical in nature. At any rate, the electrons travel in gravitational orbits, with a good deal of space between them, somewhat like our solar system—the earth, the moon, sun and planets.

"In case," John Sunlight went on, "the motion of the electrons is stopped, the result is to all practical effects and purposes a complete disintegration of matter."

Monk swallowed. That stuff about molecules, atoms and electrons was straight stuff—so was the surmise about what would happen if electronic movement could be stopped. But, as far as Monk knew, no one had ever stopped it. Still——

John Sunlight was continuing.

"Doc Savage perfected a device," he said, "which, by creating a magnetic field of superlative intensity, completely stops atomic motion, and results in the collapse of any matter in that field."

The prince wrinkled his bulbous forehead. "What is this leading up to?" he demanded.

"You read about Serge Mafnoff, the Russian diplomat?" John Sunlight demanded.

"I——" The prince looked stunned. "Look here, did——"

"He did. Serge Mafnoff was the victim of Doc Savage's death machine, as we will call it." John Sunlight moved his red cloak a little. "You see, I had a score to settle with Serge Mafnoff, and I also wished to call the world's attention to my mur—as—death device."

At this point, the plane, which had been circling repeatedly, landed. It taxied up outside, its motors died.

"Excuse me," John Sunlight said.

He went out. He was gone about five minutes. Then he came back in.

Several of his men trailed behind, all carrying rifles. Along with them, they brought the prisoners—Ham, Long Tom and Fifi.

No one happened to be looking at homely Monk at that instant. That was fortunate. Because Monk's self-control slipped; he couldn't help showing his shock at seeing Ham and Long Tom prisoners.

Doc Savage's metallic features remained inscrutable. Having failed to contact Ham and Long Tom by radio, he had half feared something like this.

"Line them up!" John Sunlight growled.

The prince looked at the captives, and was puzzled. He had never seen them before.

John Sunlight asked, "Where are Giantia and Titania?"

"They're in their igloo," a man said. "I looked a minute ago."

"Go and make sure," John Sunlight ordered. "They must not know that this sister, Fifi, is alive. They would turn on me. Later, we will take care of them."

The man left to see about Giantia and Titania.

"Now," John Sunlight said, "we'll proceed."

The prince put in peevishly, "Why not get around to the demonstration, whatever it is? This is getting me confused."

"You realize," John Sunlight said sharply, "that I have just described a scientific death machine to you."

"So what? I don't see——"

"War."

"Eh?"

"War, you fool. War."

The prince yelled, "Who you calling a fool? I'm a king; don't forget that!"

John Sunlight's grip on his patience slipped a trifle, and the snapping evil of the man showed in his eyes. He calmed himself.

"With this electron-stopping war machine," he said, "you can conquer your neighboring nation ruled by the prime minister whose agent is the Baron Karl. I believe you would like to do that."

A flash of greed jumped over the prince's dissolute face. "That," he said, "is true."

"I'll sell you the war machine," John Sunlight said, "for eleven million dollars."

"Eleven!" the prince ejaculated. "You said ten, earlier."

"I hadn't been insulted then," John Sunlight told him calmly.

Whatever the prince was going to say—it was obviously to be explosive—remained unuttered, because a man dashed wildly into the igloo. He was the fellow who had been sent to see about Giantia and Titania.

"The big women are gone!" he squalled.

John Sunlight's poetic face became ugly. "I thought you looked into the igloo a few minutes ago?"

"They had piled up snow under their sleeping robes," the man groaned. "Made it look like they were asleep!"

John Sunlight yelled orders.

"Civan!" he howled. "Take four men with guns and begin hunting those women!"

Civan shoved four men out of the big igloo, and followed himself.

John Sunlight had been trembling a little. He was a nervous man, and when excitement came, he sometimes lost some of his control. He forced himself to become calm.

"Now," he said, "I shall——"

"If you think I'll pay you eleven million for anything, you're crazy!" the prince yelled.

John Sunlight looked at the poor sample of royalty, and being short-tempered at the instant, he did not mince words.

"Remember the newspaper stories about the mysterious blackness that appeared around Serge Mafnoff's house in New York City?" he asked.

"Yes," the prince gorwled. "But that——"

"That was another war machine," John Sunlight snapped. "The blackness was caused by a combination of short electrical waves, and high-frequency sonic vibrations, which paralyze the functions of the rod-and-cone mechanism of the optic nerves in eyes. In other words—a blinding ray."

"I——"

"That, too, is a Doc Savage invention."

"But——"

"I sold it," John Sunlight said, "to Baron Karl and your enemy, the neighboring nation. They will use it against you."

The prince blanched. His mouth worked, could not make words.

"You will have to buy the electron machine," John Sunlight said coldly, "to defend your country."

The prince looked around for a seat, and sagged to it.

"Damn you!" he gritted.

John Sunlight was satisfied. He jerked his head slightly.

"Now we show the prince what happens when the electrons are stopped in a human body," he said. "I suppose we had better tie the victim."

John Sunlight slanted an arm at the huge, grotesque creature whom the prince had accepted as his bodyguard, Adonis.

"We will use that man—Doc Savage," John Sunlight said. "Fifi, he is the one, isn't he?"

"Yes," Fifi said. "That is Doc Savage."

Chapter 20
MAD HOUR

There were a few occasions in his life when Doc Savage had been caught flat-footed. This was one of them.

He began doing things about it.

Rifles were coming up. Doc whipped forward. He made for John Sunlight.

But the strange poetic-faced man with the distorted mind was fast. He was faster than even Doc had dreamed. He pitched sidewise, got behind some of his men, went on—toward the snow hole that led into one of the smaller connecting igloos.

A rifle crashed. The bullet hit Doc's chest, and he would have died then, except for the bulletproof vest from the equipment case which he had donned. As it was, the slug tilted him sidewise.

Doc went on down, hit Ham and Long Tom's ankles. They toppled. Doc had a knife out of his clothing by then. His speed was blinding. He slashed, got Ham's wrists loose—Long Tom and Ham were bound with ropes.

Doc left the knife in Ham's hands, left Ham to finish freeing himself and Long Tom.

Monk had hold of a man now. The hairy chemist's great hands made the victim scream. Monk lifted the fellow, slammed him against others.

Two men fell on Doc. They tried short-range clubbing with rifles. Doc rolled with them, all in a tangle. The bronze man was trying to reach the hole into which John Sunlight had gone.

Unexpectedly, John Sunlight came back out of the hole. He came fast, and an instant after he was through it, a gun blasted in the smaller igloo which he had just left. The bullet missed John Sunlight, but a man in the larger igloo screeched and started a jig, trying to plug a leak in his chest with his hands.

Titania came out of the small igloo. She had a rifle. Her huge sister, Giantia, was close behind, also with a rifle. They both shot at John Sunlight again. But he got out of the big igloo into the arctic night without being hit.

Giantia and Titania ran to their little sister, Fifi, and thereafter gave no thought to anything but protecting her.

Monk, Ham, Long Tom were all fighting now. Not a man was on his feet. The flailed around on the floor, and a gun banged now and then.

Doc got on his feet, turned around and around like a discus thrower, and slammed his two opponents against the ice walls of the igloo. They dropped back somewhat broken.

Then old Aput, the Eskimo, came through the igloo door like a greased brown bullet. He had few clothes, but he did have a short *oonapik*, the little hunting spear of his people.

Other Eskimos followed, some with *oonapiks*, others with only the small half-moon knives used in domestic work, called *ooloos*. They joined the igloo fray. There was no real need of Doc after that.

John Sunlight was outside. So was Civan, the pilot Porto Novyi, and——Doc did not know how many others. But a score, at least. The men who had been on the Soviet icebreaker on which the convicts had escaped from Siberia. How many of those would turn against John Sunlight now was a question. Some of them, surely. Then there were the rest of the Eskimos—friends, but unarmed.

The odds were still terrible.

Doc dived into the adjoining small igloo into which John Sunlight had tried to get. His guess was right. The apparatus for stopping electronic motion—the machine that had killed diplomat Serge Mafnoff—was there. The powerful coils and tubes were heating. That took a little time. John Sunlight had evidently switched on the device.

But Giantia and Titania had been hiding in there, and had driven out John Sunlight.

The device operated from heavy high-voltage storage batteries.

Doc picked up a battery, smashed it down on the contraption; picked up the battery, smashed again. Crushed, broken, destroyed. Until finally the death machine was a hopelessly ruined tangle that would never function again.

It was not as mad as it looked. The scientific device, as remarkable as it was, had no great value as a weapon.

John Sunlight had been perpetrating a species of hoax on the prince. For the electronic-stopping machine would not work at a distance of much more than twenty feet.

When it had killed Serge Mafnoff, it had been hidden in the unused part of the attic. The marks on the sills had been left by boards on which the device stood when it killed. It had killed through the attic wall, for it was only where the magnetic and sonic beams met, their focal point, that the effect was obtained.

Having smashed the apparatus, Doc picked a single bar of steel —a permanent magnet—out of the mess.

Then he dived back into the larger igloo.

Fighting there was done. Victims were spread out on the floor, and Monk was dancing around, tying himself into knots in an effort to learn the depth of a cut he had received in the back.

"John Sunlight!" Doc rapped. "Get him!"

Old Aput, before Doc could stop him, shot for the igloo door, hit on his stomach, sledded. He must have gone out of many an igloo in a hurry in his time to become that skilled.

A rifle whacked.

Old Aput came sliding back in, just as fast, and when he stopped sledding, began trying to straighten out his right arm, which a bullet had broken.

"They wait with guns!" he yelled.

"Back wall!" Doc said.

They went to work on the rear wall. Ice blocks were thick. There was no time to chip. They hit the wall, Doc and Monk, who were strongest. They learned that ice could be like steel. Then the ice broke, a great mass of blocks toppling outward, and they landed in the snow and cold.

For forty yards or so, Doc and the others traveled with all their speed; and Doc covered the whole distance before some of the others made half of it. Then they were down behind an ice ridge.

Giantia and Titania had remained in the igloo with Fifi.

There was a crash. A grenade. The igloo jumped apart, blocks of ice flying.

Then Giantia and Titania came running and dragging Fifi. Guns snapped, but they made it, and got down behind the ice ridge with Doc and the others.

Doc lifted his voice.

"Turn against John Sunlight now," he called, "and you will be free of the fellow."

The bronze man's voice was enormous, a rumble that carried with the volume of a public address loudspeaker.

His words were for the benefit of those who had courage to turn on John Sunlight. And they had an effect. A rifle banged, and a man screamed.

A man—it was Porto Novyi, the pilot—set off a flare, hanging it by its parachute from one of the plane wings. The glow ignited the fighting. Half a dozen men, or more, had turned on John Sunlight's group. They were fighting a strange kind of civil war of their own in the icy wind and drifting, flour-fine snow. Eskimos came running to join the fray.

Monk reared up and roared, "Boy, I ain't gonna miss this!"

"Upwind!" Doc ordered. "We have some gas grenades."

But the gas grenades did them no good. John Sunlight saw them running, guessed their intent, and shouted orders.

John Sunlight and his faction broke away and fled in retreat toward the Strange Blue Dome that was Doc Savage's mysterious Fortress of Solitude.

It was a chase, then. A wild, mad race, with death made of lead passing through the air, of hitting ice and glancing off with violinlike whining.

It was dark, the polar sky packed with clouds. That was why John Sunlight and his men managed to reach the Strange Blue Dome. Had there been light, they would have been picked off.

Doc, racing furiously, taking chances, saw the panel in the side of the Strange Blue Dome closing. It was shut when he hit it. He snatched the permanent magnet from a pocket. It was the magnet he had taken from the Death device. But it had no effect when he held it close to the door-opening mechanism.

Inside, they had jammed the door apparatus.

Doc whirled, met Monk and the others.

"Back!" he rapped. "Get way back!"

He was running with the word, going out across the stone island in what was apparently a senseless direction. Most of them stared at the bronze man in amazement. But Monk, making speed with his short legs, trailed Doc. He lost ground steadily, and began to think that Doc was going to continue out across the arctic ice.

But Doc stopped, and when Monk reached him, the bronze man was on his knees at the edge of the rocky islet. Doc was knocking snow aside with his hands, uncovering the naked stone, obviously searching.

Monk watched. There was silence, except for his breathing, and the breathing of the bronze man. The steaming plumes of their breath blew away from their lips. Once, far out in the ice fields, there was a cannon report as a floe cracked.

Then Doc found what he was seeking. A crack, apparently. He began to lay the permanent magnet on various parts of the stone, as if he were using its attraction to work a combination.

There was a crunching, and a section of the rock flew up, lid fashion. Doc dropped into the aperture.

It was only a box. In it were two switches. Doc threw one of them.

Monk, knowing something was going to happen, turned his eyes toward the great dome of glasslike blue. He waited, seemingly an age.

Finally, "Doc, nothing—nothing—" he breathed, and couldn't find the words to go on.

"Gas," the bronze man said in a low voice. "It may work; may not. When the place was built, the gas was installed against such an emergency as this."

The bronze man suddenly looked weary and battered.

"The trouble was," he added, "the place was so remote that I got to thinking no one would ever find it. So I stored those infernal machines here. I should have destroyed them."

Monk said, "We've captured some pretty devilish scientific devices in our time."

"Yes, Monk," Doc said queerly.

The strangeness of the bronze man's tone caused Monk to glance at him.

"Are all those contraptions in that blue dome, Doc?" Monk asked wryly.

"Every one of them," Doc said hollowly.

They waited. There was no sign of life from the arching blue half-sphere of the Fortress of Solitude.

Ham and Long Tom and the Eskimos, tired of waiting, moved back, some of them, and went to inspect the igloos and tents of John Sunlight's camp, searching for enemies, treating the wounded, and binding those who might offer resistance.

Later, Ham approached Doc Savage.

"The prince got his," Ham said grimly.

"Yes?"

"That grenade John Sunlight's men threw into the big igloo," Ham explained, "probably killed the prince instantly."

Chapter 21
WILL TERROR COME?

Thirty minutes later, Doc Savage opened the Fortress of Solitude.

They had to destroy a plane to do it. They sent the craft full speed against the side of the Strange Blue Dome—Doc Savage did this, selecting the spot, then leaping out of the racing craft—and the impact of the heavy motors smashed a hole large enough for them to crawl inside, one at a time.

Only Doc, Monk, Ham and Long Tom were allowed to enter. They wore gas masks. They had found the masks in John Sunlight's equipment.

Once inside, they saw senseless forms lying about, and knew the gas had been effective.

They had often wondered—Monk, Ham and Long Tom—what this Fortress in Solitude was like. They saw now, and it exceeded, if anything, what they had imagined.

Monk saw a chemical laboratory which, for completeness and advanced equipment, was far beyond anything he had ever seen, or expected to see. In America and abroad, Monk had a reputation as one of the greatest living chemists, particularly in advanced chemistry. But here, in this laboratory, he saw apparatus after apparatus so advanced that the nature of which he couldn't even grasp.

"Blazes!" Monk breathed in awe.

Long Tom, the electrical wizard, saw an electrical experimental set-up which took his breath. It made his fingers itch, drew him like a magnet. His own laboratory in New York City, and the one Doc maintained in the New York skyscraper headquarters, was a child's experimenting set, compared to this.

Ham, the lawyer, did not see any law books. Ham was no great enthusiast as a scientist.

So it was Ham who wandered around gathering up the unconscious John Sunlight faithfuls, and passing them out through the hole in the side of the blue dome.

The construction of the dome, the strange, blue glasslike material of which it was made, did interest Ham. He asked Doc about that, and learned it was a form of glass composition which could be welded with heat, and which had strength far beyond that of true glass. The welding operation explained how the dome had been constructed without joints. The stuff had the advantage of being a nonconductor, which meant that it kept out the cold.

But construction details suddenly ceased to worry Ham. He ran to Doc Savage.

"Doc!" Ham exploded. "John Sunlight—he's not here!"

"John Sunlight—not here!" The bronze man sounded incredulous.

Then they searched. Searched furiously. Doc Savage, who knew every cranny of the Fortress of Solitude, went over everything repeatedly. He examined the prisoners, to make sure none of them was John Sunlight in disguise.

Then, with breathless intensity, they began a widespread search.

They did not find John Sunlight. They did not find his body.

It was Doc Savage who located footprints that must have been John Sunlight's. And by the tracks, they knew that John Sunlight had not entered the Strange Blue Dome with his men. He had gone around the Dome, and hidden in the snow. Then, when he saw his men had been defeated, he had fled.

John Sunlight's tracks led out across the arctic ice pack.

Doc Savage followed the footprints for two days, and came to a patch of frozen red gore on the edge of an open lead in the ice. There, beside the water, the traces showed that a monster polar bear had come out of the lead and attacked John Sunlight.

They found John Sunlight's rifle, a little of his clothing. That was all.

Standing there on the edge of the lead, wondering if they were faced with evidence that John Sunlight had finally died, Monk sighed deeply.

"I pity the bear that eats that guy," the homely chemist muttered.

Doc Savage spoke quietly.

"If John Sunlight is not dead," the bronze man said, "we may have something pretty terrible ahead of us."

They stared at him. "What do you mean, Doc?"

Then he told them something they had not known before.

"There were almost a score of deadly scientific devices stored in the Fortress of Solitude," he said. "They're gone."

That didn't quite soak in.

"You mean——"

"I mean," Doc said grimly, "that John Sunlight removed the death machines from the Fortress of Solitude and hid them somewhere. If he is alive, and recovers them——"

The bronze man turned away without finishing.

The pursuit party returned to the island with subdued spirits. They returned quickly—a plane came out for them. They could not help but wonder, and the wondering was not pleasant. Evidence that John Sunlight had been killed by a polar bear seemed conclusive, and yet——

They landed on the island and guided the plane into a great hangar-room in the side of the Fortress of Solitude. It was from here that John Sunlight had secured his first plane, the craft in which he and his party had flown to New York. Doc always kept two extra planes on hand at the fortress, one a spare craft, and the other an experimental machine on which he tried out new aeronautical developments.

For the next three weeks, Monk, Ham and Long Tom flew over the arctic, searching vainly for some trace of a cache where John Sunlight might have hidden the death machines he had stolen from the Fortress of Solitude.

They never found a cache.

"What about the darkness-maker that John Sunlight sold to that Baron Karl?" Ham demanded one day.

"We will have to recover that," Doc said grimly, "as soon as we can."

There was one other problem they had to settle. Most of the value of the Fortress of Solitude lay in its existence remaining unknown to the world.

Many people now knew about it. The Eskimos did not count; they had always known, but they lived here and took care of the place. Doc had trained them for that, and they would continue, for they were well satisfied.

But the others——

"They won't keep their mouths shut," Monk muttered. "Not every one of 'em."

Doc Savage was thoughtful. When all gathered for the next meal, the bronze man made a talk. It was probably the most compelling speech Monk, Ham or Long Tom had ever heard the bronze man make.

Doc pointed out that the whole experience, from the time the convicts escaped the Siberian prison camp was so terrible that their minds would be better off if all memory of the past was wiped away. Then he explained about his brain operation, guaranteed no one would die, and promised that all memory of the past would be gone. Incidentally, no one would recall the Fortress of Solitude, either.

He sold the memory-wiping operations en masse. It was such a good talk that Monk and Ham and Long Tom were almost impelled to join in.

"It's a swell idea—for Monk!" Ham said enthusiastically.

"Why me?" Monk demanded.

"Rid your mind of the idea," Ham said, "that you're evolution's gift to the ladies."

Ham left Monk sputtering, and went away to make a little progress with Fifi. After all, Fifi had repented; and after all, Fifi was a very cute trick. Not to add that pretty soon she was going to be relieved of her memory. What more could a confirmed bachelor such as Ham look for?

The flies in the ointment—elephants in the ointment was more like it, Ham thought ruefully—were Giantia and Titania. Ham thought he'd better get on the good side of Giantia and Titania, before proceeding with Fifi.

Ham went looking for Giantia and Titania to discuss the matter. Ham was minus a front tooth when Monk saw him next.

"What happened?" Monk asked.

"Giantia," Ham said ruefully, "cracked a smile."

"Huh?"

"My smile," Ham explained.

RED DRAGON

By Thomas Harris author of **BLACK SUNDAY**

DOC SAVAGE

To the world at large, Doc Savage is a strange, mysterious figure of glistening bronze skin and golden eyes. To his fans he is the greatest adventure hero of all time, whose fantastic exploits are unequaled for hair-raising thrills, breathtaking escapes, blood-curdling excitement!

OUT OF THIS WORLD!

That's the only way to describe Bantam's great series of science fiction classics. These space-age thrillers are filled with terror, fancy and adventure and written by America's most renowned writers of science fiction. Welcome to outer space and have a good trip!

Buy them at your local bookstore or use this handy coupon for ordering:

FANTASY AND SCIENCE FICTION FAVORITES

Bantam brings you the recognized classics as well as the current favorites in fantasy and science fiction. Here you will find the beloved Conan books along with recent titles by the most respected authors in the genre.

☐	22532	THE WORLDS OF GEORGE O. George Smith	$2.50
☐	22666	THE GREY MANE OF MORNING Joy Chant	$3.50
☐	20931	NEBULA WINNERS FOURTEEN Frederik Pohl	$2.95
☐	20527	SYZYGY Frederik Pohl	$3.50
☐	14343	WIND FROM THE ABYSS Janet Morris	$2.50
☐	20672	DARKWORLD DETECTIVE J. Michael Reeves	$2.50
☐	20281	WAR OF OMISSION Kevin O'Donnell	$2.50
☐	20488	THE HEROES OF ZARA Guy Gregory	$2.50
☐	23063	LORD VALENTINE'S CASTLE Robert Silverberg	$3.50
☐	20156	BABEL-17 Samuel R. Delany	$2.50
☐	20063	GATES OF HEAVEN Paul Preuss	$2.25
☐	20870	JEM Frederik Pohl	$2.95
☐	22730	CONAN & THE SPIDER GOD #5 de Camp & Pratt	$2.50
☐	22731	CONAN THE REBEL #6 Paul Anderson	$2.50
☐	14532	HIGH COUCH OF SILISTRA Janet Morris	$2.50
☐	22557	DRAGONSONG Anne McCaffrey	$2.75
☐	20914	MAN PLUS Frederik Pohl	$2.75
☐	14846	THE GOLDEN SWORD Janet Morris	$2.50
☐	20592	TIME STORM Gordon R. Dickson	$2.95

Buy them at your local bookstore or use this handy coupon for ordering:

Bantam Books Inc. Dept. SF2, 414 East Golf Road, Des Plaines, Ill. 60016

Please send me the books I have checked above. I am enclosing $_____
(please add $1.00 to cover postage and handling). Send check or money order
—no cash or C.O.D.'s please.

Mr/Mrs/Miss_____

Address_____

City_____State/Zip_____

SF2—8/82

Please allow four to six weeks for delivery. This offer expires 2/83.